PRAISE FOR
SUZANNE BROCKMANN

HOT PURSUIT

"Brockmann continues to use her patented style of weaving intersecting story lines around a number of different protagonists and relationships. Like an excellent chocolate, a Brockmann book never disappoints."
—*Romantic Times*

"The action grabs you and drags you along. . . . [*Hot Pursuit*] will immediately grab your interest."
—*Romance Reviews Today*

DARK OF NIGHT

"Provides real chills . . . a true Brockmann masterpiece!"
—*Romantic Times*

"Once again Brockmann neatly blends high-adrenaline suspense and scorchingly sexy romance into an addictively readable mix."
—*Booklist*

"Brockmann fans will cheer."
—*Publishers Weekly*

INTO THE FIRE

"Brockmann skillfully keeps her adrenaline-rich, testosterone-fueled plot moving at a thrilling pace. With its realistically complicated, beautifully crafted characters and captivating combination of romance, suspense, and danger, it's another sure-bet winner from the always reliable Brockmann."

—*Booklist*

"A multilayered tale that includes emotion, romance, action, and pulse-pounding suspense . . . Readers will root for new and old romances and worry about what the future holds for other characters—a trademark of Brockmann's that increases fan anticipation for the next book."

—*BookPage*

"*Into the Fire* is lucky number thirteen for fans of this ever-popular series. . . . [Brockmann] juggles multiple storylines while keeping the emotional quotient intact. . . . [Her] thrillers make you think and hold your breath!"

—*Romantic Times*

"A jaw-dropping 'conclusion' suggests more fireworks ahead."

—*Publishers Weekly*

FORCE OF NATURE

"Intense and packed with emotion, this book is truly a force of nature!"

—*Romantic Times*

"Brockmann deftly delivers another testosterone-drenched, adrenaline-fueled tale of danger and desire that brilliantly combines superbly crafted, realistically complex characters with white-knuckle plotting."

—*Booklist*

ALL THROUGH THE NIGHT

"In *All Through the Night*, Suzanne Brockmann strikes the perfect balance between white-knuckle suspense and richly emotional romance."
—*Chicago Tribune*

"For the holidays, Brockmann gifts her readers with the culmination of a long-delayed love story—that of fan favorite Jules Cassidy. Of course, in true Brockmann style, this wedding tale is packed to the gills with plenty of danger, bombs, terrorists, and stalkers. But, most of all, it is a satisfying love story."
—*Romantic Times*

"A winning, innovative runup to Christmas from the bestselling Brockmann."
—*Publishers Weekly*

INTO THE STORM

"Sexy, suspenseful, and irresistible . . . [This] novel has all the right ingredients, including terrific characters [and] a riveting plot rich in action and adventure."
—*Booklist*

"Brockmann is an undisputed master at writing military and suspense fiction [with] action, danger and passion all rolled into one."
—*Curled Up with a Good Book*

BREAKING POINT

"Readers will be on the edge of their seats."
—*Library Journal*

"An action-packed and breathtaking thriller."
—*Romantic Times*

BY SUZANNE BROCKMANN

THE TROUBLESHOOTERS SERIES

The Unsung Hero
The Defiant Hero
Over the Edge
Out of Control
Into the Night
Gone Too Far
Flashpoint
Hot Target
Breaking Point
Into the Storm
Force of Nature
All Through the Night
Into the Fire
Dark of Night
Hot Pursuit

CONTEMPORARY ROMANCE

Infamous
Heartthrob
Bodyguard
Forbidden
Time Enough for Love
Stand-in Groom
Otherwise Engaged
The Kissing Game
Kiss and Tell
Body Language
Freedom's Price
Ladies' Man

HOT PURSUIT

A NOVEL

SUZANNE BROCKMANN

BALLANTINE BOOKS • NEW YORK

Hot Pursuit is a work of fiction. Names, characters, places, and incidents are the products of the author's imagination or are used fictitiously. Any resemblance to actual events, locales, or persons, living or dead, is entirely coincidental.

2011 Ballantine Books Mass Market Edition

Published in the United States by Ballantine Books, an imprint of The Random House Publishing Group, a division of Random House, Inc., New York.

BALLANTINE and colophon are registered trademarks of Random House, Inc.

Originally published in hardcover in the United States by Ballantine Books, an imprint of The Random House Publishing Group, a division of Random House, Inc., in 2009.

ISBN 978-0-345-50158-5

Cover design: Jae Song

Printed in the United States of America

www.ballantinebooks.com

9 8 7 6 5 4 3 2 1

*To the real Hot Potato Two Shoes, and Stealy Eff,
who both need nicknames for their nicknames.*

ACKNOWLEDGMENTS

Special thanks to the team at Ballantine Books: Jennifer Hershey, Courtney Moran, Crystal Velasquez, Kim Hovey, Sarina Evan, Libby McGuire, Jessica Sebor, and Shauna Summers.

Thanks, eternally, to Steve Axelrod.

As always, snaps to the home team: Ed and Jason Gaffney, Eric Ruben, Apolonia Davalos, Lee and Fred Brockmann, Kathy Lague, the patient Kuhlmans, and the ever steadfast, nearly trained, world's greatest miniature schnauzers, CK Dexter-Haven and Little Joe.

A huge thank-you to the four brave volunteers who tried to keep my Internet bulletin board open. You cannot know how much I appreciate all that you did, and you have my respect and thanks (and early copies of my books until the end of time . . .).

Thank you to the real-life Pamela Duddy, and to Timothy Woodward, for their generous donations to Greater Boston PFLAG (Parents, Family & Friends of Lesbians and Gays)—a charity that is not just one of Robin Chadwick Cassidy's favorites, but mine as well. The money you donated will help fund GBPFLAG's Safe Schools program. As a PFLAG mom, I thank you from the bottom of my heart. (For more information visit www.GBPFLAG.org.)

Pam: Jules, Alyssa, and I all enjoyed meeting you, and we wish you continued laughter and joy.

I want to give a shout-out, too, to the real-life KatiAnn

Watson. Happy birthday, KatiAnn, from Timothy and me. (And thanks for keeping Kenny alive.)

Last but way not least, I want to thank *you*, my readers, who trust me enough to follow wherever I will take you, and who continue to give me permission to write the stories of my heart.

As always, any mistakes I've made or liberties I've taken are completely my own.

PROLOGUE

Friday was going to be the night.

He knew Savannah's schedule, knew her habits, knew exactly when she'd be alone. And on Friday night, she would be. Her superhero Navy SEAL husband had planned to be in town for the weekend, but he'd cancelled.

Instead, *he* would be waiting for her.

He couldn't wait to see her face, couldn't wait until she realized that she was going to die, couldn't wait until she screamed and sobbed in fear and pain.

And oh, it had been so long since he'd last relieved the nightmarish pressure that built up inside of him, pressing out from within his chest, making it hard to breathe, hard for his very heart to beat.

And yes, he'd learned to control it, pushing it back, far back. Sometimes so far back, he nearly forgot he wasn't one of them. But he never forgot for long.

Over the past week, the pressure had returned, growing stronger and more powerful—every beat of his pulse seeming to shake him with the knowledge that it was time, it was time, it was finally time. . . .

It *was* time, and he'd take her tomorrow tonight. And although he loved to linger, this one he'd kill quickly.

And while he knew he'd regret and miss the power and pleasure he got from drawing out her pain, he'd still get some relief.

And for that alone, as short term and temporary as it was destined to be, it would be good.

But merely good—not perfect. Perfect was reserved for *her*.

Still, he'd have that perfection soon, because he knew, without a doubt, that, upon news of Savannah's gruesome death, *she* would come.

She would come, and this game he'd been playing for all this time would begin its final quarter, this play its final act.

But until then, until Friday night, he had to be patient and wait.

He had a morning ritual to help him through the day.

He'd say her name aloud—just a whisper, but it would echo in the pristine, sterile bathroom—the *S*'s gloriously sibilant, the *K* sound crisp.

"Alyssa Locke."

Then he'd go into his bedroom, and pick out a picture of her from his vast collection—some that he'd taken himself, which had been a thrill—and he'd carry it with him, all day, in the breast pocket of his jacket.

It was dangerous for him to do so. Savannah knew Alyssa well, and would ask all sorts of awkward questions if she ever saw it.

He made sure she never saw it—although there had been one particularly close call. He'd had it on the table, but had swept it into the trash before Savannah got too close. He hadn't been able to rescue it, though, before the janitor took it to the dumpster, and he'd had to print out another.

But such risks were part of the game, and carrying the photo with him gave him the comfort and strength he needed to make it through another long, dull day.

Today's picture was one of his favorites. It had run in the Manchester newspaper. In it, Alyssa was a mere shadow, a shape, standing with a number of other law enforcement officers—police and FBI—at the place where he'd left one of them. Amanda Timberman. It had taken them six months to find Amanda, and unlike all of the others, he'd hoped that they never would.

But they had, and good had come from bad when this picture was taken.

He'd since found out that Alyssa was an investigator with a personal security firm called Troubleshooters Incorporated. She'd been hired by Amanda's former fiancé—her job being to find Amanda, long gone missing. And find Amanda, she finally had.

When he'd first seen this picture, he hadn't known Alyssa from any of the other shadowy person-sized shapes in the photograph. But he knew her well now—he recognized her just from the way she was standing, from the tilt of her head.

She thought she had both the brains and the skill to stalk and capture the serial killer that the media had dubbed "The Dentist." She'd been after him for years.

But now, the Dentist was stalking her. And unlike her, he *always* caught his prey.

It had started on the very same day that this picture was taken—this journey he was now undertaking; a journey that would end—soon—with her blood on his hands and her pretty white teeth on a necklace he would wear close to his heart.

Her phone rang, shrill and startling in the darkness.

Jenn fumbled for her glasses, knocking them off her bedside table and onto the floor, peering at her alarm clock through the blur made worse by her grogginess.

2:27 A.M.

As she picked up her glasses, the phone rang again,

and she knew it had to be Maria—notorious for her insomnia. She also knew, if she answered it, that she'd be forced to recount last night's terrible, horrible, no-good date with Scooter Randall—an ordeal which she'd driven all the way out to Long Island to endure.

"Maybe he's changed since high school," Maria had said, urging her to accept the dinner invitation.

A clue that he hadn't changed might've been the fact that, after twelve years, he was still calling himself by his high school nickname. But Maria, despite being one of the smartest people Jenn knew when it came to most things, was a complete and total idiot when it came to relationships.

Jenn settled back in her bed, willing the call to voice mail. She knew that if Maria really, *really* needed her, she'd call back and she wouldn't stop until Jenn picked up.

But then, crap, her cell phone started ringing, too.

Jenn rolled and grabbed for it, because although Maria could be something of a drama queen, there had been only one other time that she'd made a two-fisted phone call like this: when Jenn's dad had been rushed to the hospital with a heart attack.

"I'm awake," Jenn said now. "I'm here, what's wrong?"

"Ford. Garage or street?" Maria's voice was tight, clipped.

"What?"

"The car, Jenn. Did you park the car in the—"

Jenn understood. "Street." She'd gotten home last night well after the time that Vincent lowered and locked the gate to the parking garage.

A few weeks ago, she and Maria had gotten a great deal from the wizened little man. For a fraction of the price it normally cost to keep a car in New York City, they were able to garage the beat-up Taurus that they bought at the beginning of the campaign and cleverly named "Ford"—

the catch being that they didn't have access to it from midnight to 6 A.M.

So far, so good—except for the many nights they missed Vincent's deadline, and had to park it on the street.

"Get dressed and get over here," Maria ordered. "On second thought, don't get dressed, just *get* here. We need a ride to the airport, *now.*"

"The airport?" Jenn asked, tucking the phone between her shoulder and ear as she pulled on the pants she'd worn on the date from hell. She kicked aside the heels she'd bought for the occasion—she was a fool to think that shoes like that made her look sexy instead of freakishly big and stupid—and stepped into her worn-out flats instead. "What airline has flights leaving at this time of—"

"We need a ride out to Westchester," Maria interrupted. "Van's grandmother's chartered a plane to San Diego, and it leaves from there. Jenn, just get over here, okay? Ken's been badly wounded. He was shot."

"What?" Despite her disbelief, Jenn had heard what Maria said. Savannah's Navy SEAL husband Ken had been shot. But the words didn't line up with what she knew to be true. "Van told me he's back from Iraq."

"He's not in Iraq," Maria said, as Jenn grabbed a sweatshirt and went out the door. "He's in San Diego. He was doing some kind of bodyguard assignment as a favor for a friend."

"Oh, my God." Jenn waited all of three seconds for the elevator, then bailed and took the stairs.

Maria continued, lowering her voice. "Jenni, it looks bad. He was hit three times, twice to the chest. He's in surgery right now, but . . ." She exhaled, hard. "I'm going to fly to California with Savannah. I'm pretty sure she's going to find out on the flight that . . . I don't want her to get that news alone."

"Oh, my God," Jenn said again. "Should I come? I could come, too."

"It was a tough enough battle," Maria said, "to talk her into letting me go. She's already said that she wants you to stay here and hold down the fort."

Which made sense. They were in the middle of a political campaign, and also, well . . . Jenn was nothing if not realistic. Because even though both Maria and Savannah jokingly referred to the three of them as "Charlie's Angels," they were just being nice when they included her that way.

A more accurate pop-culture TV reference would've been for them to sing that song from *Sesame Street* that went "One of these things is not like the others . . ." as pictures of Maria, Savannah, and Jennilyn flashed on the screen.

The drastic differences were not merely physical.

Maria and Savannah had met at an Ivy League law school, and then renewed their friendship when they both went to work, at a huge salary, for some big, sell-your-soul law firm here in New York City. They both also left, souls miraculously intact, at about the same time—Savannah to move to California to be closer to Ken, and Maria because she got an opportunity to clerk for a high-level judge.

They both came from old money and had trust funds up the wazoo, but they both never, ever flaunted it.

And then, of course, there were the physical differences.

They were both shorter than average and beautiful—Savannah blond and blue-eyed, Maria with her midnight eyes and lustrous, dark brown waves. And they were both slender; size eight or smaller to Jenn's not-quite-sixteen, yet somehow, freakishly, definitely-not-fourteen.

On top of their striking beauty and ability to wear clothes that fit perfectly, they were also both brilliant, always knowing exactly what to say and how to say it. It would have been frustrating to spend so much time with them—if they also both weren't so ridiculously nice.

So the truth was, although Jenn had been friends with Maria during high school, she'd only attended a state college and was too far in debt from *that* even to consider grad school, regardless of her near-perfect grades. So she'd gone out and gotten herself a crappy job. And then another crappy job. And then, finally, a slightly better job. And a marginally better one after that.

Last year, she'd been working as an administrative assistant at a rental car company's corporate headquarters in New Jersey when Maria and Savannah dropped by. It was a surprise visit, and they took her to lunch—and sketched out their plan to get Maria elected to the office of governor of the state of New York.

Step one was to run for state assembly in 2008—run and win.

Savannah, they'd told her, was going to be Maria's campaign manager. And they both wanted Jenn to work for them, to run their office, and when Maria won—they always said *when* not *if*—Jenn would continue on, working as Maria's chief of staff. Well, to start out, she'd be both chief *and* staff, but they were planning, here, for the long term.

And that long term included a possible run for the White House.

So Jenn had bid farewell to the land of the cubicle and had become the only paid employee in the Maria Bonavita for State Assembly office—everyone else was an intern or a volunteer. Despite that, she was still making buckets less than she had been. Plus she no longer got a huge discount on car rentals—hence the purchase of Ford.

But she was, absolutely, working to change the world—starting with their little corner of New York City—and she loved every second of it.

She'd moved into the very neighborhood they'd be representing in the state house in Albany. It was a diverse district, i.e., parts such as this one were somewhat rough. The streets were spookily empty as she let herself out of her apartment building—it was that rare time of night in the city when the late-goers had finally gone home, and the early risers had yet to emerge.

"I'm two minutes from Ford," she reported to Maria, cell phone still to her ear as she walked briskly down the sidewalk, "and two minutes from there to your place."

Last night, after driving out to the Island—to listen to Scooter whine endlessly about how he was still in love with Maria and could Jenn please, please, pretty please, put in a good word for him—she'd driven back and had miraculously found a parking space just around the block from their campaign office. Which was, in turn, just a few blocks from her apartment.

"We'll be waiting outside for you," Maria told her now. "I'm going to drive. Van's got a whole list of things she wants to review with you—the events for the next few days."

"She doesn't have to do that," Jenn said. "I know what's on the schedule."

"She wants to." Maria lowered her voice again. "She needs the distraction."

"How did this happen?" Jenn asked. She and Maria both lived in fear of Van getting this type of phone call when Ken was off on some secret Navy SEAL mission, either in Iraq or Afghanistan. This wasn't fair—he was home and safe. Or so they'd believed.

"All I know," Maria told her, "is that Ken sometimes moonlights for his former commanding officer, Tom something, who runs a personal security firm called Troubleshooters Incorporated. He was helping to guard someone, and . . . They were attacked. Tom was shot, too, but he's not as badly injured. He's in right now for a CAT scan—

a bullet creased his skull. That's really all we've heard. He's supposed to call Savannah when the test is done. Until then . . ." She sighed. "We wait and . . . Hang on a sec."

Jenn heard the muffled sound of voices, then Maria came back on the phone.

"Change in plans," her friend and boss reported. "We're not going to Westchester—well, we are, but we're not driving there. We're going down toward Wall Street. Van's uncle knows a guy who owns a building with a heliport. We're getting picked up there by a chopper that'll take us to the airport, where we'll meet the charter flight. If you're close, you can drive us, if not we can get a cab."

"I'm at the car," Jenn reported, unlocking Ford with an electronic *whoop* and sliding behind the wheel. She put her handbag on the passenger seat, locked the door behind her, fastened her seatbelt and put the key in the ignition. Dang, it smelled funky in here, as if someone had left a sandwich or a piece of fruit under the seat and it was turning into a distant cousin of gin, with a little middleschool gym locker thrown in. No doubt about it, it was time to hose this puppy down. "I have to hang up."

"We'll be waiting down in front," Maria promised, and cut the connection.

Jenn tossed her cell phone into her bag, put the car into reverse and looked into the rearview mirror.

And screamed at the top of her lungs.

There was a hulking shape of a man in the back seat— his eyes glistening in the dimness. She slammed it back to park and fumbled for the interior lights, for the door lock, for her belt release—getting everything on and opened at once.

She flung herself out of the car and into the street, with every darkly pointed comment her mother had ever made about living among all of the muggers and gangbangers and serial killers in New York City replaying loudly in her head. But she wasn't completely reduced to a terrified eleven-year-old—part of her brain was functioning clearly and calmly, assessing the situation, thank God. And thank her squad of boisterous older brothers who'd taught her self-defense by forcing her to defend herself against their teasing and taunts.

Her phone was in her bag, which was still on the front seat. Her keys were in the ignition. She could run, but she wouldn't be able to get back into her building or her apartment.

There was a twenty-four-hour convenience store two long and one short block away, but she wasn't much of a runner. Still, running—while continuing to scream loudly—was probably her best option. But before she took off, as she filled her lungs with air to scream again, she realized that the man, too, was scrambling out of the car. But he was going out the far door, on the sidewalk side—moving not toward her, but away from her.

And then she recognized him in the glow from the street light. He was the ancient-seeming homeless man that she'd seen in the neighborhood over the past few months. She'd spotted him many times, going through the dumpster in the back alley behind the office or napping in the waning sunshine in the little park down the street.

Everything about him was grayish-brown—his clothes, his long, scraggly hair and beard, his hands and face, his teeth.

"Sorry," he mumbled, slamming the car door and backing away, his hands outstretched, as if he were attempting to calm a wild animal. Or to show he was unarmed, which was good. "So sorry. Saw you park it earlier, figured you wouldn't be back until mornin'. You done scared me half to death."

She'd scared *him*?

"You were trespassing," she told him, her voice too loud to her own ears, her heart still pounding. She was still not completely convinced that he was harmless and that she was safe, so it was stupid to take such an accusing tone, but her fear was rapidly morphing into heat—into anger and indignation. "This car was *locked*."

He shrugged as he shuffled away. "Lock's not a lock to everyone, missy. Jus' wanted to be outa the rain. Stormy weather's comin'."

It *was* starting to rain, Jenn realized. It was coming down lightly in a mist that she wouldn't have noticed unless she was walking more than a few blocks—or sleeping on the street.

He faded into the shadows as Jenn exhaled hard, and—peering into the back of the car first, to make sure he hadn't left behind a companion—she climbed back in and locked all of the doors.

Her hands were shaking, but she put them on the steering wheel and forced herself to drive. Traffic was nonexistent, and in just a few minutes she made it to the building where Maria and Savannah both had condos.

Van's place was just a pied-à-terre—a home base for when she was in town—yet it still managed to be bigger and nicer than Jenn's miniscule studio apartment, and yeah, she *so* wasn't going to complain or even be envious. Nuh-uh. Not her. At least she *had* a place to live, unlike a lot of people these days, including Strong Aroma Man, who hadn't been even remotely stymied by Ford's security system. True, it wasn't close to state of the art, but still. . . . Note to self: Get one of those steering-wheel locks, ASAP.

As she pulled to the curb, there came Maria and Van out of a door held respectfully open by the always-on-duty doorman. Maria came around to the driver's side—that's right, she wanted to drive.

But that was Maria—always wanting to drive.

Jenn grabbed her bag and slid out, climbing into the back seat as Savannah and Maria took over the front. They were both traveling light and they passed their bags back so that Jenn could stow them on the seat next to her.

"Van," she started to say, "I can't imagine—"

"He's going to be all right." Savannah spoke with total conviction.

"Oh, thank God," Jenn said with a rush of relief. She looked from Van to Maria, who glanced back at her in the rearview mirror as she pulled into the street, doing a hair-raising youie that pointed them downtown. "You spoke to the doctor?"

But Maria's dark eyes were filled with warning as she looked into the mirror again and shook her head no.

"Not yet," Van admitted. "But I spoke to Meg. She's at the hospital, and she knows the surgeon. KatiAnn Watson. Meg said she's the best—Ken's in good hands."

"That's good to know," Jenn said, looking to Maria again for more information.

"Meg is the wife of one of the officers in Ken's SEAL team," Maria explained, driving as she always did—like a NASCAR champion.

"Is she the FBI agent?" Jenn asked, sitting back so she could fasten her seat belt. There was something hard back there, and she reached beneath her to pull free an old sock, its toe filled with God knows what—coins or marbles or maybe even gravel.

Ew. It obviously belonged to the homeless man, and she didn't want to look inside. She didn't want to touch the thing more than she had to. She dropped it on the floor, on the other side of the center bump.

"No, that's Alyssa," Maria was saying. "She's former FBI. She works for Troubleshooters now."

"She wasn't hurt, too, was she?" Jenn asked, as she saw that the sock wasn't the only thing the homeless man had left in the car. He'd stuck a ragged photograph of a dark-haired woman into the pocket in the back of the driver's seat. It must've slipped down during the drive, because only the woman's eyes and the top of her head protruded, as if she were peeking out at Jenn.

Van shook her head as Jenn pulled the photo free. "I don't think she was there."

The woman in the picture was African American, with short hair that framed her exceptionally beautiful face. It was hard to see in the dim light, but her eyes looked to be light-colored, and they seemed to sparkle as she looked into the camera's lens—her smile warm for the photographer.

She was young enough to be Aroma Man's granddaughter. Jenn flipped the photo over, but there was nothing written on the back—no date, no *Happy Birthday, Grandpa.* She reached over and tucked it into the top of the sock—then checked the pocket to see if he'd left anything else there when he'd moved in. But it was empty.

"Meg's married to John Nilsson," Maria explained as they sped south on the island, green traffic lights stretching out in front of them on the nearly deserted avenue, "who just got promoted. He's the new executive officer of Team . . ." She looked at Savannah. "Ten?"

"Twelve," she corrected.

"But Ken's still with Team Sixteen?" Jenn asked, and Savannah nodded.

Just last week, Van had showed her what looked like a class picture of the men in SEAL Team Sixteen—although it was unlike any class picture Jenn had ever seen before. In it the group of men were wearing swim trunks that looked as if they'd last had a design update back in 1943. Which was a good thing. The trunks—small by today's baggy standards—fit snugly and highlighted the men's amazingly sculpted bodies. Van had gone through the rows of men, name by name, teasingly picking out her choice for a potential hookup for Jenn—some junior grade lieutenant who bore the nickname Grunge.

Yes, Grunge. Thanks a million, Van.

Many of them—particularly the youngest, fresh from SEAL school, which Van had said was called BUD/S training, which stood for Basic Underwater Demolition slash SEAL—had ridiculous nicknames that made poor pathetic Scooter's self-proclaimed handle seem ordinary and lame.

Cosmo, Jazz, Gilligan, the Duke, Chickie, Hobomofo—who had a one syllable sub-nickname, Fo, for his nickname, and yes, there was no doubt a good story behind all four syllables of *that* one—Wiley, WetDream, and, of course, the esteemed Grunge. Ken's nickname was Wild-Card, which, okay, was kind of cool, but Jenn had never, ever heard Van call him that.

"Ken's going to be really angry," Van said now from the front seat, the streetlights that flashed across her face illuminating her anxiety. "Meg told me that the man he was guarding got taken. I want to be there before they tell him, because he's going to try to climb out of his hospital bed to be part of the team that goes and gets him back." She laughed, but her eyes filled with tears. "He's going to be all right," she said again, more to herself than to them. "He has to be."

"I'm *sure* he will," Jenn murmured.

"My laptop is in the office," Van turned back to tell her. "I didn't want to take the time to stop and pick it up."

"I'll send it to you," Jenn promised. "First thing in the morning."

But Van shook her head. "Let me get to California," she said, "and figure out where you should send it. I'm going to be at the hospital with Ken, and—"

"Wait to send it," Maria instructed, "until you hear from us."

"Absolutely," Jenn said. "And just let me know if there's anything else you need."

"We'll be in touch," Maria said.

"I made a list of all the meetings both Maria and I had

scheduled for the next two days." Van handed Jenn a legal pad. "Maria should be back after that."

"But if I'm not—" Maria interjected.

Jenn didn't let her finish. "I'll take care of everything," she promised again, flipping through the pad. Savannah had filled five pages with notes and lists.

"Page three and four are the interns' schedules," Van instructed. "Keep them going with the voter registration drive—these next few weeks are vital. Oh, and Douglas was helping me organize both a literature drop and weekend canvassing—again, focusing on getting out the vote. He can be a little defensive and I've found he's easiest to deal with if you give him plenty of time to talk. You don't have to do it his way, you just have to hear him out, okay?"

"Got it," Jenn said.

"Gene and Wendy are working with him to create a list of block captains," Savannah continued, "and . . . You have my number. If you have any questions—"

"Call *me*," Maria interrupted, as she pulled to the curb in front of . . . Zachary Towers?

No way. The "friend" that Savannah's Uncle Alex knew was Robert Zachary?

But yes, as they all clambered out of Ford, as Jenn humped her friends' bags out of the backseat, she saw that it was, indeed, the real-estate mogul emerging gracefully from his trademark stretch limo, dressed down in jeans and a sweatshirt. His eyes widened, as most men's eyes did, when he caught sight of Maria and Savannah. But then Savannah's uncle was there, too, pulling up in a cab, introducing them all.

Well, almost all.

Jenn wasn't affronted by the oversight, just resigned. The good news was that she would never need a cloak of invisibility when her gorgeous friends were around.

"Thank you," Van said, giving Jenn a hug.

"If you need *anything*," Jenn said again, but then they were gone, swept away into the building as the night guard leapt to unlock the door for his rich and famous boss.

Jenn climbed back into Ford and headed for home.

It was going to be a long night.

Savannah was gone.

She'd flown back to California before the sun had come up, long before he'd realized she'd escaped him and that his plan was ruined.

He'd wanted to scream when he found out. Scream, and wail, and tear at his clothes and hair.

He wanted to kill her—Jenn, the one who'd told him the news—right there and then. He hated her in that moment more than he'd ever hated anyone, as she promised all who were standing there in that pathetic little office that she'd keep them posted as to the husband's condition.

He was glad that he'd decided, back when he'd first worked out the details of his plan, not to make her his girlfriend. He'd done that before—played at normal with his victim, sometimes for weeks, before making her more permanently one of his own.

But Jenn wasn't his target and the thought of having to talk to her, to sit with her, to share her bed and make love to her . . .

He couldn't do it, couldn't settle for her mundaneness, couldn't betray his powerful emotions.

And although he wanted to, he didn't now slash Jenn into a hundred bleeding pieces—because doing so would not get him that which he wanted most.

Alyssssa . . .

He knew he was going to have to be patient again, he was going to have to wait longer. Maybe the husband would die, or maybe he'd live—either way Savannah would eventually return and he'd proceed as he'd long planned. He'd kill Savannah, and Alyssa would come.

Still, his chest was so tight and the roaring in his ears so loud, he knew he needed to find relief.

But it couldn't be now, and it absolutely couldn't be here. It had to be far enough away, and it had to be different—no long, lingering terror, no teeth.

Somehow he walked home.

Maybe . . . one tooth, broken as if accidentally, perhaps from a tire iron to the face.

Somehow he changed his clothes, changed his appearance, changed his very identity.

He knew how to not get caught, how to not get noticed, and he rented a car using a credit card he kept on hand for emergencies like this one. The camera behind the counter recorded the transaction, but its grainy images wouldn't help them find him, even if they got as far as connecting his rental to that which was to come.

He was more calm now, knowing what his immediate future held.

He left the garage, careful to obey the speed limit, careful not to cause gridlock, or to otherwise break the law.

He drove for hours, heading south through Jersey, almost to Baltimore. There was a mall in White Marsh, upscale and sprawling, with vast parking lots that became deserted at night—except for the areas near the movie theater. It had a Sears, and as the sun began to set, he parked and he went inside and bought a tire iron with cash.

And she was right there, behind the counter, as if waiting for him, a little worn around the edges, older than he usually liked and stinking of stale cigarette smoke. But she was blond and blue-eyed like Savannah—and as different from Alyssa as night was from day. So he smiled at her and she flirted with him and there was no one behind him in line, so he lingered.

She was working until nine-thirty, did he want to go out and get a drink . . . ?

It was that easy.

He went to his car to wait, and to look at his pictures—he'd taken a dozen with him for this trip—and to dream.

Of blood on his hands.

And of Alyssa Locke.

CHAPTER ONE

FOUR MONTHS LATER
MONDAY, 26 JANUARY 2009

The police detective was not impressed. "What is it, exactly, that you would like us to do?"

His name was Michael Callahan and he was young and not quite handsome, unless you went for the vaguely Popeye-esque, third-generation New York Irish cop type. Strawberry blond with blue eyes that could twinkle on command or look flat and bored, as they did right now. Lean face with sharply chiseled angular features, and a wiry, compact body. He played shortstop in the local softball league, Jenn would've bet her turkey-on-seedless-rye on that.

She answered his question with a question, aware that the interns were watching her. "What is it you usually do in situations like this?"

Situations in which a computer-printed note—obscene and rambling, but not quite a death threat—had been stuck to Assemblywoman Maria Bonavita's New York City office door with a sharply bladed knife, while Jenn and the interns had all been out at lunch.

Truth be told, Jenn hadn't expected the death threats

to start *quite* so soon. Cranky e-mails were one thing, but this . . . ?

It was only Maria's second week in office, and wasn't there supposed to be a so-called honeymoon period for an elected official? Perhaps a solid month, maybe two, before they'd have to make a call to the police?

"What we usually do is waste valuable lab time examining the fingerprints on the weapon," Callahan said, "and confirming the fact that everyone here touched it before calling us."

Ron and Gene looked abashed, and Jenn stepped to the interns' defense. "The note contains offensive language. There's a pediatric dentist's office right down the hall—"

"So you tear the paper," Callahan pointed out, "and leave the knife." He sighed again. "Not that it would've mattered. Whoever left this probably didn't leave prints. We wouldn't've found anything—at which point I would've called you back, and told you to be careful."

"Be careful," Jenn repeated.

"And to give us a call if you see anyone or anything suspicious."

"That's it," Jenn said. "Seriously. That's all you can do? I mean, thank God no one was here—"

"Whoever did this probably waited until he was sure that no one was here."

"*Probably?*"

"Lookit, for a threat this vague—" he started.

She interrupted, reading from the note, "*Next note gets pinned to your face* is vague?"

"Yeah, it is," he said. "Whose face? There's no mention of the assemblywoman. Maybe whoever wrote this was targeting the dentist down the hall and got the suite number mixed up."

"Her name is clearly on the door," Jenn pointed out.

"Okay," he said. "So when's this pinning going to take place? Today? Tomorrow? Two months from now?

Maybe you want us to post a guard in the hall, 24/7 . . . ? Of course, if we post a guard in the hallway of everyone in this city who's received a threat from some crackpot, we'll need to hire at least two million more uniformed officers. You might want to check with your boss, see if she thinks she can't find the funding to make *that* happen. Hey, I know, she could cut ammunition *completely* out of the budget, outfit both the Staties and the NYPD with swords, get one of those whetting stones for each department and boom—we're done."

Jenn had had enough. "Are you?" she asked sharply. "Done? Because Assemblywoman Bonavita was fact-finding, okay? She asked a simple question—does the State of New York really need to spend *that* much money on ammunition? She had no idea that police training was constant and required that many bullets, and when she found out, she agreed—completely and absolutely—that this was *not* a line item that could be cut or even marginally reduced. She's been vocal—throughout her campaign—about her support of New York's need for additional first responders, both in the police and fire departments, and about the *supreme* necessity of giving them the supplies and equipment required for them to do their jobs. Which is what *you* should be doing—your job. Whether or not you think that the assemblywoman asked a stupid question, whether or not you believe that questions that upset the status quo should never be asked at all, whether you voted for Maria or for the idiot, I don't care. Check it, Detective, at the door, and tell me what I need to do to keep my boss and my staff safe from *crackpots* who like to play with knives."

She'd stunned him into silence. Not so Ron and Gene, who'd expected her to blow—having seen it happen many times before. And oh, good, Hank the UPS man was standing in the open doorway, a package in his hands, grinning his handsome ass off. Gene went to sign for it, but he took his sweet time as they all just stood there, in her post-outburst silence, waiting to see what would happen next.

The detective was looking around—at the campaign posters that still adorned the walls, at the big whiteboard that they used to keep track of all of Maria's special projects, at the clutter atop Jenn's desk, at the radiator that clunked and hissed and made the office far, far too warm, and finally at her.

At her shoes, at her legs, at her dress, at the necklace she wore at her throat, and finally at her face.

And it was only then, as he met her eyes, that Detective Callahan laughed.

And it wasn't a nasty, you've-crossed-the-line-bitch laugh. It was genuinely amused—as if the mean, bored robot cop had been replaced by a real human boy.

And when he finished laughing, he was still smiling, and that smile, with the accompanying warmth in his eyes, further transformed him, and he was no longer not-quite-handsome. He was now stunningly good-looking—completely jello-knee inducing—like the even-more-attractive love child of Denis Leary and Damian Lewis. And he was particularly attractive because he was now looking at Jenn as if she were not just interesting, but an interesting *woman*.

"I voted for the idiot," he admitted. "But he was the idiot I knew, so . . ." He shrugged expansively, charmingly.

Hank sent Jenn an air kiss as he closed the door behind him. Now that the show was over, Ron and Gene, too, escaped into Maria's office with the package.

"Our website was extensive and easy to access," Jenn told the detective, hiding her fluster and resisting the urge to fix her hair. There was nothing she could do to make it look better anyway, and if she touched it, her body language would shout that she was vulnerable to his charm.

She wasn't certain of much—except for the fact that she wanted to keep that newsflash from him. Instead, she pushed her glasses up her nose and folded her arms across her chest. "It still is. The assemblywoman's positions are clearly outlined. *She's* your champion, Detective. The *idiot* thought the solution to budget cuts was to downsize the police department and instead impose a strict youth curfew. A curfew, in the city that Frank says doesn't sleep."

"Really?"

"You voted for him, and you don't know that? His position was that cuts to the police and fire department were inevitable. Maria, on the other hand, has been outspoken in her belief that New York needs to grow both departments—"

"And pay for it how?"

"We're still working on that," she admitted. "Hence the line-by-line perusal of the budget—"

"Hence," he said, with another laugh. "Who says *hence*?"

"—and the accompanying hoopla over the question about ammunition," she continued.

"*Hoopla*, I like," he told her, the twinkle in his eye on full power.

"The hoopla," she repeated, enjoying the eye contact. Was he actually flirting with her? ". . . is nothing compared to the full-on uproar over the Ten Commandments issue, which is what this"—she gestured to the threatening note and the knife—"is about."

He nodded. "Yeah, I actually heard about that one."

One of the newly elected assembly members from a more conservative upstate district wanted to reinstall an antique plaque with the Ten Commandments in the lobby of the building that housed Maria's office in Albany. It had hung there over fifty years earlier, was removed during renovations, believed lost, but had now been found.

Maria had made a statement announcing that because

her many constituents in New York City had a wide variety of religious beliefs, the presence of this plaque in a state building should also mean that other religious icons and messages could now be placed in the lobby as well.

It was then that the flood of angry e-mails and phone calls started—most of them from out of state. They'd received a number of anonymous threats, all of which they'd reported according to legislative guidelines, but it wasn't until this ugliness—delivered at the end of a very sharp knife—that Jenn became more than just mildly concerned.

Maria was worried about it, too—enough to drive back from Albany, even though Ford was developing an odd-sounding cough.

"The really stupid thing," Jenn told the detective now, "is that it's over. Completely. We all compromised—we found common ground. The plaque *is* a part of New York's heritage, and everyone agreed that in order to preserve it, it should be in a special glass case." With another plaque documenting its history, as well as a clarification from a local constitutional scholar as to the importance of separation of church and state.

"In the back of the lobby," Callahan pointed out. "Near the restrooms."

"Which nearly every guest to the building visits," she countered.

He laughed. "Nice spin."

"Both sides are satisfied," she told him. "But we're still getting the angry e-mails—more each day. I've done some research—basic Google searches—and I found out that some wing-nut radio talk show hosts are targeting us."

"Isn't that part of the job description?" he asked. "Both theirs and yours?"

"Not when it incites something like this."

She could brush aside the threats that came from

brainwashed people sitting on their sofas with their laptops, able to send an e-mail, but too lazy to actually get off their butts.

Someone clearly had, however, gotten off his butt this morning.

As Callahan glanced over again at the threatening note that was atop her desk, his expression turned rueful. "I wish there were easy answers, but . . ." He shook his head. "I'm not going to lie to you, Jennifer—"

"Jenn's short for Jennilyn," she corrected him.

"Jennilyn," he repeated, making a note on the scruffy little pad that he'd pulled from the inside pocket of his leather jacket when he'd first arrived. "Pretty name. Two words? Hyphenated?"

"One word," she told him, spelling it for him, spelling her last name, LeMay, while she was at it. "And I've found that people usually say *I'm not going to lie to you* before they actually, you know, lie to you?"

He smiled again as he nodded. "Yeah, me too. It's just . . . there's not much to go on. The paper that the note's printed on is standard copy paper. Maybe the lab could tell us whether this was printed on an inkjet or some other kind of printer. They could certainly ID the font, but—"

"I can do that. It's Times New Roman, size eighteen or twenty," Jenn said.

"There you go," the detective told her. "That's narrowed our suspects down to most of the people in Manhattan. And who's to say he or she"—he looked at the knife and made a choice—"*he* didn't come in from out of town—and don't start screaming that I'm being sexist—"

"I've been assuming it's a man, too," she cut him off, "which is definitely sexist, but probably true. Men often suck."

"Not all of 'em," he said. "And as far as the knife

goes . . ." He picked it up. "It's a Wüsthof—a high-end kitchen knife, sold not just in a set but also separately at Macy's, and the only reason I know *that* is my cousin Julie just got engaged and there was this whole crazy thing with my aunt about not giving or getting knives as a gift. Turns out if you do, the world will end and . . . Just . . . Trust me. They sell 'em, by the dozens at Macy's and God knows where else. So . . ." He shrugged again. "Short of my sitting outside your door day and night, I think the first thing you should do is upgrade your security system. Both here and at yours and the assembly-woman's residences."

He looked around the tiny front office, at the two desks and the conference table that was covered with stacks of files from the school-safety project. "Any other full-time staffers in the office?"

"No," she answered. Savannah hadn't returned since Ken was injured. With Jenn's help, she'd managed the campaign long-distance from beside her husband's hospital bed, and had only come back to town—very briefly—for election day and their victory party. She still stayed in touch by phone, though. Jenn was looking forward to her input and opinion on how to keep Maria safe. In fact, she was going to call Savannah immediately after the detective left. "Just interns and the occasional volunteer."

"And they're all people you trust?" Callahan asked. "People whose backgrounds you've cleared?"

"Yes," Jenn told him, but then shook her head. "The interns, yes. But the volunteers . . . You can't exactly grill someone who comes in to help stuff envelopes for a mailing."

"But everyone who's got a key has been checked?" he asked, as he glanced at his watch and frowned.

"I don't think so," Jenn admitted. "We were pretty free and easy during the campaign, handing out keys to just about anyone. It's not as if there was anything in here to steal, so . . ."

"Lookit, I'm sorry, I gotta go. I'm already late to a meeting and . . ." He dug in his pocket and pulled out a business card, which she took. "This is my number. If there's trouble call 9-1-1, but after that, make sure you also call me." With a nod, he turned to the door.

"Detective Callahan," Jenn said.

He turned back. "Mick," he told her. "One of my many cousins is Michael, too. He's older, so I got stuck with Mick."

"Are you going to file a report?"

"Since there's no real threat, best I can do is make a note about it," he said, apologetic. "Beat cops'll keep an eye out, but . . . It would be good if you punched up your own security."

"Yeah," Jenn said. "About that. Maria—the assembly-woman—she'll definitely get an alarm system installed here, but . . . It's her own safety that she tends to be somewhat cavalier about. I wonder if you could . . . come back and . . . maybe . . . talk to her directly?"

He glanced at his watch again, but he didn't sigh with disgust. "When's she gonna be in?"

Maria had been nearly to Kingston when Jenn had called her. She looked at her own watch. "With traffic . . . ? Probably four thirty or five."

"Keep her here 'til six," Mick said, "and I'll drop in after my shift."

"No," Jenn said. "You don't have to do that—"

"Yeah," he said, with another of those killer smiles. "I know."

"Thanks," she said, and despite the fact that her insides were melting—or quite possibly because of it—she found herself adding, "I'm also curious. I'm, um . . . What just happened here?"

Her heart was in her throat, because it was completely unlike her to be so flirtatious. She hadn't gone out on a date, hadn't so much as looked twice at a man in the four months since the tragedy with Scooter Randall.

Of course the detective didn't understand what she was asking, so now she was forced to explain. "You weren't very, um, friendly when you first got here and now you are. Friendly, I mean—and . . ." Jenn trailed off, unable to bring herself to say *I was wondering if you maybe wanted to get a drink later?*

"Yeah," he said, rolling his eyes. "Sorry about the attitude before. I just . . . It's been a bitch of a week and . . . I wasn't expecting . . . But then you kinda crushed me like a bug, and . . . You reminded me so much of my sister, it just, um . . ."

His *sister.*

"Ah," Jenn said. "Of course."

"We're twins and . . ."

"Twins."

"She moved to England three years ago, and, well, I guess I haven't had a good bug crush since." He winked at her, the way he might wink at a little kid or, yes, a sister. "I appreciate it, Jennilyn. I'll see you later."

And with that, he was gone.

She usually hated it when people used her full name—it was so feminine and flowery and it made her feel like a misnamed giant. And not a good giant like an Amazon warrior or Xena, but an ungainly one who wore sturdy shoes and support hose to keep her cankles from becoming even more sausage-like—even though her own ankles were actually quite nice.

But when Mick Callahan called her Jennilyn in his slightly husky voice, it had sounded like music.

Except he'd already gone and sistered her. He was not the first to do that—and he wouldn't be the last. In fact, the only thing that she could predict more accurately than the fact that the attractive, friendly man she'd just met was going to tell her that she reminded him of his sister, was the fact that the attractive, friendly man whom she reminded of his sister always, *always* fell in love with her gorgeous best friend at first sight.

Always.

So even if Detective Steamy Hot *hadn't* sistered her— twin-sistered her, which, okay, *was* a first—she'd be facing *that* impending heartbreak in just a few short hours.

As it currently stood, with her hopes already brotherishly dashed, she would feel no more than a pinch of regret when Mick took one look at Maria, fell to his knees, and broke into song.

It would sting, sure, but the disappointment wouldn't last long.

And one of these days, she'd meet a guy who thought of *Maria* as a sister and he'd fall madly in love with Jenn.

He was out there—she believed it. Although, truth be told, he probably didn't look *quite* like Detective Mick Callahan.

Which, frankly, was kind of a shame.

CHAPTER TWO

The man with the neck tattoo was reaching for a handgun.

It was a marvelous piece of artwork—the tattoo, not the gun—the swastika embellished and intertwined with curlicues and baroque swirls, to the point of being nearly completely disguised.

Although the handgun *was* beautiful, too. The theater's lights glinted off of it as the gunman pulled back his shirt to reveal it tucked into the top of his ragged jeans. It was a museum-quality Nambu Taisho—long and skinny, a Japanese relic from WWII—that he'd no doubt lifted from some wealthy collector's inadequately locked display case.

Alyssa Locke had already looked into this man's hazy eyes, back before he'd jumped the flimsy metal fence that still contained most of the tourists, fans, and autograph-seekers. She'd picked him out of the crowd that came to cheer or jeer the stars as they walked the red carpet that led into this Hollywood movie premiere. She knew, just from one look, that he was jacked up on something that impaired his judgment.

And in those fractions of a second after he jumped the

fence and reached for that pistol, as she sifted through her options and settled on the obvious—disarm him by force or someone was going to get shot—she also knew, without a doubt, that using reason to talk him into surrendering that weapon wasn't going to happen.

He wasn't looking to get out alive. He wanted his fifteen minutes of fame, with his picture flashed, postmortem, on AOL and CNN, his name spoken by the news anchors in hushed tones as he gained notoriety as the man who killed movie star Robin Chadwick Cassidy.

And the killing-Robin part was probably a secondary goal, since he could have taken the shot from the crowd instead of making that theatrical leap over the ineffective waist-high fence.

No, Alyssa was certain that what this man wanted, most of all, was for his life to be over and done.

He'd targeted her as the weakest link in the Robin Cassidy security chain. True, she wasn't built like her husband, former SEAL Sam Starrett, or their current team leader Ric Alvarado, or team member Jones, or even Annie, who was tall and voluptuous.

Alyssa wasn't insulted that he'd singled her out—it happened often enough. Plus, it gave her additional insight into his reasoning abilities, or lack thereof. He was not any kind of trained operative, or else he would've instantly picked up her years both as a Naval officer and as an agent with the FBI in her movement and stance.

Instead, he'd chosen to trespass into her quadrant, flinching but not retreating when she'd first hit him with the full power and volume of her "I am in charge here" voice.

"Stay behind the barricade. Sir! I said *Stay. Behind. The barricade!*" As Alyssa got even louder, she'd felt the swift movement behind her.

She hadn't had to look to know what the rest of her team was doing. They'd surrounded Robin, providing a very literal human shield as they hustled him into the safety of the theater.

Sam, she knew, would dump and run—straight back to her, to provide assistance. But she also knew that this was going to be over before it started.

Until, of course, the man pulled back his shirt to reveal that weapon.

Which was when time slowed way down, seconds stretching endlessly out, as she opened her mouth, and, as if possessed, words tumbled out.

"I have a baby," she heard herself tell him. The mother in her was as much of an infant as her son Ashton was, yet it somehow effortlessly overcame the tough-as-nails operative and even the jaded little girl she'd once been—both of whom knew that any attempts at communication with this man were useless.

It was strange to realize how swiftly her life had changed; how differently she felt inside of her more matronly body, inside of her often noisy and crowded head, simply because this miniature person who was part her and part Sam and fully his own incredible self had entered her world. At times she still felt as astonished as Ash had been months ago when he'd first flailed and spotted one of his own tiny fists, staring at it like some UFO overhead, in gleeful, wide-eyed wonder.

"He's ten months old," she told the gunman, too, because beneath the swastika tattoo, despite the drug-rotted teeth, he was a person who'd once been as small as Ash. He'd once been held in his own mother's loving arms, where she'd kissed the top of his downy, sweet-smelling head.

And despite her years of hard-earned knowledge which told her that, by pulling that weapon, he'd lost his identity and had, in fact, become *the target*, the part of her who was now Ash's mother had to try to reach out to him.

But he wouldn't hear her, or he couldn't, or he heard her and he didn't care, so she drew her own weapon—faster and in better control because her brain wasn't stuttering from alcohol and God knows what else.

Her brain was, however, fatigued from too many midnight feedings, from the strain of restricting her own diet in a hit-or-miss attempt to ease her baby's relentless gas and give them all a chance to sleep through the night. Her brain was fuzzy from the off-the-charts splatter of her still seesawing hormone levels, from Sam's wary confusion when she—usually more stoic than his teammates from his Navy SEAL days—simply couldn't *not* cry.

Because even the joy was exhaustingly overwhelming. Watching Sam with Ash—holding their baby in his big arms, singing to their son as he adeptly changed his diapers, or even asleep on the couch with Ash on his chest—the TV light from a muted football game flickering across them both . . .

This current Troubleshooters assignment was supposed to be an easy one. It was a favor, really—providing additional bodyguard assistance to the team safeguarding actor Robin Cassidy's appearance at a movie premiere while his husband, her very good friend Jules, was stuck back East.

It seemed provident: a simple assignment for her and Sam's first full night—ever—with both of them working and away from Ash.

Taking down an assailant who was armed with a Nambu pistol on the sidewalk in front of Mann's Chinese Theatre was the last thing she'd expected to be doing tonight.

And her finger was already tightening on her trigger before the trivial-seeming fact that this was a Nambu flashed through her head again, along with the thought that getting bullets for that thing would had to have been a bitch and a half.

Did they even make them anymore?

The collector he'd stolen the weapon from might've had some.

But what brain-shredded druggie, having broken into some rich guy's house, would know that the pretty, shiny handgun that he'd grabbed from the display case before he fled would need bullets that you couldn't possibly score at the nearest Wal-Mart? Bullets that you might actually need to time travel back to the 1940s to buy?

Odds were that this Nambu had no rounds in its chamber, that it was just a prop—and that this ornate man's true motive here was suicide by celebrity bodyguard.

And regardless of who she was—mother or wife or second in command of Troubleshooters Incorporated, *the* top personal security firm in the United States of America—Alyssa knew that taking this bozo down with no shots fired might not be quicker, but it would be cleaner, on so many levels.

So she launched herself at him. Goal one: get that weapon out of his hands, in case she was wrong about the bullets thing. A well-aimed kick did just that, spinning him away from her, his hand outstretched as he started to scramble after the pistol.

She was still moving and she used her momentum to block his path, her own force pushing her almost past him, so she spun again as he now grabbed for her, clutching at the front of her shirt. But she brought her right elbow up and back, putting all of her strength into a blow that connected squarely with the side of his head.

He lost his grip on her and went down, and, as she continued the turn, she saw Sam, heading back toward her, not even slowing as he bent and scooped up the Nambu, as he raced to her aid.

But she was still spinning from that elbow blast and she used the full force of the muscles in her left leg—a leg that had helped carry a very healthy nine-pound baby to term—and she kayoed the attacker with a solid kick to the chin.

He was down, he was done, but her training had been instilled in her—it wasn't over until the perp was cuffed and searched for additional weapons.

So Alyssa put the safety back on her sidearm and holstered it even as she pushed the man flat, her knee hard in the middle of his back, his cheek against Ginger Rogers' ridiculously tiny handprints, as she reached into her back pocket for one of the plastic restraints that Troubleshooters Incorporated operatives carried on every bodyguard assignment. She cuffed him quickly, easily, before Sam reached her side.

He was pissed—at her as well as at the gunman. Alyssa could read his familiar body language even out of the corner of her eye. And the crowd that had been stunned into both stillness and silence—it had all happened so fast, she was certain that most of the people hadn't even seen the assailant's gun—suddenly seemed to exhale, in unison.

"Crowd control," she curtly ordered her husband, who understood and made the weapon vanish. No point waving it around and starting a panic-induced stampede.

But it was then, as she was glancing up at Sam, her knee still pressing the gunman down, that again, almost as one, the paparazzi part of the crowd reacted.

There had to be a hundred cameras out there, and it seemed as if all of their flashes went off within the span of a few blinding seconds. But it didn't let up, it just kept coming—a barrage of flashing lights, along with a roar of questions.

"Who are *you*?" Ah, how quickly they forget—thank God.

"How long have you worked security for Robin Cassidy?"

"Alyssa Locke! Are you back to working with the

FBI?" Obviously, they hadn't all forgotten—not that it really mattered. Her picture had been splashed around enough in the past few years—thank you, Robin—that it wouldn't take a good reporter more than a few minutes surfing the net to identify her. And also to confirm that, no, she wasn't back with the Bureau.

"*How* do you spell your name?"

"Ms. Locke, have you determined the identity of the man with the gun?"

The word *gun* seemed to reverberate with a ripple, out through the throng, and as distant sirens grew louder, Alyssa finished patting down the addict—careful of potential stray needles—and, failing to find a wallet or anything at all in his pockets, stood up.

And the volley of flashes exploded again.

How did Jules and Robin live with this, day in and day out? Twenty seconds in, and it was already stale.

And oh. Great. The son of a bitch had ripped her blouse—one of the few she had that was both dressy enough for this type of event and roomy enough to wear over her still-super-sized baby boobs. She quickly covered herself by buttoning her suit jacket, which, with her blouse hanging open, made her look like the Cleavage Queen, and . . . oh. Extra great. The adrenaline or the exertion or maybe just the sheer inconvenience of the situation was causing her to leak.

The irony being that, after all these months of breast-feeding, she still sometimes struggled to relax enough to allow her milk to let down. Apparently she was going about it all wrong. No need for the soft lights and rocking chair. She just needed to throw down and kick someone's ass first.

Questions were still being shouted, to her, at her, so she folded her arms across her chest and raised her voice to be heard over them as she addressed the crowd. "Everything's under control. I'm going to ask you to clear a path for the police." She turned to Sam, lowered her voice. "Can you take it from here?"

He nodded as he looked at her, his gaze skimming down her and sharpening as he tried to see inside of her head. "You hurt?"

"No." But she was already moving toward the theater doors. "I'm fine."

But this was Sam, and he knew something wasn't right. Something besides the relentless questions and photographs, that is—which always pissed her off. He must've gotten on his radio and called Annie, because she came out of the theater, passing Alyssa, moving fast toward the sidewalk where Sam had possession of the perp.

And sure enough, Alyssa was barely into the theater's ladies' room, taking her place on the perpetual and slow-moving line, when her husband pushed open the door and followed her inside.

He was stunningly attractive tonight, dressed as he was in a dark suit and tie, with his sun-streaked brown hair tied neatly back for the occasion. His well-tailored jacket and pants made his shoulders look extra broad, his trim waist and hips extra slim, and his legs extra long. All that, plus blue eyes in a ruggedly handsome face that telegraphed both his intelligence and wicked sense of humor—even when, like now, he wasn't smiling—made the other women gaze at him with interest.

They weren't staring because he'd dared to enter this bathroom—that was no big deal. This was, after all, Hollywood. No, they were staring because they hoped that he'd come in search of *them*.

"Security," he told the waiting women. "Let's move this line outside."

"That's not necessary," Alyssa told them, told Sam. "You should be with Robin. This could've been a diversion—"

"He's secure," Sam said. "Ric and Jones have him in a

safe room. They're locked down." He stepped closer, lowered his voice, his concern radiating off of him. "Lys, if you're hurt—"

"I'm not," she said, lowering her voice, too, and pulling him back out into the lobby, because some of the women were acting as if their private conversation were the pre-show, "I'm just . . ." She uncrossed her arms to show him her shirt, and fabulous. She didn't have to bother to open her jacket. She'd leaked clear through it.

"Holy shit." Sam laughed and took her hand, pulling her toward a uniformed usher—complete with hat—who was standing guard at a cordoned-off stairway.

"Not. Funny," she said, even though she recognized that it *was* both funny and pathetic. She'd brought a change of shirt, but not a second jacket.

"Yeah, it is when you think about it." Sam held the barrier open for her, and led her up the stairs. "You're like the ultimate woman—a badass Madonna. Locked and loaded with a baby at your breast. That's my idea of the feminine ideal, by the way. It totally works for me."

"Good thing."

He still had her by the hand and he pulled her down an empty corridor, where all the doors—three of them— were tightly closed.

"And I gotta confess," he added, "that your new bra that you flashed at everyone out there? The one that's gonna show up on page three of the *National Voice* and every other tabloid rag in the country . . . ? It works for me, too."

She laughed at that. She'd gone to the store, Ash in tow, to pick up some sturdy ones that were designed to contain the problem which she was currently experiencing. But this one all but had a neon arrow pointing to it, with loopy flashing letters saying *Sam will love this! Buy it now!* Red and lacy, with panties to match, it left very little to the imagination.

No doubt about it, her husband did love lingerie, and she'd put it on this evening for the occasion—this, their first night away from Ashton. Of course, with all the parties Robin was attending after the movie premiere, Alyssa hadn't been scheduled to show it to Sam until well after 0300.

He stopped her now in the privacy of the empty hallway and tugged gently at the lapel of her jacket. "C'mon. Lemme see if you're gonna need a tetanus booster. If Swastika Boy scratched you bad enough—"

"I'm fine," she said again, but she knew only one surefire way to alleviate his concern. She opened her jacket.

"Fine," he repeated, his voice even huskier as he let his gaze turn hot, as he smiled at her, "is an understatement."

"We're working," she reminded him. She needed to find a bathroom with some privacy where she could get cleaned up and change her shirt, and yet . . . She didn't feel compelled to refasten her jacket, particularly when he ran one finger lightly along the edge of the bra in question. "We need to check in with Ric."

"Uh-huh," he said, although it was clear he wasn't listening.

"Roger." She used his given name. Sam was just a Navy SEAL nickname that had stuck. "Focus."

"I find," he murmured, as he moved in even closer, wrapping his arm around her waist, "that I'm intensely focused."

Oh, yes he most certainly was. And, God, how was it, after all these years, that this man still had the power to make her heart beat harder and her mouth go dry?

He knew it, too—she could see that as well, gleaming in his eyes as he leaned down and kissed her—a silent promise that their baby-free night was going to be a memorable one. But then he pulled her in even more tightly, in an embrace that wasn't entirely about keeping her up all night.

And it was only then, as he held her like that, that he whispered, "Jesus, you scared the shit out of me down there."

"I'm sorry." Alyssa knew from experience how hard it was to do what Sam had done—to run away from, instead of toward, the action. She knew that the adrenaline that had coursed through his system was probably still making his hands shake—it was actually far easier to be the one under direct attack than to have to watch it happen to someone you loved.

"It's stupid," he admitted as he pulled back to rest his forehead against hers. "But it's even harder now that Ash is in the picture. I'm not the only one who loses if—"

"It goes both ways," she reminded him.

"I know," he said, but he didn't sound completely convinced.

A door opened behind them, and she pulled out of his arms and buttoned her jacket.

"There you are," Robin said. "Are you all right?"

"I'm fine," Alyssa told him—it was her refrain for the evening. "His weapon wasn't loaded, it was no big deal."

"Yeah," Sam said with a laugh, as he followed her into the office where Ric and Jones were keeping Robin safe, "right. No big deal."

But she knew he didn't mean that, either.

CHAPTER THREE

Sam was out of practice.

Or, rather, he'd had a little too *much* practice, over the past ten months, in the time-honored art of the quickie.

But tonight Ash wasn't here to interrupt, as Sam tugged the last little bit of red satin and lace down his impossibly beautiful wife's long legs, as he kissed her and licked her and took his sweet time, as she dug her fingers into his hair and breathed his name in her musical voice, as he kissed her and kissed her and *kissed* her.

"Please," she was saying, "please," so he slid inside of her but he needed to take a minute—a momentary time out—to put himself back into the game, to remember the way they used to do this, but she was moving beneath him and he'd never been good at denying her that which she so clearly wanted.

Instead, he started sweating and his arms were shaking, but he was determined not to waste this opportunity. God only knew the next time they'd have a baby-free night. Which was not to say that they wouldn't have sex until then—and lots of it—because they would and they did.

Alyssa was completely up for grabbing some serious happy-fun whenever and wherever the opportunity arose, and in fact was often the instigator of the two-minute orgasm quick-fest. Over the past ten months, they'd had a lot of incredibly hot, over-too-fast sex in the bathroom, in the kitchen, on the stairs going up to the second floor, even out in the garage. She'd waylaid him more than once—pun intended—when he was taking out the trash.

They'd gotten it on at all times of day, all over their house—with the exception of here, in their bed, at night.

For some reason, it seemed that whenever they went into their bedroom and closed the door, Ashton would wake up and cry. And okay, he knew that that wasn't true. But what *was* true was that Sam would spend the entire time *thinking* that any minute the baby was going to start to wail. Either that, or before he even made it into bed, Alyssa would fall into an exhausted sleep—which kind of killed the mood.

In truth, he was beyond grateful that this woman that he loved more than life was both enthusiastic and creative when it came to getting it on. But he realized now, as he took his sweet time making love to her, that there was something that he missed almost as much as slowly sliding inside her, against her, body to body, skin to skin, her mouth soft and warm against his as she gasped her pleasure. . . .

He missed lying with their bodies still entangled, their hearts beating together, her breath warm against his neck as she sighed with contentment, the flutter of her eyelashes against his cheek, the soft rumble of her rich laughter as she felt him start to harden, again, inside of her, because he could . . . not . . . get enough . . . of her. . . .

"Ah, God, Lys," he breathed, and she opened her eyes to look up at him. She was the love of his heart, his true partner in both work and life, and the idea of losing her to the violence of the world they lived in scared the living shit out of him.

But her smile lit her eyes, her face, and he pushed the darkness away and let himself grin back at her like the damn fool that he was. This moment—now—was perfect, and he wasn't going to let his fears interfere.

Especially since it was only 2100. This perfect night was still ridiculously young.

"Thank you for talking Robin into going home early," she whispered as she moved beneath him, and the sublime magic of the fact that she was doing *that* and *thanking* him for the opportunity was not lost on him.

Convincing Robin to call it a night hadn't taken much effort. Just a few well-chosen words, and the actor—a good friend to them both—had understood completely that Sam needed to take Alyssa home. Not wanted—*needed*. Regardless of her "piece of cake" attitude toward her takedown of the gunman, regardless of her "I'm fine" pronouncements, Robin knew that Sam had to be in a safe place with her, with his arms tightly around her, for a good, oh, ten or so hours.

Robin knew that because Jules, the love of *his* life, worked for the FBI. Robin knew what it was like to witness an incident that could well have ended differently and tragically, had the luck of angels not been on their side.

Robin knew this, and had pulled the plug on the night's party-going. He'd headed back to the safety of his hotel room, where Sam and Alyssa weren't needed.

Which freed them up to come here.

"I vaguely remember how to do this," Alyssa breathed now as she wrapped her long, strong legs around him, pushing him even more completely inside of her. "And I remember why I liked it so much. The bed, the pillows, the music and candlelight . . ."

"Oh, yeah," he agreed.

"Although," she gasped as she strained against him, "there's a part of me . . . that can't stop listening—waiting—for Ash to start . . . crying." She laughed. "Followed by the sound of you . . . crying."

"If you need it, I'm happy to supply the soundtrack,"

Sam teased her back. "Wah . . . Although, this time it's tears of joy."

Still laughing, she pulled his head down and kissed him, and ah, God, it was too good, too sweet, too unbearably hot as her laughter turned to sounds of need, way in the back of her throat.

"Come on," he said into her mouth as he felt her start to unravel, as he urged her to let go. "*Come* on . . ." Because he had it back—his control. He was still sweating, but damn it, his arms were solid again and he was fully in charge. He was going to make her come, and then, he was going to make her come *again*. And only after that, was he gonna—

The phone rang.

It was shrill, it was insistent, and it was startling and disruptive in the quiet heat and intimacy of the moment.

And like one of Pavlov's dogs, after ten months of coitus interruptus and/or the very real fear of such, Sam instantly went into warp-speed autopilot.

Ringing equaled phone call.

Phone call equaled problem.

Problem needed fixing.

Fixing needed Sam and Alyssa both, up and out of bed.

Come now or don't come 'til later.

Probably much, *much* later.

As the phone sent out a second blast of ringing, his body chose *now* before his brain caught up, and he crashed into her with a shout, "Fuck!" before he could stop himself. "God *damn* it!"

Alyssa was breathless and laughing, and no doubt a little confused, because in her mind, "That was perfect timing."

The last thing Sam wanted to do was let go of her, but in order to pick up the phone, he had to roll off of her. He crawled over to the other side of their bed, away from her warmth, which pissed him off even more and made his barked greeting sound far less than friendly. "This better be good!"

There was silence on the other end, then a female voice said, "I'm so sorry, Sam, did I call too late? It's just . . . I've been trying to reach you for a couple of days. There's a bit of urgency and—"

"Savannah?" he asked.

Which was when Alyssa took the phone from his hands. "Hey, Van," she said, her voice just a tad breathless. "Is everything okay? Is Ken—"

But Savannah's husband—and Sam's friend—Ken was doing well in his ongoing recovery from last fall's near fatal gunshot wound, because Alyssa said, "Oh, good. That's . . . Oh, that's *great* news. I'm glad. Yeah. . . . No . . . No, it's okay. It's not too late for . . ." She paused longer this time, listening to Savannah, then added, "No, no—I understand your concern and . . . Navy SEALs, yeah—and Sam, yes, a former SEAL—it's a great idea, uh-huh . . ."

And okay. Now Sam was intrigued. What was going on with Ken and Savannah that was urgent, to which adding SEALs and former SEALs, including himself, to the mix would be a great idea?

"*Tomorrow?*" Alyssa said, and Sam pushed himself up onto one elbow to better watch her walk across the room. "They are? Wow. I actually think my schedule could . . . Well, child care's always an issue for short notice jobs, but . . ." Her briefcase was leaning against the wall by the door, and she dug into it, looking for something. "Oh, if we could do that, then . . . Absolutely. I'd just have to check with Tom Paoletti, see if he could spare Sam and . . . You *did*? Well, all right then."

Alyssa fished a notepad and pen from her briefcase, caught him watching her as she straightened up, and smiled. She added a little attitude to her walk as she went to the dresser, where she used the top as a writing surface.

And okay, watching his wife walk around naked was another thing Sam had missed in the past ten months. Quickies tended to involve only partial removal of clothing. And as long as Alyssa kept this phone call short, and then walked—naked—back over here to the bed when she was done . . .

His plans for the remainder of the evening were entirely salvageable.

"Hang on just a sec," she said into the phone. "I was getting a pen and . . . Can you spell the congresswoman's name for me again? Oh, it's not? She's an assemblywoman. Okay. Got it. And her website is . . . dot *gov.* Right."

She wrote it all down on the pad, and then said the words that could, absolutely, not just ruin his evening, but trash the entire rest of his week. "And the flight information . . . ?"

Sam sat up.

"Oh, that's perfect," Alyssa told her friend. "We're picking up Ash tomorrow at eight and . . . No, he's having his first sleepover tonight—with Cosmo, Jane, and Billy and . . ." She laughed. "It's really okay, but yes. Let's plan to talk again tomorrow morning and . . . After eight, yes. How about I call you from the car? All right—talk then." And with that, she hung up the phone. And turned to Sam. "Want to go to New York?"

"In January?" he asked. "Not really."

"It's almost February," she pointed out.

"Same thing."

"Please?"

"No fair," he said. "Naked begging—how am I supposed to say no?"

She snorted. "Saying *please* isn't begging."

"It is," he pointed out, "if you say it while you're naked. Although crawling across the floor would help."

She crossed her arms and tilted her head. "You *really* don't want to go to New York City?"

The idea of leaving her alone here with Ash freaked him out—which, in turn, freaked him out even more. Sam knew it was irrational. It was caused by the residual fear he'd felt when he'd watched, from a distance, as that fuckwad had pulled that weapon tonight. His brain again played the sequence, pushing it into what-if mode, presenting him with an extremely unwelcome image of Alyssa being shot, point-blank, and falling as blood bloomed on her shirt—

What the hell was wrong with him?

He pushed the unwanted worst-case scenario away, wishing he could scrub his brain clean.

The what-if hadn't happened.

But it could have.

But it hadn't. Alyssa was safe.

She was skilled. She was careful. She was smart—and she was waiting for him to respond.

"Ah, shit," he said.

"Shit is yes, right? Fuck is no? Or is it fuck is yes and shit is no," she teased. "I always get that mixed up."

"For you, sweet thing," he conceded, "it's always, *always* yes. I'll go if you really need me to."

She narrowed her eyes at him because she hated regular terms of endearment, let alone that particular one, which she felt was extra-objectifying. So he quickly pointed out that, "New York in the dead of winter—crowded, dirty *and* cold—earns me far more than one *sweet thing*."

"Yeah, poor baby, it's only the cultural capital of the entire world, and you get to go there for free, first class flight, four star accommodations . . ."

"SEALs and former SEALs?" he asked. "Who are the SEALs who're going with me?"

She smiled at his question and he knew he was right. Whatever he was being sent to New York to fix, he was not going to be assisted by his friends who were still in SEAL Team Sixteen, like Ken or Cosmo or even

Silverman. No, he was going to get stuck babysitting the young and stupid enlisted men, who were still unattached and thus willing to do Ken—or Chief Karmody, as those very youngsters called him—this kind of favor.

And yeah, it made sense that the young'uns would leap at the chance for an all-expenses-paid trip to spend a few days of their hard-earned liberty in the Big Apple. Sam knew for a fact that they'd just returned from several cold, rough months in Afghanistan. And while he respected that completely, he also knew—from the experience of having formerly been young and stupid himself—that it meant that they weren't going to be *merely* young and stupid, but rather, young and stupid and desperate to get laid.

"Jay Lopez, Dan Gillman," Alyssa listed.

"Seriously?" Lopez was okay, but Gillman totally wore him out.

"Tony Vlachic, and . . . Izzy Zanella," she admitted.

"*What?*"

Gillman and Zanella had been SEAL Team Sixteen's oil and water long *before* Zanella married Gillman's little sister, Eden.

"They're professionals," Alyssa reminded him, as she sat down, way on the other end of the bed. "They work together all the time. They'll be fine."

"Yeah," Sam said, lying back among the pillows. "They'll be fine. Except when they act like moronic children. You better come over here, woman, because I'm gonna need hands-on persuading. You'd best go fetch the chocolate sauce."

She smiled at him. "Hmmm." Oh, he loved the sound of a smart woman thinking.

But alas, she brought their conversation back to the topic at hand. "You really don't want to go?"

Sam sighed. "What's there that needs fixing so urgently?"

"Remember Savannah's candidate? The friend from law school who was running for state assembly—that's what they call their congress in New York."

He scanned his memory and came up with "Maria Something."

"Bonavita," Alyssa reported. "She won the election. She's been stirring things up in Albany, and . . . Van thinks she needs a crash course in personal safety."

"And you honestly think *I'm* the one to provide that kind of—"

"Wait," Alyssa interrupted. "No. Sam. Okay, you think I'm sending you there by yourself." She laughed as he nodded. "No, we're *all* going. You, me, Ash."

"Shit," he said again, but this time it rang with his unbridled relief. "Really? But—"

"*I'm* going to work with Maria and her office staff," Alyssa said.

"You said SEALs and former SEALs—"

"You and the children are going to stand around and look big and scary," she told him. "Van thought it would be a good idea if the people who have a bone to pick with the assemblywoman get a look at what they'll be up against if they ever decide to do anything beyond writing a nasty-ass e-mail."

"Well, shit," he said again. "If you're going, of course I'm in."

"New York—in the dead of winter," she teased. "I think maybe you talked me out of making you go. I don't want you to be cold, poor baby."

Sam laughed. "I'm pretty sure you'll be able to keep me warm," he told her.

"Still," she said. "I think it might take some *hands-on persuading* to make me change my mind back to—"

"Yeah," Sam interrupted her. "Come over here."

But she didn't. In fact, she stood up, and with that amazing attitude that he loved so much in every step she took, she crossed the room, opened and went out the bedroom door.

"Hey." Sam sat back up. "Where are you going?" he called.

"Kitchen," she answered, her laughter-filled voice trailing back as she went, still gloriously naked, down the stairs. "To get that chocolate sauce. Because that, *sweet thing*, was one *damn* fine idea."

He'd stood close enough to her, once, in Starbucks, to smell her.

She smelled clean and sweet, and he'd lurked in the shampoo aisle of a nearby Wal-Mart for hours after, searching for the brand she used.

He used it now, too, even though his hair was so different from hers.

He'd gone into the Starbucks that day, intending to surrender. He was tired, he was sick, and he'd wanted it all to be over, to end. They'd nearly caught him, thanks to her. He'd just barely escaped, and as he'd sat in his car, hands trembling on the steering wheel, he wondered why he'd run. He'd wanted—right then, in that moment of despair—for them to catch him.

He'd wanted *her* to catch him.

He hadn't known her name yet—but he'd learned that, too, in the Starbucks, where he'd smelled her sweet, clean hair.

Before he'd gone into the coffee shop, he'd thrown up, right in his car—the car in which he'd hidden Betsy Mac-Gregor in the trunk. She'd choked on her own vomit and died, alone in there, while he was evading them, evading *her*, and he'd beaten her anyway, but it wasn't any good because she wasn't afraid anymore and he'd howled his rage. *She* had robbed him of his pleasure and her pain.

So he took Betsy's teeth—all of them—but it wasn't the same. And in that moment, in the shower of his grimy motel room, as he'd scrubbed himself clean, he knew that it would never again be the same. And the despair was so heavy upon him that he'd gotten dressed, his hair still wet, and climbed into his car, to turn himself in to the police.

It was just by chance, by luck, by fate that he saw *her*, in the parking lot of that Starbucks.

She was going into the coffee shop, taking a break from their relentless but now faltering search for Betsy, so he'd parked, and then he'd puked, and then he'd followed her.

He'd stood for a moment, letting his eyes adjust to the darkness after coming inside from the bright, cold morning light.

She was standing with a man—dark-haired and short of stature—and she was nodding at something he said.

She was beautiful. As he stared at her, the despair shifted, making room for his awe. She was perfect in every way. She dressed like a man, but it didn't disguise the fact that she was slender, yet curved. Soft yet strong. And her face . . .

Sometimes, up close, women who were beautiful from a distance didn't hold up, but she was breathtaking. Magnificent. With even features that could grace magazine covers had she chosen that path, and flawless, smooth brown skin that he imagined would be soft to his touch.

Her companion leaned close to speak into her ear, and she laughed, and his despair again moved, and beneath it, like the single toll of a bell from a distant church tower, came the solidness of certainty.

Kill.

Not *her,* not yet, not here, not now.

But rather *him.*

Kill him.

He was this perfect woman's lover—he had to be. The

intimacy of their relationship echoed in the way they stood and moved, the way they talked to each other.

Or didn't talk. Whoever the man was, he'd noticed him standing here, just inside the door, staring at them, and he somehow told *her* that, with just one look, even as his cell phone rang.

"Hey, sweetie," the dead man said into his phone as he turned away, but then the rest of his words were lost, as *she* turned and looked directly at him, catching and holding his gaze.

Her eyes weren't a deep, soft brown, as he'd expected. Instead they were startlingly pale—sunlit ocean green— and he knew he shouldn't stand here like this staring, but he couldn't look away.

And he knew that it was time to surrender—or not.

Not tolled the certainty within him, and he knew just as absolutely what he needed to do. He let himself stare even longer. And then he pulled his gaze away and turned and stared, too, at the bland, boring, vanilla girl taking orders behind the counter. He made himself shuffle toward the clerk, his movement labored and jerky, and he placed his order in a voice that suggested his mental challenges were many—because no one faulted a retard who stared.

And sure enough, *she* looked away, no longer suspicious.

His reward was her name—*Alyssa*—called by the barista who then handed over her coffee.

Her dead lover was *Jules*, which was a stupid name for a man, but after he took his coffee, Alyssa spoke, her voice musical and rich. "Tell Robin to break a leg tonight," she said. And Jules nodded and said as much into his cell phone, ending the call with "See you tonight. I love you, too."

His relief that they were only friends, not lovers, made

him magnanimous. He would not kill this man now, not here, not yet.

As he shambled to the place where he was to wait for his coffee, *she* slipped past him, and he smelled her.

And it was then that he knew.

The last of his despair evaporated. It vanished, replaced by that certainty which now filled him so completely that he thought for a moment that his very skin might rupture and split. But as odd and uncomfortable as that was, he no longer felt sick or tired.

He was stronger than them, he was smarter than they were, and he knew what he wanted.

Alyssa.

The world gave him a gift as, just before she went out the door, her cell phone rang, and she reached for it. He caught a glimpse of a sidearm in a holster beneath her jacket, and it made him as hard as he would've been had she flashed him her breasts, which was odd, because the killing had never been about sex for him. It was about death and fear and power and control.

But it was what it was, and he knew not to question the will of his certainty, especially when she opened her phone, and put it to her ear, and told him her full name: "Alyssa Locke."

Alyssa Locke.

Alyssa.

Locke.

He knew in a blaze of absolute conviction that he should not give Betsy MacGregor back, as he'd always done with his victims before. But not this time. Not now.

Not until he had Alyssa Locke within his grasp, begging for him to kill her quick.

CHAPTER FOUR

Lopez kept trying to get him to talk.

"How're you doing?" he asked Dan Gillman, for what felt like the seven thousandth time in the week since the SEALs had returned from the treacherous mountains between A-stan and P-stan.

Danny nodded and even smiled as he said what he always said, "I'm good. I'm okay." But Lopez didn't look convinced, so he added, "I'm looking forward to this. It's been a long time since I've been in New York."

Start spreading the news, Izzy Zanella sang the opening to what was essentially New York City's theme song, because he was an asshole and he didn't know how to keep his goddamned mouth shut.

"Well, I *was* looking forward to this," Dan amended as he followed Zanella, Tony, and Lopez down the escalator to the airport's baggage-claim carousels. They'd traveled light, with carry-on bags only—except for Zanella the douche, who'd insisted on bringing his guitar.

Which was twice as stupid, because Dan didn't even know Zanella played the guitar until he showed up with it at LAX.

Their teammate, Mark Jenkins, was supposed to come

with them, along with his wife Lindsey, who worked as an operative for Troubleshooters Incorporated, the personal security organization they were currently representing here on the frozen island of Manhattan.

The four SEALs weren't exactly moonlighting for the firm because they weren't getting paid—just fed and housed. The "work" they had to do in exchange for that wasn't very strenuous. They were the figurative "big stick," in a "walk softly and carry a . . ." presentation that Alyssa Locke, the Troubleshooters XO, would be delivering over the next few days as she helped a newly elected liberal crybaby government official get used to the idea that some people were going to send her mean e-mails.

It was supposed to be an easy job, with a city full of upscale restaurants and bars awaiting them—restaurants and bars filled in turn with beautiful, supermodel-worthy women, many of whom would be eager to show that they fully supported the troops by taking a Navy SEAL home and getting naked with him.

After the hell of the past few months, this was going to be exactly what he needed, to start feeling like himself again.

It was going to be Danny and Jenk and Lopez, the three caballeros, together again. And yes, Jenk was married now, so the dynamic was slightly different. But Lindsey was cool. And yes, Tony Vlachic was coming with them, too, which was a little weird because he was younger than they were, he was relatively new to Team Sixteen, and he was . . . different, but it was all okay because—thank you, Jesus—he wasn't Izzy fucking Zanella.

But then Lindsey had come down with the flu, so Zanella was filling in for Jenk, last minute.

Of course.

Lopez had been apologetic on the ride to LAX, when he'd told Dan about the change in personnel. He knew—in great detail because Dan had vented to him many times—how much Dan hated his soon-to-be ex-brother-in-law.

At the top of Zanella's list of unforgivable transgressions was the fact that he'd knocked up and married Eden, Dan's younger sister. And yes, okay, there was definitely still some question as to whether Zanella was or was not the actual biological father of Eden's baby—not that it really mattered anymore, since she'd miscarried six months in.

Bottom line, Eden always *had* played fast and loose. So maybe Zanella's marrying her had been marginally gallant since the paternity was in question. But Dan suspected he'd done it, in part, to piss Dan off.

Because Zanella knew that Dan had *always* found him to be obnoxious. He was loud, he was capable of being unbelievably stupid, and he drove Danny crazy with his constant idiotic comments—not to mention his relentless singing.

Fucking Zanella had a fucking song for every occasion. And absolutely no filter through which to judge the fact that perhaps *some* occasions would be best kept song-free.

The tall, gangly SEAL had always been something of a loner. Rumor had it his BUD/S training swim-buddy rang out to get the hell away from him. But then, a few years ago, he'd gone and saved Mark Jenkins's life.

Jenk had started inviting Zanella to poker games and parties, and before Dan knew it, Jay Lopez, his tightest friend in SEAL Team Sixteen, was also inviting Zanella everywhere. And suddenly, wherever Dan went, Zanella was there, too.

He acted like he was Dan's friend, but face it, a friend didn't have sex with a friend's sister.

"When do you get the results of the latest CAT scan?" Lopez asked Dan now.

"I don't know," Dan said brusquely. "They said they'd call me. I'm fucking trying not to think about it."

"Sorry, man."

Dan sighed. "No, I'm sorry," he said. "I'm just . . ." He shook his head. "I'm really tired."

These days he was always tired, so he put his bag on the floor and sat down next to it. Lopez hovered for a moment, like the weirdest mother hen on the face of the planet.

"I'll watch your bag," Dan told his friend, "while you go babysit Zanella."

Lopez smiled at that. "I'm pretty sure he's okay."

Strains of another song drifted over from where the asshole was putting on a one-man show for the other passengers on their flight. No, make that a two-man show. Someone—Jesus, it was Tony—was beatboxing an accompaniment. Christ.

"Yeah, well, there he goes," Dan said. "And I don't trust him not to do something like get himself—or all of us—arrested. Please, I just want to get to the hotel. I'm lagged as fuck."

It was kind of crazy. They'd traveled west to east which, absolutely, according to the old saying, resulted in a coast-to-coast traveler becoming a "party beast." It was, after all, only 1930 California time.

It was extra crazy because with all of Dan's anticipation of visiting New York, he didn't want to get to the hotel so that he could shower, change, get out there, and get his ass laid.

No, what he wanted right now, more than sex even, was to sleep.

For, like, a week.

Jesus, maybe he was coming down with Lindsey's flu.

Lopez was looking at him again as if he were worried, and Dan didn't want him asking any more questions about the CAT scan or the supposed head injury that had made him lose a small but significant part of his life, so he leaned back against their two bags and closed his eyes.

He heard Lopez finally move away, heard Izzy's singing stop, thank God. But then Lopez came back. Or maybe it was Tony—the step was much lighter. Almost nonexistent, in fact.

Whoever it was, they were hovering again, and he'd had enough.

"I'm fine," he said. "Just leave me the f—"

He'd opened his eyes just before he dropped the F-bomb, and good thing, because it wasn't Lopez or Tony or even Izzy staring down at him.

It was a very little girl in a pink dress, complete with a bow in her barely there, baby-fine hair. She couldn't have been more than two, maybe three at the most. She wore shiny black shoes and white tights that were doing a kind of an MC Hammer thing with the crotch down around her knees, but she didn't seem to care. She was holding what looked like a blue stuffed bunny, clutching it to her chest.

Her eyes were blue and wide and she stared with unabashed curiosity. "Are you a soldja?"

He was dressed in civvies—well, mostly anyway. His pants were BDUs, but nothing that a civilian couldn't pick up at an Army/Navy store. His bag was military, though, with his name lettered on it—and yeah, that was what she was looking at.

"I'm in the Navy," he told her, even though she probably didn't know what that meant.

But she did. "Momma's a Ahmy soldja," she informed him solemnly. "In Wack. Her foot got bwohed up. They gon' make her a new one an' we gon' pway tag again an' wun an'—"

"Mindy!" A boy, maybe twelve or thirteen—about Dan's brother Ben's age—and clearly related to Mindy, had overheard what she'd said, which Dan had finally translated into their mother was getting a prosthetic foot, which would allow her to play tag again and run. But the boy was horrified, his thin face pale. "He doesn't want to hear about that!"

"It's okay," Danny sat up. "I've, um, been over there. It's . . . rough. Where's your mom now?"

"Landstuhl Hospital," he said. "In Germany. She was supposed to come home last month, but . . ." He shook his head, his mouth tight.

"I'm sorry," Dan murmured.

"Gwamma tooked us to Jahminny," Mindy announced, "and I kisseded Momma an' she cwied, cuz she wuvs me and Daddy stayed cuz she gotta hohd his hand and we don't gots to send her teeny shampoos no more an' hand wahmahs an' books to wead cuz the nurses wash her hair and her woom has a TV but she don't turn it on cuz she's sweepin' and I wan' say *wake up, Momma!* But gwamma won' wet me."

"Mindy, come on," the boy said. "Gram's going to be worried."

"Your mom's lucky," Dan told the little girl, "to have you and your brother and your dad taking care of her. I bet she liked those packages you sent her when she was in . . . Wack." It was a good name for it.

"Do you got packages?" she asked him.

"Yeah," he lied. "I get lots of packages when I'm over there. I've mostly been in Afghanistan, but . . . It's great to get packages wherever you go, so . . . I know your mom loved yours. Hand warmers—at this time of year, and books . . ."

"Mindy," the boy said again, but she didn't move.

She just stood there, looking at Dan, and as small as she was, she must've had a heavy-duty bullshit meter, because she held out her bunny, pushing it into his hands. "Now you gots a package too," she announced. "A bunny name

Fwed, to wuv you." She patted the bunny's head. "Bye, Fwed. Give the Naby soldja wotsa kisses in Anastan."

And with that, she was gone.

"Mindy!" Her brother turned to follow her.

"Kid," Dan called, and the boy turned back after making sure his little sister found their grandmother. Dan tossed him the rabbit. "Tell your sister thank you, but I'm pretty sure Fred will be happier staying with her."

"The real Fred's at home," the kid said. "Dad says she's the Johnny Appleseed of stuffed bunnies. He buys 'em in bulk because she leaves 'em everywhere." The boy threw it back at him. "She wants you to have it, so . . ." He shrugged. "If you don't want it, just toss it. She won't know."

He turned away, but Dan called after him. "Kid. I hope your mom comes home soon."

The boy turned back again to look at Dan, and his fatigue, his fear, and his despair were etched on his young face. "And then what? She used to run marathons. I don't think she wants to come home. I don't think she wants to *live*."

Ah, Jesus.

"I run marathons," Dan told the boy. "I would want to live, and I don't have you or Mindy or someone like your dad to hold my hand—someone more like Angelina Jolie, please. I mean, I'm sure your dad is nice . . ." That got him a wan smile from the kid, so he held up the bunny and looked at it. "All I've got is Fred, giving me wotsa kisses."

That got him a wobbly laugh, and something that looked like the spark of hope in the boy's eyes.

"Your mother definitely wants to live—and she'll be home soon," Dan reassured him. "And my bet? If she's anything at all like you and your sister, she'll be running marathons again. I bet you'll be running with her, and

Mindy'll be showering you with stuffed bunnies at the finish line. Hold *that* future in your head, kid, aiight?"

The boy nodded, turned to go, but then turned back. "Someone really should be sending you packages, sir."

Had his lie really been that transparent? Dan shook his head. "I'm not an officer. You don't need to call me sir."

"Still . . ."

"Your grandmother's looking for you," Dan told the boy. He held up Fred. "Thank Mindy again for me."

CHAPTER FIVE

He watched from the hallway, from the warmth of a supply closet that he'd discovered months ago.

It was dark, it was warm, and it was dry. He'd planned, from the start, to leave Savannah's body there, and he'd sat there sometimes, right on the dirty floor, in anticipation, alone in the darkness—picturing Alyssa's exquisite face as she opened the door and saw what he'd done.

He still sometimes sat there, sometimes all night. Waiting. Just waiting.

She was coming. She *would* come.

Today was finally the day.

He hadn't had to kill Savannah. He hadn't *had* to kill anyone at all. It was luck that Alyssa was coming—luck and a suggestion he'd made to one of the interns, who'd in turn approached Jenn. *Wasn't Savannah connected to some personal security firm—via her Navy SEAL husband? Surely she knew someone—a woman—who could come in and talk to Maria about her safety. That might go over better than advice from some cocksure police detective.*

Jenn had, obviously, taken the suggestion to heart, and here they all were.

On the verge of destiny.

He watched through a hole that he'd made between the door and the jamb, and he knew that the men in Alyssa's team—all five of them—were there as a statement. But their focus was on protecting Maria.

Which left Alyssa for him.

Provided she stayed long enough.

He'd heard—because he was always listening—that Maria thought little of the threat. It came with her job, he'd heard her argue with Savannah, who had called from California. Maria would, out of courtesy, meet with Savannah's friends, and allow them to install an office security system and update the locks. She'd even humor Savannah and meet Alyssa at the gym for a self-defense refresher.

She would give the team this one weekend, but come Monday, they'd be gone, and she'd be back to business as usual.

He'd fumed and raged because after waiting all this time, a weekend wasn't long enough. And in his fury, he'd gone too far with the blade of his knife, and his recent guest had died, her blood soaking the floorboards of his kill room.

But then with the certainty he relied on to guide him, he'd realized that it was okay. It had been time for her to die.

Because she was coming—Alyssa Locke.

And he could make her stay for longer than a weekend.

And then she would be his, forever.

It was amazing how much space five Navy SEALs took up, well, four SEALs and one former SEAL, in the outer room of the assemblywoman's tiny New York City office.

It was wall-to-wall shoulders in there, and still they came through the door: Jacked, Steamy, Parka Man, Lucky, and Hot Cowboy Dad, who was actually carrying a cheerful and heavily bundled baby in a frontpack sling thing. And okay, those weren't their *real* nicknames, but rather accurately descriptive monikers Jenn herself assigned them as they greeted her with a handshake and a smile.

Their real names were Zanella, Lopez, Starrett, Gillman, and Vlachic, and as good as Jenn was with names, they'd rattled them off so fast she'd lost track of everyone but Lopez, whose parka was the kind worn by explorers on an expedition to the summit of Mt. Everest.

The one she thought was Starrett—the Hot Cowboy Dad—had blue eyes that put Detective Mick What'sHisName's to shame. He also had that adorable baby, who looked an awful lot like the Troubleshooters team leader, a seemingly diminutive and strikingly beautiful woman with short dark hair. She came in last, shutting her cell phone as she introduced herself. She was, of course, the one and only Alyssa Locke, and she was seemingly diminutive only in comparison to her hulking team.

Jenn wasn't quite sure why, but she'd always pictured Alyssa as being a blonde, like Savannah.

Instead, she was at least part African American, which of course didn't mean that she couldn't have been a blonde, either from a bottle or even naturally. And there was something about her that was oddly familiar. "I'm Jenn. I'm the assemblywoman's assistant and—You didn't by any chance go to SUNY Binghamton?"

Alyssa shook her head.

"Or maybe to law school at—"

"No law school."

"You look so familiar," Jenn admitted.

The woman winced. "A few days ago, I did a bodyguard assignment for a movie star. There was an incident and pictures are everywhere."

Jenn shook her head. "Not in *The New York State Assembly Quarterly*."

Alyssa smiled. "Thank goodness for small favors."

"Maria's on a conference call right now. She'll be free in a few minutes, so . . ." Jenn looked around at them all. "Can I get anybody anything?"

"I would love a glacier," the tallest one—Jacked—requested, "or even an avalanche would be nice."

At first she didn't understand. Were those California drinks like wheatgrass or acai berry juice?

But then Hot Cowboy Dad chimed in. "Mind if I use the conference table," he asked Jenn in a Texas-laden drawl that on a less attractive man would have been annoying, "to peel some layers offa Ashton, here, before he parboils?"

And then she understood. "Of course. Please. Yes. Please. Take off your coats." The office *was* nearing hypertropical today. She'd taken off her pantyhose hours ago.

"Excuse me," Alyssa said as her cell phone rang and she checked the incoming number. She looked from Jenn to her husband. "I've got to take this. Will you . . . ?"

"I got him," the Cowboy said as he took the baby to the table. "You must be from Florida, Jenn. Or maybe Death Valley . . . ?"

"No," Jenn said, with a laugh. "And I am sorry about the climate in here, but this building is old. In order for the heat to reach the top floors, the radiators down here need to overperform. It's like this all winter."

"There should be a valve," Steamy said, as he went over to the ancient thing, which lurked in a grill-covered box in front of the window that overlooked the street, "to allow for a bypass."

"It doesn't work," Jenn said. "Believe me, we've—"

"Mind if I take a look?" he asked, already doing just that.

"I'll help." Parka Man was right behind him, taking off his rather ridiculous jacket and hood as he went. He had a thick sweater on beneath it, and as he pulled it off as well, his shirt nearly came with it, revealing a set of abs that could have graced the cover of *Fitness* magazine.

My goodness, he was a well-constructed man. Jenn turned away, not wanting him to catch her staring, except, whoa. He wasn't the only one eager to keep from overheating, taking off more layers than just their jackets.

"I'm so sorry," she said again, although she had to admit that she was lying at least a little, because all around her, as the SEALs stripped down to their T-shirts and jeans, the normally dingy little room was filled with a wide variety of muscles and sexy flashes of incredibly interesting tattoos on smooth expanses of sun-kissed skin.

And that, along with their many serious cases of hathead—or in Parka Man's case, hoodhead—and still rosy cheeks from the frigid outside air, made them seem a curiously attractive mix of boyishly charming and curl-one's-toes hot.

And the realization that this worked for her so completely made her pause. This attraction was, perhaps, at the basis of her failed relationships with both John One and John Two, neither of whom were particularly good at handling basic responsibilities, yet had mastered the art of using a boyish smile to get women—with the tried and true fallback being their own pathetic mothers—to do their laundry and feed them.

But both Johns got banished safely back into the distant past where they belonged when one of the SEALs all but lifted her out of his way. He was eager to help Parka and Steamy as they attempted to turn the knob on the radiator—a knob that hadn't moved a whit for the past seventy years. If not longer.

He was the SEAL she'd dubbed Lucky, because his matinee-idol face, his lush brown hair, and his long, *long* eyelashes were purely a result of genetics. He'd been lucky to get the parents that he'd had, it was as simple as that.

He'd also come in with his not-particularly-thick jacket already unzipped, as if he'd been walking around with it open, with no hat and no gloves to boot. Apparently, the minus fifteen degree windchill of the city streets didn't bother him.

But the room's current temperature certainly put him into a near panic.

"Holy shit," he muttered to Parka. Jenn clearly wasn't meant to overhear him, because he mumbled, "Excuse me, ma'am," when he looked up and saw she was watching him.

Okay, *staring* at him. She was staring, she'd cop to that. He was just so . . . stare-able.

"It's okay," she told him, pushing her glasses up her nose. "It took me awhile to get used to it, too. I went through the whole process. You know, anger, denial, bargaining . . ."

He laughed at that, and his smile—a flash of straight, white teeth—was perfect. A dash of rue and a pinch of chagrin mixed nicely with his genuine, intelligent amusement.

"The cost of replacing the heating system is astronomical," Jenn told him, told his friends, too, because she didn't want him to think she'd singled him out. Although she bet that, looking as he did, he was often singled out. "The landlord won't do it without raising the rent—at which point we'd have to move. I've got the same problem in my apartment, too. It's part of living low-budget in New York City."

"I'm not sure I could ever reach that kind of acceptance," Lucky admitted.

"You've absolutely got to want it," Jenn agreed. "Living here's not for everyone. But if you love it enough . . . Well, I've lived in Jersey, and I've found I can put up with almost anything to stay in Manhattan."

"Gilligan's okay with it being hot, hot, hot," Jacked

chimed in. "As long as he's outside. It's the heat plus no open windows thing that makes him super-squirrelly. Tight places bug him, too."

"*And* I have bad breath in the morning." Lucky wasn't very happy with Jacked. "Don't forget that. As long as you're listing my failings. Jesus, Zanella."

"And here we go," Starrett murmured to his laughing little son, whom he'd stripped down to a short-sleeved onesie and a diaper.

Okay, so Jacked was Zanella, and Lucky was also known as *Gilligan*—which had to be a nickname for Gillman. Which meant that Steamy was Vlachic by process of elimination.

He and Lopez-of-the-parka had given up on the valve and turned their attention to the window. Like most windows in elderly buildings in this part of the city, it was glued shut with around thirty coats of paint.

"Anyone have a knife?" Vlachic asked.

"Don't open that!" Starrett said, in near perfect unison with Zanella and Lucky-Gilligan-Gillman.

"Whoa," Vlachic said. "Why not?"

It was Lopez who explained, "There's no window lock. We crack the seal, we're making it less safe in here."

"You want me to find a hardware store?" Vlachic asked. "The frame is wood, a basic lock's gotta cost around three dollars." He turned to Jenn. "Are there more windows in your boss's office?"

"Two," she said. "Equally ancient."

"Do you have a tool kit or even just a screwdriver?"

"Um," she said.

"I'll get a screwdriver, too," he decided.

"Tell Alyssa where you're going. See if she wants you to get anything else while you're there," Starrett told him.

"Yes, sir." The SEAL grabbed his jacket and sweater and went out the door.

"You know, I wasn't listing your failings, Fishboy," Zanella told Gillman, giving him yet another nickname as he sat on the conference table, next to the pile of the baby's clothes. "It's freaking impressive for someone who's claustrophobic to become a SEAL. Although to be completely honest, the bad breath *has* been"—he made a face—"an issue. Glad you finally know about it, bro. Large quantities of Scope next time, before you try to kiss me good morning."

"I'll go with Vlachic," Gillman volunteered, reaching for his jacket.

But he didn't put it on.

Because Maria came out of her office, and he, like his friends, was struck dumb.

"Sorry to keep you waiting," she said. She turned to Jenn, concern on her face. "I just got the strangest phone call—"

But then Vlachic stuck his head back inside. "Sorry, sir. Excuse me, ma'am. But Ms. Locke's not out here. I don't know where she went."

"What's on your schedule for today?"

Robin Cassidy looked up from his Cheerios as Jules poured himself a cup of coffee.

"Not much," Robin answered. "I'm going to visit Art, then probably hit the noon meeting at the Arlington Street Church. If you're really going to be home by two, I'll make sure I'm here before you."

"Hat and sunglasses, please," Jules told him. "Heavy scruff—don't shave. And yes, I'll be home by then. This meeting won't take long."

"Good," Robin said. "And I know the drill. I'll be fine. Alfonse says hi, by the way."

It had snowed again last night, and when Alfonse-the-plow-guy came—while Jules was still in the shower—Robin had gone outside, too. He loved being out in the pristine, winter-wonderland cleanness of it, but Jules would've kicked his ass if he'd gone out alone, so soon after last Thursday's freakshow out in Hollywood.

Even though the investigation was ongoing, everyone and their police detective sister believed the attack at the movie premiere to be an isolated incident. Dude didn't even have bullets in his gun and was currently on suicide watch in a psychiatric hospital in Anaheim.

There was no doubt about it, some people were quite literally crazy, but with Alfonse there, handling the big equipment, Robin was safe enough to shovel the walks and porch.

Alfonse—who sported a Bahstan accent to die for and talked in telegram—was both huge and hugely disappointed that Dolphina, Jules and Robin's personal assistant, wasn't around. He was even more crestfallen to find out that she was on her honeymoon, after finally marrying her long-time boyfriend, Will.

"Didn't think that would last," Alfonse opined. "What did he, put a bun in her oven?"

"I don't think so." Robin had laughed, but then stopped.

He asked Jules now, "Do you think Dolph married Will because she's pregnant?"

Jules turned from the toaster where he was monitoring his bagel, making sure it turned the perfect shade of brown. "No. I think she married him because she loves him."

"And you don't think she's going to come back from Europe in three weeks and, like, quit because she's having a baby?"

"Why would she quit? She knows she could have as many babies as she wants, and still work for us," Jules pointed out, as always both calm and practical.

And freaking handsome as all get out, dressed for work the way he was, even though it was a Saturday.

The man could wear a dark suit and tie like nobody's business. His handgun, secured in a shoulder holster tucked neatly up beneath his left arm, barely disturbed the lines of his well-tailored jacket.

Add a pair of dark sunglasses, and the whole FBI agent look was . . . Well, it was one that Robin would never tire of.

Ever.

"I don't know," Robin admitted. "I guess I was just spiraling into worst-case scenario land. I miss her when she's not here, and now that the show's on hiatus . . ."

"Hiatus?" Jules repeated, losing a little of his calm. "Crap, it's definite?"

Robin nodded. "It will be, yeah. That's one of the reasons why I'm going over to the hospital to see Art. I gotta talk him into doing what he needs to do to get back to speed. Which is to *not* return to work until he's healthy."

Last week, Art Urban, the somewhat eccentric producer, director, and creator of *Shadowland,* the award-winning cable TV series that had helped put Robin back on the Hollywood A-list, had surprised the hell out of everyone who knew him by having a massive and near-fatal heart attack.

In true Urban fashion, he drove himself to the hospital before collapsing just inside the emergency room door.

Barely forty-five years old, he'd needed a triple bypass—and a major lifestyle change.

"He's looking at at least two months recovery at this place out near Sedona. You know, in Arizona," Robin continued. "He's been talking about putting the show into Fredo's hands while he's gone, but . . ." He shook his head. "If he's trying to de-stress, *that's* not going to work. It would probably be worse for him—attempting to micromanage from thousands of miles away . . . ?"

"*Two* months?" Jules asked as he got his bagel travel-ready, putting it on one of their plastic happy-monster plates that they used whenever Haley, Billy or any of the other under-ten set visited.

"At least two months. He really needs to go to this place—it's a ranch and . . . I checked out the website. It's like rehab for heart-attack survivors. They'll get him off the cigarettes and train him to eat healthier and start exercising. He's got to do it, or he's going to die."

"Shit." Jules wasn't happy. "This is the worst time for this—with Dolphina gone for another month—"

"Yeah, I know, but . . . He's the show, babe. I mean, yeah, it's him and *me*, but . . . If one of us is replaceable, it's definitely me."

"I happen to disagree." Jules rinsed out his mug and put it into the dishwasher. "You're the star of the show—"

"Yeah, and you're fucking the star, so you're not exactly impartial."

Jules laughed. "Sweetie, I'm pretty sure I lost starfucker status when you married me."

"Yeah, but saying that you're having marital relations with the star sounds boring."

The amusement in Jules's brown eyes glinted with something a little dangerous. "Really?"

Robin rested his chin in his hand as he gazed back at his husband. "I could just sit here all day with you looking at me like that."

Jules came over and kissed him. "No, you couldn't," he said, "and no, as much I want to, I *can't* stay home today, and while I appreciate your loyalty to Art, two months is a long time for you to be without a project. You should call Don. See if he can't find something short term for you to do."

"I know he can." Robin's agent was always trying to talk him into doing another movie. He looped his leg around Jules, keeping him close so he could straighten his tie. "Out in California. Which will suck. So, unless you can come with me, I'd rather stay in Boston."

"Yeah," Jules said, and it was a word loaded with the promise of an unhappy surprise, coming soon to this very kitchen.

"Ah, fuck me," Robin said, letting him go. "When are you going? And please tell me it's not Afghanistan— *fuck*!"

It was. He could see in Jules's eyes that not only was he going to the extremely dangerous war-torn country, but that he was going to be leaving much too soon.

"Max called just a few minutes ago," Jules told him. "The departure date's not set, but it's going to be within the next few weeks. He was giving me as much of an advance warning as he could."

Robin nodded as the Cheerios in his stomach turned to lead. Afghanistan. Again. God damn it.

"The President's going," Jules told him quietly. "He asked for me to be part of the advance team. I'll be there for about a month before he arrives, and . . . I can't turn that down."

Robin met his husband's steady gaze. "I would *never* ask you to—"

"I know," Jules reassured him.

And there they were, Robin sitting on the stool at the kitchen island, Jules standing nearby, both of them ignoring their breakfasts.

"I'm going to call Dolphina," Jules finally said, "see if she can't suggest a replacement assistant until she's back. You're going to need help picking a project and—"

"Babysitter," Robin interrupted. "Why don't we just call it what it is? We're looking for someone to babysit me while you're gone. Shit, Jules, you know if you call her, she's going to cut her trip short as soon as you say *Afghanistan*."

Last time Jules went to Afghanistan, everything had been fine. He'd come home a week later, safe and sound. But it had been a hard week for Robin—a very hard week.

Because on the trip before *that* one, shortly before their wedding, Jules had nearly died in Khandahar.

Living with the fear was part of being married to a man with an important and dangerous job. But it wasn't easy. Sure, Robin was an actor, so he could smile and exude confidence—make like he was convinced everything was okay.

Out of all of his friends, Dolphina alone knew of the toll it took on him. She helped him schedule his work while Jules was out on a perilous assignment, helping him use it as a distraction, pretty much around the clock.

But here he was, with Jules again on the verge of leaving, with no work and no Dolphina. Talk about providing a challenge for the recovering alcoholic.

But okay. What didn't kill him would make him stronger. Wasn't that how the saying went?

"We'll figure something out," Robin told Jules, and told himself while he was at it. "Any chance you can, um, get a couple days off before you go?"

"I'll ask," Jules said.

Robin managed a smile. "Thank you," he said.

Jules kissed him again and it was filled with such regret and apology, Robin knew it wasn't a few days off that Jules was going to ask for.

So he grabbed Jules by the lapels and all but shook him. "Don't you dare turn this down," he said. "The freaking President—the guy we both voted for—asked for *you*. You're going. I'll be fine. We'll figure something out. We'll get me whatever babysitters or bodyguards you think I need, so you don't have to be worrying about me while you're over there. You got that, babe? Repeat it back to me: We'll figure this out."

"We'll figure this out," Jules agreed.

Sam wasn't worried that Alyssa wasn't in the hall.

Not at first.

His wife was a big girl. She could take care of herself, and then some. If she wasn't in the corridor, it was probably because cell reception sucked in this city, with all of its man-made mountains and valleys.

Sam had tried to talk to Haley during the cab ride from the airport to the hotel where they were billeting the SEALs, and cell reception stank. After getting cut off twice, his daughter, old enough at age seven to put a little "of course my dad's a moron" into her voice, God help him, had said with exasperation, "Daddy, just call me later, when you get back from your trip to the far side of the moon."

Alyssa had probably gone looking for a signal that didn't garble her incoming call from—had to be—Max Bhagat.

She and the high-level FBI administrator had been playing phone tag all morning, and yeah, okay, the first thing Sam had thought when Tony V. had announced that Alyssa had gone into hiding wasn't *Oh, no, she might be in some kind of trouble.* No, the caveman section of his brain kicked in, as always too ready to get stuck, like a skipping record, thinking about the fact that his wife used to suck face with Max.

Forget about the fact that that had happened a million years ago, and that Sam had been married to his ex, Mary Lou, at the time. Forget, too, that Max was, himself, married now, with two beautiful kids of his own. Forget about the fact that Sam knew Alyssa loved him, loved Ash, loved this crazy life they were building together.

Sam's caveman instincts were strong, and needed to be battled daily, if not hourly.

"See if she's in the stairwell or down in the lobby," he told Vlachic, who nodded and vanished. If Alyssa *was* finally talking to Max, he didn't want to call her and interrupt. He turned to Jenn, who was responding to the assemblywoman—who, by the way, was the best-looking politician he'd ever seen in his life. Normally women who looked like Maria Bonavita were caught sneaking out the hotel room of a senator or congressman—proof that times truly were a-changing.

"On your cell?" Jenn was asking about the assembly-woman's announcement that she'd just gotten a strange phone call.

"Yeah. My caller ID said it was from Margaret Bell," Bonavita told her assistant, "but the voice on the other end was male."

"I don't think I know her," Jenn said. "Margaret Bell . . . ?"

"Of course you do. Big donor. Really big."

Jenn didn't look convinced. "Could it have been her husband?"

"Come on, Jenn, you know Maggie. She's one of Savannah's gym friends. Yours, too. Unmarried. Something of a plastic surgery addict . . . ?"

"Wait a minute—are you talking about Maggie *Thorndyke* with the collagen lips, who spends three hours, everyday, at the gym . . . ?"

"Bell-Thorndyke," the assemblywoman said. "I thought she was dropping the Thorndyke. Or maybe I got it wrong and she dropped the Bell. I should fix that on my phone."

"Excuse me." Sam interrupted the fascinating conversation. "I can't help but notice that there's not a rest-room here in the office. Is there one somewhere else on the floor? We've kind of misplaced our team leader."

"I'm sorry, you must be Ken's friend Sam," Maria deduced, giving him a smile that seemed genuine in its sincerity. "And this must be Ashton. Hello, baby. Aren't you the cutest?" She looked back at Sam. "He's beautiful, and yes, but it's kept locked. It's down the hall to the left, past the dentist's office. There's a key—Jenni . . . ?"

Jennilyn, who would've been pretty if she got a decent haircut and then didn't stand next to a woman who looked like Maria, rummaged through the clutter on her desk as Maria shook Izzy, Gillman, and Lopez's hands, introducing herself and thanking them for coming all the way from California.

"So what did he say?" Jenn resumed her conversation with Maria as she handed two separate keys on two different colored strings to Sam. "Red's the men's, blue's the ladies' room."

"Thank you," Sam said. Izzy Zanella was the only one of the three SEALs in the room who was still breathing post-handshakes, so Sam gave him a choice. "Baby or keys?"

Izzy took the keys.

"Knock first, but check 'em both," Sam ordered, and Izzy went out the door.

"He said, *Check your mail,*" Maria rasped the words in a low-pitch whisper. "Like that. It was creepy."

"Mail or e-mail?"

"Mail. I think."

"Maybe Maggie's got a new boyfriend, and she convinced him to contribute to your reelection fund," Jenn theorized.

"Where's today's mail?" Maria asked.

Lopez found his voice. "Maybe you should let me look at it first."

Gillman stepped forward too, his tongue nearly down to his knees. "Yes, you should. Let us. Help you. Please."

"Hold up," Sam said. He included the SEALs. "Everyone."

But Jenn had gone to the other desk and, no rummaging this time, picked up a small pile of letter-sized envelopes. She looked at him with eyes that were not average brown as he'd first thought, but almost golden

with a hint of green. They brimmed with intelligence—
and with her amused awareness of her boss's impact on
men like Dumbass and Dunderbrains here.

"The mail arrived right before you got here," she told
Sam. "I got as far as opening it. They're all bills." Sure
enough the tops of the envelopes were all slit.

Sam dumped Ash into Lopez's surprised arms. "Into
the hall," Sam ordered, and Lopez went.

"What's your procedure for opening mail?" Sam asked.

Jenn looked from him to Maria and back. "It arrives, I
check to make sure there's a return address that we recognize, and it gets opened. I have a letter opener that I
use—"

Sam took the mail from her. "And if there's something
suspicious?"

"I open it first," Jenn admitted. "Using a Ziploc baggie." She opened her top desk drawer and pulled out a
box of the gallon-sized. "I put the letter and the letter
opener inside, seal it, and . . . It's awkward, but do-able.
The theory being that if we do get anthraxed, we've already been contaminated by touching the envelope. But
the baggie keeps it from getting further into the air. I open
it immediately, again, because if I've touched the envelope, damage is already done, and it's better to know
about it ASAP. But there was nothing suspicious in today's mail, so I slit the tops, you know, all at the same
time. It's more efficient to do it that way."

Maria and Gillman both looked over Sam's shoulder
as he flipped through what was, absolutely, a collection
of bills and an advertisement from a local restaurant.

"I think it's highly unlikely that Maggie's rich new
boyfriend with laryngitis works for either Con Ed or
Paulo's Pizzeria," Jenn said.

But stuck between the bills for the phones and Internet
and a statement from a credit card company, Sam found
a postcard.

It was plain and white with no picture—the kind with the postage printed right on it, that you could buy from the post office. And it was addressed to the assembly-woman with her name and street address printed onto a mailing label.

The message on it was also computer printed, and affixed via a label.

Bottom drawer was all it said. There was no return address, and the postmark was from here in the city, dated yesterday.

"Bottom drawer of what?" Maria wondered.

"Your desk?" Jenn theorized, as out in the hall, Ash started to cry. "The filing cabinet . . . ?"

"Don't open anything, don't move," Sam ordered as he handed it with the rest of the mail to Jenn. He opened the door to bring Lopez and Ash back inside, taking his son from the SEAL. Ash had achieved infinity-mouth, which meant full-lung-power wailing was a nanosecond away. "It's okay, big guy. Daddy's got you now. That was a little scary, I know. I'll try to give you more warning next time. But Lopez is a good guy, okay? Shhhh, now . . ."

"Sorry, sir," Lopez apologized as Ash locked his arms around Sam's neck. "I couldn't get him to—"

Sam cut him off. "Not your fault. Go find Zanella." He'd managed to pull Ash back from going full bore into the angry-baby zone—a tremendous achievement. But the kid was now a total snot machine, which wasn't fun for anyone. "Gillman, look in the baby bag for a Kleenex," he ordered as he dug for his cell phone, because enough was enough.

Whatever was in the bottom drawer of Maria's desk or the closet or wherever, he wanted his son far from it. Which meant he needed Alyssa off of the phone with Max, now. He speed-dialed her and—shit—went right to her voice mail.

Which was when Lopez brought Izzy back from the bathrooms.

"Nope and nope," Izzy reported.

"What took you so freaking long?" Gillman asked, disgusted with Zanella as usual, as he found the container of baby wipes and was attempting to wrestle it open.

"I had to go," Izzy said with a shrug.

"That's for his butt," Sam told Gillman, as he dialed Alyssa again. They had a code. Two calls, right in a row, meant break away ASAP and call right back. Again, it went to voice mail. "I need something dry to use for his nose."

"I've got a box of tissues right here," Jenn said, adding, "Oh!" as she realized a little too late that she'd yanked open the drawer of her desk. The *bottom* drawer. "Oh, my *God*." She slammed the drawer shut.

Lopez didn't even ask. He just grabbed Ash and took him out the door, as Izzy and Gillman both reached for Maria, to hustle her outside, too.

Poor Jenn was no doubt used to being overlooked, but Gillman's brains and training overrode his hormones as he realized that he was closer to Jenn. He left Maria in Izzy's charge and turned to Jenn, but she wasn't ready to run. She moved away from him, keeping him at arm's length.

"The smell," she said. "Is just . . . God, that looked like . . . *Blood*. What is *in* there?"

The smell—which absolutely hadn't been in the room a moment ago—was fucking awful. Sam covered his nose and mouth with the inside of his elbow and grabbed the drawer-pull with his other hand and . . .

Jesus.

It looked like a human heart, lying there in a puddle of blood and gore. But it couldn't be. It had to belong to some recently butchered animal. A pig. Didn't pigs have similar hearts to humans?

Whoever had put it there had lined the drawer with plastic, to keep the mess from dripping out. And they'd caulked and sealed the edges of the drawer, too—which was why this hideous smell hadn't leaked either, despite the office's subtropic heat.

Sam shut the drawer, but it was too late. The seal had been broken. Still the odor was less awful with it closed.

Jenn had gotten over her initial shock and was both angry and disgusted, her hand over her nose. She called to Maria, out in the hall, "It's some kind of dead animal body part," then turned to Gillman to add, "I doubt it's toxic. It's just gross." She searched the top of her desk for something. "You can go out into the hall if you need air, but I have to . . ." She picked up both a business card and the telephone. "I'm calling the police."

Sam, meanwhile, was dialing Alyssa again—three calls in a row meant *pick up, now*—because this prank wasn't the act of some harmless loose-screw fuckwad. This had been planned and executed by someone who had skill, means, and will. As far as threats went, this one fell into the "take very seriously" column.

And the fact that Alyssa had gone dark was not sitting well with him. And, shit, again his call to her went right to voice mail.

"What kind of degenerate would do something like this? *God!* Yes," Jenn said into the phone. "Detective Mick Callahan, please. It's Jennilyn LeMay from Assemblywoman Bonavita's office and it's urgent."

"Stay here," Sam ordered Gillman.

"Yes, sir."

Out in the hall, Izzy had taken Ash from Lopez and, by some miracle, he was making the baby laugh instead of cry. Maria was on her cell phone, her face pale, and Alyssa was still nowhere in sight.

"Get Ash and Ms. Bonavita back in the office and lock the door behind you," Sam ordered Izzy. "Open the window in there if you have to. Lopez, you're with me. We're going to open every door on this floor, I don't care if it's locked, kick it down."

"What's going on?"

Alyssa.

Sam exhaled hard as he turned, and there she was, coming out of the stairwell with Vlachic on her heels.

She was whole, in one piece, no gaping hole in her chest where her heart had once been.

The relief that flooded him mixed badly with the god-awful smell of death and rot that clung to the insides of his nostrils. Rationally, he knew that the thing in Jenn's desk drawer couldn't have come from his wife, but his vivid imagination was linked to his inner caveman, and it often took the less-rational path.

"She was out front," Vlachic reported. "Talking to the President."

Izzy, who hadn't yet gotten to the close-and-lock-the-door part of his order, said, "That sounds like some kind of rockin' euphemism. *Stop banging on the bathroom door, homes, I'm talking to the President.*"

"No," Vlachic told the taller man. "I mean, yeah, that does sound like . . . But . . . She was actually talking. *To* the President."

Jenn appeared beside Izzy in the doorway. "NYPD's on their way."

"What," Alyssa asked Sam again, as she took Ash from Izzy's arms, "is going on?"

CHAPTER SIX

Alyssa got in the police detective's face. "I am *not* the problem here."

"Maybe not, but you're also not the solution *I* would have chosen," he retorted, and across the room, she sensed more than saw Sam shift his weight.

Oh, yeah. Good idea. Start a brawl with this fool. That would help.

But to Sam's credit, he didn't move more than that one little weight-change, and he certainly didn't speak. Even though Alyssa knew how badly he wanted to.

Before the police had arrived, they'd sent Ash and Izzy back to Savannah's pied-à-terre where Sam and Alyssa were staying. Izzy Zanella apparently had the wonder-touch when it came to the diaper-wearing set. It was pretty impressive. Alyssa had known that the SEAL babysat, all the time, for Troubleshooters CO Tom Paoletti and his wife Kelly, but she hadn't really thought about what that meant until today.

Not only did Ash take to Izzy immediately and quite warmly, but it was also clear that the SEAL petty officer was unafraid of spending an undetermined number of hours alone with the baby. He actually seemed as if he were going to enjoy the opportunity.

"I became an uncle when I was barely out of diapers

myself," Izzy told her as he gathered up Ash's bag. "I speak baby at a high level of expertise, so we'll be fine. My cell phone's on. I won't be insulted when you call to check in, so do what you need to do. Call every five minutes, if you want. If I don't answer, it's because I'm dealing with a two-handed diaper of doom. I'll call you right back if that happens."

Izzy was known in SEAL Team Sixteen as being something of a wise-ass but he leaned in close before he left, and told Alyssa quietly, "Feel free to stop on your way back to the condo and buy your husband there a drink. FYI, the whole heart-in-the-drawer, you-going-AWOL thing weirded him out way more than he's letting on. And I have no plans for any extracurricular carousing tonight, because, you know, I'm married."

Alyssa did know that he was married. To Dan Gillman's sister, Eden, no less. Who'd lost her baby six months into her pregnancy, after which she'd run off to Germany.

All of which had to suck for Izzy. But that was neither here nor there, as Alyssa stood now, facing down NYPD Detective Mick Callahan, who'd lingered after the uniformed officers had left. He didn't like the fact that she and her team were here and he wasn't afraid to let her know that.

When Callahan had first arrived, he'd all but peed in possessive circles around Assemblywoman Bonavita, who'd finally gone into her office to escape him on the pretense of making a phone call.

At about the same time, Alyssa had sent Lopez, Gillman, and Vlachic out with Jenn, to scope out both Maria and Jenn's apartments.

Mick Callahan hadn't liked the way gleamingly handsome Gillman had said "See you later," to the assemblywoman. It had made him pissy.

Extra pissy. It had been clear from that moment he'd walked in that he felt threatened by their very presence.

"I don't get," he said now, in his tough-guy New York accent, "how it's going to help Maria to have *you* here, bringing additional attention to her situation. What she needs to do is keep her head down and let this bullshit pass."

"I'm pretty sure, detective," Alyssa shot back, "that keeping her head down was removed from the options list when someone broke into this office and put an animal's heart in that desk drawer."

The entire drawer had been removed and taken to the lab to verify that, indeed, it was a pig's heart in there, as Sam had suggested. It had to be. Nearly everyone was going on the assumption that it wasn't human—the idea that it could be was just too awful to consider. But Alyssa did consider it, and until they got the results from the lab, until they located Margaret Bell-Thorndyke—aka Maggie Thorndyke—and the cell phone from which the mysterious-voiced man had made that call, she was putting both her team and the clients into lockdown mode.

And yes, it was likely that when Ms. Thorndyke was found, she would discover that her cell phone had been lost or stolen. The police were tracking it right now, hopefully to some disgruntled butcher's shop.

But until they had some solid answers, Alyssa was taking precautions.

All of the assemblywoman's interns, both male and female, had been called and advised to come into the office only if they had a scheduled interview with Alyssa. And Maria and Jenn, both, were going to have a Navy SEAL or two guarding them, around the clock—at least until the security systems at the office and in their apartments were installed and running.

"If Maria hadn't waited nearly a week for your team

to arrive," Callahan pointed out acerbically, "she would've had a security system in place. Maybe even a camera—"

"Do you often engage in wishful thinking about your cases, Detective?" Alyssa asked. "Because in my experience, I find that doesn't help."

"And what I find doesn't help," he said, "is turning something like this into a media circus. You publicize this, then we *will* have a story."

Callahan was one of those men who walked into the room and looked over the tops of the heads of all of the women as he tried to find the man who was in charge.

He probably didn't do it consciously. But he'd done it today—walking right past Alyssa to introduce himself to Sam.

It was a hot button for her, she had to admit. And it had made her put more than the usual amount of steel in her voice when she'd set him straight. "Over here, Detective. *I'm* in charge."

At that point, she still could have won him over—it wasn't too late. It was clear, just from looking at him, that he was the kind of too-attractive, too-full-of-himself man who said things like, "I have a way with the ladies," and called his spouse "the little woman."

Alyssa could have smiled at him in a way that would have made him think that she was respectfully acknowledging the obviously enormous size of his penis. And maybe she could have swallowed her ire and done it if she truly believed that he had more than a snowball's chance in hell of becoming more to Maria Bonavita than her pet cop.

But he didn't. It was clear that Maria was uncomfortable around him.

"I have no intention of publicizing any of this," Alyssa told him. "At this time, that wouldn't serve the investigation."

"And you don't think someone's going to recognize you?" Callahan asked. "And start asking questions? *Why is bodyguard-to-the-stars Alyssa Locke spending so much time with Assemblywoman Bonavita?*"

"No one's going to recognize me," she said.

"I did." He gave her an extremely inappropriate once over. "A beautiful woman like yourself . . . ? Although I gotta confess that the outfit you were wearing in those pictures in the *National Voice*? *Far* more memorable than what you've got on right now, toots."

Toots.

The police detective had called Alyssa *toots*.

Not *sweetheart* or *honey* or *sugar*, but *toots*.

And Sam knew, as he leaned there against the wall in the assemblywoman's front office, that this man's choice of belittling term of endearment was not unintentional. It was meant to be a reminder of that other word that started with a *t* and ended with *ts*.

He settled back to watch as his wife sliced and diced this prick before kicking his ass out into the street.

And sure enough, before his very eyes, Alyssa seemed to grow about six inches taller. Her eyes—usually so warmly lit with laughter, or so soft when she awoke and smiled sleepily up at him—got positively glacial as she went into ice-queen mode.

Back in the day, years before they were married, back when Sam himself had been the target of Alyssa's icicle-sharp contempt, it hadn't just scared the hell out of him when she'd looked at him like that.

It had turned him on.

It still did.

Alyssa's tone was frosty. And dismissive. "Thank you for coming in so quickly, Detective. I appreciate what seems like your genuine concern for Ms. Bonavita and her staff. I hope you can set your animosity aside as we work together toward the common goal of providing them with the best possible protection. For the moment, you *are* in charge of the police investigation, so I suggest you go investigate the whereabouts of Ms. Thorndyke and her cell phone. Nudging the lab for the results from their tests would also be a better use of your time than standing here arguing with me about something that's not going to change."

"For *the moment,* I'm in charge?" he asked, his voice loaded with amused disdain. "As full of yourself as you are, *princess,* you don't have the power to dictate who is or isn't in charge of the investigation of a crime committed—"

"The crime committed here today," she cut him off to say.

But he raised his voice to speak over her. "A crime committed in *my* precinct—"

Alyssa got louder, too. "The crime, or the *prank,* as you've dismissively referred to it more than once, was not merely facilitated by breaking and entering. The perpetrator used the U.S. Postal Service to deliver at least part of their threat. Which means, *Toots,* that this is a federal crime, and should be investigated accordingly."

Sam had—always—found it unbelievably hot when Alyssa used FBI-speak, filled with words like *perpetrator* and *facilitated* and *accordingly.*

"Oh, come on," the detective scoffed. "It was a freaking postcard, sent locally. There's no need to bring in an outside agency—"

"Someone went to a lot of trouble," Alyssa informed him coolly, "to set this up."

"You bring in the FBI," he pointed out, "this'll never get solved. They don't know the neighborhood, they don't know jackshit. They'll send in someone—"

"They'll send an agent-in-charge," Alyssa interrupted him again, "who has the experience and training to recognize the serious nature of this threat. This wasn't done, Detective, by some irate person who simply wandered in off the street. The caulking on the drawer, put there to keep the smell from escaping? Whoever did this *has* visited this office. Whoever did this knows about the overheating issues."

Sam could tell from Callahan's expression that he hadn't considered that—yeah, because he was too busy swinging his dick around like a semaphore flag, trying to catch Maria's attention. Fucking moron.

"Whoever did this got in," Alyssa continued, "with *no* sign of breaking before they entered. And I'm not willing to cross my fingers and hope this *blows over,* when every ounce of training I have is telling me that whoever did this wants something. And they're not going away until they get it. Now, if you'll excuse me, I have to call my contact at the FBI. I'll let your lieutenant know who they're sending in to take over the investigation."

Oh, snap, as Jules Cassidy would have said, were he here. And Sam was pretty certain that his and Alyssa's good friend *was* going to be here rather soon, since Jules was the said contact with the FBI to whom she referred. And he was high enough up the chain of command to ask to be assigned to this case.

To ask and be given what he'd asked for.

"Mick."

Before Alyssa could march out into the hall to make that call, Maria opened the door to her inner office. Both the detective and Alyssa turned to look at her.

"I need you to cut me some slack," she told Callahan. "I agree that some of the measures Ms. Locke is suggesting we take seem . . . a little extreme. And I also believe— I *hope*—that once we find Maggie Thorndyke, we'll find an explanation for all of this. Whether it's a joke or a prank . . . Well, we'll find that out soon enough. Until then, you need to accept the fact that as far as choices about my safety go, I've agreed to let the team from Troubleshooters call the shots."

Mick looked from Maria to Alyssa and back, and he was smart enough to know that it was time to back down. So he did.

And Alyssa took the opportunity to further dismiss him—by ignoring him as she moved toward the assemblywoman. "Is this a good time to discuss the logistics of the next few days?"

"Of course," Maria said, stepping back to lead the way into her private office.

Alyssa glanced back at Sam. "Call Jules and fill him in."

"Yes, ma'am," he said, taking out his phone and dialing.

But Mick had to have the last word. "If you reach Margaret Thorndyke before we do—"

"I'll give you a call," Maria promised him.

"We'll make sure your lieutenant is kept in the loop," Alyssa corrected, and shut the door tightly behind her, as Sam was bumped directly to Jules's voice mail.

"Call me," he said.

"Fucking bitch," Callahan added, as he gathered up his overcoat and got ready to face the cold.

And great, it was going to sound to Jules like Sam had said, *Call me, fucking bitch,* or maybe *Call me fucking bitch,* which Jules would do cheerfully and without hesitation, assuming there was a joke behind it. But before Sam could explain, Callahan added, "Have you seen those pictures of your boss, in the *National Voice? Nice* tits."

He'd caught Sam looking at him and taken the eye contact as an invitation to speak.

Sam laughed, because if this man hadn't picked up the fact that he and Alyssa were married, then he had to be just about *the* worst detective ever.

But again Callahan took it as encouragement, laughing, too. "Am I right or am I right? The woman is totally tappable, but you'd have to, I don't know, put tape over her mouth because . . . Jesus."

Sam stopped laughing and straightened to his full height, which meant he towered over the prick.

But Callahan didn't notice. He was too busy looking over at Maria's office door as he pulled on his coat. "Bitch obviously needs to get laid. Bet she's the type likes to get slapped around some, too. No problem, we can line up everyone she's pissed the shit out of, bend her over and give 'em a choice—"

Sam had heard enough. He shut his phone and hit Callahan with both hands, pushing him back and slamming him against the wall by the door, knocking both the wind and the fuck out of the fucking windbag and jamming his arm up against his throat to hold him there, gasping and choking, like the impotent misogynist bully that he was.

He knew he was supposed to use words when dealing with conflict, so he got right up in Callahan's face to ask, "Does it make you feel better? Does it make you feel like more of a man, you piece of shit? To threaten a woman with gang rape?"

"What the fuck is wrong with you?" Callahan clawed at Sam's arms as he rasped, "I didn't—"

"Yeah, you fucking well did!" Sam released him, only to slam him back against the wall again and again, as emphasis to his words. "What else is it when you *line up* a bunch of angry fuckheads and force a woman to *bend over*? And you didn't even say it to her face, you had to say it behind her back! I don't know who your daddy paid off to make you a detective—"

"Fuck you!"

"Fuck *you*!" Sam slammed him harder.

"Sam!"

He turned to see Alyssa, standing in Maria's open door, looking mighty displeased. So he let Callahan go, which was a mistake, because the son of a bitch kicked him.

If Sam hadn't moved to block it, his balls would've been lodged up in his brain. As it was he was going to have one hell of a bruise on his leg, and oh. Fantastic.

The prick actually drew on him.

"On the floor!" Callahan shouted, in between coughing for air, as he waved his sidearm around. "Get the fuck on the floor! Hands on your head! Now! *Now!*"

Sam looked at Alyssa, who was trying to shout over the cop.

"All right," she bellowed. "That's enough! That's *enough*!"

But Callahan wasn't listening, and she looked at Sam and said, "Do it," even as he was already dropping to the office floor.

Because he, too, had picked up that extra little shred of crazy in the sumbitch's eyes. And he sure as hell didn't like the way Callahan was waving his weapon in Alyssa's direction. Short of taking him down and disarming him, Sam had only one option.

So he hit the floor—hardwood and dingy—and put his hands on his head, and braced himself for it and yeah, he got exactly what he expected—a savage kick to his side that damn near lifted him off the ground. It hurt like hell, the pain hot and sharp.

It took everything in him to not grab the fuckwad's foot and do some serious damage. Maybe pistol whip him with his own weapon a time or two, because it wouldn't take much to take it out of that moronic grip.

"Stop it!" he heard Alyssa order as he breathed through the pain, staring at a paper clip and a marker pen that had fallen and lay neglected, beneath the second desk. And, Jesus, it looked like someone had lost a tooth. Not him, though—that kick hadn't come anywhere near his mouth. Or maybe it was just a tooth-shaped piece of paper there, nestled in a dust bunny.

Alyssa had more to say: "You so much as breathe on him again, and you will be in deep shit, mister!"

Maria, too, added her voice to the fracas. "Put that gun away *right now*!" She clapped her hands for emphasis, as if they were unruly dogs in a spat. "Detective Callahan, this is unacceptable!"

The pain hadn't decayed as much as it should have, and Sam knew the prick had done damage to at least one of his ribs when he felt something relatively lightweight hit his back, lighting him on fire again. Yeah, if that hurt, his rib was broken. God damn it.

Callahan holstered his sidearm—thank God for small favors—as he gruffly ordered, "Cuff him."

Who was he talking to? Alyssa?

She laughed her disbelief and disdain. "What?" as Maria still sputtered, "I can't believe you *kicked* him!"

"I'm calling for backup. I'm taking him in for assaulting a police officer. Check your rule book, Assemblywoman, I have the right to defend myself."

"Against a man who has clearly surrendered?" Maria asked.

"Oh, no," Alyssa was saying over her. "No, no . . ."

"Sam just . . . assaulted you?" Maria couldn't believe it. "Out of the blue?"

"Yes, he did," Callahan said.

"Bullshit," Sam said from the floor.

"Shut up," the detective said, and actually started Mirandizing him. "You have the right to remain silent—"

A broken rib was bearable, but pissing Alyssa off by being dragged to jail was not. "You made a joke, you dumb fuck," Sam argued, "about gang-raping my wife!"

That made them all pause—Callahan, too. "Your wife?"

Sam lifted his head and looked up at him. "Yeah, fuckwad," he said, using his eyes to point to Alyssa. "My wife. The *fucking bitch* with the *nice tits* . . . ?"

Alyssa's cell phone started ringing, and Sam told her, "If that's Jules—answer it. I left him a message you're going to want to hear about." He looked at Callahan again. "Everything you said, moron, was recorded on my voice mail to Jules. And that would be Jules Cassidy, high-level FBI? AIC, coming in from Boston to handle this investigation? Former partner and best friend of Alyssa-of-the-nice-tits, aka my *wife?*"

As Alyssa took that call—and knowing Jules, he was going to have a *lot* to say to her about what he'd heard—Sam turned to Maria, who was definitely aghast.

Callahan realized, too late, what he'd done. The final shred of his last chance with Maria Bonavita—not that he'd actually had one, but everyone had the right to dream big—was gone, baby, gone.

"You're a lawyer, right?" Sam said to Maria, mostly for Callahan's benefit. "This is a nifty new twist on the old classic case of sexual harassment, isn't it? Of course, the NYPD probably won't let it go to trial. They're not going to want a recording of one of their detectives saying—"

"I didn't know she was your *wife,*" Callahan said, like that made a difference.

"I'm more interested in pursuing the police brutality case," Maria said hotly, as Sam pushed himself up onto his hands and knees.

"He had me by the throat," Callahan told her.

"He was on the floor, following your orders, when I saw you kick him," she countered as she helped Sam to his feet.

"All right," Alyssa said, snapping her phone shut. "Mr. Cassidy, from the FBI, heard the entire conversation. He's had some experience with negotiation, and he said to tell you, Detective, that he's being extremely generous when he suggests that we simply drop all of the various court cases—both criminal and civil. We'll call it a wash. You might win one, but we'd win the others. So let's just skip it all, all right?" She tossed his cuffs back to him.

Callahan caught them, and turned to look at Maria, who shook her head at him, her disapproval still apparent. "Detective, you were leaving. I suggest you do so immediately."

Without another word, he turned and went out the door, closing it oddly quietly behind him.

Alyssa turned to look at Sam as Maria faded back into her office, to give them privacy, of sorts. "Are you okay?" she asked.

"I'll live," he said.

She narrowed her eyes at him. "He kicked you pretty hard."

"I'm fine. I am sorry, though," he told her, then qualified it, "that you had to hear what he said. Son of a bitch."

She sighed her exasperation. "You really think I haven't heard all of that before? I mean, hello." She gestured to herself. "Nice tits."

Sam laughed, but quickly stopped. Ow. "Shit."

"Hmm," she said. "You want to rewind to my question—are you all right? And maybe rework that apology while you're at it . . . ? Pull up your shirt, let me see."

He gingerly pulled up his shirt, but there was only a red mark on his side. It wouldn't be until later that it would turn the colors of the rainbow. And it would. It was going to be a piece of art. "Damn it," he swore, because it was right where he usually carried Ash.

"Does it hurt to breathe?" Alyssa asked, her fingers cool against his skin.

"Yeah," Sam admitted, drawing in his breath when she

got too close. It was his lower rib, definitely. "It's cracked." He met her eyes again. "I am sorry," he said, but then had to add, "that I got hurt." It wasn't what she wanted to hear, but he couldn't give her that. He was not going to apologize for scaring the crap out of that dipshit. And he had. He'd definitely scared Mick Callahan when he'd had him against the wall—which was what made the man get extra mean.

She shook her head, clearly frustrated with him as she headed back into Maria's office. "Call Jules back, will you? And tell him that he can cross bailing you out of jail off his to-do list."

Jenn had left her bed unmade.

"Sorry about the mess," she told the three Navy SEALs who stood awkwardly, just inside her apartment door, because, really, there wasn't anywhere else for them to go.

They'd just come from surveying Maria's condo—checking the security of the windows, doors, and even the walls, and getting an overview of the lobby, the elevators, and the hallway in the assemblywoman's building.

Jenn had witnessed the way their big brains worked as they looked around, as they evaluated the space in which Maria lived, as they thought out loud and strategized what-if scenarios.

What if they had to get the assemblywoman quickly out of the building?

There were both front and back stairways, plus a freight elevator that wasn't used by the residents, which had a lock that they could easily override if necessary.

What if they brought Maria in and discovered someone was hiding there, waiting for her?

That wouldn't happen if one of them searched the place each time they entered, which they always would do. And if they did surprise someone hiding there, whoever stayed in the hall with Maria would take her out of the building via the freight elevator, while the other dispatched the intruder.

What if they came under direct attack via the condo's single door?

They'd hustle Maria into the master bathroom, which was the safest, most secure room. Positioned in the bedroom, with the proper weapons and ammunition, they could hold off an attacking army if need be.

What about the windows?

The drapes and blinds would have to be kept tightly shut, since every building in the area was a potential sniper's hiding place.

Which was when Jenn had chimed in, because Maria, absolutely, wasn't going to like that.

They'd asked her some questions, then—did the assemblywoman live alone?

She most certainly did.

Did she have a boyfriend, either in the area or living elsewhere? Or maybe just someone with whom she was friends, with benefits?

Dan Gillman—Lucky—had asked that one, and Jenn had looked at him sideways.

It was more than obvious that he'd wanted to know this for personal reasons. But with a completely straight face, he'd explained that if they were going to be camping out in Maria's living room tonight, they didn't want to accidentally kill her boyfriend when he popped in unexpectedly from Chicago.

But no, Maria didn't have a boyfriend, not in Chicago or anywhere else. As for friends with benefits, they were going to have to ask Maria directly. Jenn knew that she *did* have an asshat of an ex-husband named Bobby in Atlanta, but he certainly didn't have a key.

And as for anyone else, besides Jenn, who might also have Maria's key . . . ?

She knew Maria paid a cleaning service to come in once every few weeks, usually while she was in Albany. And that meant that someone from the service must have a key. Plus the building's superintendent could always get in—but not while the night lock was on, of course.

As they all took one last look around, Jenn overheard the youngest of them, Tony Vlachic, comment to Jay, sotto voce, about how small Maria's place was.

With two bedrooms, a real eat-in kitchen, and a thirtieth-floor panorama of the city's skyline from its floor to ceiling windows, it was palatial compared to Jenn's studio.

Where they all now stood, squeezed in together.

Her apartment was a single tiny room, cramped even when the air mattress was deflated and folded back into the sofa. The view from *her* window was of the air shaft. In a city that was constantly changing, the ugly, claustrophobia-inducing brick and rows of other people's windows was a seasonless mix of 1890s tenement and 1960s thank-God-someone-finally-invented-the-window-air-conditioner.

And yes, to be fair, sometimes—rarely—in the winter, falling snow would settle romantically on the battered and acid-rain-scarred tops of her many neighbors' air conditioners. But Jenn could miss seeing it if she blinked. It melted quickly in the heat from the building and the humanity within.

"Nice and cozy, huh?" she said to the SEALs now as she turned on another lamp.

Dan pushed free of the others and stepped into her tiny galley kitchen. He turned around, took another few steps, which put him into the munchkin-sized bathroom. He then came back out, and opened the door to her over-stuffed closet, as if expecting to find another room, or maybe an alternative universe awaiting him there.

"Jesus," he said as he stared at her jammed-in organizational system of shelves and baskets, of which she was pretty darn proud. "You could crew on a submarine."

Jenn looked up from trying to squeeze the last of the air from her mattress, so she could fold it up and turn it back into her couch, which would turn her bedroom back into her living room. "Is that some kind of Navy insult? Your mother wears combat boots, you could crew on a—"

"No," he said with laughter, as he turned to look at her. His smile was really quite lovely up close like this. "It's not. It's . . . impressive. Those guys fit their entire lives into, like, a shoebox. Talk about close quarters—both for living and working. I couldn't do it. But you probably could."

"I bet there's not a big demand, though, for executive assistants on the USS *Depthcharge*."

He laughed again. "I don't think *Depthcharge* is on any Navy shortlist for names for submarines," he pointed out. "Depth charges are what you drop from a surface vessel to find and sink a sub."

"I knew that," she said as the metal bedframe finally folded back into the sofa with a *boing*. "I was being ironic. I'd be fine with the tight living conditions. It's the part where the sub might sink that would be problematic for me."

"Speaking of problematic," Jay pushed back his hood to say. "I'm pretty sure Ms. Locke intends for two of us to, um, camp out here with you tonight. Maybe you should leave the bed open so we can see how much floor space there is."

"There isn't," she said. "Floor space. I mean, unless we move my coffee table. We could store it over at the office, I guess, but even then . . ."

"You'll have to get sleeping bags," Dan told Jay.

Interesting, his use of *you*, as if he'd already assigned himself to guarding Maria. "One in the kitchen, one kind of halfway under the pullout part of the sofa-bed—"

"And I would step *where*, if I needed to use the bathroom in the middle of the night?" Jenn asked.

"Yeah, that's not going to work," Tony said.

"You know, I really don't need anyone to stay," Jenn said. "Let alone *two* of you. I mean, let's be realistic here. It's Maria who's being threatened. She's the one who needs protection—"

"I know that's what it seems like," Dan interrupted. "But that thing *was* in *your* desk."

"Ms. Locke is thorough," Jay Lopez chimed in, terminally polite beneath his parka. "Until Margaret Thorndyke is found—"

"I'm sure she's out shopping," Jenn said. "She shops like she's single-handedly attempting to stimulate the economy. She's got a walk-in closet the size of my entire apartment."

"Lopez has got a walk-in closet the size of your apartment," Dan pointed out.

"You're in New York City now," she told him. "You've got to readjust your definitions of small and large."

"You'd be okay if it was just one of us staying here with you?" Tony asked her. "Because, you know, some women might feel threatened by that, or be afraid some of the neighbors might think, you know, something inappropriate."

"And my bringing *two* Navy SEALs home won't make them think something inappropriate? Especially since their apartments are the same size as mine?" She looked at them. "Guys. I have brothers. You don't scare me. You don't offend me. If one of you really has to sleep on my kitchen floor tonight, I'm not going to feel threatened— I'm going to feel sorry about the fact that you obviously pulled the short straw. Just do us both a favor and don't eat dinner at the Mexican place that's down the street? When the heat finally kicks on in here, which it'll do in"—she looked at her watch—"about two hours, it's going to make the office seem chilly. FYI, my AC unit is winterized. We can't turn it on, we can't open the window. *The* window, singular. So bring shorts and ix-nay on the eans-bay, boys, because I *will* make the lucky winner go out into the hall to fart."

"It'll be rank and rating," Tony told her.

"I'm sorry . . . ?" Jenn didn't understand.

"We'll use our rank and rating," he explained, "instead of drawing straws—to determine who sleeps on your kitchen floor. Which means it's probably going to be me."

"Sorry," Jenn told him as she led the way back into the hall and locked her door behind her.

"It's okay," he said with a smile. "I'm not a big fan of beans anyway."

He remembered the day when the plan became crystal clear.

Not the details—just his goal and the potential outcome. The details came later. They always did.

He'd researched for months, every moment he could spare spent locked in his room, surfing the Internet, finding out all that he could about *her*, about Alyssa Locke.

He made lists of her friends, her family, her acquaintances, even her clients at Troubleshooters Incorporated, and he googled them all regularly, too.

He found out that Alyssa was born in Washington, D.C., that she had two sisters. Only one still lived—Tyra. Lanora, her youngest sister, had died while giving birth.

He knew that her mother had been the victim of a violent crime when Alyssa was only thirteen, that her estranged father had died in a car accident several years earlier, and that she and her sisters had gone to live with an aunt.

He discovered that, like her mother before her, Alyssa was married to a white man. Her husband's name was Roger "Sam" Starrett, and he was a former Navy SEAL who didn't deserve her, who worked beneath her, who'd planted his seed inside of her. . . .

The news of her pregnancy had made him reel with anger, with disgust, with seething hatred for this man who had the audacity to touch her, to make love to her, to defile her so completely and permanently. Swept up by his rage, he'd come to his senses in his car, driving west, toward California.

His blind urge to destroy had taken him as far as Utah, where he stopped because the certainty inside of him warned that he could not kill the husband—a Navy SEAL—without getting caught or killed himself.

And he didn't want justice half as badly as he wanted the ultimate satisfaction of gazing into Alyssa's eyes as he took out his knife.

So instead, he'd tried to relieve the pressure by killing a woman in the parking lot of a mall just south of Salt Lake City. He killed her husband, too, just to see what that would feel like, but none of it was any good. The certainty inside told him that it wouldn't be, until it was Alyssa—so he didn't extract any of their teeth or leave behind a note of any kind.

He did linger, though, and when the police came as they always did, *she* wasn't with them and he knew that they didn't connect the murders to those he'd done before.

They didn't know it was the Dentist. *She* didn't know it was him, either.

Because if she'd thought it was, she would've come, regardless of her pregnancy.

She *would* have come. She wanted him as badly as he wanted her. He was counting on that fact.

So he drove back east even though he wanted to go to San Diego, to catch just a glimpse of her. But he knew his anger at her swollen belly and his hatred of her husband would overwhelm him, so he kept himself away.

When he found out that she'd had the baby, and that it was a boy, he knew, absolutely, his destiny.

He would take her, as he'd planned, regardless of his chances of survival.

But if he *did* survive—which he was becoming more and more determined to do—he would then track down and kill the husband, and take and raise the child—*her* child—as his very own.

Jenn didn't look up from her computer as Dan went into the assemblywoman's office. Everyone else had gone for the day—she was the last one to leave.

"Hey, Tony, I'll be ready to go in . . . just a . . . few more minutes," she said, her fingers flying across her keyboard.

Danny slipped his bag off of his shoulder and put it on the floor with the sleeping bag that Lopez had picked up from some sporting goods store. He didn't bother to correct her, instead taking the opportunity to really look at her while her attention was elsewhere.

She was actually kind of pretty, in a supersized way. Not that she was fat. She was just . . . sturdy. Strapping. Statuesque.

Goddess-like—if there was a Goddess of Awkwardness.

Although the true reason Jennilyn LeMay was awkward was because she refused to embrace her extra-largeness. She tried to hide it by slouching and hunching—or by trying to make herself invisible, always jockeying for the spot in the back of the room, against the wall or over in the corner.

She didn't wear very much makeup. She didn't try at all to emphasize her eyes, which were, by far, her best feature, beneath her glasses. They were a really nice shade of light brown. Although her mouth was nice, too. It was generously wide with a default upward curve. She was quick to turn that into a real smile, which made dimples appear in her cheeks.

The dimples were pretty damn cute.

Her sense of humor was rock solid, and she clearly had a very big brain in that gigantic head of hers.

Her clothes were horrific, though—like something his older sister would've worn to the bank after getting dressed in the dark. The outfit was way too somber, as if Jenn—like Sandy—were compensating or apologizing for holding down what had once been, traditionally, a man's job.

Dark tailored skirt, starchy blouse that was buttoned uncomfortably to the neck, not-quite-matching black suit jacket over the back of her chair, ugly yet worn-out flat shoes—absolute proof that she was embarrassed to be so tall.

A little more effort, and a whole lot more daring, in bright and flowing clothes that celebrated her height, and she could've looked good. Well, interesting and strikingly eye-catching, at least.

She didn't try all that hard with her hair, either. It was shoulder length, tucked behind her ears, an almost colorlessly bland shade of light brown, and not particularly well cut. It looked, though, as if it would be baby fine and super soft to touch, but that also made it prone to getting stringy at the end of a long day.

Which this one had definitely been.

It was funny, but the fatigue that Danny had felt yesterday at the airport was . . . well, it was far from gone. But it wasn't quite fatigue anymore, either. It was hard to define, exactly, what it had turned into—this heaviness that had grown like a tumor inside of him when that kid—the private—had died from a piece of shrapnel to the throat.

It was mixed together with his current solutionless family problem with his little brother, Ben, leaving Dan angry and frustrated and depressed.

All of it had further metastasized into something that choked him from within, which, last week, had made him lose it, in front of not just his teammates, but his team's CO. Or so he was told, because he didn't remember any of it, which scared the bejesus out of him.

Back in Coronado, the senior chief had called him in to his office and tossed around words like *battle fatigue* and *stress,* and phrases like *it happens to the best of us.* And Dan had obediently scheduled a session with the team's shrink for a week from next Friday.

But he knew the truth: that the heaviness inside of him, inside of his very soul, had been there long before the goatfuck in Kabul. It had been there long before 9/11. In fact, he couldn't remember it ever *not* being there, even back when he was a little boy, entering kindergarten.

He knew what he had to do to control it, to shrink it into something that he could compartmentalize and ignore. He had to focus on the immediacy of the moment. He had to stay out of the murky shit inside of his head and instead live in the right-here and right-now.

Sex would help.

Sex always helped. Sex, and the promise of even more sex.

Unlike some of the other guys in his SEAL team, Danny had never been into one-nighters. His thing had always been the one- or two-weeker, and better yet, the always lovely vacation fling. He loved having sex with a woman for the first time while knowing that there was going to be a second, third, and fourth coming right on its heels. Best yet was experiencing this abundance of pleasure while knowing there was a concrete end date in sight.

As Dan realized that Jenn's definition of "a few minutes" was considerably different than his, he lowered himself into a chair at the conference table. He was hungry, but he'd purposely waited to eat so that he could have dinner with her. Because on his way back to this office, after picking up his gear at the hotel, he'd realized the truth.

Yes, Izzy fucking Zanella had, yet again, gotten the job that Dan had wanted—to guard Maria. But because of this, because Dan had instead gotten assigned to guard Jenn, the odds of his actually getting laid in the near future had risen drastically higher.

Because life wasn't like some stupid romance novel, or that movie with what's his name, Kevin Costner, where he was the bodyguard and Whitney Houston sang that song. *Ah-ee-eye, will always love . . .*

Yeah.

That shit didn't happen in real life.

An obscenely beautiful woman like Maria Bonavita didn't just sit around, hopelessly single, waiting for some sailor to show up. And when he did, she was not breathlessly eager to lead him into her bedroom and lock the door.

Real life was never that ridiculously easy.

Dan knew that, firsthand. He'd gone after a fairy-tale, happily-ever-after ending with the woman of his dreams—gorgeous and mysterious Troubleshooters operative Sophia Ghaffari.

She'd actually had dinner with him a few times. He'd been certain that it was destiny, that he and Sophia belonged together, that theirs would be a love affair for the ages, that their love would last a lifetime.

She, on the other hand, disagreed, and delivered the

let's be friends speech, fairly early on. More recently, she'd married a Troubleshooters co-worker—a kind of dweeby former CIA operative named Dave—with whom she was now expecting her first child.

Jesus Christ. It still pissed Danny off to think about it. It still made his inner petulant two-year-old pout and rant, because it was so goddamn unfair.

But real life was rarely fair.

And yes, here in this current configuration of real life, where there truly was no such thing as a love affair for the ages, Izzy and Lopez were going to hang out in mind-blowingly gorgeous Maria Bonavita's tiny apartment, trying to stay out of her way while she did whatever state legislators did at home in the evening.

If they were lucky, she'd say goodnight to them before she turned in.

The idea that she would stop to have a real conversation with either of them was ridiculous. And even if she did, what of it? Like she was going to risk her entire career to hook up, even for just one night, with some SEAL?

That was *not* going to happen.

The odds were better that one of them would be struck by a plummeting piece of space debris.

But the odds, on the other hand, of Dan's nailing Jennilyn LeMay, and having a hell of a two-week vacation with her . . .

That was definitely do-able.

He knew he could be exactly what she needed, exactly what she wished for and dreamed of, exactly what she never got with her classically beautiful boss always hanging around.

And it was going to be just Dan and Jenn tonight in her closet-sized apartment. They'd have a little dinner, do a little talking and a lot of laughing, lose a few clothes due to the overactive heater that she'd warned him about . . .

If he played this right, he wouldn't even bother opening that sleeping bag.

His stomach growled, and Jenn laughed and said, "I take it you haven't eaten yet—oh!"

She cut herself off when she looked up and saw it was Dan, not Tony, sitting there.

And there he was, staring into Jennilyn's pretty eyes, and everything he'd intended to say to make her laugh and get them moving toward the night's inevitable conclusion vanished. It was gone, clear out of his head.

So he sat there in silence, just staring back at her, like the village fricking idiot.

She looked away first, as if embarrassed by the extensive eye contact. "I'm sorry, I thought . . ."

"Yeah." Danny found his voice, but his brain was still set on totally stupid and lame. "But I'm it. I'm your, you know . . ."

"Bodyguard," she supplied the word. "Wow. I'm so sorry."

"No," he said. "It's . . . why I'm here, you know? In New York. To work and, um . . . Vlachic—Tony—actually had plans for tonight, so . . . That's how we're going to do it until the security systems are in place. Three of us on, one off. At night. During the day we'll . . . probably do two off, two on, because Sam and the team leader will be around."

She nodded as she shut the top of her laptop. "Well, that was . . . really very sweet of you," she said. "To let Tony have the first night off."

"It's not a big deal," Dan said. In truth, he had nothing to do with it. It was entirely Alyssa Locke's decision. But sure, if Jenn wanted to give him credit for it . . . He'd take it.

She laughed with both derision and genuine amusement. "Tell me that again, later, when you're trying to sleep on my kitchen floor."

"Trust me, I've slept in plenty worse places," he told her.

"I bet," she said, and behind her glasses, her eyes softened. "Tony told me you just got back from . . . well, he didn't say *exactly* where, but . . ."

"Yeah, we can't . . ." He shook his head. "Talk about that, but . . . Hey, I was thinking," he said, "that if you haven't eaten, we could, I don't know, get some take-out. Maybe . . . rent a movie?"

He'd said it in a manner that was completely casual and totally friendly, but the look she gave him was a mix of amazement and disbelief, with a little bit of disgust thrown in, as if he'd instead suggested take-out followed by her dancing naked for him, culminating in a BJ.

And that was—okay, he'd admit it—the subtext of his suggestion, because yes, he wanted her mouth on him, but in a vast variety of interesting and creative places.

"Or not," he continued. "I just . . . don't get a chance to see a lot of movies while I'm . . . overseas."

Her suspicion and doubt was instantly erased, and he knew that all he had to do was whisper the word *Afghanistan*—or even imply it—and victory was within easy reach.

Because now she was apologizing to him. "Sorry. I'm just . . . I've got about an hour more of work to do," she told him. "I'm writing this . . . Well, it's going to take at least an hour to finish and . . . I lost a lot of my workday today, so . . ."

"Oh, right, of course," he said. "*I'm* sorry, I shouldn't have—"

"No," she cut him off. "Please. If you rent something that I've already seen, then I can kind of do both at once."

"If it's only an hour," Dan told her. "I can wait. You've got a lot of books on your shelves. I'll borrow one"—women always liked men who read their books—"and stay out of your way." He laughed. "Or at least try. You know, until you're done. But I've really got to eat first. Or at least get something to tide me over if you're not hungry—"

Her stomach growled, and she rolled her eyes. "There's your answer to that."

"Let's get take-out," Dan said again. "We can eat and then you can get back to work, and when you're done, if there's time—if we want—we can rent a movie."

She smiled at him then, those dimples appearing. "How's Chinese sound?"

"Sounds pretty perfect," he told her, smiling back, testing his theory again by adding, "Not a lot of Chinese food where I've been lately, either."

And oh, yeah. Sing alleluia and praise the Lord. He was *totally* getting some tonight.

"If we call ahead, it'll be ready when we get there." She pulled a take-out menu from a file on top of her desk and held it out to him. "My treat."

That wasn't going to work. "Not a chance," he said as he glanced at it. It wasn't too pricy, but still . . . "I've seen where you live, Jenn. This one's definitely on me."

She laughed, but she shook her head. "Dutch, then," she said.

Dan glanced up from the menu and into her eyes, and he knew with the instinctive certainty that had rarely failed to guide him into a woman's willing arms, that this was not a point to push her on. He'd let her win—this one. "Fair enough." He reached for his cell phone. "You want me to call . . . ?"

"*I* will," she said, already dialing the office phone. Obviously the restaurant was on speed dial. "They know me. They'll throw in extra rice."

"Extra rice?" he scoffed. "Come on, LeMay. Get 'em to give you the good stuff. Extra fortune cookies. I want at least three."

"You can't have three fortune cookies," she said in

obviously mock outrage. "I mean, is that even legal? What do you do with three fortunes? Average them?"

"No," he said, laughing, too, teasing her back. "You pick the best one and throw the others away. Didn't your multitude of brothers teach you anything?"

"Apparently not," she said. "Their brotherly advice handbook didn't include a chapter on fortune cookies."

"Then thank God I'm here," he told her. "And not a moment too soon."

"Believe me, I really don't need another brother," Jenn told him, but before he could respond, she turned her attention to the phone. "Yes, hi, Mrs. C., it's Jenn. I'd like to place an order for take-out. No, I'll pick it up. And oh, the gentleman I'm dining with tonight? He'd like *three* fortune cookies, so we'll need four altogether." She smiled at him, and those dimples reappeared. "He likes a choice when it comes to his destiny."

CHAPTER SEVEN

Maria Bonavita caught him getting all weepy.

It was embarrassing as shit, and he should have known better, because babies were total chick magnets. Izzy had learned *that* truth long before he'd learned the true value and power of actually having a chick magnet at his command.

Women loved to hold babies, to hug them, to smell them. It was, Izzy was pretty certain, a biological imperative, a brain-stem reaction—particularly among women in their early thirties, such as the assemblywoman.

Izzy had brought Ash into the kitchen to get out of Maria's way. They'd come over—Maria lived just down the hall from Savannah's condo, so it wasn't much of an "over"—when Alyssa found out that Tony Vlachic had tickets to see *Avenue Q*. Tickets, plural. The kid had a date, too, with the same "friend" he'd been seeing off and on for the past year.

Not that Izzy'd asked and not that Tony had told.

But everyone knew, and he'd even made plans to meet his "friend" here in town, so. . . . In order to not let the T-man get hosed for the outrageous price of two seats in a Broadway theater, Alyssa had given the tadpole the night off.

Which meant that Izzy was doing double duty here

with Ash in Maria's condo, until Sam and Alyssa got back from their visit to Maggie Thorndyke's townhouse, because she and her cell phone still hadn't turned up.

Ash had gotten fussy, so Izzy'd adiosed him out of the living room and into the kitchen, which was when Maria had announced that she was taking a shower.

But it seemed as if she were that amazing and rare creature: a person capable of taking a true five-minute shower. And not five minutes under the spray. Five minutes from disappearance to reemergence. Pretty dang impressive.

He'd just given Ashton a bottle, and the little guy's eyes had rolled back in his head as he'd fallen into a post-feeding, full-belly coma of happiness. So Izzy'd sat there, at Maria's kitchen table, holding the sleeping baby in his arms, looking down into that happy, chubby little face as Ash occasionally, dreamily sucked on some giant, perfect, invisible breast.

Izzy had smoothed back the baby's hair, and touched the unbelievable softness of his cheek, aware that Eden's baby—had he survived—was supposed to have had this same perfect, smooth, mocha-colored skin and dark curly hair.

Which was when Ash, no doubt now dreaming of his mommy or daddy, had smiled in his sleep—a big, goofy baby smile. And he'd sighed and nestled even closer to Izzy.

And the possibility of everything that might have been had rushed through him, and he'd gotten all teary-eyed.

Which, of course, was when Five-Minute-Maria waltzed into the room.

"Oh," she said as she realized that Ash was asleep, and she cut herself off, whispering, "Sorry."

It was obvious that she was apologizing, too, for walking in on Izzy while he was on the verge of sobbing like a little girl.

He turned his head away from her so he could wipe his eyes, which was idiotic because as long as he *didn't* wipe his eyes, he could've pretended that he wasn't crying—that is, as long as he could keep his head turned away until his cheeks air dried. But it didn't matter, because he *did* wipe his eyes, so now there was absolutely no doubt in the assemblywoman's mind that he was, himself, a total baby.

But she was a highly skilled people person, and she didn't catapult herself from the kitchen, screaming "Oh my God! A crying man is in my kitchen! Someone make him stop!" Instead, she turned her back on him, giving him privacy of sorts, murmuring, "Just getting some tea," as she quietly got a mug from the cabinet and put some water on to boil.

His embarrassment was stupid, because it wasn't as if she'd walked in on him in the bathroom, taking a dump or even jerking off.

Both of which he did on a fairly regular basis. Although, come to think of it, crying over Eden and Pinkie—which was the baby's in utero name even though he was a boy—was also something Izzy did with some regularity, but usually always in the bathroom with the door securely locked.

The silence was awkward, so Izzy broke it. "I fell in love with this girl who was pregnant," he said, "and convinced her to marry me, but the baby was stillborn."

Maria turned to face him, surprise and sympathy in her eyes. She had her hair up in a ponytail and she was wearing a Union College T-shirt with a baggy pair of sweatpants. With her face clean of makeup, she was freshly, gleamingly, classically beautiful like some thirteenth-century Italian painting come to life.

"I'm so sorry," she said so sincerely that he kept going, even though he knew that he'd already said more than enough.

"I thought I was going to have this," he admitted, gesturing to Ash, "but now . . . They're both gone."

And now the silence was even more awkward, and he knew he should turn away—maybe say *Excuse me*, and take Ash back into the living room, where Lopez was sitting by the door.

But before he could move, she spoke. "Both?"

Izzy nodded. "She, you know, split. She didn't love me—it was kind of obvious and . . . I'm sorry—you must think I'm, like, creepy TMI guy, sitting and crying in your kitchen. I'm usually less of a load."

"No," she said, laughing quietly, so as not to wake the baby. "It's actually . . . No. It's refreshing. You're . . . Irving, right?"

"Well, that's what it says on the birth certificate." He looked down at Ash again. "I must've been one butt-ugly kid. Can you imagine looking at something as beautiful as this and going *I know, let's name him Irving*."

She laughed again. "Is it a family name?"

"Yeah," he told her. "Although that makes it even worse. My maternal grandmother had a brother named Irving who died before his first birthday. *I know, let's give the kid the name with the built-in curse of doom*."

On the stove, the kettle started to sputter, and Maria quickly took it off the flame before it woke Ash.

"I used to think it was wishful thinking on my mother's part," Izzy mused. "I was pretty much an accident. An afterthought, but . . . Now I know that's not something you wish for. Not ever."

His dickhead brother-in-law, who was none other than his teammate and nemesis, Danny Gillman, had made the mistake of uttering the sentiment that maybe it was for the best when Eden had miscarried. *Maybe it was for the best?* Holy Christ. At the time, Izzy had come close to beating the shit out of him.

It was only in hindsight that Izzy realized that Danny

had no frame of reference. He and Eden were far from close. Same with Izzy and Dan, so . . . Dan had no clue what it felt like to want something as much as Eden had wanted Pinkie; as much as Izzy had wanted both Eden and Pinkie—regardless of who the baby's father was—to be part of his life.

"The peeps call me Izzy," he told Maria. "From my initials—I.Z. I also answer to Zanella and *hey you*. And a bunch of other things, too, but you're unlikely to use such crass language, so I won't bother listing 'em."

Her smile was lovely.

"You want to hold him?" Izzy asked her.

But she actually seemed startled, and shook her head. "I don't want to wake him," she said. "I'm not very good with . . ."

"That's how you get good with 'em," he pointed out. "You get to practice on other people's kids. You sit, so there's no chance that you'll drop him and—"

"Is that how you got so good at it? Practicing on other people's babies?"

He nodded. "It's not a skill set I get to use too often in the Navy, but I also answer to *Uncle Izzy*. You know, it's probably not a good idea to let him sleep too much now, or he'll be up all night, so it's okay if you—"

"No," she said, all but making the sign of the cross. "Thank you, but . . . No." She turned away and poured herself a cup of tea. "You want some?"

"Despite my tendency to weep at the sight of sleeping babies, I'm not really much of a tea guy. But thanks for asking."

"You know, a long time ago," Maria said, with her back still to him, as she added some sugar to her cup and stirred, "I ran away from someone because . . . everything seemed so complicated, but . . . I wanted to be followed—chased—pretty desperately." She took a sip, turned to face him. "Are you sure that your wife—"

"No," Izzy said. "Believe me, I chased her." He shook his head.

"Is she . . . with someone else?"

"No," he said. "But she's in Germany. She's doing some kind of nanny thing for a friend—some woman who just had twins. She's getting room and board and . . ." He looked down into Ash's serene face. "She doesn't need me. She won't see me, but she's been pretty clear about the not needing me thing, so . . ."

"I'm sorry," Maria said again.

"Best I could do—via e-mail to her friend—was talk her into not immediately filing for a divorce or an annulment or whatever—I don't even know which it would be. We were only married for, like, two days."

"It could be simple. And inexpensive," Maria said. "If you need a lawyer, I could—"

"No," Izzy said. "Thanks, but . . ." He shook his head.

"If she doesn't love you," she said, not unkindly, "she's probably not coming back."

"I'm aware of that," he told her. "Which is why I go to see her every few months or so. Not that I actually *see* her, but . . . I try. I'm going there in about a week. Depending on how long Troubleshooters needs me here, you know."

It was much cheaper to fly to Europe out of New York. This unexpected trip east was a godsend.

Maria was looking at him, sipping her tea as she leaned against her kitchen counter, speculation in her extremely pretty brown eyes.

"You think I'm a loser," he said. "That's okay. I definitely am, so . . ."

She laughed. "Part of me is still waiting to be chased—waiting for that *I can't live without you* proclamation that another, more sane part of me knows I'm never going to hear. So if you're a loser, honey, I'm one, too."

Izzy nodded and gave her his valley girl imitation.

"Then, you're, like, totally a loser. Ew. Don't, like, talk to me. Loser."

Maria laughed—a burst of amused surprise, that of course woke Ashton, who started to cry.

"Shoot," she said, wincing. "Sorry. I'm so sorry—see? I'm terrible with kids."

"Shhh," Izzy told Ashton, bringing him up onto his shoulder as he got to his feet. "It's okay, little boy. Everything's okay. Just because I'm a loser and the loud lady is a loser doesn't mean you'll grow up to be one, too. Both your mom and dad are really, *really* cool." He looked down at Maria, who was shorter than she'd seemed when he was sitting down. "I want to give her time—my wife—but I don't want to become the creepy ex who just never goes away. The stalker ex, you know?"

She nodded. "I had one of those once. It wasn't a lot of fun, for either of us."

He rocked back and forth—a move that never failed to quiet even the fussiest of babies. And sure enough, Ash gave him a huge burp and a little frothy regurge, and then settled down.

"I think this might be my last trip to Germany," Izzy said, as he used a paper towel to clean the baby-blurp from his shoulder. He'd been thinking about it for a while, but this was the first time he'd said the words aloud, and he couldn't stop the rush of tears to his eyes.

"That sounds like a healthy decision," Maria said quietly. "Made by someone who's definitely not a loser." She gave him a sad smile. "Good night, I.Z."

"Good night, Assemblywoman," he answered as she left the kitchen, as he held tightly to Ash, as he breathed in the baby's sweet, warm scent.

And he knew that he'd return from Germany as he always did—empty-handed, save for his crushed and broken heart.

But the truth was that he'd already lost everything, months ago. He'd simply refused to believe it, to acknowledge it. Which made him the biggest loser of all.

"There was nothing unusual about it at all," said the head doorman of Margaret Bell-Thorndyke's apartment building, on Central Park. "She left as she always did, around nine, nine-fifteen. She had her bag for the gym—the one with the wheels. She was pulling it behind her. She was underdressed as she always is, and we had our usual chat about the weather as I called her a cab. *Cold one this morning, Miss Maggie, and you without a coat.* . . . I could always tell when she was planning to come straight home from the gym. She wouldn't take a coat, and she wouldn't take Lulu."

"Lulu?" Alyssa asked, looking from him to Margaret's obviously worried personal assistant, who'd joined her and Sam there in the sitting area of the ornate lobby.

Sam kept shifting in his seat like his side was hurting him, but at least he wasn't in jail. And yes, she *had* just thought that. *At least Sam wasn't in jail.* Of course the day wasn't over yet.

"Her dog," the woman—a Miss Gwen Endercott—answered in her vaguely British-sounding accent.

"If you can call it that," the doorman added. He wore his name pinned onto his heavy maroon uniform overcoat—Mr. Robert Jackson. He set his hat onto the table, and unfastened some of the coat's gleaming gold buttons.

He was African American and one of those men whose age was difficult to guess, with just a touch of gray in his closely cropped hair. He could have been anywhere from a worn-out forty-five to a well-preserved eighty.

Alyssa suspected he was somewhere in the middle since he'd proudly informed her that he'd been working there for thirty-five years without a single sick day. He claimed he knew the missing woman quite well, and she believed him.

"It's about yay big"—he cupped both of his big hands together to show how small Lulu was—"and ugly as sin, but don't tell Miss Maggie that. She takes that animal nearly everywhere—slips it right into her handbag."

"Is the dog upstairs?" Alyssa asked.

"Along with quite a mess." Gwen Endercott sniffed. "Her coat is up there, too."

"Unless, of course," Mr. Jackson interjected with a wink, "she was meeting a gentleman friend. Then she'd leave both the coat and the dog at home."

Apparently, Margaret Thorndyke—she'd recently decided to drop both the Bell and the hyphen from her name—had left in the morning, as usual. Miss Endercott, also as usual, had arrived at 10 A.M. and had gone about her morning chores, expecting her employer to show up as she usually did, for her daily luncheon.

Not lunch—luncheon.

Prepared by a chef who arrived at eleven o'clock.

"Can you tell me what she was wearing when she left?" Alyssa asked the doorman.

"Most women dress in black. It's slimming. That's what they tell me when I ask." He winked at her again. "You don't need to worry about that, Miss PYT."

"Her standard gym clothes," Miss Endercott said, "were black yoga pants, black boots, black fleece top—"

"Sounds about right," Mr. Jackson agreed. "Just once I'd like to see a woman wearing something *red*."

Sam cleared his throat and Alyssa met his eyes—and knew exactly what he was thinking. Despite his recent injury, he was, no doubt, contemplating the existence of her now-famous red lingerie that he'd watched her pack in their suitcase, on the off chance that they'd be able to grab a few minutes of private time while camping out with Ashton in Van's little apartment.

What were the odds of *that* happening? Especially now, with Sam's broken rib. Cracked. Cracked rib. Funny how his ribs were always cracked, not broken.

"You said she took a bag." Alyssa asked, "Could she have brought a change of clothes with her to the gym?"

"Yes, she usually did," Miss Endercott replied. "She didn't always shower and change there, in fact, more often than not, she didn't. But she liked to have that option."

"A bag that size"—the doorman put in his two cents—"could have fit changes of clothing for the entire week."

"But to leave without specific instructions for me to get a sitter for Lulu, or to cancel the chef," the personal assistant argued, "is *most* unlike her. I assumed she'd be back, so I put the dog in her crate. Which she soiled because no one attended to her until I came in again this morning."

"Wait a minute." Sam spoke up for the first time since they'd arrived. "Are we on the same page here? Margaret Thorndyke was last seen leaving for the gym *this* morning. Right?"

The doorman and the assistant exchanged a look.

"No, sir," Mr. Jackson said.

"It was *yesterday* morning," Miss Endercott informed them.

"Okay," Alyssa said, sitting forward. "We've definitely got our wires crossed. The police detective helping with this case told me that Ms. Thorndyke was seen by the doorman, leaving for the gym around 9 A.M. *today*." Mick Callahan had left a monotone message on her voice mail, obviously only because he'd been ordered to do so by his lieutenant. "Could someone else have seen her? Is there another doorman—"

"There is," Mr. Jackson interrupted her. "But the detective spoke to me. Our conversation was very brief, though, and he put me on hold in the middle of it."

Alyssa glanced at Sam again. Clearly Mick Callahan wasn't interested in doing them any favors—let alone doing his job. She was going to have to call his lieutenant, get someone else assigned to the case. Even though the FBI was taking charge of the investigation, they'd still want the help and cooperation of both city and state police.

"Did a police detective named Callahan get in touch with you?" she asked Gwen.

She nodded. "He called about an hour ago. He didn't seem overly concerned. He said he'd be by in the morning, if Ms. Thorndyke hadn't shown up before then." She looked to Mr. Jackson. "It was Ms. Bonavita who called to say that you and Mr. Starrett would come by with some questions."

Jackson nodded. "I got a call from Miss Maria, too."

"Let's start over," Alyssa said. She looked at the doorman. "The last time you saw Margaret Thorndyke was *yesterday* morning."

"Yes, ma'am."

"And it was yesterday that you arrived at 10 A.M.?" she asked the assistant.

"I arrive at ten every day, including weekends, so yes. That's correct. At 2 P.M.—yesterday—I called Ms. Thorndyke's cell phone but went right to voice mail. So I called the gym," Miss Endercott continued, "to see if she'd left a message for me at the front desk, which she sometimes does. But she hadn't. I inquired—had they seen her that morning—which was yesterday—and they had. She signed up for her usual spinning class, which ends at eleven-fifteen. Which doesn't mean she didn't stay longer. I knew the young woman to whom I was speaking, and she . . . bent the rules and checked their computer system. And told me that Ms. Thorndyke had left the gym just after noon.

"At 6 P.M., I still hadn't heard from her, so I called her

cell phone a second time. Again I went right to voice mail, so I crated Lulu and left for home."

"She's basically off the map," Sam's voice was loaded with his incredulity, "and you only call her twice before just . . . going on home?"

Gwen Endercott looked at him with a smile of condescension and barely concealed disdain. "Clearly you don't move in Ms. Thorndyke's circle."

"That's true," he said. "So enlighten me. In your little circle here, when a friend disappears you just—"

"She's not a friend, she's my employer."

"Did you call her later that night?" he asked.

"I absolutely did not," she said, her pinched mouth looking as if it were going to purse itself into oblivion. "Ms. Thorndyke has given me specific instructions forbidding me to pester her with phone calls. I had already pushed the boundaries—and risked my position—by phoning her twice in one day."

"And you didn't think it was unusual, or cause for alarm," Sam asked, "when you arrived the next day— *this* morning—to find that she hadn't been home last night? Does she do this all the time? Maybe hook up with one of her *gentlemen friends*?"

Gwen Endercott now looked at Sam as if he were something nasty she'd found on the bottom of her shoe. She clearly disapproved—of her employer's vanishing act, of the current sheer tastelessness of this situation, and particularly of Sam's blunt questions. "I'm afraid I can't say."

"I can," the doorman chimed in. "It's been a while, but yes."

"A *long* while," Miss Endercott said sharply.

Alyssa looked at Sam, who received her silent message and nodded. Divide, and get more accurate information— at least from Robert Jackson, who didn't share Gwen Endercott's inclinations to hide the truth about her employer's love life.

"Miss Endercott," she said with a sympathetic smile. "Perhaps you and I could go upstairs. I'd like to get a current picture of Ms. Thorndyke, and take a glance at her appointment schedule, if I may . . . ?"

The assistant rose to her feet with a sniff and led the way to the elevators as Alyssa glanced back at her husband, who was shifting his position again on the couch, and wincing because he'd thought she wasn't watching.

Miss Endercott wasn't the only one soft-pedaling the truth.

Sam was definitely hurt worse than he was pretending. Although getting him to admit it, or even take a few days of bed rest, was never going to happen.

"And she goes, *His name is Fwed*."

"Oh, my God," Jenn said as she gazed into the black button eyes of the stuffed rabbit that Dan had pulled from his bag to show her. "That's so cute. Fwed."

"Yeah, she was unbelievably adorable," Dan told her as he zipped his bag back up. "I tried to give it back, but her brother said she's got, like, duplicates and the real Fred stays safely home. She told him to give me *wotsa kisses in Anastan*."

"Anastan?" Jenn asked, but got it as the word left her mouth. "*Afghanistan*. Wow."

It was easy to forget that the too-handsome, too-charming man who was going to spend the night sleeping on her kitchen floor was a battle-hardened soldier. A highly trained commando type, who regularly risked his life for their country. A skilled and deadly operator who was staying here with her tonight, to make certain that she remained completely safe.

So why did she feel this sideways-slipping sense of impending danger every time she met his too-warm brown eyes?

Because he was funny and smart and nice, and the

very fact that he had shown her Fred-the-bunny, that
he'd chosen to share that story with her gave her the
biggest case of warm fuzzies that she'd fallen victim to in
a long time.

She'd thought she was tougher and more cynical than
that, but apparently not.

"Her mom was Army," Dan told her as he straightened back up. He was tall, too. Taller than she would be,
even if she got crazy and wore heels. And dressed as he
was in a snug-fitting T-shirt and standard green army
pants, clunky boots on his big feet, he looked like he belonged in some fictional TV-show-world like *Battlestar
Galactica* or *Army Wives,* where everyone was beautifully
Hollywood-perfect. "She was in the hospital in Germany
and . . ."

He shook his head and took his empty plate and went
into her kitchen to get more of his General Tso's
chicken. He raised his voice so she could hear him from
her seat on the sofa, where they were tray-tabling it. Not
that there were other options. Jenn didn't have a dining
room table, let alone a dining room.

"I mean, she gave me the rabbit because she somehow
knew—Mindy, the little girl. I don't know how, but she
somehow knew that I, you know, don't get a lot of packages when I'm over there. I mean, it's no big thing. I'm
fine with it. It's actually better that I don't. We move
around so much anyway, it can be a pain in the ass to
track a package when you're out there and . . ."

He came back out with his plate reloaded, a charmingly
sheepish expression on his face, his eyes filled with chagrin. "Jesus, listen to me. Did you believe *any* of that?"

Jenn silently shook her head, no, as she hugged Fwed
to her chest.

Dan nodded. "Yeah, I thought I'd gotten really good
at lying about it, but . . . Somehow this kid knew it was
crap, too." He forced a smile as he put his plate on the

tray table and sat back down on the other end of her couch. "You know you're in trouble when you can't even fool the toddlers, right?"

"Your girlfriend doesn't send you packages?" she asked, inwardly wincing because her words sounded like exactly what they were—a fishing expedition.

She'd caught him with his mouth full, and as he chewed and swallowed, he looked at her with those eyes that were the color of really expensive chocolate. He took a slug of his Coke before saying, "I'm not very good at long-term or long-distance, so . . . I'm kind of . . . perpetually between girlfriends when I'm over there."

"Ah," Jenn said, even though she wasn't quite sure exactly what he'd just told her. There had definitely been a message in there, but she wasn't sure how it fit with the fact that any minute now he was going to ask her for sisterly advice.

It was going to be about Maria. It always was. He was going to confess that he'd fallen instantly in love with Maria's beauty and intelligence, and could Jennilyn take her friend's pulse, see if Maria even noticed whether or not Dan existed.

Being friends with Maria meant spending her life locked in Limbo's torturous eighth-grade room. She'd had more phone calls start with the man on the other end saying, "So, what'd she say . . . ?"

"How about your family? Don't they send care packages?" she asked Dan, because the conversation was lagging. That, plus she really couldn't believe he didn't have *some*one sending him *some*thing while he was overseas.

"Highly dysfunctional," he said. "Trust me on that one. I don't want to bore you with the details, but . . . In a nutshell, it's a nightmare."

"Do you really know anyone," she asked him, "whose family *isn't* dysfunctional? And what's functional, anyway? The Cleavers? The Huxtables? I think real life for most people is probably closer to the Sopranos."

He laughed, flashing his gorgeous white teeth. "Should I be worried about that? LeMay doesn't sound like a big Mafia name. Although it's clear you're living *way* beyond your means in this palace."

She laughed, too, as she narrowed her eyes at him. "Mock me all you want. I'm exactly where I want to be."

"In a steam box," he teased as he sipped his soda again. "If this is *really* where you want to be . . . ? I'm pretty sure that in your past life you were a microorganism on Mars."

"Oh, please," she said. "The heat *just* clicked on. If you think *this* is a steam box, wait an hour."

He laughed, but then realized, "Are you serious? It *just* went on . . . ?"

She nodded. "But I didn't mean *this* is where I want to be," she said, gesturing to her apartment around them. "This is temporary. This is unimportant. What I *mean* is working with Maria. Doing something that matters." She smiled at herself, rolling her eyes and adding, "She said to the Navy SEAL who recently returned from a war zone." Talk about doing something that mattered.

But Dan was still focused on the heat. She could already feel it getting even warmer in there, and she shrugged out of the sweat shirt she'd pulled on when she'd first come home.

"You know, this is something I've definitely never said before while having dinner for the first time with a nice-looking woman," he told her, "but . . . when it hits eighty-five, I'm going to *have* to take off my pants."

"I told you to bring shorts," Jenn said, laughing. "And let's keep the conversation bullshit free, okay?"

"What, you don't think you're nice-looking?" he asked, glancing at her before shoveling more chicken into his mouth. "God, this is delicious." He filled his fork again and, cupping his hand beneath it, held it out to her. "It's awesome. You gotta try it."

"No," she said, holding her own hand up to stop him. "Thank you. I *still* don't want any. It's too spicy."

"For you," he said. "But not for me."

"Oh," she said. "Yeah. Right. I get it. It's subjective. You like General Whoever's chicken and you think I'm . . . whatever. Like I already said, let's keep this conversation bullshit free, SEAL-Boy."

"Fair enough. Tell me about your daddy, the Mafia hitman."

Jenn laughed. "He wasn't."

"So what was he?" Dan asked with his mouth full. "An alcoholic?"

She looked at him. How could he possibly know . . . ?

He correctly interpreted her incredulity and smiled. "I was checking out your bookshelf before. You have some of the same books as I do. That, plus an Al-Anon handbook . . ." He shrugged. "Raise your hand if you have a family member who's been through rehab." He lifted his hand, too, adding, "That's good that he's, you know, gotten through the denial stage."

"He's done better than that," Jenn admitted. "Was *your* father . . . ?"

"Sister," he told her. "My older one. Sandy. Although my father might've gone to rehab, too. I don't know. He definitely needed to, but he dropped out of our lives a long time ago, and hasn't bothered to drop back in."

"Not a twelve-stepper, then," she said.

"Sandy is," Dan said. "She tried to do that . . . whichever step it was. I forget. The making amends thing. She came to Vegas, to visit my mother and husband number four. That's where they're living now. It used to be New Orleans. Sandy and *her* husband—ex now—had a sporting goods store, but then Katrina happened, and—"

"Oh, God," Jenn said.

"Yeah," Dan agreed. "Anyway, two days in Vegas and Sandy relapsed. It was . . ." He shook his head—apparently words couldn't describe the awfulness. "She's back on track now, thank God. She sends me an e-mail every few months, but other than that, she's done what my father did. Total non-contact. I don't blame her. She's got to do what she needs to do to stay sober." He looked down at his plate, as if he'd suddenly lost his appetite. "I wish I had an excuse like that to, you know, stay away. Husband Four follows my mom's marry-an-alcoholic-dickhead pattern. But my little brother Ben is stuck there, so if I just never showed up, he'd be on his own—which he is most of the time, anyway, who am I kidding?"

She exhaled. "Wow."

He glanced at her. "I win, right? In the dysfunction-off?"

Jenn nodded, unable to not smile. "Among other things, yes."

"Yeah, I've learned that it's pretty much a lock when I mention Hurricane Katrina," he told her. "I get extra pain and suffering points for being in Iraq at the time."

"Oh, my God, Dan . . ."

"Yeah, I didn't know if they were dead or . . . Sandy and her husband—like I said, ex now, because he sucked—*their* two kids, my mother and Ben, and Eden, my younger sister . . . No word from any of them. Total radio silence. So I'm over there, right? And all these stories started coming in about people drowning in their houses, trapped up in their attics because the water rose so high. And then we saw the news footage about people dying at the Super Dome and Ben's a diabetic, so . . ." He laughed ruefully at the face she was making. "I don't talk about it a lot, because it's so fucking pathetic—excuse me."

"Brothers," she reminded him. "Lots of them?"

"But I'm not one of them," he said. "So I don't have those same privileges."

Jenn was so surprised, she spoke without thinking, "I don't remind you of your sister?"

He laughed loudly at that. "Jesus, no. Not even close. Eden—she's . . . gone." His smile faded. "I lost her a long time ago, before Katrina even. And Sandy . . . ? You dress a *little* bit like her, but . . ." He turned slightly to face her, to look at her appraisingly. "She's about four hundred years older than you are. In substance abuse years, I mean."

Jenn nodded. She understood. Her father's heart wasn't the only thing that was failing on him, relatively early in his life. He'd abused his body, and it showed. Even fifteen years sober, next month.

"You've got this . . . I don't know, freshness," Dan continued. "It's not really innocence. . . ."

He was studying her face, and she had to look away, embarrassed and oddly shy.

"You're . . . unbroken," he told her.

It was such a strange word for him to use, and she looked back at him, deep into his eyes, and something shifted inside of her. Was he . . . ? Seriously . . . ?

"Whatever happened with your father," he continued, holding her gaze, "you survived it with your faith intact. You know, faith in the basic goodness of humanity?"

"You can really tell that, just from looking into my eyes?" she asked, putting Fwed-the-bunny down on the empty seat between them, because it looked as if he were going to move closer. And she wasn't sure how she felt about that.

"Absolutely." Dan nodded. And he did move, but it was only to turn to face her. He pulled his right leg up on the couch, moving Fwed so that the rabbit now sat on his knee. "And from talking to you. Although, you know, I read palms, too."

He held out his hand as if he expected her to offer up hers for him to read—yeah, right. She laughed, because it was all so . . . ridiculous.

"Are you right- or left-handed?" he asked.

"Right," she told him. "Extremely. Like, my left hand is useless."

"Oh, man," he said, "mine was, too. But when we train—you know, the SEALs—we have to be as ambidextrous as possible. So before I even applied to be a SEAL candidate, I spent two weeks with my right hand tied behind my back. I'm talking fully tied, 24/7. I started out at about the speed of a clumsy first grader. Now I can do just about anything with my left hand that I can do with my right. You gotta keep practicing though. I still give myself what I think of as left-hand training days about once a week."

God, he was charming. And handsome. And he was talking to her as if there were nowhere else he'd rather be, no one else he'd rather be talking to.

And she didn't remind him of a sister. *Not even close,* he'd said.

"Gimme," he said, holding his hand out to her again. "Your right hand. Come on, LeMay. Let's have it."

Jenn didn't put her hand in his. That felt too weird. Instead, she just held it out, palm up, as she laughed to show that she didn't take this—or his bedroom eyes and quicksilver smile—at all seriously.

But he took hold of her, pulling her closer, the heat of his own palm warm against the back of her hand. And again, something moved inside of her.

It was a swirling mix of attraction and desire, because instead of looking down at her hand, he was gazing into her eyes, and he smiled as if he liked what he saw. Which was, again, ridiculous. He was Brad Pitt handsome, and she was . . .

Available.

Ah. There it was.

He was spending the night here, and he wanted to spend it *not* on the kitchen floor.

"You know, I'm not an idiot," Jenn said, but the words came out sounding breathless and, yes, faintly idiotic. Because even if he were the absolute King of Immediate Gratification, ruler of Love-the-One-You're-with-Land, and even if she *were* the Queen of Available—which, okay, she was—this was far from the way the scenario usually ran.

That look in his eyes was anything but brotherly.

He was, as the saying went, a Sure Thing.

Assuming she was into a really hot night of completely casual sex, no strings attached.

"I can see that you're not," he told her, glancing up from her palm. "An idiot. This right here"—he traced the line in the middle of her palm—"is your head line. Not headline, like, *extra extra, read all about it.* But the line for your head, as opposed to the line for your heart— which is this one, right here." Again he traced her palm— at the top this time—with the tip of one big finger.

His hands were really huge, she realized. Bigger than hers, with her long, skinny, ET-phone-home fingers. They were callused, too, his hands—with nails that were neatly trimmed. His skin was quite a few shades darker than hers, as if he spent a lot of time in the sun and tanned effortlessly.

She burned and peeled, so she usually remained pretty solidly cavefish white, even in the heat of the summer.

"Both your head and your heart lines are well defined," he told her. "You're well balanced—maybe even a little too pragmatic. See, your heart line goes straight across. If it goes up here"—he traced his finger up between her first and middle fingers, which felt sinfully good—"moving away from your head line, you're more of a dreamer. But look at how close the two lines come together. Judging from that, I'd say it's highly unlikely you're going to run off with Emilio, the man on the flying trapeze, to join the circus."

She leaned over to get a better look, and when she glanced up at him, their faces were much too close, so she backed off. It was hard not to smile, though, when he was smiling at her like that. "I think you're making this up."

God, but he smelled good—like her brother Alan's best friend John, a John that she didn't ever actually date, but had desperately wanted to. He was an avid snowboarder, and he, too, always smelled like a mix of sunscreen and fresh air, even in the winter.

"Wait, I'm not done," Dan said, laughing as she tried to pull her hand free. He wouldn't let her go. "And I'm not making this up. I've spent some serious vacation time in N'Orleans. I've had my own palm read plenty. And I paid attention."

"And what did they tell you—the myriad of wise palm readers who bamboozled you? *You will go to New York,*" she intoned, *"and have Chinese food in a very small, very hot studio apartment . . ."*

He laughed. "It's never that detailed. Although one of them said—I'll remember this one forever. Wait, let me get it right . . ." He paused, and then recited, *"You'll get what you want, but whether or not you realize, before it's too late, that you truly* want *what you* get, *is up to you."*

"Ooh," Jenn said. "Deep. And how much did you pay for that gem of wisdom? Because I got a fortune cookie? In the kitchen? That's probably going to be just as profound, but mine came free with my dinner."

"Scoff all you want," he said. "But you might want to be careful because look, your fate line is pretty fractured."

He pushed the palm of her hand slightly together, then traced a jagged line that appeared right down the center, going from her middle finger to her wrist.

"It's solid to your heart line," he informed her, "and

solid *after* your head line, but in between the two? It's a mess."

It was. "Let me see yours," she said, and he finally let her go, in order to hold his hand out for her.

"Solid fate line, right here," he said, pointing to it.

"I don't know why I'm looking. For all I know, mine's the way it's supposed to be and you're the one with the crazy fate of doom or . . . whatever." She had to get closer to see it, and as she peered down at his hand, she laughed. "Here's where, if you were one of my brothers? You'd smack me in the face and shout something like *Boo-yah! You share the fate of the moron!*"

Jenn felt the exhale from his laughter move her hair—he was that close. And when she looked up at him, he didn't move back. He just smiled into her eyes.

"Your brothers were harsh," he said.

And he kissed her.

Jenn saw it coming. He telegraphed it, totally, his gaze flickering down to her mouth, once, twice, lingering that second time before he looked into her eyes again and leaned toward her, catching her mouth with his.

It was gentle and sweet—reverent, almost. As first kisses went, it was quite possibly the loveliest she'd ever had. He smelled even better up close, his lips a soft contrast to the stubble on his chin.

She kissed him back, until the logical part of her brain overcame her total surprise and she pulled away, but she was still dumbstruck, so all she did was stare at him. He'd just *kissed* her. He'd just kissed *her*.

"Sorry," he said, but it was supremely obvious that he didn't mean it. "I couldn't resist. I just . . . I like you. You're . . . really cute."

It was his word choice that brought the fantasy crashing down around her, and gave her back her ability to speak. *Cute?* Was he serious?

"Unbroken," she reminded him. "Fresh and unbroken. Cute tends to be petite or maybe . . . freckled. With curly hair. But definitely petite."

He actually had the balls to argue with her. "Cute has nothing to do with—"

"You should've gone for *funny*," she said. "I've been called funny before, and that works. Particularly when it's combined with *smart*. I like *smart*."

"Petite's way overrated anyway," he insisted. "I'm not petite, so why would I want—"

"What *do* you want?" Jenn asked.

Of course, that question, direct and to the point, silenced him.

She waited, raising her eyebrows.

"Well," he said. He took a deep breath. "I want to get to know you better, so—"

"Bullshit," Jenn said. "At least be honest. Are you going off assignment here, or is this, like, a standard part of the Troubleshooters *save me from the pig-heart-wielding madman* personal security package? Round-the-clock bodyguarding with an optional bonus orgasm. A *Save me, Fuck me* two-for-the-price-of-one?"

He laughed at that. "You *are* funny," he said.

"Too late," she told him. "You went with *cute*."

"I went with *I like you*," he countered. "You *are* cute, and I *do* like you, and I guess I thought you maybe liked me, too—"

"No, thank you," Jenn said. "Okay? I'm going to make it easier for both of us, and just say *no thanks* to whatever you have in mind. Yes, you're a fabulous kisser and I'm sure I'll regret this for the rest of my life. But I have a set of rules and guidelines for how I live my life and I absolutely do *not* have one-night stands with—"

"I've got two weeks." He interrupted her. "You want honesty, Jenn? I'll give you honesty. I don't do one-night stands either and, okay, for the sake of transparency and full disclosure, I've done plenty of one-nighters in my life, yeah, but I don't like 'em. Well. I don't *not* like 'em, but . . ." He exhaled hard and started over. "I like the kind of sex you have around day five, you know? The kind where we're out at a restaurant and we order dinner and we're talking about movies or books or something and you look at me and smile and there's this crazy spark and the waiter brings the food right at that moment, and we both go, *We'll take it to go,* and the anticipation is so sweet, because we both know *exactly* how great it's going to be when we get home and fall into bed."

Jenn was silent and he just waited, watching her with those eyes and that face and that incredible body beneath that T-shirt and those cargo pants.

"You're good," she finally said. "You're *really* good. My bullshit meter's totally pinned, and yet a part of me's still going, *wow, yeah, day five* . . ."

"It's not bullshit," he said, and his nose should have grown a good ten inches, and God, don't think about *anything* growing like that, but he *was* a rather large man, with those big, *big* hands, so it was hard not to think about it . . . "I like you, Jenn. So I'm going to put it all out on the table and be completely honest here. I would love to hook up with you, starting tonight. I can stay in town for two weeks, if you don't mind me crashing here with you when the Troubleshooters assignment ends. After that, though, I'm heading back overseas, and although I can't tell you exactly where I'm going, it'll probably be to Afghanistan, and I'll probably be there for months."

Oh, God. It was as if he knew exactly the kind of chaos she felt when he so much as mentioned Afghanistan.

"Two weeks," Dan said again, as if he also knew she was actually considering his crazy proposal. "I can't promise you longer than that. I'm not going to lie to you—"

"Yes, you are," she said. "You're lying your ass off right now."

"No, I am not," he insisted.

"Yeah, you are," she said again, "but even if you weren't, you don't know me. How can you sit here and know that day . . . *three* I'm not going to be driving you crazy because I laugh like a horse or . . . or . . ."

"You don't laugh like a horse," he said, laughing himself.

"Or do that awful baby talk thing and call you *pookie* in public," she continued, "or . . . dress up your penis in Barbie clothes?"

He laughed again at that. "Wow. That's, um . . ." Still grinning, he scratched his head.

Jenn was laughing now, too. "Crazy? Yes. It's definitely crazy. And that's my point. How do you know I'm not crazy?"

"I don't," he said. "But I think that Barbie clothes thing might really work for me."

"Yes," she said. "Right. *You* might be crazy. That's an equally good point."

"Okay," Dan said. "Here's the deal. If I turn out to be crazy, then you say—on day three—when the, um, fucking you're getting isn't worth the . . . fucking you're getting, if you'll pardon the crassness of my French, then you say, *Pookie, it's just not working out,* and I'll immediately slink off into the sunset."

Jenn shook her head. "I just don't—"

He kissed her again.

This time she didn't see it coming. This time, he grabbed her and locked lips before she knew what was happening. This time, it wasn't sweet or soft. This time it was a kiss for the record books, with his arms tightly around her, his body—all those muscles—against her, and his extremely talented tongue in her mouth.

And this time, that treacherous desire that had started heating her from the inside out didn't just shift in her chest. It slid through her, leaving her breathless and weak, clinging to him, her fingers and toes tingling.

"All the words in the world," he said between kisses, "can't explain this. It's not rational. It's fire—it's hot and I *know* that it's mutual." He pulled back to look into her eyes. "And we can tiptoe around it and waste this precious time, or we can be honest about it, and have the greatest two weeks of our lives. You're not looking for forever, and you know it. What would you do with a boyfriend who hung around for more than two weeks, anyway?"

She didn't say anything, because she was afraid if she opened her mouth, *Kiss me again* would come out. And there was *so* much about this that absolutely didn't work, she didn't know where to start.

"Dan. I don't—"

"If we do this," he cut her off, "and right now, I'm praying that we do, because I like you and I really want you, but if we do this, it needs to be exclusive, because I don't share well. And I know you have a crush on that detective—"

"What?" she said, pulling free from him—something she should have done many long moments ago. "I do not."

"Yeah," Dan said. "You do. But he's all about Maria—"

"*You're* all about Maria," she said. "Or you were, before you got stuck here, guarding me!"

"Okay," he said. "You know what? Yes. I will cop to the fact that I noticed her. But I would bet my entire savings account, which is undeniably meager since I currently pay my mother's rent, that Maria—and she is beautiful, that's a fact—but she would never, in a million years, make a joke about dressing my penis in Barbie clothes."

Jenn laughed. "Okay, the way you keep bringing that up is bordering on frightening."

"I love that your brain came up with that. It's the funniest thing I've heard in a long time and . . . Jenni, I want to laugh," he said, and it was, quite possibly, the most honest, most serious thing he'd said to her all evening. "I want to get laid, yeah, it's true, but I also want to laugh. I got two weeks where I know I'm not going have to watch one of my friends die—which is *the* fucking worst thing that can happen to you. Trust me on that."

"Oh, God," she said.

And there they sat, just gazing at each other.

He broke the silence. "I want to kiss you again," he said. "Please don't say no."

"Dan."

He moved toward her.

"No."

He backed down, but said, "Not a lot of conviction there, Jenn."

"I can't," she said.

"But you want to."

God, he was arrogant, but he was also right. She didn't stand up. Didn't take her plate and his back into the kitchen. Didn't put some distance between them— between herself and the most attractive man she'd ever met, let alone who wanted to kiss her.

She just shook her head.

He nodded as he took a pen from his pocket, took her hand, uncapped the pen with his teeth.

"Dan," she said, letting her exasperation sound in her voice. What was he doing? "Don't."

But all he did was draw a very small X, right in the middle of her palm.

"That's me," he said after recapping the pen, as he repocketed it. "Right there. Right in the chaos of your fate line, between what you really want to do, and what you think you *should* do—based, I would bet, on someone else's set of rules—rules that have nothing whatsoever to do with Jennilyn LeMay, who is independent and strong enough to recognize that a two-week relationship with a man who will be the best lover—and the best boyfriend—she's ever had, is exactly what she needs to bring balance and passion and vitality to her equally chaotic life."

She laughed, because . . . dear God . . . She had to give him huge points for persistence, creativity, and sheer chutzpah.

He let go of her hand, and she looked down at that mark, despite her attempt not to. *That's me* . . .

And he wasn't done slinging the bull. "Just because it's not serious, just because we're not going into this with the idea that it's forever, doesn't mean it's not special. Because it is. It will be."

"God," she said again. "You are *so* good."

"Two weeks," he said. It had become his refrain. "Please, Jenn. I don't get a chance like this very often. I really like you. And I want to spend this time with you before I go back to the war."

CHAPTER EIGHT

The crazy-ass bastard started screaming at them, his speech slurred and his words almost impossible to understand.

"Don't touch her!" Sam had thought the man was saying, over and over. "Don't you touch her!"

He'd first spotted the homeless man quite a few blocks back, as he and Alyssa had walked—slowly, because his entire right side was stiffening up and hurting like a bitch—from Margaret Thorndyke's digs, which overlooked Central Park, to this comparatively crappier neighborhood where Maria Bonavita resided.

And that *crappier* was a relative one.

Because it was a case of super-fucking rich versus merely fucking rich, with a universal truth that the streets below both majestic buildings belonged to everyone. Including Don Quixote de la Crazy-Face, here, who was shouting what definitely sounded like, "Don't you dare touch her!"

It was Sam's fault, completely.

He'd stopped with Alyssa, there on the sidewalk a few blocks shy of Maria's apartment building, because he hadn't had time, during the long, frozen walk from Central Park, to say what he'd wanted to say. *I'm not going to ask you not to go to Afghanistan. In fact, I think you should go. But as much as it scares me not to be part of your team and go with you, I think it would be selfish to do that. It would be unfair to Ash.*

He'd stopped Alyssa from walking those last few blocks, and he'd pulled her close and kissed her—something else he couldn't do once they were inside. He'd gotten as far as a variation on *In fact, I think you should go,* when old Don Q made himself known by starting his tirade from way down at the other end of the block.

He and Lys weren't the only ones there on that sidewalk, but Sam knew that he wore his Texas roots pretty much stamped on his forehead. Yeah, he could conceal it when he wanted to. He'd learned to blend in to his current environment, both as an operative in the SEALs and working for Troubleshooters, but this job wasn't about blending so he hadn't bothered to try.

And right now, what he was trying to do was have a conversation with his wife.

When he'd first noticed the homeless man, he'd dismissed him. And although he'd learned early on in his life never to dismiss anyone completely, his training and instincts had told him that Don Q wasn't a threat.

Sam had first thought the dude was a lady, with that froth of wild gray curls exploding out from beneath his grungy knit cap, with its dingy Marines patch sewn on, right in the center. The puffy purple-and-grime-colored woman's down-filled overcoat that flapped around his legs helped with the whole gender-bending effect. But the guy had a beard—unkempt, sparse, and gray. That and his shoulders—former linebacker wide, despite the fact that he now walked hunched over—screamed dangling genitalia.

He was African American, and about the right age to be a Vietnam vet.

Back about seven blocks, before the shouting had started, Sam had assumed that they were being approached not just because of his Texas tourist attitude, but also because both he and Lys were former Navy. Even though neither of them advertised that fact the way some folks did, with the word NAVY stitched across their jacket or the seat of their pants, there were just some people, usually former servicemen or women themselves, who simply *knew.*

So yes, Sam had assumed that the Don had targeted them as compatriots—*and* as likely candidates in his quest for donations to buy tonight's swerve-on, in its delivery vehicle of a bottle of Wild Turkey.

And while Sam would've been fine with buying the man a roast beef sandwich, he had more than his share of friends and family members who were recovering alcoholics, so the idea of funding this man's addiction didn't sit well with him.

So he'd picked up their pace, because La Mancha Man had a bad leg. His gait was unbalanced and although he could manage a surprisingly quick shuffle, he couldn't possibly keep up with them—even with Sam's pain-in-the-ass cracked rib.

He'd made another mistake then—he'd believed that they'd left the Q-ster far behind. Part of it had to do with Sam's being distracted by a wide variety of discussion topics—none of them easy or fun.

It had started with a phone call Alyssa had received, back at the beginning of their walk, before Don Quixote had appeared, as they left the lobby of Margaret Thorndyke's swanky apartment building, over in the *super*-fucking rich part of town.

Unlike other fairly important breaking news of the day—such as the info about the impending A-stan trip coming directly out of the Oval Office in Washington, D.C.—this time, Alyssa relayed the news from her call to Sam as soon as she got off the phone.

"Margaret Thorndyke's cell phone was traced to

Nicco's, a restaurant not too far from Maria's office, where she lunches somewhat regularly," Alyssa had told him, her unhappiness clear in her tone. "It was on the floor, under a table—its ring set on silent. The proprietor couldn't remember if she was in today or even yesterday. We should get a cab."

She stepped to the curb, probably because she knew that the arm motion necessary for flagging down a taxi might make Sam vomit from the pain. As it was, the cold was making him shiver, which wasn't working well for him, either. Of course, with the weather being what it was, there were no unoccupied cabs in sight.

Sam zipped his jacket up and tucked his scarf more securely around his neck. "I'm okay to walk. It's not that far."

She gave him her *what kind of fool do you think I am* look—the one that he'd learned not to laugh at—so he tossed a little truth out there. "It'll feel better to walk. It'll help me keep warm. This shivering shit is killing me."

He headed south, and she fell into step beside him.

"So," he said, before the main topic of conversation became his rib, "Maggie's cell phone. They find any prints on it?"

"It's at the lab," she said. "They'll run fingerprints, and a DNA test."

Lotta DNA and other crud on a cell phone.

"That's good," he said. "And the restaurant . . . ?"

"It's a popular place," she told him. "Upscale. Good food. Gourmet Greek, and always crowded. Lots of regulars, including Maggie Thorndyke. The owners are checking their records, see if whoever sat at that table today paid with a credit card. If she was there with a date . . ."

"We might also want to check to see if anyone sat at the bar in the late afternoon, running up a tab, waiting for a table to empty so he could plant that phone," Sam suggested. "We should talk to the bartender, too."

Alyssa was silent as they maneuvered their way around an oncoming woman with a double stroller, which held an obvious set of twins, a little older than Ash. God help the poor woman. He loved his son dearly, but if there were two Ashes, he'd have long since been driven mad from sleep deprivation.

"I'm not saying that it happened that way," Sam continued as they waited at an intersection for the light to change. "But it's definitely possible."

"I prefer the scenario where Maggie Thorndyke had lunch there today, with her new boyfriend," his wife said. Sam had told her that Mr. Jackson reported that when "Miss Maggie" was younger, every so often—every two months or so—there would briefly be a new man in her life. Very briefly, and usually accompanied by two or three days of massive alcohol consumption and possibly even drug use.

It was a pattern that the doorman had seen again and again through the years.

But he'd also reported that it had been years since she'd last run that pattern.

And this time, although the disappearance felt familiar, he hadn't seen her with anyone on the day she'd vanished—not man or woman.

"And what?" Sam asked Alyssa now. "She lost her phone, which was coincidentally and immediately found by Mr. Pig Hearts R Us, who used it to make that call to Maria before he tossed it under the—"

"No," she said. "No, you're right. It's not a coincidence. Whoever took Maggie's phone took it because he knew Maria uses caller ID. They also knew that as a big donor to the campaign, Maggie's phone number was one that Maria would always pick up.

"So really the two most likely scenarios," she continued, "are that whoever did this stole Maggie's phone on purpose. And yesterday, after literally years of being single, she hooked up with some new guy and is so totally in love that she still hasn't noticed her stolen phone—" She broke off, shaking her head in disgust. "I don't like *that* coincidence any better than the first one."

"Which leaves the second most likely scenario," Sam said, "that whoever did this took both Maggie's phone *and* Maggie."

Alyssa hated that idea, just as he'd known she would. "In which case, we've got the phone back, but where's Maggie?"

He'd reached over and taken her hand, squeezing her gloved fingers, and she'd looked at him.

"We'll find her," he said.

"So far this trip sucks," she pointed out. "Are you having fun yet? Because I'm not. I particularly hated the part where the police detective threatened to shoot you."

She was fiercely, grimly pissed, but that, in combination with the bright red fleece hat that she'd bought in Times Square, made Sam smile. The hat was complete with earflaps, a little yarn ball at the top of an elfin point, and the eternal message *I (heart) New York*.

Despite being one of the most beautiful women he'd ever known, his wife had nearly always forsaken fashion for comfort or convenience.

She rolled her eyes at him. "Yes, I know the hat's plenty foolish-looking, thanks."

"I was actually thinking it's hot," he teased. "With the right outfit—or lack thereof . . ."

Alyssa laughed, but it was all too brief before she sighed her frustration. "I honestly thought this job would be easy. I like Savannah, I really do. But she's gotten a little"—she searched for the right word—"hyper-cautious ever since Ken was injured. I expected to have to give a few lectures on personal safety and pick out a relatively inexpensive alarm system for Maria's office and maybe go see *Wicked* and have dinner at Sardi's and visit MoMA and the USS *Intrepid* and . . ." She exhaled hard. "Okay, I'm done whining. Sorry. I honestly didn't expect this threat to be reality based, so . . . And I *really* didn't expect you to immediately become one of the walking wounded."

"I am so sorry that I got hurt," he said.

"People, particularly men like Callahan, are going to say all kinds of nastiness about me, and you're going to have to—" She cut herself off. "I don't want to talk about this right now. Did you speak to Jules?"

Oh, glorious segue on a shiny silver platter.

"I did," Sam said. And it was right around then that he first noticed Don Quixote watching them, muttering, "It's you, it's you," as he headed toward them, no doubt looking for a handout. "He and Robin are driving down from Boston tonight."

"Robin's coming?" Alyssa asked, surprised.

"His show's on hiatus." Sam reported what Jules had told him as he picked up their pace—ow—and steered Alyssa across the street to avoid the homeless man. "Art Urban had a heart attack—a bad one, so . . . Robin's coming along to babysit Ash, if we want it, and, you know. *Be* babysat. I think Jules is looking at this like a vacation, too. A chance to hang with us."

"I'd heard Art was in the hospital," she said, "but I had no idea it was so serious. Is he going to be okay?"

Sam nodded. "He will be—if the show goes on hiatus. Which leaves Robin with a lot of free time on his hands. Jules didn't say it, but . . . he's a little worried."

She was silent, lost in her own thoughts, so he cleared his throat and added, "Especially since he's heading overseas pretty soon. He told me about the assignment in Afghanistan."

Alyssa looked at him then, and at that moment the sky opened up and started dropping big, fluffy, fake-looking snowflakes all around them. It was ridiculously pretty.

"I'm assuming," Sam continued, "that that was what the President called you about . . . ? You know, earlier today . . . ? Jules told me Max recommended you as an additional security consultant. Sounds like they're creating one hell of a team."

"Oh, my God, Sam, I'm so sorry," she said. "I didn't have time to tell you, and then, to be honest, I completely forgot."

"The *President* called and you forgot?" He believed her, but forgetting a phone call from the President deserved a certain amount of mocking.

"Yeah, I know." She looked at him, amusement, chagrin, and apology in her eyes. "I need a vacation. Oh, wait. This was supposed to be one. Instead I got a break-in at a public official's office, a missing socialite, rotting animal organs, and, speaking of guts, an uncooperative police detective who apparently hates yours now even more than he hates mine."

He nodded. "Total suck-ass day. We're going to find Maggie Thorndyke, you know."

Alyssa nodded, too, but he could tell that she wasn't convinced. "Have you ever seen a pig heart?" she asked him, and he wasn't surprised at all that *that* was the cause of her distraction, and that even now that he'd brought it up, her trip to Afghanistan was getting pushed back to the bottom of her priority list. "You grew up kind of in the country."

"Kind of? It was the suburbs," he corrected her. She'd lived in a city for most of her childhood. To her, the burbs of Ft. Worth, Texas, where he'd grown up, had no doubt seemed positively rural.

They'd rented a car once, during a lengthy layover in Dallas, and they'd driven past Sam's childhood home.

They'd also gone past the house where his beloved Uncle Walt and Aunt Dot had spent the bulk of their laughter-filled lives, and past the dusty airfield where Walt had first taken Sam and his cousin Noah up in a Cessna—where Sam had first discovered just how wide the world truly was.

"But didn't you say there was some kind of farm that you used to go to?" she asked him. "Wonderland Farm or . . ."

"Wonderville Farms," he said, amazed that she remembered that. He'd mentioned it maybe once, a few years ago. "It was a glorified petting zoo." His elementary school had gone every year, in the spring, after the baby animals had been born. "And yes there was a pig there, but they never put its heart on display, if that's what you're asking."

"You studied some anatomy, though," she persisted, "right? In the Navy? Basic stuff about the circulatory system?"

Sam knew where she was going. "I've seen pictures of a human heart, sure, and, yeah, it could've been. In that drawer. Except . . ."

"It *couldn't* have been," she finished for him. "I keep thinking that, too. Unless some total psychopath has targeted Maria."

"So okay," Sam said. "When we get back to Kenny and Van's, we'll jump online and find a picture of a pig heart, so we can compare."

"What I need is the fucking lab report," Alyssa said, her strong language betraying her frustration. "How hard could it be? Human—yes or no? I don't need to know what kind of animal, just that no, it's not human."

"When Jules gets here," Sam said, "we can ask him to make some calls, apply some pressure."

"That," Alyssa said, "would be good."

They walked in silence for a block or two before she spoke again.

"I didn't tell him yes," Alyssa told Sam. "The President. I didn't tell him no, but I didn't tell him yes. I said I'd have to talk to you. He knew about Ash, and he knew we haven't taken any overseas jobs since he was born. And he also knew that you're usually my XO. But since this would be mostly advisory, the Troubleshooters team would be a small one, so—"

"Mostly?" Sam asked.

She nodded. "We'd be working with the advance unit, offering suggestions that the task force as well as the Secret Service would consider when making the final plans. Any red-cell work would be done with the assistance of SEAL Team Sixteen."

Oh, that hurt, way worse than any broken rib ever could.

Red-cell assignments were those in which a group—in this case his former SEAL team, led by Alyssa—would attempt to breach the organized security, in order to illustrate the system's weaknesses, flaws, and outright failures. Sam loved being part of a good red-cell attack, and in this one, he'd have had the chance to work with his friends from Sixteen.

Alyssa frowned. "Did Jules say that he was definitely going to be part of the FBI advance team? Even while Robin's on hiatus?"

They both loved Jules's husband, Robin. They truly did. But they were also both well aware of the young actor's weaknesses, and of how hard it was for him when Jules willingly put himself into danger.

Hell, it was hard for Sam when Alyssa did it, and he *wasn't* a recovering alcoholic, like Robin.

"Jules told me he was going to be over there for at least a month," Sam reported.

"I wouldn't have to be gone for that long," Alyssa told him. "More like a week, maybe ten days."

"But they want you for the full month." He'd gotten that info from Jules, too.

She shook her head. "That's too long. I'm not willing—"

"You could make your own schedule." Sam knew that, too, and he'd already done the math. "24/6 it for three blocks of time, with four days off between each."

"Four days isn't enough to get me back home."

"It's enough to get you to Greece. Or Italy. I was thinking," he said, tugging her to a stop and pulling her out of the flow of pedestrian traffic because they were just a few blocks from Maria's building, "that if Ash and I went somewhere safe, but close enough for you to fly into . . . ? Robin, too. I was thinking of seeing if Robin wanted to hang with Ash and me. You know. While you and Jules are over there."

She was so surprised on so many levels. It was rare that he rendered her speechless, and this time he clearly had, so he kissed her.

And then, because he couldn't ever just kiss his wife once, he kissed her again. Longer, lingeringly.

"I'd never ask you not to go," he told her quietly. "I'm proud that you got called, and I'm glad that the CIC's smart enough to recognize that you're the right person for this job. And I want to go, too, I do, pretty damn badly, but . . . Jules'll be with you, so—"

"Don't you touch her! Don't you dare touch her!"

Sam turned, and sure enough it was the homeless man who was, also surely enough, shouting—at them.

Alyssa turned, too, as the man shuffled toward them, his puffy coat billowing out behind him like the weirdest version of a superhero cape that Sam had ever seen.

"I'll kick your ass!" he was saying now. And there was

no doubt whatsoever that he was talking to Sam. Except with his slurred speech, he might've been saying, "I'll *kill* your ass."

Bottom line, there wasn't much chance of either of those two options happening, given that Sam was nearly six and a half feet tall, and—despite that cracked rib—in the best shape of his entire life.

But his inner caveman—the part of him that often spoke or reacted before employing full use of his brain—stepped in front of Alyssa. And bumped into her trying to step in front of him. She shot him a look of exasperation and he shifted his position so that they were both facing the attack, even as he scanned and analyzed the threat.

The man's left leg was a weak point, and his limp telegraphed his pain. He was carrying what looked like a piece of paper, and he was waving it at them angrily. His other hand was empty—at least there appeared to be no glint of knife-blade, or handgun, or broken bottle, or even a tin can. And he appeared to have nothing up his sleeve, since the coat was too small for him and the sleeves ended well above his hands, exposing quite a few inches of his bony wrists.

Wads of newspaper that he'd packed inside that coat for extra warmth fell around him in a surreal shower as he charged them.

Alyssa tried reason and called out to him, her voice clear in the cold night air, "Are you former Marine? We're both former Navy."

But the man didn't answer or slow as he shouted again, "You get the fuck away from her!" And yeah, he was looking right at Sam. Anger mixed with a serious dose of crazy in eyes that were framed by a heavily furrowed brow and bared teeth—signs that, despite the lack of weapon, Don Quixote de la Crazy-Pants here wanted to do them—or more accurately Sam—some serious harm.

The old adage "once a Marine, always a Marine" was

true even among those that the system had abandoned and discarded, and because of that, Don Q had the unerring aim of a heat-seeking missile.

"Stop right there!" Alyssa stepped in front of Sam.

But he didn't stop. And it was more than clear that this guy was going to go right through Alyssa to get to Sam, which meant they really only had one option.

Turn and run.

Sam grabbed Alyssa and beat feet toward Maria's apartment building, as fast as he could move it.

Which was pretty damn fast, despite the obstacle course created by the relentless crowd of pedestrians, despite the fact that Sam's side shrieked with pain, with every step he took.

"Excuse me," he said. "Sorry. Coming through!"

Lys was as smart as she was beautiful, and she understood why he'd chosen to retreat, but she couldn't resist asking, "Didn't think you could take him, huh?"

Caveman Sam, who had the IQ of a pinhead and the emotional maturity of an eight-year-old, answered with, "Oh, I coulda taken him." More highly evolved Sam recognized that she was teasing, and turned it into a joke. "But I've already hit my quota and beaten up my allotment of old men for the week."

But then she said, "Oh, no!" as she dug in her heels and slowed him down.

And he turned back to see what she was looking at, and he saw, too, that Don Quixote had taken a tumble and was lying on the sidewalk, motionless and silent.

Alyssa wasn't the kind of woman who took kindly to phrases like, "Wait here," or "Stay back." So Sam didn't bother to say anything that stupid. He just made sure she didn't get too far out in front as she jogged back toward the fallen man.

New York was supposed to be the city of zero eye contact, zero connection, but two men and a woman, all apparently strangers to each other, had already stopped to help.

The younger of the two men was either a doctor or a nurse, his scrubs hanging out from beneath a pair of sweats he'd pulled on, on his way either to or from work. The other man was a cab driver, his Indian accent thick as he used his cell phone to call 9-1-1 for help. The woman was digging in her pack and pulled out an energy bar and a bottle of water, offering it up to the man in the scrubs, who was unafraid of DQ's stench and grime and had loosened the purple coat in order to put a finger to the old man's neck.

"His pulse is steady and he's breathing easily," he announced in a New York accent nearly as difficult to understand as the cabbie's, who relayed that information to the emergency operator.

"He was chasing us," Alyssa volunteered. "He was shouting and seemed angry, so we ran. He's got a bad leg—it didn't take much to get away. I think he tripped, though, and hit his head when he fell."

Dr. Bronx reached to examine the back of the homeless man's head by touch, and nodded. "He's definitely got a contusion. Although it's also obvious that he's severely inebriated."

"I've seen him around," said the woman, who looked young enough to be a high school student. "He's usually got a bottle of something in a paper bag."

And okay, her backpack advertised NYU, so she was probably a college student. Sam was just getting old.

The doc shook his head at her offering. "He's out cold. But thanks."

"Police and ambulance are on their way," the cab driver told them.

"What are they going to do with him?" NYU worried.

Alyssa spoke up. "They'll take him to the ER, make sure he's okay. And if his blood-alcohol levels come back as elevated as I think they're going to, they'll most likely transport him to a city drunk tank so he can sleep it off before they release him."

The doctor looked up at Alyssa, puzzlement on his face. "Are you sure you don't know him?" he asked her in his extra-on-*Rescue-Me* voice. "He's not a . . . relative or . . . ?"

"Not all black people are related," Sam felt inclined to point out.

The doc shot him a *no shit you asshole* look.

"We're from San Diego," Alyssa said, including Sam in her statement with a glance. "I've honestly never seen him before tonight."

"Well, he seems to know you." The man held out a crumpled piece of paper. "He was holding this in his hand."

Sam leaned forward so that he could see, too, and his heart damn near stopped in his chest.

It was a photo of Alyssa. It wasn't a clipping from the newspaper. It wasn't one of the recent paparazzi shots snapped just last week in front of Mann's Chinese Theater. It was, in fact, the photo from the Troubleshooters website. Someone—and it was hard to believe Don Quixote had the money or means—had printed it onto photo-quality stock.

"Hmmm," Alyssa said, as Sam put it a little less succinctly.

"What," he said, "the fuck . . . ?"

The drive from Boston to New York was a relatively easy one.

And, of course, nothing was ever really all that difficult when Robin was sitting next to Jules—not even the relentless traffic at the Mass Pike toll booths at the exit for Route 84, not even the fact that the rain that relentlessly fell was beginning to turn into what the New England weather people cheerfully called a "wintry mix," but was in truth a lot like getting pelted with someone's syrup-free Slushee.

It was barely eight o'clock, but the late January sun had long since set and it felt more like midnight. The defroster in the car was cranking, and the windshield wipers kept a ragged rhythm as they finally made it through the toll and headed into Connecticut.

"Where would someone go to buy a pig's heart?" Robin wondered as the road started to open up. "Are there really still butcher shops where butchers actually . . . butcher, instead of just getting large slabs of already dead meat?"

They did most of their grocery shopping at Whole Foods, or at the Shaw's at the Pru. Robin couldn't remember the last time he'd seen a butcher shop, let alone shopped in one.

"There're mostly the dead meat kind left." Jules glanced at him as he moved the car into the left lane. "But Yashi did some research for me and found out that there *are* still a few in New York City that do the actual butchering of the livestock. Although he also found out that most of *those* are kosher, owned by Orthodox Jews, so . . ."

"Probably not a lot of pigs being slaughtered there," Robin surmised.

"Definitely not," Jules agreed, glancing over to give him a smile.

"I love that we're doing this," Robin blurted out. "It's great that we're going to see Alyssa and Sam and Ash, and . . . I just . . . Thank you for letting me tag along, babe."

Jules reached over and took Robin's hand, interlacing their fingers.

Every now and then—like right now—Robin got this sudden flash of disbelief, of pure dumbfoundedness, that this truly was his life now. He got to sit here in this car, next to Jules, because Jules *loved him, too.* It seemed so surreal—and like one of the world's best miracles—that when they reached the hotel and checked in, he'd share Jules's room. It was completely, wonderfully incredible, too, that ten years from now, he'd wake up in the middle of the night and Jules—his lover, his best friend, his husband—would still be there, lying next to him, solid and warm and funny and kind, and ready and willing to help him chase any lingering nightmares away.

"Sam's a little freaked out by the pig-heart thing," Jules said now, breaking the comfortable silence that they'd fallen into.

"It's definitely freak-out worthy," Robin agreed. All of it was—including the fact that the police detective assigned to the case wanted to *tap* Alyssa, and had tried to drag Sam to jail, after breaking his rib. "So what's the plan when we hit town? Visit the shops where someone could've bought a pig heart and . . . see if they used a credit card to make the purchase? See if there was a security camera running, see if . . . ? I'm not sure what. If they were wearing their *I hate Maria Bonavita and her ass-face* T-shirt?"

Jules laughed. "I don't know," he admitted. "Yashi got me a list of all the farms and butcher shops and slaughterhouses—the porcine ones—in New York as well as Jersey, Connecticut, and Pennsylvania. I think it's more likely that our guy brought the heart with him, wherever he came from."

"That's pretty gross," Robin said. "How do you transport something like that? In a cooler, inside a plastic baggie?" The logistics of it all suggested advance planning, which was creepy.

"Alyssa's more concerned about the fact that whoever did this got into the assemblywoman's office with little to no effort," Jules told him. "Tomorrow she's going to interview the interns and volunteers who've spent any time in the office over the past year—and I'm going to help. Apparently quite a few people have had access to the key. The woman who's missing did."

"She's still missing?" Robin asked. Something Thorndyke. Margaret—that was her first name.

"Yup," Jules said. "And it turns out she borrowed a key, back during the election campaign, to drop off something for some fundraising party. The assembly-woman's assistant, Jenn, said she returned it, but . . ."

"Margaret could've copied it," Robin deduced.

"A lot of people could've copied the key," Jules confirmed. "Alyssa thinks it's personal—the fact that it was a heart in that drawer instead of, I don't know, large intestines or brains or liver or . . ."

Yeesh.

"If this were a movie," Robin pointed out. "Pig-heart-man would be a jilted lover, driven mad by his unrequited love for Maria—"

"If this were a movie," Jules cut him off with a laugh, "this four-hour drive to New York would be edited down to a four-second crane shot of the Mass Pike, an *Entering Manhattan* sign, and then the car pulling up to the valet at the hotel."

"Maybe not. Maybe this is a really boring movie," Robin teased him back. "Or maybe—I know—it's *porn*. We're going to pull off on some secluded exit ramp and . . ." He did a little dance right there in his seat. "Get this car rockin' and rollin', bay-bay . . ."

Jules laughed.

"Or it's a horror movie and we're part of the alien abduction subplot," Robin kept it going because he loved making Jules laugh. "Any minute now the alien claw is going to appear and pluck us off the road and pull us up into the bowels of the mothership."

"Maybe it's not a pig heart," Jules said, playing along. "Maybe it's an alien heart."

Robin held his hand up to his ear. "I think I hear Oscar calling . . ."

But it was Jules's phone that suddenly rang.

"Wait a minute," Robin said. "He's supposed to be calling me!"

"Shhh!" Jules was laughing as he put in his earpiece. "It's Yashi. Hey, Yash. Whatcha got for me, baby-cakes?"

But then, as Robin watched, Jules's smile vanished. In fact his entire face and body language changed. He morphed from Robin's husband and lover into pure FBI agent.

"What?" Jules breathed into his phone. He checked the rearview mirror for the traffic behind them, signaled, and moved all the way over to the right lane as he said, "Holy shit, are they sure?"

He kept the turn signal on because there was an exit coming up, as he asked Joe Hirabayashi, aka Yashi, who worked for him at the Boston FBI headquarters, "Are we running the DNA—" He cut himself off, nodding as he listened. "Yeah," he said. "Yes. *Shit.*" Another pause, then, "No, no, I'll call Alyssa and tell her . . . No, it's going to take me longer to get there . . . No, I've got Robin with me and I've gotta . . . Yeah. *Yeah.* Call me as soon as you . . . Thanks, Joe." He ended the call. *"Jesus."*

He took the exit, glancing at Robin. "We're turning around. I'm taking you home," Jules said, even as Robin spoke past his heart, which had lodged tightly in his throat.

"What's going on? Why do you have to call Alyssa? Are Sam and Ash all right?"

Something was horribly wrong, but Jules glanced at him again to say, "They're fine."

"Thank God." Robin's relief allowed Jules's words to penetrate. *I'm taking you home.* "What happened? Why can't I—"

"*Shit,*" Jules said again, the muscle in his jaw jumping as he braked to a stop at the traffic light at the end of the ramp. It wasn't obvious which way to go to get back on the highway in the reverse direction, and he jabbed at the GPS screen, trying to get a better-proportioned map.

"Jules," Robin said as the light turned green and the car behind them honked. He pointed across the street to a restaurant with a nearly empty parking lot. "Pull over there."

Jules took his foot off the brake and pulled into the lot, jerking to a stop and throwing the car into park. He canceled their current route on the GPS, and pushed the button that would program the thing to return home. Only then, as it was calculating the route back to Boston, did he look over at Robin.

"It wasn't a pig's heart," he said quietly. "The lab report's in. It was human."

CHAPTER NINE

When Dan took off Jenn's glasses and kissed her again, and she didn't push him away, he knew that he was in.

He knew, too, that he couldn't hesitate, that he shouldn't give her too much time to think this through and maybe change her mind.

Which meant that he had to get enough of their clothes off to get himself inside of her as quickly as humanly possible.

But Jesus, her mouth was so soft and sweet, and he wanted her to kiss him like that for about three hours. But right now that was going to have to be something to look forward to. It would happen. He was as certain of that as he was of the fact that once he made her come, he would be getting it on as often as he wanted until the day he said good-bye.

She was, after all, pragmatic—and he knew that not just because of the lines on the palm of her hand. He knew because he knew women. He knew, too, because he truly liked women—all shapes and sizes of them—provided they had a brain and a healthy sense of humor. A pretty face and bikini-worthy body was a bonus, sure. But if had to choose between fucking a woman who looked like a supermodel but was in fact a royal bitch on wheels, or fucking someone who looked like Jennilyn and made him laugh and enjoy the non-sex time, too, well . . .

Here he was, wasn't he? With his hand up her shirt, beneath her bra, her breast so soft, her skin so smooth, and yeah, she liked that he'd found her nipple. He liked it, too, and Jesus, she was so freaking hot, the way she was moving beneath him, as he pushed himself more tightly between her legs, as she let him come closer, welcoming him.

Tomorrow was his scheduled night off. He could've waited one more day, hit a bar or two tomorrow night, and absolutely, positively gotten his ass laid with someone prettier and skinnier and allegedly sexier, but probably not smarter or funnier.

That, combined with his not wanting to wait another freaking minute longer to get some, made this a no-brainer.

Because he wasn't lying when he'd told her that he wanted to spend the next two weeks laughing.

Right now, though, he wasn't laughing at all. He was afraid to stop kissing her—afraid that if he didn't keep her mouth fully occupied, she'd tell him to stop or at least to slow down, and he didn't want to do either. So he kept on kissing her, even though he wanted to lick that tight little nipple into his mouth, even as he pushed her skirt further up her legs.

She'd shed both her shoes and her pantyhose upon arrival in her apartment. He'd noticed that she hadn't been wearing stockings in the office, but she'd gone into the ladies' room to put them on for the frigid walk home.

Her bare legs were long and smooth and her panties were small and loose enough—alleluia—to be pushed aside, so he went to unfasten his pants, and ran into her hands, reaching to do the very same thing.

He was so surprised that she would choose to participate rather than lie back and let this happen to her, that he forgot to keep kissing her, and in fact, pulled back and got instant eye contact.

He should have closed his eyes and kissed her again, but he froze, unable to look away.

"This is crazy," she breathed, her fingers suddenly still, too, on the buckle of his belt.

And he knew as he gazed down into her eyes—and they were such a beautiful shade of brown, with swirls of green and yellow—that whatever next came out of his mouth was going to mean the difference between life and death.

And okay. All right. He'd been in life and death situations before, and he *wasn't* going to die if he didn't have sex with this woman in the next forty-five seconds. He was just going to *feel* as if he were going to.

And for one insane moment, he considered just whispering *Afghanistan,* but he knew that he'd ridden *that* horse as long and as far as possible. She wasn't stupid, and if he made it too obvious, she wouldn't be able to let herself be played.

And she *was* letting him play her. Despite his saying that she was both strong and independent, there wasn't a woman alive who didn't harbor a secret wish for forever after meeting a man that she liked enough to have sex with.

Which was why he needed to be careful, over these short weeks, to mention, frequently and gently, of course—that he would be leaving.

But as for what to say right now . . . ? He knew that if he waited too long to respond that that would end his chances, too, so he did the only thing he could do.

He agreed with her. "It *is* crazy," he whispered.

It must've been the right answer—thank you, Jesus—because she pulled his head down and kissed him again.

So he dug into his pocket for one of the condoms that he'd put there a few hours ago, as she reached again between them and unfastened his belt.

God, he wanted her to touch him. He wanted her to reach into his pants and wrap those long, elegant fingers around him. But she stopped well short of that.

She let him pull down his own zipper, instead skimming her hands up and over the muscles in his back, beneath his T-shirt, her fingers cool against the heat of his skin. That felt unbelievably good, too, as he freed himself and covered himself and he pushed aside the silk of her panties.

And goddamn but he loved fucking women who hadn't had sex in months, or probably more accurately *years*. She was so ready for him—she moaned at the lightest touch of his fingers. And oh, yeah, this was already going to be one for the record books. She was wet and hot and damn near pulsing with her desire for him.

Later tonight, he'd fuck her again, slowly—the way he really wanted to, just pushing the tip of his dick inside of her and then taking it back. Giving her a taste of what he had to offer, and then a little bit more and a little bit more, until she was begging, until he filled her completely, until she took him fully—which, by the time that it happened, would make both of them come in a rush.

He wanted to do it while he looked into her pretty eyes, while he smiled down at her, while she smiled, too, giving him a flash of those dimples.

He wanted her clothes off, too—although women her size usually balked at complete nakedness, especially while all of the lights were blazing, the way they currently were. It would take him a while to convince her he found her attractive, just the way she was, but two weeks was plenty of time to get that job done.

But right now, his goal was to make her come fast. To go for *good,* not *great*. To leave her wanting more, so that there would be not just a *later tonight,* but two weeks' worth of *laters* in his golden, shining future.

So he guided himself, and she shifted her hips to help line him up, and then there he was, poised on the brink of exactly what he wanted, knowing how good it was going to feel when he slid inside of her, and then doing . . . just . . . that. . . .

"Oh, God," Jenn breathed, as she took him, all of him, and *Oh, God* was right, because she was so freaking tight, but she had him so damn deep he wanted to say it, too—*Oh, God*—but he couldn't do more than moan, it felt so amazing.

He knew he was going to come too soon if he moved, but he moved anyway, in part to explode his theory that nothing on earth could feel better than this, because it could and it did.

Sweet Jesus, it did, and the way that she was touching him, kissing him, gasping her pleasure into his mouth as she moved with him and against him in a perfect rhythm, was exactly what he wanted and needed.

There was only this, only pleasure, only now, and everything else—all of the bullshit of the past few months, no, all of the bullshit he'd endured over the nearly three decades of his life—evaporated.

He wasn't even thinking about Sophia—sometimes he closed his eyes and pretended he was making love to her. But it wouldn't be like this, because she was tiny and delicate and fragile—emotionally as well as physically—and he knew that if he ever made love to her, he'd have to be cautious and careful, but not so with Jenn. She was solid and large and enthusiastically, aggressively unbreakable.

Unbreakable and unbroken, and he opened his eyes to look at her. Her face was so close to his, and her skin was smooth and clear. Peaches and cream, it was called. Her eyelashes were dark against her cheeks, and her nose was a little too small for her face, although maybe not, because along with those dimples it added enormously to her entire cute factor.

"Oh, God," she was saying as she wrapped those killer legs around him, her hands on his ass as she tried to pull him even closer, to push him even deeper. "Oh, yes! Oh, *yes* . . . "

Her voice was rich and husky and very sexy—although right here and now there was little about her that he didn't find overwhelmingly hot.

Even her sofa, as ancient as it was, was sexy—particularly the way they were making it creak and rock as she urged him faster, harder, deeper. Jesus, he was slamming himself into her—no fragile flower, she—like this was day four, as if she trusted him completely. And he could only imagine what kind of sex day four would really bring, and he wanted to cry, because he knew it was going to be unbelievably great.

This was, without a doubt, the beginning of the best two weeks of his life.

He'd found out, from some article online, that while in the Navy, Alyssa had won awards and acclaim for her marksmanship. He read in another piece about Troubleshooters Incorporated, the company for which she was currently second-in-command, that she still spent a lot of time at the firing range, perfecting her skill.

He liked that about her. As deadly accurate a shot as she was, she still worked to achieve perfection. He could relate.

The article also mentioned that, while working for the FBI, she was one of two snipers who'd helped in the takedown of a hijacked commercial airliner in Kazbekistan.

She'd killed—Alyssa had—more than once. But the act of taking another's life hadn't crippled her. It had made her stronger.

He loved that they had that in common, too.

As he worked to learn more about her, he'd made lists of her friends, of her acquaintances, of the people she worked with. He'd spent hours combing through Troubleshooters Incorporated's website.

It was there that he'd found his very favorite photo of her.

And any time the firm was mentioned in the news, he saved the articles and cross-referenced the people mentioned.

That was how he'd discovered the link to Maria Bonavita. It had started, months earlier, with yet another photo of Alyssa, taken while providing security for überwealthy Savannah von Hopf, while Savannah's Navy SEAL husband was out of the country. He'd then found an interview with Savannah, in which she mentioned her longtime friendship with her temporary bodyguard. And then, last year, he'd read the press release stating that Maria Bonavita was running for the New York State Assembly, with Savannah von Hopf leading her campaign.

He knew, right away, that this was what he'd been waiting for.

No doubt about it, the world had handed him a shining, perfect gift.

So he'd packed his bags and headed home, to New York, for the first time in many, many years.

"Please don't take me home," Robin said to Jules, putting his hands over the GPS screen, as they sat in the parking lot of the Vernon Diner, somewhere just east of Hartford, Connecticut, with the car's windshield wipers continuing to sweep away the falling globs of wintry-mix-turning-definitely-to-snow. "This weather's only going to get worse. We're two hours from Boston, that's four hours before you're right back here, at which point the roads'll be even more slippery, and you'll still have nearly two more hours to go. And that's driving at your usual healthy *yes, officer, this* is *an official FBI vehicle* speed, which you won't be able to maintain without going into a ditch."

"Robin," Jules started.

But Robin had a litany of reasons, and he'd only just gotten started. "I can help," he said. "With Ashton. I'm good with him, which frees up both Sam and Alyssa, and yes, I know we'll still need a guard, but we'll only need one guard, because Ash can stay with us in our hotel suite, so we'll have hotel security looking out for us, too. He'll be safe there, and I will be, too. Even if it's just for a day or two until they decide how they're going to handle this, if they're maybe going to take him back home—at which point, if you haven't caught this guy by then, I'll go, too. I promise. In fact, I can help by seeing if Ash and I can't go stay with Janey and Cosmo in L.A."

Robin's sister, Jane, was married to one of Sam's former SEAL teammates.

"*If* you don't catch this guy by then," Robin said again. "Besides, are you really going to just drive me back to Boston and drop me off, like, *Good luck sleeping tonight in our really big, really empty, really spooky old house, knowing for certain that there's some freak out there who cut a woman's heart out of her chest and put it in an assemblywoman's desk drawer. Love you, too, sweetie! Buh-bye!*" He switched back to his regular voice. "I'll be safer with you than I would be at home, all alone. I always am."

Jules just sat there silently, letting Robin argue, waiting for him to finish.

"I am, and you know it," Robin felt compelled to emphasize, adding, "Call Alyssa, will you? She needs to know that this is now a murder investigation, so she can increase the assemblywoman's security. Ask *her* if I can help with Ash. If she says no, I'll take the LimoLiner back to Boston in the morning."

Jules sighed and nodded. And dialed his phone.

Sam was waiting with Alyssa for the elevator that would take them up to Assemblywoman Bonavita's apartment, when her cell phone rang.

"It's Jules," she informed him, and opened her phone. "Hey, where are you? Have you left Boston yet?"

Sam took out his own phone, intending to call the number that the police officer had given him, in order to keep track of Don Quixote's whereabouts. To say that Sam was eager to speak to the old man in the morning, when he was sober, and ask him why the hell he had a picture of Alyssa clenched in his grimy hand, was an understatement.

The homeless man hadn't awoken, not even when the ambulance came. He was being taken to St. Sebastian's Hospital, but Sam was going to have to call and check to find out where he'd end up after that.

The beat officer who'd shown up when the homeless man had collapsed wasn't particularly apologetic, and Sam knew he suspected that the old man was Alyssa's father or grandfather or maybe her crazy Uncle Bob— and that they didn't want to admit it so they didn't get stuck paying his hospital bill.

Sam had taken the opportunity, though, before the police arrived, to search Don Quixote's voluminous pockets. The man had no wallet or identification. He *did* have a diverse and interesting collection of beer-bottle tops in one pocket, and about a ton of weird trash—like he'd recently gone dumpster-diving outside of an office building—in his others. A broken ruler, an empty computer ink cartridge, a variety of paper clips, some plastic file-folder tabs in a rainbow assortment of colors, an unopened pack of Post-it notes, about twelve different pencil stubs.

He had no other pictures—not of Alyssa or anyone else—and Sam wasn't sure how he felt about that.

But before he made his phone call, Alyssa caught his attention from where she was now standing, over on the other side of the building's small elevator lobby.

She hadn't said a word—in fact, she'd gone dead silent, which in itself was attention-grabbing. Usually her conversations with Jules were animated, with lots of laughter. She'd also shifted and had crossed her arms, her neck and shoulders suddenly tense, as if she were listening to Jules with every cell in her body.

"Any results from DNA—" She cut herself off to listen, but then asked, "When?" She listened some more, nodding, her hand against her forehead as if she had one hell of a headache. "Okay. Okay. Yes. I don't . . . I don't know, Jules. Let me . . . Let me talk to Sam and . . . Yeah, I'll call you back and Jules . . . ? Thanks for calling me first."

She snapped her phone shut, and when she turned to look at Sam, he knew that Maggie Thorndyke was dead. He could see it in her eyes, in the sorrow that she let him see on her face.

"Ah, fuck," Sam breathed, as he crossed to put his arms around her, as she allowed herself—careful of his rib—to hold onto him, too, even if just for this brief moment that they were alone. "I'm so sorry."

"I didn't want to be right," she said, her voice muffled as she spoke into the folds of his jacket. But then she looked up at him, a trace of chagrin in her eyes. "I like being right, you know that I do, but not this time."

She sighed, stepping back because fifteen seconds of comfort was fifteen seconds more than she usually gave herself when there was evil out there in the world—evil that needed to be stopped, and justice that needed to be served.

"DNA test still hasn't come back, but the heart was human," she told him, morphing back into the killer's worst enemy—tough, strong, resilient, and determined to track him down. And, according to Sam's watch, probably painfully in need of feeding Ash, or at least using the breast pump to expel her milk if Izzy'd already given their son a bottle.

She pushed the elevator button again. "I have to go break the news to Maria. I need you to call Gillman, give him a sitrep and have him bring Jennilyn back here—no. Wait. Call Jules back and find out where he and Robin were planning to stay. Let's upgrade his suite to a bigger one. I want to move the assemblywoman there. At least until we can sweep her apartment, make sure no one's listening in. Let's move her first, before we say anything about Maggie Thorndyke, and let's not discuss where we're going while we're upstairs."

Sam nodded. "What about Tony?"

"Call him. Let's get him back in. And we have to decide what to do about Ash. Robin's still offering to babysit, at least until we can find an alternative source of child care. I'm thinking Noah and Claire . . . ?"

"They're in London," Sam reminded her that his cousin and his wife had finally, after many years of marriage, taken the honeymoon they hadn't been able to afford when they'd first gotten wed.

"Mary Lou . . . ?"

He shook his head. Sam's ex-wife, Mary Lou, was closing in on the end of what had been a difficult pregnancy. Her new husband, Ihbraham, had just left Sam a message, asking if he and Alyssa could take Sam's daughter for a couple of days. Sam was going to have to call him back and tell him no.

"She's just been put on bed rest," he told Alyssa now. "Is she all right?"

"Yeah, but the doctors expect her to go into labor early. She could pop any day. Why not just keep Ash here with Robin? We'll make sure they're both safe."

Alyssa nodded as the elevator door opened with a ding. "Don't take too long," she said.

"I'll be right up," he told her, knowing that despite all the orders she'd just fired off—call Jules, call Gillman, call Tony—she'd given herself the hardest job of all: Get Maria to leave her apartment and, once at the hotel, break the news to her that her friend was probably dead.

Jenn came.

She came, and immediately after, even while the rush of intense pleasure was still fluttering and feathering through her, she was instantly mortified by what she'd just done.

She'd just had sexual intercourse with a man she'd met for the first time, just a few hours ago.

She'd had nothing to drink, not tonight or even for the past two weeks, so she couldn't blame it on any alcohol.

Yes, she'd discovered a gruesome surprise in the bottom drawer of her desk today, but that was hardly a good reason to hike up her skirt and go at it like a dog in heat, with some sailor.

Some incredibly handsome sailor, and okay, not just a sailor but a Navy SEAL—although Jenn wasn't sure if that made it better or worse.

Worse. Definitely.

There was not much here that was going into the *better* column any time soon, as he—Dan Gillman, aka Fishboy, aka Gilligan, aka Lucky, aka the man she'd just had crazy, loud, boisterous, furniture-banging sex with—lay with his head down, face against the pillow of her couch, depleted and breathing hard. He was still between her legs, still inside of her, still warm and large, although much less solid.

Any second now he was going to lift his head and she was going to have to look into his eyes and say . . . what? She would have to say something. Maybe *See? I told you it got hot in here.*

But, God, that would make her sound as if she did this a lot—had sex with a near stranger at the drop of a hat, or the drop of a zipper, as it were.

She could say *If that was day one, day five could darn well kill us both,* but that presupposed that he'd told her the truth, that the BS he'd laid on her about being her "boyfriend" for two weeks—yeah, right—wasn't merely just part of his attempt to get her to have sex with him tonight and only tonight.

But he didn't lift his head, and he *still* didn't lift his head, and Jenn realized with a sudden jolt of shock that his ragged breathing wasn't stopping. That . . .

He was . . .

Actually . . .

Crying?

And suddenly it wasn't so hard to figure out what to say. "Are you all right?" she asked.

And suddenly she wasn't the one who was mortified—he was.

"Oh, shit," he said. "I'm sorry, I just . . . I . . ."

He rolled off of her, rolled away, pulling out and leaving her scrambling to push her skirt back down as she fought her way free from the cushions so she could sit up next to him there on the edge of the sofa, where he was now perching.

He'd turned away from her just a little—just enough to hide his face. But it was more than obvious that he was wiping his eyes with the heels of his big hands.

She touched his shoulder, solid beneath the soft cotton of the T-shirt that she'd never managed to get off of him, much to her disappointment at the time. Now, she was enormously glad that he still had it on. "Dan . . ."

He laughed a mix of his disgust and disbelief, glancing at her with eyes that, yes, were rimmed with red. "Jesus Christ," he said. "You must think . . . I'm some kind of . . ."

"No," she said, running her hand down his broad back, as if he were one of her six-year-old nephews who'd just gotten teased by the fifth graders on the school bus. She could hear her cell phone buzzing at the bottom of her purse, but whoever was calling—her mother, one of her brothers, even Maria—could just leave a message. Now was not the time to go scrambling for her phone.

"I just, um . . ." Dan looked down at his hands, at his open right palm as he sat with his elbows on his knees, his pants pulled back up but still loose and unfastened around his ridiculously trim waist.

As Jenn watched and waited, he traced his own unbroken fate line with his thumb. "I don't get why I'm alive and . . ." He turned to look at her, letting her see that, again, there were tears in his eyes.

And okay, he was gorgeous when he was smiling and laughing, he was hot as hell when he was reading her palm and attempting to seduce her. But with those midnight eyes brimming with that heartfelt emotion, he was human, and that made him even more beautiful.

It made him . . . real.

And it took her breath away.

"I was right next to him," Dan told her haltingly. "This kid, he was maybe nineteen, twenty tops. Private Edmund Williams. His friends called him Eddie. And I'm the SEAL, you know. So Williams and his Marine buddies are trying to impress me by taking me to this restaurant where the food is so spicy your eyes water for three days after eating it. It was my idea to go. I love eating the local food, and the way they were talking about it . . . It was supposed to be safe, in the part of town where they like Americans but . . ."

He looked away from her, down at the floor, but his eyes were out of focus and she knew he was thousands of miles away, in the dust and heat of some ancient, poverty-stricken city on the other side of the world. Her phone was ringing again, and she reached out with her foot and kicked her bag farther away from her. If it was Maria, she'd call on the landline. And if it was the Trouble-shooters team, they'd call Dan directly.

Her family could wait.

"I don't remember the explosion," he was saying as he shook his head. "I don't remember very much about the entire incident at all. I know from the report that it was an insurgents' munitions dump, hidden in a school base-ment." He looked at her again. "Can you imagine that? In a fucking elementary school? That's where they kept their stockpile of rockets and grenades and even dyna-mite."

"God," she said, because she could not imagine that.

"It was a block away," he continued. "If we were closer, we would have been vaporized. As it was, shrap-nel went everywhere, and the entire squad of Marines was hit—everyone except me. But Eddie, who was right next to me, *right* next to me—he's hit in the throat, and he's down and . . . His friends are all looking at me like I'm Jesus, like I can save him because I'm a fucking SEAL. God, I do remember flashes of that. I can't god-damn forget it. . . . But there's no corpsman, no medevac team in the world that can get him to a surgical station quickly enough to keep him from bleeding to death."

He looked at her again, wiping his eyes again before his tears fell. "At least that's what I read in the report. I don't remember much of it, but I apparently carried him all the way back to the hospital on the base and tried to beat the crap out of the triage corpsman who told me it was too late. That Eddie was already gone."

"Oh, Dan, I'm so sorry." Jenn's heart was in her

throat, and she had to wipe away the tears that had welled in her own eyes, but she didn't stop touching him, her hand now in the softness of his hair at the nape of his neck.

He was back to looking at his hands. "I can't stop thinking about it. He was three inches away from me, and the shrapnel hit *him*. Three inches, and *he's* the one in the body bag. I'm three inches to the left of him, and I'm the one who walks away without a scratch. I mean, yeah, I got tossed around and they think I must've hit my head pretty hard, because I blacked out but . . . I'm the one who gets to keep breathing, to come here to New York, to meet you"—he glanced at her again—"and yeah. To make love like that. It's been a while since I've . . . been with anyone and . . . It was unbelievably great and . . ." He laughed, running both hands down his face. "Jesus, maybe now I'm embarrassing myself even more because you didn't think so—"

"No," she said. "It *was* great. It was. It was *incredible*."

"Yeah?" he asked, and this time when he turned to look at her, he didn't look away. He held her gaze with eyes that were softly uncertain, as if he didn't dare believe her. At least not completely. But he reached over and took her hand, bringing it to his mouth, to kiss her knuckles, her palm, her wrist . . .

Oh, God. His lips were so soft. "It's been a while for me, too," she admitted. "A *long* while. So it wouldn't take much to rate two solid thumbs up. But that was truly inspiring." She laughed even as she felt herself blush. "I wonder what my downstairs neighbor thinks. She opens her door and glares at me when I make too much noise getting my mail."

He smiled, a boyish mix of relief, amusement, and pride. "Yeah, I thought we might actually put this couch through the floor. Damn, woman . . ."

"Okay, so I guess I know what Mrs. Harrison thinks."
She rolled her eyes.

But now he was looking at her like he maybe wanted
to try it again—putting the couch through the floor—
and she was the one who had to look away. "But I *do*
wonder what *you* think," she said softly. "I've never
done anything like this, not with anyone. Of course,
that's probably what I'd say even if I did it all the time,
right?"

"Jenni, don't worry. I believe you, completely," he said.
"Although, really, if you did . . . ? So what, you know?
Women are allowed to have fun, too."

"Yeah, and what planet are *you* from?" she asked.

"Haven't you watched *Sex and the City*?"

"Of course," she deadpanned. "Can't you tell? I'm so
obviously into expensive shoes and designer handbags."

Dan smiled. "I'll take that as a no."

"It's a hell no," she said. "I mean, I've seen a few
episodes, and it's funny enough, and well-acted, but excuse me, the women are all beautiful. Even the one who's
supposed to be plain is drop-dead gorgeous."

"Which one is supposed to be plain?" he asked.

"See?" she said. "It's a fantasy, totally. But it's not
mine. It's not one I can relate to."

"I think they're all supposed to be hot," he said.

"Great," Jenn said. "I think I'll invest a hundred hours
watching extremely beautiful women floundering around,
making messes of *their* lives, and then I'll go buy twenty
cats and never leave my apartment again."

"So what *is* your fantasy?" he asked. "*The West Wing*?"

She did have the box set of that, and he'd apparently
spent some time looking at her bookshelves.

So she answered him honestly. "Yes. I want Maria in
the White House. Obviously, it's not going to happen tomorrow, but in fifteen or twenty years . . . ?"

"I'll be a senior chief by then," he said. "If I stay in the Navy. If I'm—"

He broke off, and she knew what he was thinking. *If I'm still alive. If, next time, I'm not the one standing three inches to the left. . . .*

But he forced a smile, and then he leaned forward and kissed her.

It was such a sweet kiss, so different from the way he'd kissed her before.

And when he straightened up to look into her eyes, that uncertainty was back.

"I'm a mess, Jenn," he said quietly. "I've got so much noise in my head, so much crap to sort through. But all I want, right now, more than anything, is to make love to you again. On your bed this time, so I can fall asleep after, with you in my arms. But . . ."

Her heart lurched, the way she'd heard it described in romance novels. She'd always rolled her eyes at the description. As if a heart could actually lurch.

But she was wrong, and all those writers were right.

He had more to say, and she waited, watching as the muscles jumped in the side of his jaw, as he struggled to find the words.

"I have these . . . nightmares," he finally admitted, "that I haven't been able to shake, and—"

"It's all right," she interrupted him. This time she leaned in to kiss him. "Just wake me if you have a bad dream, okay?"

"That's not what you signed on for," he said.

She narrowed her eyes at him. "I don't remember the part where I signed anything."

"Yeah, thanks, Ms. Literal, but you *know* what I mean. This is supposed to be two weeks of fun. It's not going to be fun for you if—"

"Oh, it'll be *plenty* fun," Jenn said, more than half amazed at the words coming out of her mouth. A few short minutes ago, she'd been convinced that his talk of two weeks was just that—talk. She'd been certain that he only wanted what she'd already given him, so he was going to fade away into the night.

But now? She believed him, too.

She believed him and she liked him—this beautiful, sad, funny, damaged yet so-courageous man. And even though she knew that two weeks was nothing, that it was a heartbeat of a relationship that would be over too soon, she didn't care. She wanted him to stay with her for every second of the precious time that he had, before he had to go back to that horrible, dangerous world where standing three random inches to the left meant the difference between living and dying.

She kissed him again, and with a confidence that would have astonished her had she been watching this play out from afar, she reached down into his still unfastened pants to find him and wrap her fingers around him.

Because he'd said it himself—that he wanted, more than anything, to make love to her again.

"Oh, yeah, I like *that*," he breathed into her mouth, as his body confirmed his words.

"Good," Jenn said. "Help me get this bed opened up, and we'll give Mrs. Harrison downstairs something to *really* complain about."

CHAPTER TEN

Maria wasn't used to cloak and dagger. She also wasn't used to not having the final say.

"Ma'am," Alyssa said, gently but firmly. "It's important we don't talk about this here, but I *will* explain when we get where we're going."

"How about you tell me what's going on in the cab?" Maria suggested.

"Fair enough," Alyssa conceded, even though they weren't taking a cab. They were being met, at the service entrance of this building, by several cars from the FBI. But she didn't want to tell Maria that. Not here, where it was entirely possible the killer was listening in. "Pack only what you need for tonight and for the morning. Our team will be available to come back here and pick up anything else you might need, but we must get out of here. Now. Without any further discussion."

The assemblywoman was a few years younger than Alyssa, but she hadn't gotten to where she was by being a fool. She knew something bad had gone down, and she had about a million questions in her eyes, but she finally nodded.

"I'll get my bag." She turned back, though, to ask, "May I bring my laptop?"

"No, ma'am," Alyssa said. "But we'll make sure you

have access to a computer and to the Internet when we get . . . where we're going."

"What about Jenn?"

"She'll meet us over there." Alyssa prayed that that wasn't a lie. Sam hadn't been able to reach Danny or Jenn, and had sent Izzy and Lopez out to kick down her apartment door, if need be.

Someone capable of kidnapping and killing Margaret Thorndyke could damn well target Maria's chief of staff next.

But Maria nodded—she wanted to believe Alyssa—and vanished into her bedroom.

Sam, meanwhile, was bundling Ashton into his cold-weather-wear, the hood of which had little mouse ears. Despite the awful news, it was hard for Alyssa not to smile at Ash, especially when the baby, perpetually cheerful, delivered up one of his silly, drooly smiles. And especially when Sam smiled back at him, talking to him the whole time he dressed him.

"You know I'm gonna take a picture of you in this thing. And when you're thirteen and permanently mortified, I'm gonna post it on your facebook page." He glanced up as if he knew Alyssa were watching, and told her, "Tony just called. He's two minutes away. When he gets here, we'll go. I've got all of Ash's gear. When we get where we're going"—a location that only Sam and Jules knew—"I'm going to recommend that we call a time-out. Just a short one," he added when she started shaking her head no, "We don't want you wrecking another shirt."

"Too late," she told him. "Besides we don't have time for even a short break."

"Tough sh . . . sugar." He made a face at Ash. "Daddy almost said a bad word." He looked back at Alyssa. "We'll make time. While we're waiting for . . . you-know-who to arrive."

Alyssa glanced at her watch. Jules's ETA wasn't for another few hours.

"There's plenty for the team to do between now and then," Sam said, somewhat cryptically. She knew he was talking about getting hold of an electronic surveillance device and doing a sweep of this apartment, as well as Jenn's place and the office.

Maybe there *was* time for a break, of sorts.

Sam knew that Alyssa didn't like breast-feeding Ash in public. Not because there was anything wrong with it, but because she felt it undermined her authority as team leader. Particularly when her team consisted of several extremely immature Navy SEALS.

It was tough enough, being a woman in charge of a truckload of testosterone, without rubbing their faces in the fact that she was female by feeding her baby in front of them.

She'd tried the discreet blanket thing, but Ash was a grabber, prone not just to exposing her to the world, but to waving the blanket gleefully in the air and drawing everyone's attention.

Maria came back out of her bedroom, rolling an airline-carry-on-sized bag behind her. She'd changed out of her yoga pants and sweatshirt, and into standard Manhattan-wear: black pants, black blouse, black jacket, black high-heeled boots.

It was the kind of outfit Alyssa would've worn to a meeting at the White House, and Maria had put it on, along with makeup, just in case someone spotted her during the fifteen seconds they were going to be out in public.

What a life she'd chosen for herself.

Although she probably thought the exact same thing about Alyssa.

Sam's phone beeped and he answered it, relaying to Alyssa, "Tony's here."

Alyssa reached into her jacket and drew her sidearm from the holster she'd stopped to put on after that phone call from Jules. She didn't mind so much being seen without makeup or underdressed, but getting caught unarmed—that was a potential career killer.

In fact, it was a potential killer, period.

She'd gone into Savannah's little apartment and picked up the suitcase with which the TS Inc team always traveled—even on a so-called low-key assignment such as this one. It contained a wide variety of weaponry, including a small amount of that old SEAL favorite, C4 explosives. A Navy SEAL could use it not just for big explosions, but for little ones, too. Like, to open a locked door, fast. So it was, and would continue to be, a staple in the Troubleshooters equipment locker.

She hefted the bag now, setting it on the floor by the door, which she knocked upon twice.

Tony knocked back, also twice, from out in the corridor, and she unfastened the variety of bolts and nightlocks.

He was dressed up, shivering slightly. He probably didn't have an overcoat, just a utilitarian cold-weather jacket that wouldn't have worked with the nicely tailored suit and tie he was wearing. He'd fixed his hair differently, too. It was gelled to be artfully messed, and he looked adorable.

"Sorry to have to call you," she said.

"So am I," he said sincerely, and she knew Sam had told him why he'd gotten called in. "But my friend knows that I have to go when I have to go, and this was—"

She put a finger on her lips and he nodded. He also patted his left shoulder, and she knew that he, too, was now armed.

"Let's move," she said, glancing back at Sam, who nodded. He was ready—although she knew that carrying Ash had to hurt.

Maria had put on her coat, and Alyssa walked beside her as Tony led the way to the elevator.

It was being held by a woman and a man—both of whom were so clearly FBI agents that they might as well have had the letters tattooed on their foreheads.

Was I ever that obvious? she wanted to ask Sam as they rode down thirty floors in silence.

He looked at her, one eyebrow raised as if he knew exactly what she was thinking—which he always did—as he rocked back and forth to keep Ash from fussing until they reached the lobby. The female agent took Maria's bag from her as they exited the elevator, leading the way to the back of the building, where the cars were waiting.

As they stepped outside, the snow was still falling, but the heat from the passing traffic kept it from sticking to the street. On the sidewalks though, it was turning into something thicker and darker—and slippery, without a trace of pristine winter wonderland.

They rode together—Tony, Sam, Maria, and Alyssa—in a car that had, thanks to Jules's thoroughness, a car seat ready and waiting for Ash.

The phone call came just as the luggage was loaded, the baby strapped in, and the doors were locked, as the driver pulled away from the curb.

The number on Alyssa's cell screen was Jules's. Her stomach sank as he didn't say hello. He just said, "Bad news."

"The DNA test?" she asked.

"Yes," he told her. "It's a match."

"Margaret Thorndyke," she confirmed. Sam, who was sitting across from her, shifted his foot. Just slightly. So that his boot was touching hers.

"Yep," Jules said. "It's her. Was her. Shit, you know what I mean."

"Yes, I do," Alyssa said. "Thank you for calling. I have to go. I'm with the assemblywoman and, um . . ."

"I'll be there soon," Jules promised.

Yeah, but not soon enough. Back when she was partnered with Jules, when she, too, had worked for the FBI, he was always the one who broke the bad news to murdered loved ones. He was good at it—if someone could be good at that kind of thing.

Alyssa closed her phone and met Maria's eyes.

"They found Maggie?" the assemblywoman asked.

"Not exactly," Alyssa said. "Ma'am, the news isn't good. We know, for sure, that Margaret Thorndyke is dead. The . . . body part . . . from your office was human. It was hers."

Maria drew in her breath sharply, and turned pale. But other than that, her composure was remarkable. She nodded. "I knew it was bad," she said. "When you took me out of . . . But I didn't think . . ." She cut herself off to ask, "Do you honestly believe that my apartment is bugged?"

"I don't know," Alyssa said, another thing she'd learned from working with Jules. Being truthful about what they did or didn't know helped win hearts and ensured cooperation. "We're taking precautions, though," she continued. "Being extra cautious."

"I'm so sorry for your loss, ma'am," Tony murmured.

"I don't understand," Maria said, and her voice shook only slightly. "Who would do this? What do they want?"

"I don't know that either," Alyssa admitted. "But we're going to find out. And then we're going to find him. Count on it."

Alyssa was good.

He knew when the news about Margaret's heart came back from the lab, because she immediately circled her wagons.

They gathered—all of them—not in the office, and not in Maria's condo either, but in a different location, probably a hotel room, which was smart, because he couldn't listen in on them there.

Not that she'd had a chance to look for the bugs he'd planted, both in the office and in Maria's condo—but she'd find them soon enough, unless he could get there first.

He didn't need to hear what she was saying. He could imagine it, and imagine what she was doing, and he floated in the euphoria, knowing that now—right now—she was, at long last, thinking of him, too.

Izzy was worried.

Whoever they were dealing with here, he was a psycho. "How hard is it," he asked Lopez, who was a trained hospital corpsman, "to cut a heart out of someone's chest?"

"In one piece like that?" Lopez answered. "It's hard."

That's what Izzy had thought.

It wasn't just hard, it was gruesome and macabre. And freaking twisted.

And if they got to Jennilyn's apartment to find the place in a shambles and Jenn and Gillman hacked into little pieces, it would be yet one more way that he'd failed Eden. Despite the animosity between his wife and her brother, Eden loved Danny. Izzy knew that. He understood it on a visceral level, because he, too, had brothers who could treat him like royal shit, and yet he still loved them.

The walk over to Jennilyn's apartment was a relatively short one—just a few city blocks, but Izzy wanted to get there, fast. He wanted to break into a jog, but Lopez wanted to walk—and to keep calling Danny's cell phone. Again, and again, and again.

"Holy shit," Izzy realized. "You think they're doing it? You think Fishboy's already talked his way into her pants, and . . . what? The music's up so high and they're both screaming so loudly they can't hear their phones ringing?"

Or they were singing along.

Jennilyn LeMay didn't exactly strike him as the Celine Dion type, but for some reason, that was the picture that immediately leapt to mind. Dan Gillman leaning buttoned-to-the-neck Jenn over her kitchen counter, banging her while singing along with *My Heart Will Go On* at the top of his lungs.

The mental image would have made Izzy laugh his ass off, if there weren't some psychopath looney-tunes nut-fucker out there, carving people's hearts out of their chests.

Lopez sighed as he shut his phone, and Izzy knew he was right—or at least that Lopez thought he was right, and that Lopez believed that Gillman and Jenn were bumping uglies.

"Wow," Izzy continued, "I didn't see *that* one coming. I mean, Danny was practically doing the cartoon wolf thing with Maria. You know, *ah-roo-ga, ah-roo-ga,* the heart thumping out of his shirt, the salivating fangs, and the bulging eyes—*the better to see you with, my dear . . .*" He broke into song: "*If I can't have you, I don't want nobody baby, except your assistant, uh-huh!* What a douche bag. Talk about the big bad wolf, Jenn was practically wearing a little red riding hood and skipping through the forest."

Lopez usually didn't say much whenever they were paired up together without the rest of their merry band, apparently preferring to let Izzy narrate away to his heart's content. But right now, he actually spoke. And it was chiding, which hurt. It always hurt when Lopez—whose real name was Jesus—did the disappointed thing. "People who live in glass houses, man."

He didn't bother with the rest of the adage—*shouldn't throw stones.*

"What?" Izzy asked defensively, even though he knew damn well that Lopez was talking about Eden, who had been seventeen and 364/365ths, when Izzy'd first met her.

Eden, who was also Danny Boy's little sister, which had been a huge no-no, but also Eden, who had never in her life worn an innocent little red riding hood, not even back when she was ten years old.

Eden, whom Izzy had married because she was in trouble, knocked up and carrying some sleazebag's kid; because her parents were assholes; because her own brother had washed his hands of her, leaving her to suffer her stepfather's ongoing emotional and physical abuse.

Bottom line, though, Izzy had married Eden because he'd wanted her, and marrying her had made her his— even if only on paper, if only for a very short time.

"I'm just saying," Lopez told him, dialing Dan again. "You might want to shine a little of your indignant light onto your own inner cartoon wolf, Zanella, and see what you find growing there in the darkness."

But Izzy wasn't buying it. "I loved her," he said. "Eden. You honestly think Gillman feels anything for this girl besides *ooh, baby, yes, baby . . . Near, far, wherever you are . . .*"

"I think this *girl*," Lopez said, not batting an eye over the fact that Izzy had broken into song, "is a woman, while Eden *was* a girl. Don't get me wrong, I agree with you. Gillman *is* a douche bag. I just happen to think you're one, too."

"And what are you?" Izzy asked as they went up the stairs to the front door of Jenn's building. "The king of perfect? Pope Jay Lopez, the first?"

Lopez didn't answer that, because on the other end of the phone, Gillman had finally picked up. He wasn't chopped up into little pieces after all.

"Dan," Lopez said. "It's Jay. Where the hell have you been, man?"

Jenn threw up.

Maggie Thorndyke was dead. With her silly collagen lips and her perpetual hope that if she could just get a little bit more in shape, spend another hour a day at the gym, take one more DVD lecture course or this time really learn to speak another language, then Mr. Right would finally find her. She'd lived all of her years waiting for the moment that her life would begin.

But it hadn't begun. It had ended some time in the past two days, at the hand of a horrible murderer.

And Maggie's eternally hopeful heart had ended up in the desk drawer of one of the few people she'd let get close enough to maybe—almost—be called a friend.

The last of the Chinese food Jenn had eaten two orgasms ago left her stomach, and she flushed the toilet, wiping her mouth with a damp facecloth that Dan had left in reach, on the edge of her sink.

"Don't touch me!" she'd told him when he'd first followed her into the bathroom. "Don't! Just, *don't* . . . " So he hadn't touched her, but he hadn't run away, either. He'd stayed there in the bathroom with her, closing the door to give her some privacy.

Privacy. Right.

His friends were out there in that room that surely smelled like sex, with her bed pulled out, sheets rumpled and damp—as if they couldn't guess what Jenn and Dan had been doing, pretty much constantly since they'd gotten home, several hours ago.

It hadn't seemed so sordid back when Dan was kissing her, when she was lying in his arms.

But now it was just another blot of awfulness in a night that was up for the all-time awfulness award.

After Dan had finally answered his phone and realized

that Jay Lopez and Izzy Zanella were moments from knocking on her door, they'd both scrambled to throw on some clothes.

He'd all but ripped open his sleeping bag, too, flinging it onto the kitchen floor in an attempt to make it look as if they'd been sleeping separately. At 8:45 at night. Gosh and gee whiz, they'd both been plum tuckered out, and they'd fallen right to sleep. Which was why neither of them had noticed the forty-plus phone calls they'd each gotten on their cells.

Maybe Alyssa and Sam's infant son Ash was naive enough to believe that, but the two SEALs who'd been sent out on this search and rescue team certainly weren't.

Nor was it likely to be believed by anyone else back at Maria's condo. Including Maria, who would be a mix of astonished, ecstatic, approving *and* appalled at Jenn's impetuosity.

Although, why Maria hadn't called on Jenn's landline, she didn't know. Unless . . . She always turned the ringer to silent when she left in the morning, so as not to disturb Mrs. Harrison, her downstairs neighbor, who complained at the slightest noise from upstairs.

When Jenn had arrived here tonight, with Dan and a bag of Chinese food in tow, she'd neglected to turn the ringer back up.

Even then, she'd been overly distracted by the incredibly good-looking guy whom she'd then had sex with. Twice.

As she sat on the bathroom floor, leaning back against the ancient black and white tile on the wall, she realized that she'd buttoned her shirt wrong. She was off by one button, all the way up. Perfect.

Dan was sitting on the floor across from her. There was just enough space in the tiny room for them both to sit without touching.

He spoke. "I'm sorry you had to find out about your friend that way. Zanella's an asshole, with the sensitivity of a retarded amoeba."

His teammate, Izzy Zanella, was also his brother-in-law. Or rather, soon to be ex-brother-in-law.

They'd talked a bit more about their families in between orgasm number two and Dan's realization that the weird buzzing sound across the room wasn't the radiator, but rather his phone vibrating in his pants, jangling against a few coins he had in his pocket.

Before the sky had fallen, and Izzy and Jay had come in, announcing that the heart was not just human but had belonged to Maggie, she and Dan had laid there together, in her bed. He'd had his arms around her as, with her head on his broad shoulder, she'd traced his various muscles and tattoos.

He'd asked about her family, and she'd told him how lucky she was that her father had gotten the help he'd needed as early as he did, about how, despite that, her oldest brother had been badly damaged, about how, being the only sister among her four brothers, she'd always had her own bedroom, while her brothers had had to share. She'd gotten used to having privacy and to this day, preferred it—which was why she lived here in this utility-closet-sized studio rather than sharing an apartment with Maria or another friend.

In turn, he'd told her a little bit more about his severely dysfunctional family. He'd said that he worried about his little brother, Ben, who lived with his clinically depressed mother and his Nazi of a stepfather—a man who'd started mean and gotten meaner after being injured in a car accident.

Dan told her that he sent money home every month, but he wasn't sure if Ben ever benefited—other than having the rent paid and a roof over his head.

They'd been talking—really talking—and, God, she liked him so much. Too much.

"Maggie wasn't really a friend," Jenn admitted now as she rebuttoned her blouse. "I mean, I liked her, but I didn't really know her that well. I don't think anyone did. She had trust issues—trouble letting people in, you know?"

Dan nodded.

"So we didn't exactly hang out together," Jenn told him. "But she was a huge part of the campaign. She didn't just donate money, she spent a lot of time volunteering in the office and . . . Why would someone kill her? God, Maria must be so upset." She pushed herself to her feet and found her glasses on the edge of the sink. Putting them on made the world go back into focus. "I've got to get to her."

Dan stood, too, still not touching her. But he also didn't move to open the bathroom door. He just stood there, in front of it. "That's where we're going. The team leader moved her out of her apartment, too. Lopez said you should pack an overnight bag."

"Have the police been called?" Jenn asked, realizing immediately it was a very stupid question. "Of course they have. They were probably the ones who called with the lab results. Sorry, I'm . . . just really rattled."

"The FBI AIC should be arriving soon," he told her. "He'll be able to answer all your questions."

"AIC?"

"Sorry. Agent in charge. His name's Cassidy. He's good. He'll be taking over the investigation. He'll probably bring a whole team in. They'll catch whoever did this."

They. Not *we.*

"Does this mean that the Troubleshooters team is going home?" she asked.

"I don't really know," he said. "Maybe. Probably."

"Ah." She looked away, afraid of what he might see in

her eyes, and he stepped forward and touched her, gently lifting her chin so that she had to meet his gaze.

"I'm here, Jenn," he told her. "For as long as you need me. Regardless of whether the team stays or goes. Okay?"

He was tall enough that she had to tilt her head up to look into his eyes. He was perhaps even more handsome with his hair a mess from her running her fingers through it, and from his lying back in her bed to smile up at her while she'd climbed atop him.

He hadn't bothered to button the overshirt that he'd pulled on when he'd been unable to find his T-shirt, and it now hung open, revealing tantalizing glimpses of his sun-kissed chest.

She'd gotten him naked for that second time, but he hadn't pushed to get her clothes all the way off, which was a little weird, but nice. Even though they'd had sex twice in a very short amount of time, she wasn't sure she was ready for him to see her naked. And somehow he seemed to know that.

He, however, had a body that was meant to be on display as frequently as possible, with sculpted muscles and smooth, tanned skin, and quite a few intriguing tattoos— among them a chain of barbed wire that circled the big bicep of his right arm; and a single word—coexist—made up of a variety of philosophical and religious symbols, on his back, between his shoulder blades.

"Okay?" he asked again when she didn't answer.

He'd just promised that he'd stay as long as she needed him—as long as it fell reasonably within the boundaries of his ridiculous two-week time frame.

She sighed and answered, "Dan. I, um . . ."

He cut her off. "Just say *okay*—that, yes, you hear me. You don't need to decide anything right now—in fact you shouldn't. Just . . . pack a bag so that we can get out of here."

Jenn nodded. "Can you ask your friends to wait for us in the hall and . . . may I have the bathroom to myself for a minute, please?"

"Absolutely," he said, and let himself out, closing the door behind him.

She locked it, and only then did she let herself cry.

CHAPTER ELEVEN

"I'm sorry," Assemblywoman Bonavita said, sitting forward in her chair and looking from Alyssa to Sam to Jules and back. "Are you actually questioning . . . *me*? I'm a *suspect* in Maggie's murder?"

Sam shifted in his seat, trying to find a position that didn't hurt, glad he didn't have to answer her, that he could just sit there and look pretty.

The hotel had upgraded them to this super-fricking-deluxe suite that actually had a separate conference room they could use for these preliminary interviews of both Maria and Jenn. The upgrade had been all on account of Robin being an Emmy-winning TV star, and hadn't cost him an additional dime.

There was an irony there, in that once you got famous and rich enough, people started to give you all kinds of shit for free. But only after, of course, you were rich enough not to need it.

Alyssa was tired. Sam could hear it in her voice, and he could relate. He was tired, too, and his side was hurting badly enough to make him wish he'd gone to the drugstore and picked up an Ace bandage and about a truckload of ibuprofen.

Not that either of those things would help.

"It's standard procedure, ma'am," Alyssa was telling

Maria, "in any murder investigation. It's more often the case that victims are killed by people they know, so—"

"I'm aware of that, yes," the woman said. "So, okay. How do we get me off the suspect list as soon as possible? How do we clear me?"

"We'll need a record of your whereabouts from the time Ms. Thorndyke went missing, to this morning," Jules said, "when the, um, evidence appeared in your office desk drawer."

Evidence?

Jules caught Sam's eye and shrugged, his movement almost microscopically miniscule.

Not that Maria would have noticed had Jules done a full Fonzie, complete with two thumbs up and an *Ey*. She was a little wrapped up in making sure her political career didn't end before it started.

"That's easy," she said earnestly. "I was in Albany for most of that time. My schedule of meetings is posted on my website. It wasn't nonstop, but it's close. I attended a dinner party that got me back to my hotel late. I still haven't found an apartment in Albany, so I've been getting a room at one of those extended-stay hotels. I checked out early this morning, to drive back to Manhattan—I spoke to the desk clerk when I left. You can also check my E-Z Pass account for the exact time I came in over the bridge. I drove straight to the garage where we keep the car, and I walked to the office from there. When I arrived, Jenn was already in, along with several of our interns and volunteers."

"About what time was that?" Jules asked.

"Probably . . . nine? Maybe a little after. Oh, I stopped at the Starbucks on the corner, and used my credit card, so I can get that time for you, too. It should be posted online by now."

"Do you recall which of your interns were in your office when you arrived?"

"Ron," she said, "and Gene. Wendy . . . And Belinda," she recalled. "Oh, and the new UPS man, Hank something, was delivering a package. I chatted with him and the interns, had a brief schedule update with Jenni, then went into a meeting with Douglas. Forsythe. He was there, too. He's a volunteer—the way Maggie was. He's also a major donor." She looked at Alyssa, alarmed. "Should we warn him? Is it possible that whoever killed Maggie is targeting the big donors to my campaign? Oh, my God, has Savannah been told?"

"Savannah's safe," Alyssa reassured her. "As for Douglas . . . I don't think we have enough information to come to any conclusions, but . . ." She looked at Sam. "Have we called him?"

Sam nodded, checking the list he'd made. "Yeah. We'll be meeting him, tomorrow afternoon, in the office." He deferred to Jules. "If you want to stick to that schedule. Mr. Cassidy. Sir."

"Yeah, that's good," Jules said, ignoring him. "We're going to want to talk to him, as well as all of the interns. And the UPS man."

"To corroborate my story?" Maria asked. "They'll all confirm what I've told you."

Jules smiled at her. "I don't doubt they will. But since they were there before you, one of them may have seen something or someone suspicious."

She nodded. "I'm sorry if I seem ignorant. I was a lawyer for quite a few years, but I never practiced criminal law. It was all taxes and insurance and real estate."

Alyssa looked at Sam and nodded—which was his cue to leave. It was, she'd said, "time to give the assemblywoman some privacy," but he suspected her real goal was to get him into bed. And not in the good way.

"Now we get to the hard part," she told Maria as he went to the door, trying not to scream or walk bent over. *Damn,* he hurt. "Past relationships. Ex-boyfriends—"

"Ex-significant-others," Jules interjected.

"Or maybe even current significant others," Alyssa continued, using his more PC language. "Any enemies, any incidents that you may have made note of, both during the campaign or since you've taken office?"

Sam closed the door behind him and—holy fuck. In just the short time he'd been sitting there, his body had further stiffened to the point that walking had made him see stars.

He had to take a moment, leaning back against the wall and closing his eyes, breathing through the pain— something valuable that he'd learned from Alyssa's Lamaze class, not that he'd ever tell anyone that.

There was a low dresser type thing with a mirror above it, right there in the foyer to the suite, and he pulled up his shirt to look at his ribs and—

"Holy shit!"

Sam dropped his shirt and turned to see Robin standing there with Ash in his arms. Jennilyn was standing slightly behind him, still looking a little shell-shocked that she was in TV star Robin Chadwick Cassidy's hotel suite.

Or maybe the real reason she was looking shell-shocked was standing behind her—Danny Gillman, fuckhead extreme. Rumor had it Gillman had seduced sweet little Jenn in record time, and that they'd been too busy going at it to answer either of their phones.

"Don't say *shit* in front of the baby," Sam reminded Robin, then pointed at Gillman. "You and me, later. In the conference room."

"With the candlestick or the rope?" Robin quipped, but then answered his own question. "I suppose, Colonel Mustard, that either one will do."

"Da," Ash said gleefully, holding out his arms.

"Hey, Little Bit," Sam told his son. "You're gonna have to stay with Uncle Robin for a while longer, okay?"

"Yeah, Daddy can't hold you when he's on the verge

of falling over," Robin said, then addressed Sam directly. "Shouldn't you go to the hospital when your body starts inventing new colors like that?"

"And have them tell me what? *Your rib's broken. Don't take a deep breath for the next two weeks. Fifty dollar co-pay, please.* No, thanks."

Jenn pushed her hair behind her ear. "Mind if I, um, see?"

"What am I?" Sam asked. "A freak show?"

She didn't back down. In fact, she laughed, which made her eyes come to life and sparkle, and he understood—a little—why, out of a city filled with millions of women, Gillman had chosen her. Other than the fact that she was convenient, which she certainly was.

"One of my brothers wanted to skateboard, you know, professionally," she said. "Extreme sports. He never qualified, but he did break his ribs five, no, six times. I used to tape him up. I got pretty good at it."

"Yeah, tape doesn't really help," Sam said, but he lifted his shirt again for her to see.

She drew in her breath through her teeth at the sight of the rainbow-hued bruise that covered his entire side. "That's a broken rib, all right."

"Thank you, Dr. House," Sam said as he lowered his shirt again.

"When I broke a rib," Gillman volunteered, "it helped me to wrap it. Having the bandage on reminded me not to jar it, or move too fast."

"Or to cough or sneeze," Jenn said. "Or laugh. Don't laugh," she told Sam. "You're breathing okay?"

"Yeah," he said. Broken ribs could puncture lungs, so in the big picture, he was absolutely doing fine.

"You should let Lopez look at it," Gillman said, then called, "Hey, Jay. C'mere."

"I should start charging admission," Sam grumbled.

"We were actually coming to find Jules and Alyssa,"

Robin said. "But you'll do." He looked at Jenn. "Show him."

She held out the photo of Alyssa that Sam had taken from the homeless man he'd dubbed Don Quixote.

"Where did you get this?" she asked. "I saw it on the table out in the living room and . . ." She looked back at Robin. "He really needs to sit down."

The *he* she was talking about was Sam, and damned if she wasn't right. His knees were pretty fucking wobbly. But Lopez was there, and he and Gillman helped him into the living room, like he was some kind of ancient grandpa. But when Lopez looked at Sam's side, he tsked and then called in a drugstore order to Izzy and Tony, who were out tracking down a bug-sweeper.

"Tell him what you told me," Robin prompted Jenn, now that Sam was sitting down and no longer in danger of face-planting on the carpet.

An act that would have further pissed off Alyssa.

"It was months ago," Jenn said. "In September. I remember because it was actually the night that Savannah's husband Ken got shot."

Sam remembered that night. In vivid detail. Ken, who was a chief in his old SEAL team, and a good friend, had nearly died.

"Maria called me," Jenn continued, "because she and Van needed a ride to the airport, so they could go to California. She told me to get the car."

Robin was nodding as if these details were both interesting and important to the story that Jenn was telling. So Sam didn't interrupt. He just let her tell it as she got a bottle of water from the mini-fridge.

"I'd parked it out on the street," Jenn continued, as, in a surprise move, she handed the bottle to Sam, "a few blocks from my apartment, and when I got there, I got in and started it, and I looked into the rearview—and saw a man sitting in the backseat. It was this homeless man I've seen around. I still see him around. Not all the time, but every now and then."

Okay. Sam was now extremely interested. "Black guy?" he asked. "In his sixties or early seventies?"

"Crazy hair and funky beard?" she said, nodding.

"Puffy purple coat?" he asked.

"That's him," Jenn said. "He didn't have the coat then, but I've seen him with it since. He broke into the car—it was raining and he was going to spend the night in the backseat. I startled him as much as he startled me. Okay, maybe not, but he got out of there fast, and one of the things he left behind was that picture. Of Alyssa. It's funny, I knew when I met her that I'd seen her somewhere before—and I was right."

"He's where we got that," Sam pointed to the picture of Lys. "We were just walking down the street, and he comes at us. At me, really. He was screaming *don't touch her*. Crazy shit." He looked at Ash who was laughing as Robin bounced him on his knee. "Stuff. *Her* being Alyssa. We ran, and he tripped and knocked himself cold. We went to see if we could help, you know, get the police there, or . . . That was when we found the picture. Talk about weird. But he was pretty drunk. He never regained consciousness, at least not before they took him to the hospital."

"Which hospital?" Jenn asked, her eyes somber.

"St. Sebastian's," he told her. "You know it?"

She nodded.

Gillman had picked up the picture and was looking at it. "If he left it in the car," he asked Jenn, "how'd he get it back?"

"I gave it to him," she said. "He left some other things, too. A sock filled with . . . well, treasure, but probably only to him, you know? Military ribbons, some marbles, buttons—things like that. I saw him a few days later at the dumpster behind the building—the window from the ladies' room looks out over it. I guess he goes through it pretty regularly. But he was gone before I got down there. I actually ended up tracking him to a men's shelter at a church not far from here. I never actually spoke to him—I think he was afraid I was going to get him into trouble or something, you know, for breaking into the car. So I left the sock and the picture with one of the workers at the shelter. He must've given it back to him." She took the picture from Gillman. "I'm pretty sure this is the same photo. It's a little more ragged, but . . ." She looked from Gillman to Robin to Sam, her eyes wide. "Do you think he killed Maggie?"

"I don't know," Sam said. "But you better believe that Alyssa and Jules both are going to want to bring him in and ask him a whole lotta questions."

Jennilyn was nervous as she went into the conference room to talk to the FBI agent and Alyssa. Dan knew this, because she'd told him as much.

"They have to make sure that I'm not the one who killed Maggie," she said, dead serious, "and I don't have an alibi."

He tried not to laugh in her face. "Jenn, they know it wasn't you."

"But . . . I can't prove it. I could have made up that story about finding that photo of Alyssa, and—"

He leaned forward and kissed her, right there in the living room of the hotel suite, and she looked at him as if he'd taken a crap on the coffee table, then furtively looked around to see if anyone had seen them.

He lowered his voice to say, "Sorry, that was stupid. I didn't, um, realize you didn't want anyone to know you're, you know, seeing me."

She stared back at him. "What? No! I didn't think *you* wanted anyone to know. I mean, the whole thing with your sleeping bag back at my apartment . . . ?"

Had she really thought . . . ? "Jesus," he said. "Jenn. No, I was trying to protect you. That didn't have anything to do with *me*. It was all about you."

No wonder she'd been distant and weirdly too-polite ever since they'd left her place—always moving to the other side of the hotel suite whenever he approached.

And here he'd thought she was just horribly embarrassed because it was pretty obvious that everyone knew they'd hooked up. Lt. Starrett definitely knew. That comment he'd made about talking to Dan later . . .

Danny was *not* looking forward to that.

And talking about future unhappiness, the bedroom count in this suite was definitely lacking—despite it being the biggest suite Dan had ever been in, in his life. There were rooms for the Cassidys, for Alyssa and Sam and their baby, and a third room that Jenn would be sharing with Maria.

Everyone kept stressing that it was temporary. Which meant what? Just for tonight or for the next week? Dan couldn't get anyone to say.

The SEALs were grabbing any available sofa or floor space, and fucking Izzy had already laid claim to the conference room—which was the only other room with a door.

Which meant that the hard-on that Dan was walking around with wasn't going to go away any time soon.

It was screwed up—the fact that having sex again, after going without for a long time, got him instantly revved up for *more* sex. Most of the locker room talk that he'd ever listened to—and he tried to avoid it whenever possible—had been about the huge relief that came with finally getting some.

Not so much for him. He could go months without getting laid, and be fine with self-delivered maintenance, a mere couple times a week, as the need arose.

But as soon as he got the real thing, all he wanted was

more. Which was another reason why the two-week plan worked best for him, rather than one-night-and-good-bye.

And finding a woman as enthusiastic as Jenn had been . . . ?

Danny could imagine, had they been allowed to stay in her apartment, them tearing through all of the condoms he'd put into his pocket earlier this evening. And buying plenty more in the morning.

Before breakfast, even.

Jenn now smiled, and he looked up, realizing that he'd been sitting there, staring at her mouth. As he met her gaze, it was clear that she knew exactly what he'd been thinking about, and she was both amused and perplexed. But mostly perplexed.

"You know what really bothers me?" he asked. "Like, to the point of adrenaline rush? And *adrenaline rush* is testosterone-talk for near panic, I might add."

She shook her head, one of her dimples coming briefly out to play. It vanished quickly, because she was still vastly uncertain as to where their relationship stood.

It was hard not to smile back at her, and what he *really* wanted to do was talk her into going into the bathroom with him, perching up on that granite counter, and wrapping her long legs around him.

But this was pretty serious shit, and he needed to talk to her about it.

"It bothers the hell out of me, that that guy was in your car, and you just got in," he told her. "It's a basic safety rule, Jenn. Especially for women. You always make sure that opening the door triggers the overhead light, and you always, *always* check the backseat. Even if you just got out of the car for a half a second."

"I was in a hurry," she tried to explain.

Danny shook his head. "It doesn't matter. He was in

there, and you didn't know it. Do you know how lucky you are—"

"I know," she cut him off. "Believe me, I've been thinking about that. A lot."

"I like your heart right where it is," he said, and it didn't take much for his voice to ring with sincerity. In fact, it didn't take any extra effort at all.

If they'd been alone, he would've reached for her, pulled her close, and kissed her. He'd have gently tugged her shirt over her head and kissing away any protests she might make, he'd have unfastened her bra and . . .

"You gotta stop looking at me like that," she whispered. She was laughing a little, but she was also looking around again to see who might be watching.

No one was. Maria was still in the conference room with Alyssa and Jules. Sam had vanished—probably into his room to take a hot shower, to try to loosen up his injured muscles. Robin was putting Ashton to bed. Izzy and Vlachic were still out and about playing counterspy, and Lopez was over by the door and out of sight.

"Sorry," Dan told her, but he knew that *she* knew that he didn't mean it. "I know there's supposed to be this meeting later, after Zanella and Vlachic get back, but I was thinking, regardless of what's decided, I could maybe install a security system in your apartment myself. Tomorrow. So we could, you know, stay there. Tomorrow night, at least."

She smiled her surprise again. "You're in an awfully big hurry to get back there."

"Damn straight," he said, tracing the side seam of her jeans with his finger, down near the cushions of the couch, where no one could see, even if they were there and looking. "And I'm pretty sure you are, too."

But Jennilyn hadn't just put on her jeans when they'd both hurriedly gotten dressed. She'd also slipped into some too-serious sanity, and it had been reinforced as they'd left the safety of her apartment. It was a shame, after all the work he'd done to make sure that she'd take the lead when it came to having sex that second time.

Danny still wasn't sure where the idea to cry had come from. He'd felt her get tense, mere moments after they'd both climaxed that first time, and he knew he had to do something, or he wouldn't get the repeat he already wanted.

At that exact moment, he'd felt the odd pressure of tears, back behind his eyes, and just like that, he knew what he had to do, even though he'd never done anything like it before. It had been instinct, and since he trusted himself completely when it came to women, he'd gone with it.

He'd let himself cry.

He hadn't meant to tell her *quite* so much, though. And at one point, he'd actually been afraid that, now that he'd started, he wasn't going to be able to *stop* crying. That had been a little scary.

But he'd managed to stop, mostly because it had worked like a freaking charm. She was all over him.

Until Lopez and Zanella made the scene and got Jennilyn tense all over again.

"Dan," she said now, and paused as if carefully considering what she was going to tell him, and he knew that the next words that left her mouth were going to include the word *talk*.

So he spoke over her. She said—ding, ding, ding—"I really think we need to talk about—" as he said at the exact same time, "It'll be easier to talk at your place, you know, in private and . . ."

He laughed and added, "I'm glad we're on the same page, you know, about talking."

But the look she shot him made him laugh. "You want to go there to have privacy to *talk*," she said.

He nodded. It wasn't a lie. "Among other things."

"Like . . . baking cookies?" she asked.

"I could make that work," he told her. "Although turning the oven on? That would heat up the place even more. I'd probably have to be naked. You know, beneath my *Kiss the Cook* apron."

Jenn laughed. "I don't have any aprons, so unless you carry one with you—"

"Always," he said, "along with Fred the bunny and my favorite book of poetry—*Limericks from the Isle of Nantucket.*"

She laughed again, shaking her head, and he could tell that she wanted to say something, but that she was holding back.

"What?" He nudged her. "Just say it, LeMay."

She looked down at her hands, clasped in her lap. "I just . . . I'm surprised," she admitted, glancing up at him almost shyly. "I thought this was where you'd be running away. I mean, really Dan. You and me . . . ? And if the team's going back to California . . ."

"The team's not chained together," Dan told her. "I already told you—if you want me to stay, I'm gonna stay."

"But what about what *you* want to do?" she asked him. She was serious, looking searchingly into his eyes.

For someone who liked to talk, she hadn't been listening to what he'd told her.

So he took her hand—the one that he'd drawn that *X* on. It had faded from washing and other activities, but it wasn't completely gone. And he put it directly on top of the wood he was concealing in his pants, which of course made him even harder, especially when she laughed and squeezed him.

"Wow," she said.

"What I want," he said, "is to take you into that bathroom over there, right now, and—"

The conference room door opened, and Jenn snatched her hand back and leaped to her feet.

"Jennilyn, if you're ready," Alyssa said, as Maria came out.

There was no way on earth that Maria had seen Jenn touching him, but she surely knew that something was up from the way that Jenni was blushing. Her face was almost fire-engine red.

It was cute—although he'd never tell her that. Not using that word.

But then Jenn turned back to Danny to say, "This could take a while. So in case you get bored . . . You know, when I was in second grade? My best friend Debbie and I would make Barbie clothes from paper towels and Kleenexes." She smiled sweetly at him. "Toilet paper works, too."

Dan laughed, and Maria smiled, but it was clear that she was clueless, thank the Lord above.

Dressed the way Jenn was, in jeans and a T-shirt, sweatshirt on top, sneakers on her feet, hair pulled back in a ponytail, no makeup on—she'd sweated off what little she'd worn to work—she looked like nothing special walking away.

Particularly next to Maria, who remained unbelievably beautiful, with a body that was, undeniably, world-class.

But even if everything were completely equal and no feelings would be hurt, no promises broken; if Dan had a choice between fucking Maria or fucking Jenn . . .

He'd pick Jenn. No contest.

Go figure.

As the door closed behind Jenn, Dan could feel the assemblywoman looking at him appraisingly, as if she, too, were planning to lecture him.

But—oh, fantastic—before Maria made up her mind about whether or not to approach him, Sam came out into the living room wearing one of those thick, white hotel bathrobes, his hair still wet from his shower, and slicked back from his face.

He sat down, gingerly, in the easy chair to the left of Dan as, across the room, Maria disappeared down the hall to her bedroom.

They both heard the door click gently shut before Sam spoke.

"Danny Gillman," he said.

"Conference room's still not free, sir," Dan pointed out.

Sam had been one of the officers in Sixteen, when Dan first joined the elite SEAL team. This was back when legendary Lieutenant Commander Tom Paoletti led the team, before 9/11—when life seemed so much simpler.

To a very young enlisted man like Dan, Lt. Sam Starrett had been a superhero. He'd been the CO on one of Dan's first major assignments, the takedown of a hijacked airplane. It had been what the world now thought of as an obsolete and old-style hijacking—the kind where an airliner, filled with civilian hostages, was held by terrorists after landing on the tarmac of an airport in a dangerous third-world country.

Sam had drilled the SEALs in the takedown team over and over and over and over, until they could have burst open the airliner's doors in their sleep, to take out the terrorists and leave the hostages unharmed.

It was due to Sam's diligence, his tenacity, and his ferocious insistence on perfection, that his SEAL team rescued all of those hostages with minimal loss of life.

Like a lot of the enlisted men in Team Sixteen, Dan had been upset when Sam resigned his commission as an officer. But he'd had to leave. He'd gotten into some trouble, having to do with his ex-wife.

A lot of Sam's trouble through the years had had to do with women.

So it seemed kind of ironic that he was going to lecture

Dan now about . . . what? A woman. And sure enough, he jumped right in.

"Jenn seems nice," Sam said.

"She is, sir," Dan agreed. "Very nice. I like her, very much."

Sam cleared his throat. Here it came. "She's not exactly in your league, though, is she?"

He purposely misunderstood. "I always aim high, sir."

"I meant—" Sam started, but then stopped himself. "You know exactly what I meant, dipshit, so don't play dumb. You're way out of *her* league."

"I'm sure she'd find that insulting, sir, and I do, too, on her behalf."

"Cut the *sir* shit," Sam said, "I'm talking to you here, Danny, man-to-man."

"With all due respect, sir, I've got to disagree. I think your tone is condescending. I don't like your implication that Jenn's somehow not good enough for me, and I think your intention here is to interfere in my personal life, which you have no business doing."

"She's *not* not good enough for you," Sam said, crossly. "You know damn well that that's not the league I'm talking about. I'm talking about experience, about expectations. About her being *nice*, and you being a walking dick."

"Takes one to know one, sir," Dan said.

Which was when Sam surprised him. He agreed. "It does," he said. "I've played your game, Danny. What are you going to do if you get this girl pregnant?"

Dan laughed. Jesus. "I'm not, sir. I'm always careful."

"Accidents happen."

"Sir, I appreciate your concern—"

"Imagine yourself married to her," Sam said. "If you can't do it, if it doesn't at least make you go, *Huh, maybe* . . . then you need to rethink what—or who—you're doing."

"I'm pretty sure if Jenn got pregnant, sir, she'd want to be in on any decisions, any choices. Just because your first wife—"

"Let's not go there," Sam said.

"I thought this was man-to-man, *Sam*," Dan said. "Just two buds, shooting the shit. I'm not sure why you have the right to criticize my relationships when I don't have the right to—"

"You're not a kid anymore." Sam got in his face. "You're fucking thirty years old, and you're still playing it like you're twenty-two, like you're *Gilligan*, the fuckup, the green-behind-the-ears dipshit, who gets away with being stupid because he's so goddamn adorable." He changed both tone and direction. "When are you taking the chief's exam?"

"What?" Dan said. "I'm not."

"Why not?"

"What is this?" Dan asked. "Attack Danny Gillman day?"

"Why the fuck not?" Sam repeated his question more forcefully.

"Because I don't want to be a chief, all right? What does this have to do with Jenn? I'm careful, I like her. And she likes me. What's the big deal?"

"The *big deal* is when you're working for Trouble-shooters—"

"I'm not exactly getting paid here, sir," Dan told him. "And by the way? I was planning to mention this—I quit. If you need me to, I'll reimburse Commander Paoletti for the airfare."

Sam was really baffled. "So . . . what? You're just going to leave?"

"No, sir," Dan told him. "I'll be staying here in New York. With Jenn. We hooked up and . . . like I said, I really like her and she likes me. I've got about two weeks of liberty left, and I'll be spending that time with her. I'm happy to help you out if you need me, but I don't want to be paid, in any way, for protecting my own girlfriend. That's kinda weird, sir. Could be kinda awkward."

"Just like that, she's your *girlfriend*?" Sam said.

"Not only do I aim high," Dan told him, "but I work fast. Sir."

Sam sighed. "Dan, look. What I really wanted to talk to you about is . . . Lopez told me about what happened in Kabul."

Shit. "Lopez had no right to—"

"Lopez is your friend, and he's worried about you," Sam said. "As he should be. You ever black out like that before?"

Ah, God. "No, sir."

"Just that once?" Sam asked.

Dan sat forward, on the edge of the couch. "Are we done here, sir?"

"Lopez said it happened twice."

Fucking Lopez. "Then why are you asking, if you already know? Are we *done* here?"

Sam sat forward, too. "Head injuries can be tricky."

"It's not a head injury," Dan said. "I wasn't injured—"

"So then it's what? PTSD?" Sam offered up the career-flattening acronym for post traumatic stress disorder that no one—including Danny—had dared to utter aloud before this moment. "If I were you, I'd go with mild head injury. An explosion with that much force? Your brains got temporarily scrambled. But either way, it never occurred to you that this might be information you'd need to disclose to Troubleshooters—to Tommy Paoletti?"

Dan *hadn't* considered that. And fuck, that pressure was back behind his eyes, only he was pretty sure that his bursting into tears wasn't going to work to manipulate Sam the same way it had with Jenn.

"Has it happened again?" Sam asked, his voice suddenly gentle.

Dan shook his head. No. At least he didn't think so.

"You've got to tell someone if it does," Sam said.

"No, sir," Dan said, his voice tight. "The way it usually works is that someone tells *me*. I don't remember *shit* when it happens."

Sam sighed. But then he nodded. "If you black out again, make sure it gets to me or Alyssa."

"Yeah, well," Dan said, "Lopez is here, so . . . No worries about that, right?"

"He's concerned about you," Sam said again. "He says you won't talk to him."

"I've got an appointment with the team shrink, sir," Dan said. "In a few weeks."

"That's not the same," Sam pointed out, "as talking to a friend or . . . If Jennilyn's really your girlfriend, Danny, you should tell her what's going on. At the very least so she knows what to do if you *do* black out again."

Dan looked at him. "Are we done here?" he asked again, and this time he didn't wait for Sam's answer. He just stood up and walked away.

CHAPTER TWELVE

He watched from the closet as two of the SEALs returned, as he knew they would.

When they first came down the corridor, he'd thought,
with a flash of heat and rage, that the taller one was
Starrett—the husband. And even though he knew they
must be armed beneath their winter jackets, he almost
ruined everything by bursting out at them, just to stab
Starrett in the throat.

But it wasn't him. It was the other one, who was just
as tall, but not as ruggedly handsome.

He thought about killing him anyway, about the way
his blood would spray, hot and thick against the wall
and in his face, coating him and staining his clothes.
That would make it hard to escape, but first he'd have to
kill the other—the one who was fumbling to get the key
into the lock.

He could do it. He wanted to do it. He had his Taser
with him, which would give him the advantage.

And killing them would confuse the issue and keep
Alyssa from realizing, too soon, who he was, because
the Dentist had only slaughtered women.

True, he'd killed that man in the mall parking lot, and
of course his father—but they hadn't connected those
deaths to him. Not yet, anyway. And yes, there was also

that one horrible man, years ago, with Amanda, but he'd hidden him well and they hadn't found him.

Right now though, he wanted to surprise Alyssa, and the bodies of these two—gutted and left in Maria's office—would help him to do just that.

It was a good idea—of that he was certain.

But he was also just as certain that he couldn't kill them both and be sure he would survive.

Wait. He needed to wait.

"In this lifetime, Chick," the tall one said impatiently as the really young shorter one tried a second key.

At last the door opened and the light went on, stabbing into his brain, but he didn't look away.

They wouldn't be in there long. He'd left nothing for them that would lead back to him. He'd even found the tooth he'd dropped some days ago. It had cut its way free from his pocket, dropping onto the floor from the leg of his pants—a ghost from the past biting him and making this adventure even more lively and nerve jangling, since he couldn't go searching the floor for it with Jenn sitting at her desk. And he hadn't had time in the early morning hours when he'd left his gift in the drawer. As it was, he'd almost been seen.

But he'd found it tonight and it was back in his pocket, where it belonged.

He'd cleared his listening devices out of Maria and Savannah's apartments, too—taking a moment to stand there, breathing in Alyssa's sweet scent. She hadn't been there long, but it was enough for him to feel her presence.

The tall one came back out into the hallway, looking at his cell phone. "Here we go," he said. "Now I've got bars. Wait—bar, singular. What is with this city? I get better reception in frakking Mumbai. Let's see if it'll let me dial out . . ." He held the phone to his ear. "Yes! Jackpot! Yeah, hi, Mr. um, Cassidy . . . Yeah, it's Zanella. Nope, nothing here, either." He paused, listening. "Yes, sir, we'll stop there on our way back to the . . ."

He waited, holding his breath, hoping to learn where they'd all gone, but the tall man—Zanella—didn't finish his sentence. But he did provide other information.

"If you're right, and this homeless guy's our man, he's either in St. Sebastian's or the drunk tank, so he couldn't have cleared the place. Of course, if he *is* our man, he's not likely to have access to high-tech equipment—No, no, I know it's not a done deal. We were thorough. Yup. Okay. Roger that. I mean, shit, I *didn't* mean . . . I'm just going to hang up now." He closed his phone. "Holy Jesus. *Roger that.* Things *not* to say to your gay boss."

"You need to lighten up," the shorter man—Chick, he was called—said from inside the office. "He's a nice guy. Just treat him the same way you treat everyone. With massive disrespect."

"Ha-ha, you're so fucking funny. What I *need,* right now, is to tinkle." Zanella stepped inside and returned almost immediately with the key to the bathroom. He vanished into the darkness down the hall.

And he knew that this was what he'd been waiting for. He could do this. While they were separated. Kill the shorter one, put on his jacket, and wait for the tall one to return.

He was already euphoric from the news that they thought *their man* was a street person—probably the very one who lived in the basement of a nearby building. That was brilliant, perfect, tremendously good news. He wished he could listen in further, to find out more. What were they planning? Were they still interviewing the staff tomorrow? Although, he'd find that out, soon enough . . .

He heard the bathroom door slam shut down the hall, and he knew he didn't have much time if he was going to do this. He pushed his door open a crack, but then stopped.

Because he realized that if he *didn't* kill them now, he could follow them. They would lead him back to wherever Alyssa had gone.

And he wanted to know where Alyssa had gone more than he wanted to feel the spray of blood in his face, more than he wanted to confuse and surprise.

He wanted Alyssa.

Alysssssa . . .

"Hey, how was the end of the show?" The shorter one came out of the office, carrying the bag they'd brought in, and setting it on the floor. He laughed as he spoke into his cell phone. "Yeah, I wish. I've heard the soundtrack and . . . Ah, I love that song—was it great?" He turned off the office light and shut the door, searching the ring for the right key. "No, baby, I'm glad. I just wish . . . No, shit's kinda hit the fan here, so . . ." He laughed again, as he put the key into the lock and just let it hang there. "Oh, you're not, are you? Ya *think*? No, no, it's better if you don't. I mean, I'm okay with it, of course I am." He got quiet. "No," he said. "No, no, I just don't want it to be hard for *you* . . . " He exhaled. "Yeah, great, dick joke, thanks. I'm being serious here, and you're . . ." He drew in his breath. "Yes, that does sound . . . *really* nice. All right, all right, look. It's the Hilton on Fifty-third and Sixth Avenue. Yeah, yeah, West Fifty-third. That one. If you really want to get a room, I should be able to get away for at least an hour, maybe longer. . . ."

And there it was. He didn't need to follow them. He could kill this one right now.

He pushed the supply closet door open a little bit more, but the other one, Zanella, was already coming back down the hall, singing. "*Every night in my dreams I see you, I feel you . . . And why can't I get this song out of my head? Oh, I remember.*" He kept singing, putting his own words to the familiar tune to that blockbuster movie, "I was picturing Danny Gillman singing this song, as he shagged Jennilyn LeMay. . . ."

"I gotta go," the one named Chick said into his phone as Zanella put the bathroom key back in the office, locking the door behind him, and handing over the key ring. "I'll see you later." He smiled, then lowered his voice. "Love you, too."

"Whoa. *That* sounds pretty serious, T-Man," Zanella said, as Chick pocketed his phone and the keys and zipped up his jacket.

"It is," the shorter man admitted. "It's, um, been, yeah, pretty serious for . . . a while now, actually."

"That's great," Zanella said. "I'm . . . really happy for you, man."

The SEAL was standing right in front of the storage room door. He was going to turn, and he'd see that the door was open—just a crack, but it *was* open—when it hadn't been open before.

Sometimes destiny happened, for reasons that he couldn't question.

He'd kill them both. He had to, so he would.

If it was meant to be . . .

He readied his Taser and braced himself, silently shifting his feet, knowing that he couldn't wait for them to pull their weapons free from their jackets, knowing that he had to move first, to surprise them.

But then Zanella said, "So when are you going to bring him by? Let us meet him. Make sure he's good enough for our little Tony."

He?

"I . . . don't think I'm ready for that. Not this trip. Maybe back in California. He lives in L.A., so . . ."

That was definitely a *he* that they were talking about. The shorter one had said *Love you, too* to a *he*.

His surprise and disgust floored him, and he lost his advantage, lost his edge, lost his opportunity to strike first.

But they didn't notice the door, didn't find him, didn't kill him.

They just moved off down the hall, as Zanella hefted the bag, saying, "Maybe we could have a cookout after we get back from this godforsaken land of ice."

"Yeah," the homosexual said, "maybe."

"No pressure. Let's get to that drugstore—what's it called, Duane Reade?" Zanella's voice echoed down the hall as they went to the elevators. "What the fuck kind of a name for a drugstore is Duane Reade, anyway?"

Jenn was exhausted by the time she closed the bedroom door behind her. And yet she knew Maria was infinitely curious, and probably had a million questions for her, starting with *Dan Gillman—oh, my God—seriously?!?*

They'd both survived their interviews with FBI agent Jules Cassidy, who was adorable and married to movie and TV star Robin Chadwick, which was pretty unreal.

Robin had come from Boston to New York with his husband to babysit for little Ash. Which was also unreal. Jenn wondered who would come in to do Alyssa and Sam's laundry later in the week—maybe Colin Firth? And perhaps Susan Sarandon would be by in the morning, to serve them all some breakfast.

And okay, Robin had explained that he and Jules had been close friends with the Troubleshooters team leader and her husband for years. They were, in fact, not merely Ash's godparents, but, should anything happen to Alyssa and Sam, Robin and Jules would be given full legal custody of the child.

Which was a real possibility, considering the line of work Alyssa and Sam were in.

So considering that: yes, that was one very solid, very tight friendship the four of them had going on.

"Are you all right?" Maria asked, as Jenn unzipped her overnight bag and pulled out her pajamas.

Jenn shook her head. "I just . . . I still can't believe Maggie's really dead." She turned to face Maria. "Everyone's all solicitous and *sorry for your loss,* but I didn't know her very well. I think I had lunch with her three times. Total. And she always brought along someone who ended up donating big money to the campaign, so we never really talked about anything personal. Did you have any idea at all that she was a recovering alcoholic?"

"None," Maria admitted. "I just remember that her lips kind of scared me, and she always had that little ugly dog with her."

"Do you really think that homeless guy killed her? You know the one, right? With the wild hair and . . . He just . . . He didn't seem . . ."

"People are crazy," Maria said. "And people *get* crazy from seeing and doing terrible things. God only knows what he lived through in Vietnam." Alyssa and Sam both had been pretty certain he was a veteran of that war, from Jenn's description of some of the ribbons and medals he'd kept in his sock. "And the system clearly isn't set up to provide him with the care he needs, so . . ."

Jenn knew this was a sore point for Maria, whose younger brother Frank had deployed to Iraq in 2004, and hadn't been quite right since he'd come home. It had been months since he'd last left his room in their parents' house in Glen Cove.

And look at Dan—a Navy SEAL—highly trained, highly skilled. A professional warrior. And yet still capable of being badly damaged by the relentless violence of life in a war zone.

One of Maria's goals—set out early in her campaign—was to help change the system. She wanted to make sure that all servicemen and women, even those whose injuries were not apparent, got the long-term, expert care that they deserved.

"Can I ask you something a little . . . unusual?" Maria

said. She was sitting on her bed the way they used to sit in high school when they had a sleepover. Legs crossed, pillow on her lap.

Despite sitting that way, and even with her hair neatly braided so it wouldn't tangle in her sleep, Maria looked like the grown-up that she was.

Although, come to think of it, she'd always come across as being mature and full grown. It was Jenn who was still being carded when she was long past twenty-five.

She sat on the other bed and cut to the chase. "Is your question about Dan?"

"What?" Maria said. "Who? Oh. No, but go, Jenn. He's pretty cute, I mean, as long as you know what you're doing. . . ."

"I have no idea what I'm doing," Jenn admitted, flopping back on the bed. "At all."

"You'll figure it out," Maria told her. "You always do. I have faith in you."

"It's not serious," Jenn said, saying the words aloud for the first time. Testing them out. "It's short-term. We've already agreed not to try to do the long-distance thing. Which means it's just going to end in two weeks when he goes back overseas."

And okay. She hadn't quite sounded convinced, even to her own ears. And the words definitely triggered a sinking feeling in her stomach, a sense of dread. It came from that last word she'd uttered—overseas. Despite the relationship's lack of seriousness, she was definitely daunted at the idea of Dan leaving to go back to the war.

And then, of course, there was the possibility that the awful sinking feeling was triggered by the idea of his leaving, period.

Countered by the very non-sinking feeling she'd gotten when Dan had met her eyes from across the room during tonight's meeting.

They'd all gathered in the living room, where Jules,

who was going to continue working closely with Alyssa, had admitted that they were all still pretty deeply in the clueless zone. They didn't know who had killed Maggie, although they had a list of people they were going to be checking out, including the homeless man who'd had Alyssa's picture.

They didn't know *why* Maggie was killed, either, but they weren't ruling out that the motive could be political. It was possible that the murderer had taken to heart some lunatic fringer's diatribes of hate, ignorance, and fear, and had chosen Maria as his target, with Maggie as collateral damage.

Jules and Alyssa expected some further contact from the killer. He'd caught their attention, but he hadn't yet delivered his real message. That, they both believed, was yet to come.

Tomorrow, their priority was to interview Maria's interns and volunteers, and to install high-tech security systems in both Maria's and Jenn's apartments, and in the office, too. The goal being to get them back to work, and back to living their lives, as quickly as possible. Although neither Jenn nor Maria should plan on going anywhere without a bodyguard any time soon.

Despite that, the consensus was, absolutely, to get them back to sleeping in their own beds by tomorrow night.

And yes, that was when Dan had looked at Jenn.

And the world had tilted, because, God . . . She didn't know him all that well, but she knew exactly what he was thinking from that look he'd given her.

I don't think I can wait until tomorrow night. . . .

"Not every relationship needs to be serious," Maria was saying now. "Two weeks could be a perfect length."

Jenn turned to look at her friend. She was trying to be supportive, but she sounded just as lame as Jenn had.

"It could be just exactly right," Maria insisted. "As a professional, you don't want a relationship that's *too* short. It'll raise eyebrows. But two weeks? You can come off of two weeks of great sex with the really hot guy, and look pensive and a little sad, and say, *We tried, but it just didn't work out,* and everyone'll call you *brave* instead of *slut.*" She smiled. "Except for me, slut."

"Shut up." Jenn threw a pillow at her.

"On a scale from one to ten, with ten being phenomenal," Maria started.

"Don't ask me that," Jenn protested. "I'm not going to answer. It would be crass and undignified."

"I'll take that as an eleven," Maria said.

"No comment."

"What's that you're implying? A never before reported twelve?!"

Jenn laughed. "Stop. I'm not doing this."

"May I change the subject?"

"Please."

"Are you sure? It's to something much less pleasant than fabulous sex with unbelievably hot guys."

"*Please,*" Jenn said. "Change the subject, already."

"Sam Starrett's broken rib," Maria stated.

Jenn sat up. "Yeah. I saw that bruise. Did it happen in the tussle with the homeless psycho-killer guy?"

"No, it did not." Maria had on her super-serious face. "Jenni, Mick Callahan did it."

"*What?*"

Maria nodded. "Jenn, I know you like him, but there's been something . . . off with him, right from the start. He freaks me out."

"Because he's in love with you," Jenn said.

"This isn't just socially awkward unrequited love," her friend told her. "He really clashed with Alyssa in the office today—while you were out showing the SEAL squad my apartment. You were probably getting jiggy with Dan Gillman underneath my bed. Which also freaks me out, but not as much."

"I was *not* getting jiggy with anyone," Jenn said. "It wasn't until later that . . . Never mind what happened *when*. Mick clashed with Alyssa how?"

"To start with, they just both really rubbed each other the wrong way," Maria said. "Alyssa got kind of icy while Mick went directly to pretty rude. And then, when she came into my office to talk to me, he said some things about her, to Sam, that were shocking."

"To *Sam*?" Jenn couldn't believe it. "What is Mick? An idiot?"

"He claims he didn't know they were married," Maria said. "But I don't know what to believe anymore when he's around."

"God," Jenn said. "And what about Sam? I know he's a friend of Savannah's, but why do we just trust what *he* says over—"

"Jenn, Sam was leaving a voice mail to Jules Cassidy, and everything Mick said to him about Alyssa was recorded."

And *that* would be a good reason why they believed Sam over Mick.

"It was ugly and misogynistic and violent," Maria continued. "Sam lost his temper and pinned Mick to the wall, which got kind of noisy, so we came out, and there they were, and then Alyssa said *stop*, so Sam let him go, at which point Mick actually drew his gun—"

"Seriously?" Jenn said. She closed her mouth. She'd been sitting there with it open.

"I was there," Maria told her. "He made Sam get on the floor, hands on his head, the whole perp position, you know? And when he was down there? That's when Mick kicked him and broke his rib."

Oh, God, no . . .

"I saw him do it, Jenni," Maria continued. "It was vicious. I know you like him, but we need to put some distance between him and us. I don't want him coming into the office anymore. He makes me uncomfortable."

"Mick's a constituent," Jenn pointed out. "I don't think we can—"

"I don't want him coming in to see *you*," Maria rephrased her request. "He's just pretending to be friends with you—"

"He is not."

True, Jenn hadn't known Mick for all that long, but their friendship was the instant kind. Mere days after they'd first laid eyes on one another, she'd bumped into him in the bookstore. They'd ended up at O'Brien's, a local bar, where he'd told her all kinds of tales, both harrowing and funny, of life as a New York City cop.

"Okay, fine," Maria said, although she clearly didn't believe it. "He's not pretending. But this latest incident was too much. Don't encourage him."

"Are you telling me that, as my boss—"

"No," Maria said. "As your friend. And I will kick your butt if you go out with him again to that bar where he drinks, which I *know* that he does too much and too often, and you, of all people, should know better than to go there with him."

"I just . . . I like him," Jenn defended herself. "He's a good person—"

"Jenni, you didn't see him—"

"Who isn't perfect," Jenn continued, "and doesn't always make the right choices. His job is impossible—"

"He told Sam that what Alyssa needed was a good gang bang."

Oh, Mick. Jenn sighed. "He can be a real jerk, but I'm sure he didn't mean it."

"Then he shouldn't've said it," Maria countered. "Will you please do me a favor and not call him anymore? At least not until the FBI catches Maggie's killer."

Jenn looked at her. "You don't actually think that Mick . . . ?"

"You should've seen him," Maria said again. "Frankly, I don't know what to think. He's on my list of suspects."

"Maria, come on, he's a *cop*!"

"Well, Jules and Alyssa asked me about relationships, and Mick's asked me out about four million times in a very short amount of time. He actually cornered me—on Thursday—in my office. You weren't there and . . . I honestly didn't know what he was going to do. Thank God Douglas came in. Which was awkward, because I'm not sure *he* didn't think he was interrupting something mutual but inappropriate. But my point here is that Mick makes me uncomfortable. Plus he's got a better motive than some crazy homeless man."

"Crazy is motive enough," Jenn said.

"But crazy plus motive needs to be investigated."

"What's Mick's motive?" Jenn asked. "Spurned suitor?"

"It's a classic," Maria pointed out, "on the motive's list of greatest hits."

"He's going to love being investigated," Jenn told her.

"It's his fault," Maria said, "for being mean and vicious. Just promise me that you'll—"

"I promise," Jenn said, lying back on the bed again. "I'll keep my distance. God."

They sat—and lay—in silence for several long moments, then Maria said, "Assuming I don't end up with my heart in, like, the mayor's assistant's desk drawer—"

"Don't say that!" Horrified, Jenn turned her head to look at her friend. "You're safe, and we're going to make sure that you stay safe."

"Assuming that we do," Maria said, "do you honestly think that an unmarried woman, or even a married woman without children, could ever get elected President?"

Jenn sat up again. Where had *that* come from? "I'm not sure of anything," she answered, "since we haven't gotten as far as *woman* yet. Although I'd bet the big bucks that having a family could be extremely important to some of the more conservative voters."

"And I don't have one," Maria pointed out the obvious.

"I said *could be*," Jenn pointed out. "And *some*."

"If I'm going to have a baby," Maria said, "I should have one soon. Before we position me for the senate run."

"All this talk of crazy people," Jenn said, "is making you crazy."

"I'm just trying," Maria said, "to make sense of all of this. Everything happens for a reason, doesn't it?"

"Except for the things that happen for absolutely no reason," Jenn countered. "Of which there are an awful lot in this whacked-out world."

"But what if my being targeted like this, and what if Maggie's murder," her voice shook, "for which I will never forgive myself—"

"Maria, my God, honey, this isn't your fault," Jenn interrupted her. "Not at all. You didn't ask for this, you don't deserve it, and you are absolutely *not* responsible for it."

Maria nodded, as if she were trying to convince the emotional part of her to embrace what her logical side surely already knew to be true. "It feels like my fault," she said quietly.

"It's not."

"But what if," Maria said, "something good can come from it? Like you and Dan."

"Okay," Jenn said, "I don't think the whole twelve on a scale from one to ten thing really counts as something good coming from Maggie's murder."

"But what if you fall in love with him," Maria persisted. "Dan. And what if he falls in love with you—"

"That's not going to happen," Jenn told her. The second part, anyway. The first part—what if she fell in love with Dan—was already dangerously close to moving from possibility to reality. Oh, God, she was in trouble here. And if that first part happened without the second part, that wasn't exactly good news either.

"But it's not impossible," Maria said, and she was so fierce in her hope, in her belief that light could come from darkness, that Jenn couldn't bring herself to argue.

"You're right," she agreed. "It's not impossible."

It was, however, very, *very* highly unlikely.

Hospital bed number 14C held a weeping, vomiting toddler and her extremely concerned parents.

"Excuse me," Jules said as he knocked softly upon the door and leaned into the tiny room. "I'm so sorry to bother you, but . . . have you been in here long?"

"About an hour and still no doctor," the girl's mother said grimly.

"An hour." Jules looked at Alyssa, and then tried to intercept a nurse. "Excuse me . . . I'm sorry, would you tell me . . ."

The nurse sped past him.

The emergency room here at St. Sebastian's was crowded. The waiting room was wall-to-wall people of all ages, from crying babies to gangbangers to dazed-looking elderly men and women—all jockeying for their chance to see a doctor.

When Jules had called, he was told that their John Doe—a homeless man brought in with a possible head injury—was in bed 14C.

There was no sign, either, of the FBI agents who had been sent in from the New York City office to guard him or take him in for questioning, should he be released from the hospital.

Another aide approached, pushing a computer on a rattle-wheeled cart, and Jules tried again. "Excuse me." He leaned in to read the name tag pinned to her chest. "Ms. Duddy. Pam."

"Can't stop," she told him.

But he stepped in front of her, and it was stop or run him down. She stopped. She was in her early forties, with a sweet, round face that broadcasted her exhaustion. She was clearly overworked and overwhelmed and she sighed her exasperation. "Sir . . ."

"Nice socks," Jules said, and Alyssa looked down to see that she was, indeed, wearing unusual socks—adorned with little dolphins. She also had a *Mister Spock Rocks* sticker on her computer cart, along with another that said *Fan of All Things Joss*.

"I really can't stop," the woman told Jules.

"Maybe not for a fellow *Buffy* fan," he said as he took out his ID and held it out to her with an apologetic smile. "But for the FBI?"

That got him her full attention.

Particularly when he added, "We're looking for the man who's supposed to be in fourteen C, because we think he might be connected to a murder in which a woman's heart was cut from her chest."

"Connected to?" Pam Duddy asked.

"As in he might be the killer," Jules told her. "Which is why we're kind of perturbed that he's not actually *in* bed fourteen C."

He pointed to the occupied bed, and she pulled her cart out of the stream of traffic.

"What's the patient name?" she asked.

"You have him as Doe, John."

She shot him a humorous look. "Oh, good," she said, fingers moving across her keyboard, "that makes it so much easier. We have seven different Does, Johns tonight. He was brought in . . . what time?"

"Around twenty hundred," Alyssa said, translating to civilian, "Eight P.M."

"This him?" she asked, spinning her laptop to face them.

There was a slightly blurry digital photo of the man that Sam had dubbed Don Quixote in the right corner of her computer screen. He was on a gurney and unconscious, his eyes closed, but . . . "That's our man," Alyssa confirmed.

Pam pulled her computer back around, and typed in several commands and . . . "Got him," she said. "He's in . . . bed fourteen C, which is what you already knew. Sorry. I'm not finding . . ." She looked up from her computer, an apology in her warm blue eyes. "Here's what we do know: He wasn't released. At least not officially. He might have done what we call a self-release. Also known as a walk-away."

"Has the hospital been this busy all night?" Alyssa asked, as Jules took out his phone.

"Yes, and sir, there are medical reasons why you can't use that in here. We're not just being difficult, I promise you."

"Sorry," Jules said, adding, "Thank you so much for your help, Pam." With a keep-talking-to-her nod at Alyssa, he headed back out into the waiting area. He was, no doubt, calling his contact at the FBI headquarters, hoping that the confusion was only on the hospital's end.

Although he was supposed to have gotten a call, should the homeless man be taken into FBI or police custody.

Pam looked as if she were getting her computer cart ready to roll, so Alyssa stepped forward to block her path. "Do you get many indigent patients here?" she asked.

"We're one of the few hospitals in this part of town that takes them," Pam told her. "So again, yes. But we don't go to Herculean efforts to keep them from wandering off."

"Is it possible he's doing his wandering in the hospital?" Alyssa asked.

"That's unlikely," she said. "With his wrist bracelet on,

he'd be easily ID'd as an ER patient, and brought back down here."

"Unless everyone's too busy," Alyssa pointed out, but Pam shook her head.

"With that hair, wearing a hospital gown . . . ? He's gonna get noticed," she said.

"Is it possible he was moved to another location in the hospital, or even to another hospital, but the transfer's not in your records?"

"Anything's possible," the woman said in a tone that was heavy with *no way*, "but our system's pretty good. I can check with the nurse's station, see if they know anything—"

But Jules was already coming back, his normally cheerful face a complete thundercloud.

Pam correctly read his expression, too. "Or . . . we'll certainly keep an eye out, and let you know if he comes back."

"We'll be issuing a BOLO," Jules said, having overheard her. "And an APB."

"Good luck finding him," the woman said, and took the opportunity to escape, rattling her cart away.

"What happened?" Alyssa asked Jules, who was already leading the way back to the lobby.

But he didn't answer until they'd made their way out of the front doors and into the street.

It was still snowing, so Alyssa pulled her hat back on. Jules had earmuffs. As high-level FBI, he couldn't risk getting hat hair. Or so he claimed.

"What happened?" she asked again.

"They were delayed getting here—the agents who were assigned to make sure our John Doe didn't go anywhere," he reported. "They were coming in from Queens, and a semi jackknifed on 495. They were stuck in traffic, so they called the hospital and spoke to a nurse who told them our man wasn't going anywhere. Except he did. When they arrived, his bed was empty. They didn't call me, because they didn't think he'd go far. They expected to find him. But . . . they didn't. And go on. Ask me what I know you're dying to ask me. Why, dear Jules, didn't they think he'd go far?"

Alyssa didn't have to ask, but she made it a question anyway. "Because he left without his clothes?"

"Correct! Ten points to the woman in the funny hat." Jules was furious about this. "Our man is now wandering Manhattan in a knee-length hospital gown with his ass hanging out, two very thin blankets around his shoulders, and a pair of paper booties on his feet."

It was cold tonight and getting colder. As if to punctuate her thought, the wind whipped down the city street, rocking a sign.

"Are they still looking for him?" Alyssa asked. It was a relatively stupid question, considering how angry Jules was. In fact, it was likely that every available person in the local Bureau office was getting called in to assist in the search. The real question was, "How can we help?"

"I'm going to hit the local subway stations," Jules said, heading briskly down the sidewalk. "Although if he got on a train, he could be anywhere."

"If he got on a train," Alyssa said, scrambling to keep up, "at least he's warm."

"Why do I care?" Jules asked, talking more to himself than her. "If he killed Maggie Thorndyke, freezing to death would be letting him off easy."

"Because if he *didn't* kill Maggie," Alyssa answered anyway, "and I don't think you believe he did, anymore than I do—then he's just another wounded vet who sacrificed nearly everything for our country, and you don't want him to die in the street. What I can't figure out is why he'd have my picture."

"Because you're pretty?" Jules said. "Oh and nice tits, by the way, I've been meaning to say that."

She went to smack him, but he danced, laughing, out of the way.

"Sorry," he said, "I couldn't resist. Seriously though, that photo *is* a nice one. Maybe *too* nice. It's from the TS website, right? Maybe you should ask Tom to pull it down."

Alyssa nodded. "I've already spoken to Tracy about it. She's going to take all of the personnel photos off the site."

"Judging from the length of our John Doe's beard and hair," Jules said, "I think it's safe to guess he's been on the street for a while. Do you agree? That, like, he's not some wealthy stockbroker or computer programmer who's recently gone off his meds?"

"I would guess that he's not, yes," Alyssa said. "His teeth were in bad shape. And his skin . . . ? Let's just say he's sporting years of harsh weather and neglect."

"So where does he get anything that he has?" Jules asked. "His winter coat? His collection of beer-bottle tops?"

Not only had Sam found beer tops in his pockets, but Jenn had also said that he'd had quite a few in an old sock he'd left in her car.

Bottle tops, a small pile of military ribbons, some Monopoly game pieces, several shiny stones . . .

"He gets it from the Salvation Army," Alyssa said, "or from a freebies box at a shelter."

"Or he goes through the trash," Jules pointed out. "Jenn said she'd seen him diving the dumpster outside Maria's office. We should check with Savannah, see if she had a picture of you, maybe to show to Maria."

"Back in September?" Alyssa asked.

"Maybe they were talking about hiring additional security," Jules suggested. "So she had your picture, but they went another route, it got thrown out, and our homeless guy found it and kept it."

Alyssa shook her head. "Why would he keep it?"

"Because you're pretty," Jules said again. "Or maybe because he has a daughter or granddaughter who's about your age, and he likes pretending that picture is of her."

"I don't know," Alyssa said. "It's all just so weird."

"Check with Savannah," Jules said.

"I don't know—"

"Another possibility," Jules pointed out, "is that the whole homeless guy thing is an act, a costume that he puts on. And he's really some diabolical and insanely wealthy—and insane—killer who's been tracking you for years. And he didn't wander off from the hospital. He escaped, and his trusty minion picked him up in his Rolls Royce and took him back to his mansion, where he's plotting against you as we speak."

"But of course, you're really Batman, so you'll stop him."

"It has been suggested," Jules noted, "that I could be Batman."

"I'm liking the first scenario better and better," Alyssa admitted.

"Then call Savannah," he said again.

"I will. Hey! I thought we were searching the subway stations."

Jules had stepped to the curb and neatly hailed a cab. He opened the door and gestured for her to get in. "*I'm* doing that. You're going back to the hotel to feed your giant, hungry, adorable baby. Sam made me promise I wouldn't keep you out past pumpkin-time. He said if I didn't send you back you'd ruin another shirt, and we can't have that." He turned to the driver. "Hilton Hotel, West Fifty-third and Sixth." Back to Alyssa. "Go back, make sure Sam's okay, too. Although if he needs a hospital, we're not coming back to St. Whatsis. Oh, and tell Robin I'm about two hours behind you. If I'm going to be later than that, I'll call."

"I'm not leaving you," Alyssa said.

"I'm a gay man, trolling subway stations in Manhattan," he said. "What could go wrong?"

"That's supposed to make me feel better—"

"It was a joke, oh, humorless one," he said. "I'm meeting a team from the Transit Police, they're going to take me to a couple of popular subterranean homeless hangouts. Hey, when you were a kid, you ever watch that show, *Beauty and the Beast,* with Linda Hamilton?"

"The woman from the *Terminator* movies, yeah." Alyssa had. "My sister was *really* into it."

"If this were an episode," Jules told her, "I'd be indoctrinated as one of the mutant underground people and given a hobo name, like . . . Hot Potato Two Shoes, and be forced to choose between my loyalty to my new brethren, and my life up above. FYI, hands down I'm picking my life up above. Unless, of course, I find out that all along, Robin has secretly been a mutant, too. In which case, I'll communicate with you in the future via whispered messages through the sewer drains."

"I thought you were Batman," she said, laughing despite her trepidation.

"Are we getting in or are we talking?" the taxi driver asked petulantly.

"She's getting in," Jules said, and Alyssa reluctantly did just that.

"Be careful," she told him.

He nodded. "I'll call you if we find him."

CHAPTER THIRTEEN

It had been a long time since he'd seen them—his *mère et papa*.

It was stupid of them to make him speak French at home. Spanish would have served him better. But they'd never known what to do with him. He'd arrived late in his father's life—an unexpected and unwanted surprise.

His mother was already dying. The cancer that killed her had started before he'd appeared in her womb.

He wondered sometimes if it was that, the death that had already claimed her, that touched him and marked him, an unborn babe, for its own.

He was barely two months old when she'd died.

His nannies, of which there were many, never stayed for long. His father couldn't keep his pants zipped. He'd heard one of them say as much, as she angrily packed her bag, long before he understood what the words meant.

His father had finally married one of them—his *mère*—but she was more interested in his father's money than in his child, and she hired more nannies to care for him while she shopped.

As the years passed, he'd learned to move silently about the rambling old house, exploring its basements and attics, but spending most of his time in the windowless Prohibition Room, built during the 1920s.

He'd learned to speak French, and to avoid the biting and scratching of his *mère*'s angry, spiteful cat, Monsieur Henri, and he'd learned that school was a place to be taunted and abused—unless you were the taunter and abuser.

He'd learned he was very good at both.

When he was twelve, they'd shipped him off to boarding school after they found the box that he'd kept in the crawl space in the basement. It held what was left of Monsieur Henri, gone missing four years earlier, and his replacements, Tinkerbell and Jolie.

Even then, he'd loved their teeth, loved that they would try to bite him as they screamed in pain.

It was his fault for not hiding his box well enough, and he'd learned from it, learned that he must keep his secrets more carefully hidden.

At first he'd gone home for the occasional rare holiday, until Suzette, *Mère*'s new poodle—a vicious little thing that barked and snarled at him incessantly—was hit by a car in the busy street in front of their house.

It wasn't his fault that she'd raced out the door every chance she could get. Although it *might* have been his fault that he'd held the door open. . . .

They'd sent him to doctors, who recommended they ship him off to a school for troubled youth—where he'd learned, even better, to hide his secrets from the world. And then they'd set up a generous trust fund for him, available upon graduation from college, on the condition that he not come home again.

A condition he'd kept, until last year.

His *mère* didn't recognize him when she opened the door.

He'd told her he was from the bank, that there was an identity theft problem. There were papers she and her husband would need to sign immediately.

She'd welcomed him in, and together with his father—a

stinking old man in a wheelchair, peering at him through cracked and grimy glasses—signed papers that gave him, their only son, power of attorney.

It was only after that, that she recognized him.

He'd made sure of it.

"No . . . *No!* Listen to me!"

That was Gillman's voice, low but urgent, from out in the living room.

Izzy was instantly awake and sitting up—and damn near knocking himself out by hitting his head on the bottom of the conference table. Mother*fucker*. And it had seemed like such a good idea to put his sleeping bag under here.

He kicked his legs free as he scrambled toward the door that he'd purposely left open.

It was Lopez who'd asked him to play the selfish asshole and claim this room for his own. It was also Lopez who'd been the mediator for the dispute that followed, and who'd made the decree that Lopez, Tony and Izzy would all share the conference room floor, in between their shifts guarding the suite, while lucky Gillman would get to sleep on the comfort of the couch.

It was, absolutely, a concerted effort to keep the Fish-boy from taking sweet Jennilyn by the hand, and locking her in here with him. Lopez thought, and Izzy had to agree, that the two lovebirds might benefit from a night of enforced apart-ness, which really translated into time for Jenn to come to her scattered senses. Assuming she had any.

Also assuming that getting banged by Danny was something she really didn't want to do—which was a very big assumption Lopez was making here.

It was entirely possible that knocking knobs with Gilligan was no big thing for her, and that Fleet Week was her mostest favorite-est time of year.

"You get the *fuck* back over here!" Danny said from the sofa as Izzy approached. The lamp on the far end table was on—he'd clearly fallen asleep with it burning. He wasn't shouting yet, but his mutterings were getting louder and more clear.

Lopez had said that Dan had been having nightmares, and if they were anything like the ones Izzy had had a few years back, dude was going to scream the place awake, and then, when the lights were blazing and everyone was staring, he'd be sitting there, shaking and sweating, with tears icing the cake of the *what planet is this again?* expression that was all over his bewildered face.

"I don't give a good goddamn!"

"Hey, man," Izzy said as he got closer, because it seemed like a good idea not to startle him, Dan being a Navy SEAL and all. He wasn't quite sure the best way to do this—to shake him awake, or to turn on another light, tell him a joke, sing him a song . . .

Lopez probably knew, but he was out in the hall. Vlachic was no help, since he was making use of his non-watch time by meeting up with Mr. Serious, elsewhere in this very hotel—lucky bastard, gettin' some.

Alyssa still wasn't back from wherever it was she'd gone with Jules, and there was no sound or movement from behind any of the three tightly shut bedroom doors.

Izzy tried again. "Hey. Earth to Gillman."

Dan sat up—a shadowy, backlit shape on the couch. Although he didn't get louder, his voice was a ferociously menacing growl. "Keep your fucking hands offa her, you piece of shit!"

Ooo-kay.

That was a little too weird—like Dan was going to start speaking in tongues, or maybe his head was going to spin completely around, or his eyes were going to glow bright red-orange with an unholy flame. . . .

Izzy turned on the other lamp that was right next to him. "Yo, Dan-o. Wake—"

"No, you know, I *don't* believe you—"

"Up." The additional light didn't seem to work to rouse him, although that really hadn't been its purpose. It was doing just fine, though, in its job of assuring Izzy that Dan wasn't in the throes of demonic possession. At least not yet.

"Dan. Look at me, bro."

His eyes were open, but unfocused. He was in some crazy kind of deep sleep.

Maybe if Izzy just kept talking to him . . .

"You know, back when I was little," he said, sitting down across from the couch, in the chair that swiveled, "When I was around eight—and pretty much right up until I turned twelve—I was a sleepwalker. To this day, my brothers won't let me forget this one time I got out of bed. They were all still up, watching TV—they were older than me. And my mother's like, *What's that sound?* It was this crinkling noise, like plastic being wrinkled or shaken, and she gets up to see WTF. Turns out it's moi, young Irving, fast asleep, and taking a whiz into the kitchen trash."

Dan was silent—no more muttering—but he still didn't give Izzy any eye contact.

So Izzy kept going. "I continue to point out—whenever they bring it up, which they do, like, every fucking time they see me—that it was better that I chose the trash over my brother Martin's sock drawer, right?"

He'd actually stopped his sleepwalking through sheer will when he hit the early stages of puberty. God forbid he wander the house—filled with his brothers and their various girlfriends and wives—in his thin PJ pants, with one of his relentless tweenage boners.

"You couldn't pay me enough money," Izzy told Gillman, "to make me go back and be a twelve-year-old again."

Still nothing.

"Why don't you lie down, Dan, and get some sleep," Izzy suggested.

No movement.

He tried again, pitching his voice higher. Because maybe if he made himself sound like Dan's mommy . . . "Go back to sleep, honey. Everything's okay. Daddy and I can't plan our surprise trip to Disneyland unless you're in beddy-bye."

Nada.

So Izzy moved onto the floor in front of Gillman and tried a little physical contact. Just a hand against Dan's T-shirt-clad shoulder as he leaned in to try to catch his eye . . .

Big mistake.

Gillman came to life with a move that pushed Izzy's hand away, even as he lunged forward, slamming Izzy into both the chair and the coffee table, taking him down to the carpeted floor with a shout and a crash that also took out both lamps—how the hell had he managed *that*?—and plunged them into darkness.

"Get your fucking hands off me, douche bag!"

Whether Gillman knew who he was wrestling with or not, Izzy didn't take the time to find out. He had almost two inches and quite a few pounds on Gillman, but that didn't exactly make for an easy contest. Izzy may have had clarity about where he was and even *who* he was, but Gillman had his nightmare-induced rage. And that was assuming he'd even truly emerged from his dream-world.

Besides, Izzy wasn't looking to beat the crap out of Gillman. In fact, he was working hard *not* to hurt the foo'—as well as to not get hurt *by* him. Yes, he liked his testicles right where they were, thanks, so he struggled and rolled and pinned and finally got Gillman into a headlock with his left arm, while using his legs to trap the other man in place.

It was like holding onto a beached shark, or maybe wrestling an alligator, only Izzy was also trying his damnedest to not trash the hotel furniture.

"Gillman, you're safe," he tried to tell him, "you're okay, Danny, come on, come on, come *on,* will you chill, you fucking idiot?"

Those last few words seemed to echo, because the lights went on—all of 'em, not just one little lamp. It was suddenly blazingly bright, and just like that, Danny stopped fighting him. He was looking up and . . . Izzy turned to see Sam Starrett's incredibly angry-looking bruise, and yes, Sam's equally angry face not too far above it.

"What," Sam said, "the *fuck* . . . ?"

He wasn't the only one who'd come out of their room at the sound of the mêlée. Robin was there, too, his eyebrows raised. And Maria—looking more beautiful than a woman had a right to, with night cream on her face. And there, indeed, was wide-eyed Jenn, and yes, even Lopez had come in from the hall.

He stood there, just shaking his head, radiating disappointment.

"And you were there, and you were there, and *you* were there . . ." Izzy said, because there were just too few times in life when quoting from *The Wizard of Oz* worked so beautifully. He added "Ow!" as Gillman elbowed him in the gut.

He let go of the other man, who scrambled away from him, looking about as shell-shocked as Izzy had ever seen him.

And, shit, the whole sweating and shaking thing that Izzy had been trying to avoid was happening. In fact,

Danny looked as if he were in danger of barfing, right on the rug.

"It was my fault," Izzy quickly announced, so that the asshole didn't have to endure the added humiliation of copping to a nightmare of epic proportions. "Completely. I should know better than to ask Gillman about Eden—you know, his sister and my, um, wife? When we're both tired, it gets . . . Well, you see how it gets. I just . . . I haven't heard from her in a really long time, and I couldn't sleep and he was still awake, so . . . I made the mistake of asking him. I'm sorry, sir and . . ." He looked at Dan. "Sorry. Dan."

The look Gillman shot him was one that Izzy had never seen before, and couldn't quite read. Was that gratitude for covering for him, or horror that he now owed Izzy a great big one, or was it just stunned hatred? It was hard to tell. Perhaps a mix of all three . . .

But Gillman then glanced up at Sam. "I'm sorry, too, sir." He included the others. "I'm sorry we woke you. It won't happen again."

"Damn straight it won't," Sam told them both. "Stay away from each other. This *does* happen again? I'll send you both home."

"Yes, sir," Izzy said, as Dan echoed him.

"And," Sam continued, "you might want to send up a thank you to whichever god you pray to, that you clowns didn't wake up Ashton."

But of course, as if on cue, from the other room, the baby began his siren-like wail. It started low, but quickly grew in both volume and intensity.

The look on Sam's face almost made Izzy laugh. Almost.

Instead he got to his feet. "Sir, if you want, I'd be happy to take care of—"

"You're bleeding," Sam said tersely, and went back to

deal with the kid, closing the door none-too-gently behind him.

Bleeding?

Izzy did a quick inventory of all of the places that made him go *owie,* and discovered that he was, indeed, bleeding. His elbow was rug-burned like a son of a bitch, the skin broken and oozing blood. Not a lot, but enough.

He retreated back toward the conference room, unwilling to be in Sam's line of sight in the event that he came back out.

Robin, too, had vanished into his room, and Lopez had returned to his post. But Maria lingered. "You should clean that out. You need help?"

Wacka-chicka-wacka-chicka. If life were porn . . . But it wasn't. She was just being nice, and elbows were a bitch to see.

"Nah, I'm good with the bathroom mirror," he told her. "This is not my first scraped elbow."

She smiled at that. "I didn't think it was. Dan Gillman's really your brother-in-law?"

"Yes, he is." Izzy glanced over to where Jenn was talking to Danny. He was back sitting on the couch, his body language almost as shut down as it had been when he was sound asleep. "It's been the source of some friction. Truth is, he didn't like me very much to start with, so . . ."

"Ah," she said. "And there you were, you know . . . Mmphing his sister."

"Mmphing?" he repeated, delighted.

She smiled back at him, and quite possibly even blushed a little. "There are certain words a politician should never say."

"Even when they're mmphing?" He couldn't resist asking, but to his complete surprise, as she laughed, she actually held his gaze longer than she should have.

In fact, he was the one who looked away first. He tried to see his elbow again, and used it as an excuse. "I should, um, go and . . ."

Across the room, Dan and Jenn's conversation was over, too. Izzy wondered if he and Maria looked as stiff and awkward standing there.

"Good night," Maria said, and he nodded, but then she added, "For the record, if you got sent back home, I'd be disappointed."

Izzy looked up at her, surprised, but she was already heading for her room, and she didn't look back.

As Jules closed the taxi door, the cab lurched away from the curb. Alyssa fastened her seat belt, then checked her messages on her phone.

Max had called with more information about the job in Afghanistan. Her boss at Troubleshooters, Tom Paoletti, had left a long message, too, about the very same thing.

And . . . oh, good. Detective Mick Callahan had called, four different times, but he'd left only one message.

"What the hell is going on?" his voice was raspy with anger, his speech slightly slurred, as if he'd been drinking. "Suddenly *I'm* under investigation? Do you know how badly that jams me up? I got guys from my own house looking at me sideways, as well as I-fucking-A coming in on Monday to *evaluate* whether or not I need a fucking round of sensitivity training. *This* is the thanks I get for walking away from an assault?"

It took her a second to translate I-fucking-A as IA, which was short for Internal Affairs. Every police department had a division whose focus was to shine a spotlight onto their own, to ferret out possible wrongdoing. And while Jules had told her that he'd kept his promise and hadn't released the voice mail with Mick's *Nice tits* rant to the detective's superiors, he *had* sent over a request for an evaluation and review.

"Make this go away," Mick's message continued. "You are going to make this go away, you understand? Or I will have that asswipe husband of yours in jail so fast, your head will fucking spin."

Click.

Well, wasn't that just fabulous?

Mick Callahan was a drunk dialer. How charming.

It was still relatively early out in California, so Alyssa punched in Savannah's number. The call went right to voice mail, and she left a message asking about that photograph.

As she put her phone away, she noticed that the cab had come to a complete dead stop in rush-hour-worthy traffic. Of course, they were on a one-way cross street that *was* only one lane wide.

"Is this theater traffic?" she asked the driver. They weren't too far from the hotel, which was near both the theater district and Times Square. But as she looked at her watch again, she realized it was too late for that. The theaters had let out well over an hour ago. In the distance, she could hear approaching sirens.

"Accident," the taxi driver reported.

She opened her wallet. "I'll get out here."

The night air was cold, and the street *was* slippery as she made her way to the sidewalk. And yes, she could see that there was a multicar fender bender completely blocking the intersection.

As she got closer to the hotel, she realized that she was approaching it from the back. This time of night, for security reasons, she'd have to enter through the front doors into the main lobby, and show her key card to a guard.

Which meant that, for security reasons—oh, the irony—she was going to have to walk another block and a half along streets that were suddenly empty.

Alyssa didn't have what she thought of as a high fear factor, but for some reason, tonight her spidey senses—as

Jules would have called them—were tingling. Maybe it was the cold, or maybe the uncertain footing of the ice- and snow-covered sidewalks, but she was on edge, unable to shake the feeling that someone was following her. So she straightened up, walking taller.

Not that she couldn't kick the butt of anyone who tried to mug her. And not that anyone was actually out here, following her. Nothing was moving and the only sound was that of her own feet, crunching in the snow.

Still, the best time to stop a mugging was before it happened. And it definitely helped for a woman walking alone down an empty street to walk with shoulders back, head high. To look more like Superwoman with a don't-mess-with-me attitude than a weak, helpless victim.

And to be aware of all the places where someone, about to jump out at her, might hide.

Between two parked cars.

From the alleyways, and even from darkened entrances of businesses that had closed shop for the night.

Most merchants had metal shields that went down over their windows and doors, but one of them, just up ahead, hadn't locked the rolling awning-like metal to its anchors in the sidewalk. It was up slightly, just enough for someone to crawl into and . . . Okay, paranoid much?

If someone were hiding there, they were lying on the cold cement of the sidewalk, and *had* been lying there at least since Alyssa had turned onto this block. They also would have left footprints in the snow. Which they hadn't.

Still, she picked up her pace as she went past. Another quarter block and she'd turn the corner, and the hotel entrance should be right . . . there . . .

It was. It was well lit and there were signs of life— taxis and a cold-looking bellman unloading a late arrival's luggage onto a cart.

Alyssa stamped the snow off her boots, went through the revolving door, flashed her key card at the guard, took off her hat, and headed across the lobby to the bank of elevators, which was over by the bar.

"Alyssa Locke. I was hoping to run into you."

She turned, and yes, it was none other than Mick Callahan—a bottle of beer in his hand.

"What are you doing here, Detective?" She kept her voice cool and unemotional.

"Looking for you," he said, with a smile that had, no doubt, charmed a lot of women. He *was* a nice-looking man, and had, also no doubt, learned from an early age to use his appearance to his advantage.

Funny how it was okay for a man to do that, but for a woman . . . ? The double irony was that Callahan himself would lead the angry mob, pitchfork in hand, to discredit any such woman for being calculating, manipulative, and insincere.

And a ho. He'd also call her a ho.

"Who told you we'd be staying here?" she asked.

"My lieutenant," he said, his smile slipping somewhat, and she knew that was a lie. Jules had spoken to his lieutenant, who had immediately agreed to keep Callahan away from the case. So the detective must have gone to some trouble to access the report that contained their current contact information.

"He thinks the idea that I'm a suspect in your murder is bullshit, too," Callahan added.

"*My* murder?" she said.

He laughed. "Whoopsie. What's that called when that happens . . . ? A Freudian slip."

Alyssa called it being drunk and a complete fool. Although his speech wasn't as slurred as she'd expected it to be. It actually wasn't all that much worse than it had been when he'd left that message on her cell.

Of course, everyone got their drunk on in their own unique way.

And she knew that, in his current state, talking to him

about any of this—even calling him out on his lie about getting their hotel information from his lieutenant—was a waste of her time.

"You'll have to excuse me," she said. "It's been a long day. I suggest you call it a night, too. There are plenty of cabs out front."

"Yeah," he said. "Yes. I am going to . . . I didn't come here to . . . I, um, just wanted . . ." He cleared his throat. "How 'bout I ride up with you? That way I can say what I came to say and . . ."

She was shaking her head. Not a chance. "You can tell me tomorrow."

But one of the elevators opened with a ding, and he gestured toward it. "I don't mind."

Alyssa didn't move, and before she could rephrase *no fucking way* into a less Sam-like and more diplomatic statement, Callahan realized, "You don't want to be alone in an elevator with me. Am I right? I'm *right*. You actually think I might've killed that woman . . . ?"

"You've had way too much to drink, so, yes, I'm not interested in going anywhere with you," she said. "As for what I think . . . You'll have the opportunity tomorrow to provide the FBI investigators with an alibi."

"Which," he said tightly, "I don't happen to have. I was home—under the weather. Stomach flu. I took a coupla sick days."

"Really," she said. Stomach flu or hung over? "You seem well enough now to have a beer. Or twenty."

"Yes," he said earnestly. "Yes, okay. I *have* had too much to drink tonight. And I shouldn't have called your cell phone and left that message. I was really angry at the time, but I've had some time to cool off and, you know, think about it, and I, um, came here to, um, apologize. Both to you and your asshole husband—and okay, you probably don't think he's an asshole because you married him. Or maybe you do and you're sick of his bullshit.

But, all right. I shouldn't have said what I said about you, even if it's true. The, you know, *nice tits* part."

Good God. *This* was an apology?

He realized that perhaps he shouldn't have said that. "Sorry. I'm just . . ." He started over. "I've been having some personal issues lately, and my judgment's been a little . . . off."

You *think*?

He staggered slightly, and Alyssa knew that any minute he was going to start crying on her shoulder. His second—no, make that his *fifth* wife had left him. Growing up, his family life had been awful. He'd lost all of his savings in the recent stock market crash. . . .

"Go home, Detective," Alyssa said again. "You want to try again with your apology at the meeting with the FBI investigator? I'll certainly be willing to listen. But right now, you're not doing yourself any favors."

Another elevator opened, and he backed away, seemingly genuinely apologetic.

So Alyssa got on, and he still didn't move, except to say, "I *am* sorry."

But right before the elevator doors closed completely, she heard him mutter, "Fucking bitch," so that *seemingly* was in serious question.

Shaking her head, she used her key card to access the VIP floor where they were staying, checking her phone to see if maybe she'd missed Savannah's return call, due to slipping into one of New York City's many dead cell zones.

But no. She put her phone back into her pocket as the elevator opened, and she got out.

Jay Lopez was sitting in the hall outside the entrance to their suite, and he stood up respectfully as she approached, using his own key card to unlock the door.

"How can you be sure," Alyssa asked, "that I'm not some evil twin robot version of myself?"

He looked startled for a moment, but then smiled as he realized she was making a bad joke. "I'm pretty sure, ma'am, that if I worried about that particular possibility, I wouldn't be sitting out here. I'd be off trying to sign up as our Don Quixote's Sancho Panza."

Alyssa laughed. "Yeah, but first you'd have to find Don Quixote."

"Uh-oh," he said.

"Yeah," she told him. "It was not a good night."

He was holding the door open just a few inches, and he didn't open it further and she knew her *not good* was going to get worse.

Sure enough—"Zanella and Gillman mixed it up a little," Lopez reported. "Just about fifteen minutes ago. Gillman's having some . . . issues."

Terrific. Maybe Gillman and Mick Callahan could start a support group.

"I've spoken to Lt. Starrett about it, at some length," Lopez continued. "I'm sure he'll fill you in. I just wanted to give you a heads-up, ma'am."

"Thank you," Alyssa told him, as he opened the door for her.

Whatever had happened, it was now quiet. There was a single light on in the living room, and someone was in the guest bathroom. She could hear the fan running.

Two of the bedroom doors opened, and both Sam and Robin looked out at her as if they'd been waiting and listening for her return.

Well, in Robin's case, for Jules's return.

"He's a couple of hours behind me," she told him. "He's safe. He's with the Transit Police. They're looking for our John Doe, who wandered out of the hospital."

"Aw, shhhoot," Sam said as Robin said, "Thanks."

Robin closed his door as Sam opened theirs wider, and sure enough, Ash was burbling over in the portable crib that the hotel had provided.

"Hey, baby," Alyssa called to him. "Mommy's home. I'll be right there. . . ."

"Let me get some clothes on," Sam said, closing the door behind her, as she shrugged out of her jacket and went into their bathroom to wash that dreadful hospital off of her hands. "And I'll go out and find Jules. Watch his back."

Said the man who was looking a little gray-green just from the effort of getting out of bed.

He was also the man who'd used the bathroom sink to wash out not just several of Ash's onesies and bunny suits, but also the blouse Ash had spit up on, during the airline flight east. He'd hung them all neatly over the shower curtain rod—except for her blouse, which was carefully drying on a hanger.

He'd gotten the stain out, completely.

"Thank you for doing this," she told him, gesturing toward the drying laundry as she met his eyes in the mirror.

He shrugged it off. "No big. Do you want me to go . . . ?"

"No, Jules is fine. Your shirt's on inside out."

He usually didn't wear a T-shirt to bed, and it was obvious that he'd quickly pulled this one on when he'd heard her coming in.

"It looks worse than it is. The bruise," he said, not trying to play games, which was nice. "It's about as subtle as a tattoo saying *I'm an asshole.*"

"Funny, that's the very word Mick Callahan used to describe you," Alyssa told him. "He was down in the bar, waiting to ambush me."

"*Son* of a bitch," Sam said, then looked at her hard. "Are you all right?"

"Yeah," she said. "It was just . . . not what I needed."

"I'm gonna kick his ass—"

"Also not what I need," she told him. "Really, Sam.

He's coming in tomorrow to be interviewed. I want you to stay far away from him."

From out in the other room, Ash's babbling had taken on a tinge of anger.

"Na-na-nah," the baby said, with a hint of tragedy in his voice. "Ning-a-nang."

"Whoa, you hear that?" Sam asked. "He said it. *Ning-a-nang*."

Sam had told her, just yesterday, that Ash had been trying out a whole bunch of new sounds—including *ning-a-nang* when he was mad.

Alyssa hadn't quite believed him. She'd never heard Ash say anything like that. But Sam's theory was that the baby was never all that angry when his momma was around.

"Ninga-ninga-ninga-nang!" the baby shouted now, definitely PO'ed that they were taking so long to go over to him.

Alyssa had to laugh. "I heard that," she said, following Sam out of the bathroom. "What are you saying?" she asked Ash, but then nearly ran into Sam's broad back.

He'd stopped short.

Ashton had pulled himself up, so that he was standing in the portable crib, his tiny hands gripping the top rail as he gazed at them, wide-eyed—as if he couldn't quite believe what he'd managed to achieve.

"Has he done this before?" Alyssa whispered.

Sam shook his head. "Holy shit," he mouthed the word he didn't want their son to hear. He started to laugh. "He's on the verge of both talking and walking. We are *so* screwed."

CHAPTER FOURTEEN

"You okay?" Jenn asked Sam as they went up the steps into the vestry of yet another church shelter.

"I'm fine," he said shortly.

Broken-rib-day-two sucked. Although it was probably day three that was the absolute worst. At least it had been for her brother, but Jenn wasn't about to tell Sam that.

They were out and about, in the company of the youngest SEAL, Tony, searching for the homeless man who'd had Alyssa's picture. The man had gone AWOL last night, disappearing from the hospital. Despite a pretty huge search effort, he hadn't yet turned up.

Jenn was taking Sam and Tony on a tour of all the shelters and soup kitchens she'd visited, back when she was trying to return both that photo and the man's treasure-filled sock.

Their first stop had been the place where she'd actually found him back in September, but unfortunately, he wasn't there now. The volunteer workers knew him, but hadn't seen him in quite a few weeks.

So on they went.

The day had started off weird and had just kept on getting weirder.

Dan had already left the hotel by the time Jenn got up, and it wasn't as if she'd slept in.

True to his word, he'd gone with Lopez to see about putting security systems in Maria's office, as well as in both Maria's and Jenn's apartments. They were doing the actual installation themselves, with equipment that could be tied into one of the big-name security company's grids—if that's what Maria decided that she wanted. For now, all three systems were going to be connected directly to a mainframe that the Troubleshooters team would monitor from the hotel.

That seemed like relatively good news. Jenn knew that being away from both her home and office was a hardship for Maria, who took her job very seriously, and worked around the clock.

But it was the *only* good news of the morning.

The first bit of weird if not outright bad news came directly to Maria, who got a call from her father, reporting that Frank, her younger brother, had disappeared. After well over two years without leaving the house, months since he'd come out of his room, he was gone. No note, no missing clothes besides a pair of jeans, his combat boots, some long underwear, a sweater, his winter jacket and a Glock automatic pistol. Maybe a hat and gloves— Maria's parents weren't sure. The Glock, however, they *were* sure of.

It was missing from its case in their bedroom closet.

They didn't know exactly when Frank had left. Last time anyone had seen him had been quite a few days ago.

Which was before Maggie Thorndyke went missing. And okay, yes, no one had actually pointed that out, but Jenn knew they were all thinking it.

In the "That's Crazy" column was the fact that Frank didn't seem to have a motive for killing Maggie. He loved his sister—or at least he had back when Maria and Jenn were in high school.

But a lot had happened to him since then. So Alyssa and Jules both quietly passed around a recent photo of Francis "Frank" Bonavita to the members of their teams, advising that he was believed to be armed and dangerous.

Weird and/or discouraging news item number two was the fact that the lab tests on Maggie's cell phone had come back. The only fingerprints and DNA on the thing belonged to her. Which meant whoever had made that call to Maria had been careful and used gloves and probably even worn a face mask.

It confirmed that the crime was premeditated, although Jenn didn't really think much confirmation was needed. The caulking around the drawer and the postcard sent through the mail took care of that.

Although, tipping heavily on the weird scale was the fact that the caller had said *Check your mail,* not *Check your bottom desk drawer.* Jenn had pointed that out during breakfast, and Jules had agreed that it was definitely a question they were pondering. His best guess— and he admitted completely that it was only a guess—was that the killer knew the office schedule. He knew when the mail arrived, and he also knew that it was sometimes ignored until later in the day. Using Maggie's phone to call had been a risk, but one he'd been ready for. Because— Jules theorized—for some reason, the killer wanted his so-called gift discovered while the Troubleshooters team was there.

What reason that was? No one had a clue.

Weird and/or discouraging news item three was encouraging at the outset. A New York City webcam was positioned on the corner, looking down the sidewalk directly in front of Nicco's, the restaurant where Maggie's cell phone had been found.

The FBI, under Jules's direction, had requested and obtained archived footage from that camera.

The discouraging part was that there had been some kind of glitch in the archival system and the digital recording for the past month had been scrambled, with seventeen minute segments randomly mixed and completely out of order. The footage was clearly time and date stamped, but someone was going to have to sort through all of it and pick out the bits that were pertinent. In other words—Jules had said—they shouldn't hold their collective breaths, waiting for a close-up of the killer's face.

Which they might already have in a photo that Jules had gotten from the hospital where their man had been admitted but walked away. His eyes were closed, but it was a good enough likeness, and they were leaving it, with a contact phone number, at all of the shelters.

"His name's Winston. I don't know if that's a first name or last. It's all I ever got out of him. He used to be a regular here," the tall man with the prison tatts on his knuckles told Sam now, as Jenn and Tony hovered in the background. "But not so much anymore. It's been awhile since I've seen him."

"About how long?" Sam asked.

The man scrunched up his face as he thought about it. "Since New Year's—maybe even Christmas? Sorry, I can't be more specific. We get a lot of traffic through here."

"I appreciate even that much info," Sam said.

Jenn spoke up. "What does it mean?" she asked. "In your experience? When someone like Winston suddenly stops showing up?"

"Usually, it means he's dead," the man said somberly. "Mortality rate on the streets is high, particularly in winter. But it could also mean that he found Jesus or, more accurately, Jesus found him. That some Good Sam plucked him off the street and put him in an in-patient program. Or he caught a case—accidentally on purpose, you know?—and went up river for a little state-supported vacation for these colder months."

"I'm sorry." Jenn shook her head. "I don't know. Caught a case . . . ?"

"Got his . . . self arrested," the man told her. "For something with a nice little two-to-three-month jail term. Which someone like Win would spend in the psych ward, first detoxing, then getting his head shrunk. If the doctors are good enough, they might even find the right cocktail of meds to bring him back to earth. Only he'll walk out of there in the spring, with a pile of prescriptions he can't possibly pay for—and a half-year wait for the paperwork to go through if he tries to get his meds through the VA. And by the time they get around to reviewing his file, he'll have already slipped away again, and be back on the street, talking to himself."

"He's not in-patient," Sam said. "And he's not in prison. I saw him just last night."

"Another possibility is that he got himself a warm place to sleep," the man told them. "Somewhere the police haven't found yet—because once they find these places, they clear 'em out, regular. Could be someplace only he knows about—like there's a broken window, lets him get into the basement of a building."

"How well did you know him?" Sam asked. "Did he ever show you a picture of a woman—"

But the man was already shaking his head. "Took me two months to pry the name Winston outta him. And then, like I said, he's been gone."

"Thank you," Sam held out his hand, and the two men shook. "If you see him—"

"I'll give you a call."

With that, they all trooped back out into the cold.

"That was good," Jenn said.

Sam wasn't as enthusiastic. "You know how many basements there are in New York City?" he asked.

And yes, the information they'd just received definitely fell into today's *even good news is bad* arena, but wasn't it about time they got lucky? "If we start by searching the basements near the office," Jenn began, but Tony interrupted.

"It's not that simple," he told her. "Even if we find a broken window, we can't just enter the building without the cooperation of the super or owner. So it's not just a matter of you take one side of the street, I'll take the other. It requires a team of at least three per building. One person to find the superintendent, one to watch the window, and one to watch other escape routes. I'll tell you this, if I were setting up camp in a basement? I'd make sure I'd have at least one other way to get out."

"Well, we can check *our* basements, right?" Jenn refused to take this as a loss instead of a win. "Plus, we now have a name. Winston."

"Google that," Sam said dryly, "and see how many million hits you get."

"I absolutely *will* see," she responded, undaunted. "Winston, Vietnam vet, New York. You never know."

Sam stopped at the top of the stairs, clearly bracing himself for the jarring trip down them, and Jenn stopped beside him.

"Do not," he said, "ask me if I'm all right."

"I was actually thinking that it's time for lunch," she lied. "We're right around the corner from the office. Why don't we go in, get warm and . . . maybe order pizza?"

"Nice save," he said.

"Is that a yes?"

"It's a hell yes," Sam told her.

She smiled back at him, and he added, "I can see why Danny Gillman likes you so much. I mean, aside from the obvious fringe benefits."

His words made her face heat, but he wasn't finished.

"It's been awhile since I've kept up with who he's dating," Sam continued, "but you're pretty different from his usual victims, I mean, girlfriends."

And, yes. He'd completely meant *victims*.

"Most of his exes," he told her, "had an IQ just a little higher than a mushroom."

Jenn laughed at that. "And I'm at *least* as smart as a rutabaga. Or maybe . . . a stalk of celery?"

Now Sam laughed, too. "Nah, you're much higher up the evolutionary chain."

"Have you and Dan been friends for a long time?" she heard herself ask. Oh, God, was she really doing this?

Sam thought about it as he went down the stone steps, one at a time, leaning heavily on the railing. "It's going on eight years now," he said. "We were both in Team Sixteen for a while."

"Dan's SEAL team," she clarified.

"It was mine first," he said, taking the edge off of his words by smiling. "Back when I was a junior officer, he was an FNG—an effin' new guy. He was enlisted, I was older, so . . . We were never really friends."

"That's too bad," Jenn said as he hit the sidewalk and started moving a little faster. "He could use a friend like you. Someone who's got their shit together."

"You've got your shit together," Sam pointed out.

"But I'm just a temporary friend," she told him, and at his *oh really* look, she added, "I went into . . . whatever this is that we're doing, well aware of that."

"So . . . what?" he asked, his incredulity all but dripping off of him. "You're just gonna let *him* define the parameters of your relationship? His head's so far up his ass he doesn't know if it's night or day." He paused, then added, "Unless, of course, you're *good* with it being temporary. "

"I don't know," she admitted. She'd met Dan, what? Just over twenty-four hours ago . . . ? God, the thought of what they'd done—twice—last night still made her blush. "I don't really know him that well."

Except she *did* know him—enough to know that he

listened when she talked. And that he was capable of expressing his honest emotions. God, when he'd cried . . .

He'd nearly broken her heart.

Sam stopped outside of Maria's office, and Jenn realized that Tony had given them some distance to talk privately. He now stood several yards away, speaking to someone on his cell phone.

"What do you like on your pizza?" Jenn asked Sam. It was a polite way of signaling that the personal part of their conversation was officially over. She added punctuation by starting up the stairs.

"Jenn." Sam gestured her back over to him with a tilt of his head. And although she stopped, she wouldn't move toward him, so he came to her, exaggerating the degree of pain it caused him to climb each step.

It was meant to make her feel guilty, which she refused to do. He was going to have to climb these stairs anyway, if he wanted lunch.

"I don't mean to scare you off," he said, which was right up there with *I'm not going to lie to you* and *I'm telling you this for your own good* when it came to things people said that were the exact opposite of what they meant.

"I don't scare easily," she told him, "so you should probably save your breath."

But he was bound and determined to say his piece. "But if you notice Danny acting oddly or erratically—"

"You mean *more* oddly or erratically than his hooking up with someone with a higher IQ than a mushroom?" she asked.

He looked surprised, but then laughed. "Touché."

"You know, I don't really know what I'm doing," Jenn told him, "but I *do* know that it would be a lot easier without everyone butting in."

"He had a head injury recently," Sam told her flatly, "and several incidents in which he blacked out. I think it's related—that the blackouts are a result of the injury. But they might be a symptom of PTSD instead, which could end his career. I apologize for *butting in,* but I thought you'd want to know."

With a nod, he moved past her, and went inside the building, leaving her standing on the stair with Tony watching her, out in the cold.

Jennilyn came into the office.

It wasn't until she did that Dan realized he'd practically been holding his breath, waiting for her.

She was dressed down in jeans again today. They suited her far better than the ill-fitting business clothes she'd been wearing yesterday.

When they'd first met.

Huh.

It felt as if a full week had passed between his walking into Assemblywoman Bonavita's office for the first time and Jenn coming through that door, but it had barely been twenty-four hours.

It was Day Two of Fourteen, and Day Two should've started with them waking up in her bed, legs intertwined. She'd stretch and smile at him sleepily, and he'd smile too, and pull her close, spooning her back against him, and they'd both say *Good morning,* and he'd murmur into her ear about how great he'd slept and how she shouldn't go anywhere, because he was going to get up and make some coffee and bring her a cup, but in truth the coffee would have to wait, because with very little effort, he'd be getting his happy on all over again.

Only, he'd woken very much alone on the couch in the living room of that hotel suite, after having another one of his goddamn blackouts.

Which was a crying shame, on so many levels.

"We were thinking about ordering pizza," Jenn told him as she took off glasses that were fogging from the tropical heat, adding, "Oh," as she saw the pizza boxes that were already on the conference table.

She also seemed a little taken aback by the fact that the room was nearly filled to overflowing by a large group of people, all wearing dark suits.

"FBI agents, from the local office," Dan told her. He leaned closer, lowered his voice. "I can't remember their names. I think there's at least one John and maybe a Matt and a Carol. The cool thing is they all answer to *sir* or *ma'am.*"

She smiled at him. "Good to know."

"We were a step ahead of you with the pizza," Lopez pointed out. "There's plenty left. You may have to re-heat, though. It might be a little cold."

Jenn opened one of the boxes. "Might be . . . ?" she asked, shooting Lopez a questioning look as she slid a slice on a paper plate, maneuvered around a man in a dark suit, and put it in the microwave. "It's stone cold. What time did you guys eat lunch? Nine-thirty?"

"Ten-forty-five," Dan admitted. "We were up early."

"I can see," she said, looking around the room at the se-curity equipment—movement detectors, window alarms, the control panel they'd installed right by the door. "You gonna tell me how this stuff works, or just let me guess? Maybe trial and error it, until the neighbors complain?"

"Not a chance," Lopez told her with a smile. "But we'll wait until we can show it both to you and the as-semblywoman at the same time. Over the next few days, you're not going to be in here without one of us. Excuse me. I have to . . ."

He dodged several of the suits on his way into Maria's inner office, where the Troubleshooters and FBI team leaders, plus Sam Starrett, were giving each other sitreps, aka situation reports, aka discussing the big nothing they'd uncovered since the day began.

Jules and Alyssa had been talking earlier about how

they expected Maggie Thorndyke's killer to contact them. But Dan had been here for most of the morning, and the phone didn't ring. And it still didn't ring. And it apparently didn't ring over at the hotel where Maria had her cell phone, either—although she *had* found out that her mentally ill brother had gone missing, so they were now searching for him, too.

But the Troubleshooters team was in wait mode—his least favorite part of an op. Although truth be told, Dan *had* given Sam his official resignation. So technically, he wasn't part of this op anymore. Which meant that wait mode was about to become his new favorite time of year.

"If you want," Dan said, praying that Jenn did, "after you eat your pizza, I can take you back to your place and show you how *that* system works."

She looked at him, but before she could answer, the microwave dinged and Lt. Starrett came out of Maria's office and used his outdoor voice.

"All right, we've got interviewees coming in, in about fifteen minutes. Who's supposed to be here and who's not?"

Jenn looked to Dan for guidance, which was nice. "I don't think I'm supposed to be here," she said.

"I know I'm not," he told her.

"Do you have time," she asked, her brown eyes so serious behind her glasses, "to talk?"

"Yeah. Sure," he said, taking a mental inventory of the condoms he'd stored in the side pocket of his cargo pants.

"*Really* talk," she told him, taking her slice of pizza from the microwave. She looked at him again. "Really," she emphasized.

"I'd like to talk," he said, which wasn't quite a lie, because the verb he really meant also ended in a hard *K*.

"Good," she said, pizza in hand as she gestured to the door. "Then let's go."

Was this really going to be this easy? They were just going to stand up and walk out of here, walk around the corner to her place where—thank you God Almighty—they would finally, finally, *finally* be alone.

To talk.

He would talk. Absolutely. Hell, he was a freaking Navy SEAL. He could multitask.

Dan shrugged on his jacket and followed Jenn out the door.

"What time is that dickhead Mick Callahan coming in?" Sam asked.

Alyssa looked up at him from her seat behind Maria's desk. "When you say things like that," she started.

"I'm not going to kick his ass," he promised her and Jules both. "I'm just going to sit here, very quietly, and rip him a new one with my eyes."

"And that's what I'm afraid of," she said. "He's just crazy enough to take offense to that kind of—"

"See?" Sam told Jules. "She thinks he's crazy, too."

"You manhandled a cop, SpongeBob," Jules pointed out, using the silly nickname he'd assigned Sam years ago, even though Sam already had way too many nicknames. His real name, that his parents had bestowed upon him, was Roger. He'd been called a lot of things over the decades he'd been alive though, and somehow *Sam* had stuck. Thank God. Because he'd always hated Roger.

Although he did truly love it when, at certain times, Alyssa caught his attention by addressing him with it.

And Jules's nickname, SpongeBob, as ridiculous as it sounded, was in truth a term of endearment that Sam appreciated far more than the man's standard, which was *Sweetie.*

"Is it really all that crazy that Callahan reacted the way he did?" Jules continued.

Alyssa actually came to Sam's defense. "It did have a . . . certain unstable quality to it," she admitted. "A . . . what's that word? Not tinge. Like a sepia tone, only a coating . . ."

"Patina," Jules suggested.

"That's it." She smiled happily at him. "A patina of instability. Lots of little cracks that you can't see unless you look closely."

Sam sighed. "Sometimes you guys wear me out."

"You're just not gay enough," Jules told him.

"No, no, he's *exactly* the right amount of gay," Alyssa countered.

"There are some who would disagree," Jules said. "But isn't diversity grand—that we can sit here and treat him like an equal?" He lowered his voice to a stage whisper. "Even though he's not?"

Alyssa's cell phone rang, interrupting. "It's Savannah," she told them. Taking it into the outer office, she answered it. "Hey Van, thanks for calling me back. . . ."

Please, God, let Savannah have printed out that picture of Alyssa so that they'd have an answer to at least one of their mysteries.

Jules sat down next to Sam. "FYI—I told Alyssa this earlier—the hospitals and morgues are all on alert," he said, "but there's been no word from any of them. So, I really like the idea of Winston having a home base in some local basement. That explains why no one's seen him."

"Either that, or the homeless thing is a disguise." Sam laughed at himself. "And yes, I've been watching too much TV."

"I tried that one on Alyssa," Jules said. "It's pretty far out there. It defies Occam's razor."

Occam's razor was a theory that said that any time there was a question or a problem, the simplest explanation or answer was usually the correct one. In other words, if there were two possibilities—A) that the killer was a reincarnation of Jack the Ripper, born again into the body of a priest who dressed as a homeless man and who had access to his church's antiquities which he was quietly selling on eBay to pay for his bloodlust; or B) that the killer was an estranged family member who'd killed Maggie accidentally in anger, and panicked—it was probably going to be B.

"But not everything's always as simple as it should be," Sam pointed out. "Why cut out Maggie's heart?"

"Because . . . he's a showman," Jules postulated. "He wants to make an impact, to be noticed."

"A dead body'd do that," Sam said.

"I haven't told Alyssa this yet," Jules said, "but there's something about this case that's . . . not right."

Sam looked at him.

"I know," Jules said. "That sounds stupid. Of course it's not right. A woman is dead, her heart cut out and stashed in a desk drawer." He sighed. "I spent the morning at the local Bureau office, and they've looked hard at everyone who benefited from Maggie's death, including Lulu, her dog. Okay, kidding about that, but . . . still. There's no one and nothing that points to anyone who knew her. Her brother's her heir, and he doesn't even want the money. He's giving it all to UNICEF."

"Out of guilt?" Sam asked.

"I don't think so," Jules said.

"Are we looking at this wrong?" Sam asked. "Is it possible it was a burglary? Or maybe Maggie saw something that she shouldn't've seen, and this is the killer's way of throwing us all off track?"

"Occam's razor," Jules said again.

"Okay," Sam said. "If the killer's not a family member, then the simplest explanation is . . . that Maggie was a pawn. That someone wanted to put a human heart in that desk drawer, and Maggie became an unwilling organ donor."

They sat in silence for a moment.

Then Jules said, "So who's our target? Maria or Jenn?"

"It was Jenn's desk," Sam pointed out.

"But Maria's office door was locked," Jules said.

True. The assemblywoman's inner office, where they were sitting right now, needed a separate key to unlock its door.

"Why stop with Maria and Jenn?" Sam asked. "Maybe the target is one of the interns or volunteers." All of whom they'd be talking to, this afternoon.

"Or maybe the target is Maria *and* Jenn," Jules was thinking aloud. "Someone who knew them both."

"Like Mick Callahan," Sam pointed out as he stood up and went to the door.

"Yeah," Jules said, "but I was thinking more along the lines of the assemblywoman's missing brother. I don't buy into coincidences. Why should he pick right now to disappear?"

Alyssa was still on the phone, over by the coffee station, pouring herself a cup.

Their most likely scenario was that back in September, Savannah had printed out a picture of Alyssa to show to Maria as part of a pitch to use Troubleshooters Incorporated as security for a campaign event. Maria had decided against hiring the team, and the picture had been thrown out. It had made its way, with the rest of the office trash, into the dumpster out back where Winston, their homeless man, had found it while sifting through the garbage.

As if Alyssa felt Sam's eyes on her, she turned—still talking to Savannah on the phone—to look at him.

And she shook her head, no.

So much for Occam's freaking razor. Unless someone else in the office had checked out the Troubleshooters website and printed out that picture. Or . . .

"What if the killer's real target," Sam said, "isn't Maria

or Jenn." He turned to look at Jules. "What if his target's Alyssa?"

"So that's how it works," Dan told Jenn, shutting the cover of the control panel on her new alarm system. He'd cleaned up her apartment while he'd been in there this morning—taking out the Chinese food containers and the garbage, washing the dishes that had been in the sink, and turning her bed back into a sofa.

It was extremely thoughtful of him to have done that.

"There's also a remote control," he added, shrugging out of his jacket and tossing it over the arm of her couch before picking up a little keychain-sized device from the table upon which she kept her alarm clock. He held it up for her to see as he crossed back toward her.

"Why," she asked, trying to focus on it instead of the way his T-shirt fit snugly across his broad chest, "is there a remote control? In case I'm too lazy to take the four steps from my couch to the panel, when I'm ready to go to bed?"

"Oh," he said, as he handed her the device, "no, you should turn the system on as soon as you get inside. Not the motion sensors, but the rest of it. Remember, there're two settings. Home and away."

The thing he'd given her looked like a miniature version of the control panel. "Yes, I remember. Home is when I'm here. Check."

He smiled, which worked well with the whole nicely fitting T-shirt thing. "The remote's main purpose is the panic button," he said, taking it back from her and pointing to the red button on the side. "If you wake up in the night and someone's between you and the control panel, you just push this, and the alarm'll go off—silently though. It sends a message—*send help*—to the monitoring system. Push it twice in a row, and you get the message plus the full sirens, which sometimes helps scare away a potential attacker."

"But why didn't the sirens go off when whoever's standing there first broke in?" she asked, watching him put it back on her bedside table. And why hadn't he jumped her the moment they got inside? She'd fully expected him to.

"It's really just a hypothetical," Dan said.

"In other words, I don't really need the remote control."

"It's definitely designed for people with bigger homes," he said. "It's . . . just a second line of defense."

"But if our psycho-killer got in by disabling the alarm system," she pointed out, "it's unlikely that anything'll happen when I push the panic button, because the system's been disabled, right?"

"Maybe he cut a hole through the floorboard and climbed up through Mrs. Harrison's apartment."

"Maybe it's Mrs. Harrison who cut the hole and climbed through it," she said. "Okay, that seems to be an appropriate reason to panic. You sold me."

"Good," he said, laughing. But it faded quickly, leaving behind . . . heat. Yet, he still remained all the way across the room.

"So," Jenn said, with a bravado that was as completely manufactured and as false as her request that they come here merely to talk had been. Yes, she definitely wanted to talk to Dan. There was a lot she wanted to ask him. Later. "Day two. What kind of sex do we have on day two?"

She barely saw him move, but he had and he was now kissing her, his tongue in her mouth, his body hard against her, his hands on her butt as he pulled her more tightly to him.

God, yes. She opened herself to him, kissing him back as ferociously, pulling his T-shirt up and over his head as he deftly unfastened her jeans and yanked them, with her panties, down her legs.

This was what she'd expected instead of that tutorial he'd given her on her security system, and she realized that he wasn't as cocksure as he pretended to be.

And if she truly had wanted merely to talk, he would, indeed, have merely talked—a thought that warmed her the same way his showing her Fred-the-bunny and cleaning her apartment had done.

Which was nice, but not as nice as his exploring fingers between her legs, or the solid smoothness of his bare back beneath her hands, or the way he seemed to inhale her, each kiss longer and deeper and more possessive than the last.

Jenn tried to kick off her shoes, but she was wearing her bad-weather boots, and the laces of the right one were too-tightly tied. She got the left one off though, but remained hobbled by her jeans, even as she pulled Dan free from his briefs.

He was as rock hard as he'd been last night when he'd placed her hand on him, and she wondered if he knew how close she'd been to going into the privacy of the bathroom with him, right then and there—to hell with the fact that everyone would've known exactly what they had been doing when they reemerged.

"Ah, God, Jenn," he broke their kiss to say as she touched him. "I want . . . I need . . ."

She knew, because she wanted and needed, too. She tried to kick her jeans free from her shoeless foot, intending to wrap her leg around him and push him deeply inside of her, even as they stood right there, by her front door.

But she wasn't quite tall enough, and it wasn't just her jeans that hindered her. Dan pulled back, too.

"Condom," he said, fumbling in one of his cargo pockets for the little foil package.

Good idea. As he covered himself, she used the opportunity to push her jeans off her left leg, nearly falling over and hopping into the kitchen to catch herself on the counter. "Oh, my God. *That* would've been an embarrassing trip to the emergency room." She was laughing, and he was, too, as she finally got free and could then focus on untying her boot.

But he came up behind her as she was leaning over, and pushed himself inside of her.

"Oh," she gasped, as he said "Gahd," and this time she *would* have fallen, if he hadn't been holding her tightly around the waist.

"Oh, my God," she said again, her voice filled both with her laughter and her surprise.

He'd started to move, but now he froze. "Oh, shit," he said his breath warm against her ear. "That wasn't, like, an invitation?"

She laughed again—she couldn't help it. Invitation? "Yes and no. The whole taking-off-my-pants thing was definitely an invitation, but—"

He started to pull out, but she pushed back against him, not letting him go, and in fact driving him deeply inside of her.

"*That,*" she gasped, "was an invitation."

"Uhn," he said, and she had to grab for the counter, using it to brace herself, as the force of him thrusting into her, again and again and again, pushed her forward.

It felt unbelievably good, his hands holding tightly to her hips, but then it felt even better as he moved to touch her—exactly where she wanted to be touched.

"Jenn," he rasped. "Jesus, Jenni . . ."

She knew that she liked it when he called her Jenni, but she'd had no idea that hearing him say it could actually make her come—in combination, of course, with the not-very-gentle sex they were having, and the exquisite placement of his fingers and thumb.

Her orgasm ripped through her, and she stopped thinking, stopped analyzing, stopped doing everything but *feeling* as she shattered into a million pieces, as she shook and gasped and wanted more and more and *more*. . . .

Even after it was over and done.

Her face was practically pressed against her toaster—in fact, she could see herself oddly distorted, reflected in its chrome sides. She could see Dan, too. His eyes were closed and he'd let go of her to hold himself up on the very countertop that she was practically lying on. The muscles in his arms and chest were taut as he worked to catch his breath.

But then he opened his eyes, and looked directly at her and smiled, and had he been someone who was sticking around for longer than two weeks, she would have imagined herself someday telling her children *and then our eyes met in the reflection of the toaster, and I knew he was the one*. Without telling them what they'd done right before their eyes met, of course.

Instead, she made herself think about all of the great sex they could have in twelve and a half days. And she smiled back at him. "No RSVP jokes, please," she told him.

Dan laughed and opened his mouth.

"Or apologies," she cut him off.

"That doesn't leave me much to say," he pointed out. "Except . . . Jesus, I need a nap. After which, can we *please* do that again?"

CHAPTER FIFTEEN

Nearly everyone had something they wanted to hide. That was just a fact of life, and it applied to the assembly-woman's interns and volunteer staff.

Alyssa and Jules settled into a pattern of questioning. She acted as the primary interviewer for the men, and he took on the same job for the women.

Sam sat quietly and observed—and ruminated on the seemingly absurd idea that Maggie Thorndyke's heart had been put in that desk drawer specifically for his wife to find.

It was one of his crazier thoughts, for sure, but he couldn't shake it, and as Maria's staff came in, one at a time, he watched them closely as Jules introduced him-self and Alyssa with handshakes. At Sam's request, Jules tossed out a quick "That's Sam Starrett from Trou-bleshooters, he'll be observing today," so he could stay as much in the background as possible.

He would've liked to have been behind a one-way win-dow, but Jules had pushed to do these interviews in the familiarity of Maria's office, hoping for greater candor.

The big money questions that Alyssa and Jules were asking were: What time did you arrive at the office yes-terday morning? Did you see anyone entering or leaving the building when you arrived? How well did you know the victim? Did you see Winston, the homeless man, that morning? And the classic: Can you account for your whereabouts between 9:00 A.M. Friday and 7:30 A.M. Saturday, during the time Maggie Thorndyke was abducted and murdered?

And then there were the little questions, too, about each individual's background. When did they first meet Maria and Jenn? Did they have any crazed stalkers or, more likely, any relationships recently gone south? What did they think about the other people with whom they worked?

Everyone who'd been in the office the morning of the grisly discovery had made note of the others who'd also been there. Their list was unanimously complete. It had been a Saturday, after all, and they'd come in to assist with a mailing that was finished before 10:00 A.M. At which point, they'd all—except for Jenn and Maria—left before the Troubleshooters team had arrived.

There were four college interns, one volunteer-slash-major donor, the UPS man, Jenn, and of course Maria.

The two female interns—Wendy Ramirez and Belinda Davidson—were interviewed first. They were roommates, living not far from the office. They were also both poli-sci majors at NYU. They'd arrived together on the morning in question, coming in after everyone but Maria was already there.

Neither of them knew Maggie Thorndyke well, although Wendy had run into the woman a time or two on campus because she was an alum. Wendy admitted to giving Maggie her phone number and angling for a dog-sitting job. It was, she told them, with wide-eyed sincerity, probably inappropriate for her to have done so, but the potential pay was too good to pass up. But the one time Maggie had called her—back in December—it had been exam week, and Wendy couldn't spare the time.

Belinda was as blond and blue-eyed as her name

implied—which probably said more about Sam's youthful love of the Go-Go's than anything else. *She* had a secret having to do with Winston. Even though she hadn't seen the homeless man on Saturday morning, she had, in the past, brought him with her into the office. He would wash in the men's room, she told them earnestly, while she'd make him coffee and microwave him a meal. He'd even helped her, a time or two, stuffing envelopes for a mailing like the one they'd done yesterday. He was, she insisted, a damaged but gentle soul.

Both women were enthusiastic in their support of Maria. They lit up as they talked about her. They also had gaydar worth shit, because they both relaxed enough to flirt a little with Jules.

Neither gave Alyssa much more than a glance, and both had solid alibis during the hours Maggie was believed killed, and little information beyond that.

Next up was intern Ron Reed, who was a curious contradiction. Despite his laid-back look of long hair pulled back into a ponytail, torn jeans and a Heifer International T-shirt, the law student brought with him a complete written account of his whereabouts over the past week. The details were precise and clearly organized, down to the minutiae of what he ate, when.

He'd merely printed out his log from his phone's calendar program, he told them this was no problem for him at all, and he could go back further if they needed that information.

He admitted to having a bit of OCD which, he insisted, would work to his advantage when he was employed by a big firm and reporting billable hours.

Ron had brought copies in triplicate, and as Sam glanced through the pages, he saw that on Saturday, the kid's morning bowel movement had been a little bit loose, perhaps from the sushi he'd had the night before.

Okay.

And yes, Friday night Ron had been in the company of his girlfriend, Amy, *and* all four of his roommates, one of whom was celebrating her birthday. The party had continued in his living room, well after 2 A.M., when Ron and Amy went to bed.

Like Wendy and Belinda, he was enthusiastic when asked about Maria. He didn't know his fellow interns very well, though, he tended to keep to himself. Amy could get jealous.

Especially of Maggie Thorndyke. She was a cougar, and all the male interns had learned to stay away from her.

Although maybe not Gene Ivanov, because he was older so she didn't flirt with him the same way, but back during the campaign, when they had more volunteers coming into the office, Ron and the other guys had put a strict "no one is left alone in the office with Maggie" policy in place.

Not that he had anything against cougars, Ron had added, pointedly giving Alyssa a once-over, as if to say *if you're on the prowl, baby, I'm game. . . .*

It was strangely discordant, like a three-year-old flipping someone the bird. Yet it was still disrespectful on top of being flat-out laughable. But Alyssa didn't immediately bitch-slap him the way Sam would've, if he were her.

He honestly didn't know how she did it—how she kept her cool in this fucked-up world where nearly every man, including little frightened dweebs like this one, saw her first and foremost as a sex object. And some of them— like Mick Callahan—never managed to see past her beauty to the strong, smart, capable person that she was.

Sam had to count to twenty to keep himself from slapping the punk for her.

But Alyssa just went on down their list of questions until, with a smile, she showed Ron Reed to the door.

At which point she waved Gene Ivanov in, and shook the fourth and final intern's hand.

Like Ron had said, Gene *was* older than the others. In his early forties, he was a graduate student at Columbia. Tall and thin, he was quietly handsome. He'd also dressed up for the occasion, as if this were a job interview, or maybe even a date. He wore a suit and tie, and his dark hair was carefully combed.

He was also nervous as hell, his hands clasped tightly in his lap, his voice shaking every now and then as he answered Alyssa's questions.

Where was he on Friday night? At home, with his parents.

He'd been the first one into the office on Saturday morning, but he hadn't seen anyone out front, or leaving the building, or in the elevator, or in the hall outside of the office. According to Jenn, who signed off on the interns' time sheets so that they got proper credit for their work, he'd arrived and opened up the office at 7:30 A.M.

But when Alyssa asked, Gene cleared his throat and told her that he didn't actually arrive until a little after eight-thirty. He'd worked that extra hour, however. He'd written a rough draft of a speech for the assemblywoman during his commute. He lived out in Brooklyn—he'd moved back in with his parents after his dot-com business failed—and he always left early because sometimes the subway was delayed. But sometimes it wasn't, so sometimes he'd stop at the Starbucks near the office and set up his laptop on one of the tables there. There was this girl, who worked the counter, that he—ahem—liked. . . .

Sam then cleared his throat, too, and Jules glanced at him, no doubt thinking the same thing: That Gene was covering something up.

Did he stop at Starbucks on the morning that Maggie's heart was discovered in Jenn's desk, Alyssa asked him and he blanched, but said yes, adding that he was happy to give them a copy of the piece he'd written, if—ahem—they needed to see it.

Some people were naturally nervous, and some got more nervous when facing authority. Others' nerves were ramped up when they lied, which Gene seemed to be doing.

Would his parents verify that he was home Friday night?

His parents would, he told them. And he gave them his home phone number, but added that they were—ahem—pretty hard to reach. If Alyssa and Jules wanted, Gene could maybe get them to write a note . . . ?

Like this was high school, and he'd cut gym class.

But the man's face flushed, as if he were embarrassed to be living at home at his age, and without even waiting for Alyssa to tell him, gently, that a note wasn't going to cut it, he promised her that he'd make sure his mother would return her call. His father was elderly, but even when he was younger he'd had trouble remembering what he'd had for lunch, let alone when Gene was or wasn't home.

Sam looked at Jules again. Maybe now was the time to point-blank it and ask the guy if he'd killed Maggie Thorndyke. . . .

But Alyssa didn't go there. She just kept asking Gene questions about Savannah. Did he know her well—Maria's campaign manager?

He hadn't known her well, but he'd certainly met and talked to her a few times. She seemed nice. It was hard for everyone after her husband was injured and she'd run the campaign via phone, from out of state. But she'd clearly gotten the job done.

Had Savannah ever talked to him about Maria's safety, or security for any of the campaign's fundraising events? Had she spoken to him about her friends in Troubleshooters Incorporated, or shown him the TS Inc website?

He gave them a lot of no's without any throat-clearing.

Still, after Jules showed him to the door, Sam called a time-out.

"This one's hiding something," he said.

Alyssa smiled at him. "Gene was nervous," she agreed. "But that doesn't make him a killer."

"We'll check his alibi," Jules told him. "I'll send someone out to his house, see what his parents have to say about his whereabouts Friday night."

"That's assuming he hasn't already buried his parents in the basement," Sam pointed out.

"If so," Alyssa said, "why get them involved as his alibi?"

"Good point," Sam said.

"You want to take a break?" she asked him. "Maybe go check on Ash or join the search for Winston—"

"No," he told her. "I'm with you."

"It's important," she told him, "in an interview setting like this, to allow the person to talk, without feeling threatened."

"Got it," Sam said. "Hate it, but got it."

"We ready?" Jules asked, and the next person—Douglas Forsythe, a volunteer and big donor—was ushered in.

He was around Gene's age, or maybe even a little older, with a receding hairline and a serious dash of salt at his temples.

Despite that and his nerdy glasses, he was a good-looking son of a bitch, and a complete contrast to both Gene and Ron in that he moved with the absolute self-assurance of the ridiculously wealthy. He was actually wearing a bow tie and it didn't seem out of place around his neck. The rest of his clothes were what Jules and Alyssa would call *shabby rich*. And if they asked, Doug would no doubt tell them that the tweed jacket he was wearing was the very one he'd gotten back at Yale, when he was the captain of the rowing team.

Like Gene, Douglas, too, still lived with his parents—although he made sure Alyssa and Jules knew that he'd returned to his childhood home to help care for them in "these, their twilight years." His father had Alzheimer's, and his mother, although still chipper—his word, too—struggled to get around, even with the walker he'd bought her.

Maria had described him as *long-winded*. Jenn had been less kind, calling him *pompous and opinionated*.

Whatever he was, it was clear that the man loved to hear himself talk.

Yes, he knew Maggie. In fact, they'd dated once while they were both in college and home for the holidays. It was years ago, back before she got kicked out of Vassar. She was into drugs at the time, and he was and had always been on the straight and narrow. Although he was quick to reassure them that he didn't believe her death was drug-related. She'd changed a great deal in the past few years, and had been a valuable member of the election campaign, fully clean and sober.

She didn't seem to remember him, and he'd never bothered to remind her, since the evening had been embarrassing. And of course, he was only bringing this up now for the sake of full disclosure. And god forbid she kept a diary that mentioned him by name, ha ha ha.

Yada, yada, yada, he talked and talked and *talked*. No, he was unfamiliar with Troubleshooters Incorporated, although he was on their website just this morning. His mother—of all people—had recognized the name both of the company and of Alyssa Locke. Her only vice was that she was a tabloid reader. She'd told him all about Alyssa's heroism in saving the life of the movie star that Jules was . . . somewhat flamboyantly connected to.

It was all very frightening, although Mother found it thrilling, but was it possible that he and his parents were in danger, too? Not that he wouldn't leap to help if

Maria needed him, but he'd been leery enough to ask a friend to come and stay with his folks while he was out this afternoon. Their townhouse had a security system, of course. And his father hadn't been a Republican his entire life for nothing. He had a hunting rifle over the fireplace in the back parlor.

Douglas's secret was that he hadn't told Mother and Dad that the candidate he'd convinced them to support—Maria—was a left-leaning Independent. If they saw the need to speak to either of them, perhaps to verify that he was indeed home with them at the time of poor Maggie's murder, would they do him a favor and leave that little detail out?

But then it turned out that he had *another* secret. His mother was a pack rat, and he was attempting to clean out sixty-five years of Wonderbread bags and cat-food tins, by carrying bagloads here, to the office dumpster. If he tried to put them out with the trash, Mother would see and raise a stink. This way, she would never know.

But the point of this was that he *had* brought several bags to the dumpster yesterday morning, and while there, he'd been startled almost out of his wits by that homeless man who often hung about.

Winston was at the dumpster on Saturday morning?

He was, Douglas told them. The man was limping, as if he'd recently hurt himself. He'd seen him several days earlier, and he wasn't. Limping. Despite the limp, he ran away as if he were afraid of Douglas.

He'd followed the homeless man—but not entirely because he was being a good Samaritan, he had to confess. In fact, he followed him more out of wariness that the fellow was up to no good. But by the time he followed him out of the alley and down to the side street, he was gone. He'd vanished, as if he'd hopped into a cab. Which was ridiculous, of course.

It was then that Sam stood up. "Show me."

Douglas was startled. "My goodness, I'd forgotten you were sitting back there."

"Show me where you saw him, and where he ran," Sam said. "Right now. Let's go down to the dumpster."

Douglas looked from Sam to Alyssa, who stood up, too. "We'll all go," she said with a reassuring smile.

Dan forced himself to sit on the very end of Jenn's sofa.

He'd gotten up from a nap and taken a shower, opening the curtain to find her digging through her medicine cabinet, looking for a bottle of pills. She'd found them and celebrated with a brief but heartfelt version of the "Hallelujah Chorus." He'd pressed, and she finally admitted that she was prone to bladder infections—particularly post-sex, after a long period of celibacy.

But these pills would take care of the problem in no time.

Still, it had given him a solid case of the guilts because he hadn't exactly been gentle with her. He must've looked stricken, which he had to remember to do more often because she'd kissed him and reassured him that it absolutely wasn't his fault. And then she pulled him back to bed and proceeded to give him the hummer of the century. Which was saying something because he'd had some extremely talented women go down on him.

And maybe it was her inexperience that made it so rockin' great—the way she'd asked him to tell her what to do; asking what he liked, what felt good. Because not only did she ask, she also listened. The end result was her giving him head that was mind-blowing, and made even more so by the fact that she kept him laughing the entire time.

Okay, not the *entire* time, but damn close.

But now she was done with *her* shower, coming out of

the bathroom with a cloud of steam, wrapped in a towel, hair slicked back from her face.

She smiled at him, and the sight of that dimple in her cheek made his chest feel tight, which was stupid because he didn't do love. Not post-Sophia, anyway.

He liked Jenn, though. A lot.

That was what it was—it had been awhile since he'd been with a woman that he'd genuinely liked. His last two girlfriends had been all about the physical attraction, and as hard as he'd tried, neither had lasted even a week—thank Jesus for volunteer assignments.

"You put the sofa back together," Jenn stated the obvious as she opened her closet and got out some clothes.

"Yeah," Dan said. "I wanted to make sure you didn't ravish me again. You animal."

She laughed even as she saw right through his lame attempt at a joke.

"The medicine works fast," she reassured him. "I'm fine. It's not your fault. And it's not contagious—"

"God," he said, "no, I know." He'd used her laptop to google bladder infections while she was in the shower, but not because he thought it was contagious. He gestured now to the screen, which still held a list of facts from WebMD. "Did you know that it's called honeymoon cystitis? It's not just from making love, it's from making love with too much frequency, which means it *is* my fault."

She didn't even glance at the computer. She just sat down next to him on the couch, leaned forward and kissed him. "Do you hear me complaining?"

He smiled into her eyes, loving that she was comfortable enough to sit there with him, wearing nothing but that towel. Of course, he had to sit on his hands to keep himself from peeling it off of her. "No, but the website said the condition was pretty uncomfortable."

"I caught it early enough," she told him. "So it's not that bad. I've already taken the first pill—which works pretty quickly. Until then, it'll help if I drink a lot of water. And cranberry juice."

"Yeah, I read that, too," he said. "But I checked your cabinets. You don't have any cranberry juice."

"So we'll go get some," Jenn told him. "It's not like I can't walk." She kissed him again, and he found himself closing his eyes and enjoying the softness of her mouth. But then she pulled back to say, "The I-can't-walk sex doesn't happen at least until Day Ten, right?"

Dan laughed as he looked into her dancing eyes. "Baby, with you, I'm not sure. *I* may not be able to walk to-morrow." But he made himself get up and as he pulled on his T-shirt, he told her, "I'll run down to the bodega and get some cranberry juice while you get dressed." He paused. "I mean, if you *want* to get dressed. If you don't, I'm cool with that, too."

"Actually," she said, and her inflection and the way she shifted on the couch—sitting up and keeping her towel from falling off, and then holding it there, in place—set his girlfriend drama-meter twanging. Not that Jenn was big with the high drama, or with any drama at all. In fact, she was remarkably drama-free. "I was wondering if you, um, wanted to talk about what happened last night. You know. With Izzy."

He was silent, and she added, "It's just, it took a nap plus, well, *plus,* to make you seem like yourself again. Except, I don't really know you that well, so maybe *that* was Dan and this is just an act—" She broke off, laugh-ing and rolling her eyes. "Okay so that was a preview of what I'm going to say. Feel free to pretend to go to the store and then keep running. Or you can tell me that it's none of my business, except I have a confession. It's been bothering me that I haven't told you already, but Sam Starrett told me a little bit more about what happened in Afghanistan. . . ."

Dan turned away, he couldn't stop his reaction, and

she quickly added, "*He* approached *me*. He said that he thought I should know, and I disagree. If you want me to know something, then *you'll* tell me, but . . . I just wanted to make sure you knew that if you want to talk, I'm happy to listen. I know this is just a game we're playing here. I know it's not real. I'm fully cognizant of the fact that it's not going to last beyond our end date, and I'm not advocating that it should. I'm not. I'm just saying that Maria and I used to play Monopoly with her brothers and there were games that lasted longer than two weeks and . . . My point is that even though this is short-term, it doesn't have to be just great sex and a good time. If you want to talk to me, about *anything*, it won't go any further—I promise you that."

"I blacked out again last night." The words came out of him in a rush, like a helium balloon no longer tethered to the ground. But saying it aloud didn't bring relief. It brought shame and fear and a terrible, overwhelming despair because he knew he would be derelict if he *didn't* tell someone who *would* take it further.

"With Izzy," she said, confirming what was pretty damn obvious.

"Just . . ." Danny said, not meeting her gaze as he jammed his arms into his jacket. "Let me get you that cranberry juice."

Jenn stood up. "Dan—"

"Please," he said, forcing himself to look at her. "I need to get that for you. It'll take me ten minutes. I'll be right back. Set the alarm behind me."

He keyed in the alarm code so he could open the door and went out, shutting it tightly.

He went down the stairs instead of taking the elevator, needing to not put himself in that confining little box, even for just a short time. He rushed through the lobby, too, bursting out onto the sidewalk and into the cold, fresh air—taking deep, steadying breaths as he headed to the store on the corner, trying to calm the pounding of his heart.

It was actually kind of funny—the way that he hated tight spaces. If he could, he'd live most of his life out-of-doors. Maybe in a tree house, like the Swiss Family Robinson.

When he was a kid, that had been his favorite movie, and he'd longed to be shipwrecked—but with the Robinsons instead of his own crappy family.

But what was funny was that now, here he was, willingly hooked up with a woman who lived in a place the size of a closet, and it didn't bother him. Not a bit. In fact, he liked it. Even when she wasn't there, because the entire place reeked of her. Not just olfactory-wise, but cosmically. The place was drenched in her presence, and despite the miniscule square footage, it didn't feel confining.

It felt safe.

The door to the store was standing open, as if the clerk behind the counter, like Dan, preferred the bracing winter air to canned heat.

One entire wall held refrigerated sodas and juices, and he found an organic cranberry-pomegranate mix that looked good. There was no just-plain-cranberry juice, so he took it to the counter. He'd bring it to Jenn, and if it wasn't right, he'd look online and find the nearest health food store.

His cell phone rang as he was handing a ten dollar bill to the clerk. It was Izzy fucking Zanella, and he almost didn't answer it.

But he knew it wasn't a social call, so he tucked his phone between his shoulder and his ear as he took his change and the juice in a bag. "Gillman."

"Dude, are you at Jenn's?"

"Why?" Dan asked. "What's it to you?"

"I'm not trying to pry, you paranoid asshole," Izzy said cheerfully. "Although maybe I should be if you're having so much fun that you don't notice the alarm system's malfunctioned."

"Malfunctioned?" Dan repeated.

"Check the control panel," Izzy instructed. "There must be some kind of short in the panic button function."

"In the what?" Dan said.

"Read my lips, my challenged brother," Izzy said, which was a stupid-ass thing to say during a phone conversation, but that was Zanella. "You've got a hardware problem over there, because from *my* end it looks like someone hit the panic button."

Holy Jesus. "I'm not at Jenn's, I'm at the store, send backup—*now*!" Dan told Izzy as he started to run.

Of course Mick Callahan chose that exact moment to show up—as Alyssa was escorting Douglas Forsythe outside, where he'd seen Winston the homeless man by the dumpster on the very same morning that the killer had put Maggie Thorndyke's heart in Jennilyn's desk drawer.

She felt Sam's tension level ratchet up, and she attempted to control any potential confrontation by getting out in front of it.

"Detective," she greeted Mick as pleasantly as she could, considering that the pain from Sam's injured rib had awoken him repeatedly in the night. She'd heard him get up quite a few times. "Why don't you go on upstairs? We'll be back inside, in a few minutes."

Callahan looked like hell, like he hadn't gone home after their conversation by the hotel bar. In fact, Alyssa was willing to bet that he hadn't gone home at all last night. He was still wearing the same tired clothes and he hadn't shaved.

He wasn't standing close enough for her to tell if he was still drunk, but he could well have been.

He all but ignored her, nodding a greeting to Douglas. "Hey, Dougie," he said, tsking his mock disappointment. "You been killing people again? I thought I told you to stop doing that."

Douglas's mouth tightened. "This is hardly a joking matter, Detective."

"You're so right," Mick said. "And I have to confess I feel *much* better knowing that you're on their suspect list, too."

And, great, now Douglas was alarmed, his eyebrows raised. Alyssa stepped closer to him, murmuring, "Sir, you're not on our suspect list," as Jules stepped forward—and up.

"Jules Cassidy. I'm with the Bureau," he introduced himself to Mick, using their handshake to somehow gracefully maneuver the detective back toward the building's front door.

It would have worked beautifully. Jules would've taken Mick Callahan upstairs while Alyssa and Sam did a tour of the dumpster with Douglas, who clearly had made a sacrifice to move home to care for his parents, instead of yachting off the coast of France, or whatever it was that people did when they had more money than the queen and the pope put together.

Although, if he really had that much money, wouldn't Douglas simply have arranged for in-home care? Of course, maybe he had, and his presence provided emotional support. Except he had said he'd made arrangements with a friend to stay with his folks while he was out this afternoon.

Alyssa was just about to ask him about that, when Jay Lopez came barreling out the door, nearly wiping out both Mick and Jules.

"Izzy called. Panic button's activated in Jenn's apartment," the SEAL announced, loudly enough for both Alyssa and Sam to hear. "Gillman's on his way. He needs backup."

"I'm with you," Jules said, except Mick took off with them.

"Stay back, stay here—God *damn* it!" Alyssa heard Jules order the detective, who did not obey.

"Son of a bitch," Sam said and she met his eyes and knew exactly what he was thinking. He wanted to go and back Jules up, but he didn't want to leave her alone with a potential suspect. And until they spoke to Douglas's mother and confirmed his alibi, he *was* still a suspect, regardless of how ridiculous that seemed.

"Go," she told Sam, but he hesitated. There was something about this entire case that had him really spooked. And he didn't spook easily. Or at least he hadn't before Ash was born.

She didn't know what to make of his theory that whoever had killed Maggie was, in truth, stalking her. It seemed absurd—the idea that someone had engineered the series of threats in order to get her to come all the way out here from California.

Okay, unless they hadn't engineered it, but instead merely found out that she was coming here, and took the opportunity to send that bloody message by leaving Maggie's heart in that desk drawer. . . .

And now she was getting as bad as Sam. Yes, a bloody message had been sent, but she didn't speak Psychokiller, so her ability to translate and understand was severely hampered.

And the idea that Winston, their homeless man, was the psycho-killer in question was as absurd as the idea that Jules truly was Batman, which she knew with almost one hundred percent certainty that he wasn't.

If Jules really could fly with his batwings, he would

have done so in front of her, many times throughout the years that they'd been friends.

And okay, now she was losing it.

Except the concern in Sam's eyes was very real.

"I'll take Mr. Forsythe back upstairs," she assured him. "We'll wait for you to get back." She turned to Doug. "Do you have time—"

"Of course," he said, taking a cell phone from his overcoat pocket, and dialing. "Just let me call Marileni. Make sure she can stay a bit longer with Mother and Dad." He held up one finger as, phone to his ear he spoke rapid-fire in a language that wasn't quite Spanish, it was. . . .

"Portuguese?" Sam murmured.

Douglas heard him and he smiled as he shut his phone. "Very good. Marileni was my nanny growing up—she's from Brazil. And yes, she's able to stay."

"Go," Alyssa said, and Sam took off at a run that, with his broken rib, must've brought tears to his eyes.

Jenn shouldn't have opened the door.

She knew she shouldn't have opened the door, and yet she did, because she thought it was Dan and that he'd forgotten his keys, and now here she was.

With little Frankie Bonavita, who wasn't so little anymore, and who'd wanted her to go with him up to the roof, where they wouldn't be overheard.

"Give me the gun, Frank," she told him as they climbed the stairs.

On the way out the door of her apartment, she'd managed to hit the panic button—the one that rang silently. She'd also taken her coat and had dropped one of her gloves in the hall outside of the stairwell, and another on the stairs heading up.

"I didn't know where else to go," Frank told her. "They said they were watching Maria, so I couldn't go to her. . . ."

"Who said that?" Jenn asked. "But please, just, first—give me the gun?"

"I can't," he said tightly. He'd lost a lot of weight since he'd been home, and his face was gaunt, his eyes sunken as if he were already dead. He was a mere skeleton of the vibrant young man he'd once been.

"Sure you can," she said. He was using again, that much was clear. Probably crystal meth—a side effect was this kind of paranoia.

"It's not safe," he told her. Definitely meth.

"Frankie, look at me," she commanded, stopping there on the landing to the seventh floor. Her voice held far more authority than she felt. "You trust me, right? You came to *me*, right?"

He nodded. "I don't want to hurt anyone else."

Oh, God. "Then give me the gun."

He was going to do it. She felt it—he was wavering and he was going to hand it to her. But then he shook his head. "I can't. It's not safe."

"Why isn't it safe?" she asked, holding her ground. "Who told you that it's not safe?"

He shook his head.

"They," she said. "You said *they*. Who's *they*, Frankie?"

"I don't know," he said. "They sent a letter. To me. They said I killed her but I didn't." His face crumpled. "Jenni, I didn't, but they said they have evidence. And they said that instead of going to jail, they would send me back. I'm not going back! Christ, what's that?"

Having his gun back in her face was not conducive to clear thinking, but it soon became obvious that *that* had been the sound of someone opening the stairwell door from a floor or two above them. Whoever had opened it was whistling, making no attempt to be stealthy coming down the stairs.

"Someone's coming," Jenn whispered to Frank. "Hide your gun."

He put it into his pocket, but he didn't let go of it, and she knew that his finger was still on the trigger.

The tune being whistled was familiar, and Jenn suddenly recognized it. It was the theme from the old TV show, *Gilligan's Island*. And she had to fight so that she didn't simultaneously burst into both laughter and tears.

Gilligan was one of Dan's many nicknames. It was Dan coming down those stairs, and his whistling was his way of telling her he was on his way to her rescue.

Except, God, the last thing she wanted was for him to get shot.

But there he was, rounding the corner and stopping short, looking down at them as if surprised to see them there.

"Oh, hey, Jenn," he said. "How are you? It's, you know, Danny, your neighbor from the ninth floor . . . ?"

He was sweating, but his gaze was steady, his face calm. She knew he'd run back here, as fast as he could, to help her, and she couldn't keep tears from flooding her eyes.

He was so tall and hard-muscled, with such broad shoulders—but that meant nothing in a situation like this one. Dan may have been strong, but he wasn't bulletproof.

His face was so familiar to her. In just a short time he'd gone from being some too-handsome player to her lover and dear friend.

But she forced a smile as she met his dark brown eyes, playing along and trying to give him as much information as possible. "Of course. We met at the Halloween party. You were the cowboy with the *big gun*."

He smiled and even laughed a little as if she'd said something extra funny, but he nodded at her, saying "That's right. Big Gun Gillman—it's one of my nicknames." He looked over at Frank and then back to Jenn, and then over to the railing, and she realized that he, too, had his hand in his jacket pocket.

The silent message he'd just sent her was obvious—move out of the way in case violence erupted.

But even as she moved, she told Frank, "Dan just got back from Iraq." She looked at Dan. "*Frank* was over there, too. You know, I used to babysit for him. Remember, Frankie? We used to play those epic games of Monopoly with Maria?"

She could see the *oh crap* in Dan's eyes as he realized that this was Frank Bonavita, Maria's missing brother.

"Where'd you serve?" he asked Frank.

"I don't talk about it," Frank said tightly. "You should go."

"Hey, Jenn, I've been meaning to drop by," Dan said, his gaze solidly on Frank, "to pick up that book you were going to lend me. The one about the, um . . ."

"Yes," she said. "The, um . . . book I was going to lend you . . . *Cooking Crystal Meth for Dummies*."

Dan shot her a *what?* look.

And yes, that *was* way too obvious.

"I'm not cooking again," Frank said fiercely. "I'm not. And I don't buy it. I don't leave the house so I *won't* buy it, but it just keeps showing up. And I'm not an idiot. I saw you with Jenn," he told Dan. "I saw you go in, and I waited for you to leave. So just go, so I can talk to Jenni. I need to talk to Jenni."

He was extremely agitated, and Jenn looked at Dan, afraid for him. "You should do what he says."

"Yeah, that's not happening," Dan said. "I'm not going anywhere. As long as it's confession time, Frank, I know you've got a weapon, I've got one, too, and mine is aimed right at your chest. Do not move, do not even *look* at Jennilyn or I will drop you where you stand. I'm an active-duty Navy SEAL and I am good at what I do." He kept his eyes firmly on Frank as he added, "Jenn, go down the stairs."

She hesitated, because she didn't want to leave him.

But then he looked at her—just a glance. And in that moment, as their eyes met, Jenn realized that she'd been wrong about the toaster. *This* was the moment about which she'd tell their children—the moment she truly *knew.*

"Here's where we find out if you trust me," Dan said, still talking to Jenn with his gaze glued to Frankie, who, motionless, had started to cry.

"I do," she told him. Oh, God . . . "I just don't want either of you to get hurt."

"No one's getting hurt," Dan said. "Right, Frank?"

"I'm not going back," Frankie whispered. "You can't make me go back there."

"That's right," Dan reassured him. "You're *not* going back. I can promise you that. I can help you, Frank, I want to help you. Whatever you were going to say to Jenn, you can tell me, and I will help you. But first Jenn's gotta get the hell down those stairs. Say yes if you understand."

"Yes," Frank whispered, his eyes tightly closed.

Dan glanced at her again. "Jenni, *go.*"

Heart in her throat, Jenn turned to leave. But she couldn't do it without saying, "Frankie, don't you dare shoot him—I love him, okay?"

With that, she didn't look back. She didn't want to see the horrified surprise on Dan's face. And she didn't just go down the stairs.

She ran.

CHAPTER SIXTEEN

Marileni called back.

It was not even three minutes after Sam left to follow Jules and Lopez and Mick Callahan over to Jenn's apartment, where the panic button had been pushed.

The elevator hadn't even arrived. Alyssa was standing with Douglas Forsythe in the lobby, asking him about the different types of health-care providers who came in to assist him with his parents, while trying not to seem too obvious about the fact that she kept checking her phone, hoping for a text message from Sam or Jules.

The problem was probably just a bug in the newly installed system, and Jenn was going to answer her door, perplexed by the crowd of operatives standing there.

That was better, of course, than yesterday's fiasco, when Alyssa had sent Lopez and Zanella over because neither Jenn nor Gillman were answering their phones.

Alyssa didn't know Jennilyn LeMay at all, but Sam had told her about his little talk with Gillman—who was going to reimburse Troubleshooters for his airline tickets to and from New York. Apparently, he was unwilling to get paid, in any way, to protect his "new girl-friend." Except he wasn't exactly protecting her. Lopez had said Gillman was "on his way," which meant he'd left her alone.

And even if the problem wasn't more than a bug or a glitch, Gillman needed a good lecture about properly testing the system before leaving the client—girlfriend or not—unprotected.

Alyssa surreptitiously checked her phone again while Douglas droned on and on and on.

Currently, he told her earnestly, he was doing most of the work himself.

What were they talking about? Oh, right—caring for his parents.

Nurses aides, nursing assistants, visiting nurses—he'd tried all of them, in a variety of combinations, but his mother was something of a pickle, when it came to having strangers in her house. Marileni, of course, they'd known for years.

And to be fair, they *had* found a nurse's aide his mother had liked, but she'd just had a baby of her own and was officially on maternity leave. Still, she managed to come in once a week to help his father with his bath. His mother was still doing all right with a walk-in shower . . .

Douglas was giving Alyssa details about the shower stool he'd ordered from a medical-supply company when his phone rang and he'd started speaking Portuguese again. As he got off the phone, his expression was apologetic.

"Marileni's grandson's school just called. Umberto seems to have caught that awful stomach flu that's going around. She's got to go pick him up," he told her. "I really must head home."

And *that* was not good news.

Sam was completely wigged out by the fact that Winston had had her photograph. It was hard to say which would bother him more—Alyssa taking Douglas out to the dumpster by herself, or letting him go home without following a possible lead that could provide them with some answers.

She checked her phone again, and Douglas asked, "Any word about Jenn? I hope she's all right."

"Nothing yet. Can you give me five minutes?" she asked him as she called the main line of Maria's office, knowing that one of the FBI agents who were on hand would pick up. Carol or John. "To show me—right now—where you saw Winston yesterday morning?"

He frowned as he looked at his watch.

"Three minutes," Alyssa bargained, leading him to the front door of the building, as indeed it was Carol who picked up Maria's office line. "Hi, it's Alyssa Locke. I need you or John to join me and Douglas Forsythe out back by the dumpster, right now. Can one of you do that?"

"Yes, ma'am. I'm on my way."

"I want one of the FBI agents with us," Alyssa told Douglas. "But she'll catch up."

"I really have to hurry," he said.

So they hurried.

In order to access the back alley, they either had to go through the building's basement, or they had to walk down to the cross street, take a left and another left. But Alyssa had been with the team that checked out the basement earlier that morning, and even as innocuous as Douglas appeared, she wasn't going to risk Sam's wrath by taking the man through what could have been a perfect set for a horror movie.

As opposed to a narrow back alley that smelled like urine and rotting food, covered in ankle-deep slush that they'd have to slog through.

They were retracing Douglas's route in reverse, and Alyssa stopped briefly at the entrance to the alley as she narrated what he'd already told them.

"When you got out to the street," she said, "here, right? He was gone?"

"That's correct," he said.

This entire neighborhood consisted of older buildings, some of them crumbling, some exquisitely preserved. Some had wrought iron fences and gates that locked, but some had gates that hung permanently open on broken hinges. Steps led down to what looked like basement apartments—again in a wide variety of upkeep.

There were dozens of places Winston could have hidden from Douglas's untrained eye.

He glanced at his watch again, and Alyssa gestured for him to lead the way into the alley.

"How often have you seen Winston in the area?" she asked as she followed him.

"Oh . . . at least several times a week," he told her. "He's something of a local institution, although I had no idea his name was Winston. Savannah was right—you *are* good. You're here only two days, and already you know more than we do."

"How well do you know Savannah?" Alyssa asked.

"Are you sure I'm not a suspect?" he countered, and it was weird, his demeanor was almost flirtatious or coy—as if, after thinking it through, the idea of being a suspect was titillating.

He was not unattractive, though, and maybe that was the problem she had with him. A man who looked like Douglas Forsythe—a man as wealthy as Douglas Forsythe—was used to getting whatever he wanted.

And she just couldn't see him providing intimate care for his elderly parents.

"Just making conversation," she told him.

"Oh, and you're quite good at lying, too, aren't you?" he teased.

What she needed to do was meet the parents, and get a look at the place where he lived with them. Because right now she just could not imagine it.

She made herself smile at him, though. Where *was* Carol . . . ? "I've been friends with Savannah for a long time. Our husbands were both with SEAL Team Sixteen. Well, Ken still is. For a while, I thought that Savannah was going to run for office, but then she got behind Maria . . . Is that how you met?"

"At a fund-raising event, yes. Back in . . . what was it? May, I think. Right after Maria announced her candidacy. I'd just come home. Mother had fallen and fortunately *hadn't* broken her hip. But it was a very close call." He pointed down the alley. "Fourth dumpster's ours. Or rather, Maria's. I tend to get possessive, but I have to admit that the campaign kept me sane. When he's lucid, Dad's stuck in 1975, and Mother's happy enough to join him there. It's been a challenge—and that's aside from having to learn how to properly fasten an adult diaper. I've come to value my extracurricular activities quite highly. And I'll answer your next question before you ask it: It's only been recently that I've had to have someone stay with them when I go out. Dad's gotten much worse. Mother's afraid he's going to wander off."

"That can be a serious problem," Alyssa agreed, then got the conversation back on track. "You approached the dumpster . . . how?"

"Just as we're doing right now," he told her. "I came in from the street, as we just did."

It didn't make sense for the homeless man to run *past* Douglas, when the alley extended down in the other direction, all the way to the next side street. Why not run that way?

As Alyssa stood, gazing down the alley, a car pulled in to the far end, followed by a police car, its lights spinning.

Douglas saw it, too. "Wonder what's going on," he murmured. "Should we run? *You'll never catch me, coppers.*" He did a terrible imitation of James Cagney.

She smiled, because it was polite to do so, especially

since this was taking far longer than the three minutes she'd promised. "So . . . Winston was where, exactly?"

"He was standing over here." Douglas put himself at the closest end of the dumpster. "I must have gone right past him, to get over here"—he moved again—"to the recycling bin. The bag of tins I was carrying was heavy, so I didn't see him until I'd dumped it in. He startled me—I may have screamed. I'm rather glad no one heard me. *He* took off, running back the way we came."

He peered down the alley at the cars that were still parked there, clearly distracted by them, and the people who'd gotten out of them—several of them uniformed officers.

"At which point you followed?" Alyssa asked him.

"Not immediately, no," he told her. "I had one more bag that I disposed of before heading back toward the street."

"Could you still see him at that point?" she asked, turning to look down the alley, toward the street where they'd entered.

"No, he was already out of sight. He was moving quite quickly." He added, "Despite his limp, of course."

Of course. "Could he have hidden behind one of the other dumpsters?" she asked, as she walked back a bit in that direction. There were other access doors in the buildings on both sides of the alley. Some had steps leading down, some had old-fashioned bulkhead entrances. But every door that Alyssa could see had extremely secure-looking locks.

And it was true that plenty of people could get past even the most secure-seeming lock, but doing so would take even an expert lockpick a longer amount of time than Douglas had described.

"I suppose he could have," he mused. "I have to confess, I was somewhat leery of being alone in the alleyway with him. I didn't look for him too carefully. Do you really think he might be the one who did that awful thing to Maggie?"

"We're looking for him for a variety of reasons," Alyssa said, checking her phone yet again.

"Which you can't tell me about," Douglas said. "Of course. Any word?"

"Nothing yet," she said, as what looked like an ambulance joined the two vehicles at the end of the alley. "Thank you for your time. I know you need to get on your way. I'm going to see what's going on down there."

"I'll walk with you," he said. "With the one-way streets, it's actually easier to get a cab going home if I go out this way."

As Alyssa got closer, she could see yellow tape, marking the area as a crime scene. A crowd had yet to form, but there were police officers standing by the open door to the basement of the building at the very end of the alley.

A woman was nearby, her jacket unzipped, her face pale and her eyes bright with tears. Her hands were trembling as she used a tissue to blow her nose.

"Are you all right?" Alyssa asked her.

"I never seen nothing like that," the woman whispered. "Never in my life. They're dead. They're both dead."

"*Two* bodies," Alyssa clarified. "And you found them?"

She nodded. "Tenant in 1B was complaining of the stink. Something died in the wall, she said. Or maybe in the basement . . . I knew he'd been living there—the old homeless man. I thought he was harmless, but he wasn't. I never seen such a thing as what he did to that woman . . ."

Alyssa opened her phone and called Jules.

Who answered on the first ring. "Shit," he said. "Sorry, Sam asked me to call you, and I totally spaced. Jenn's fine. Maria's brother Frank showed up packing heat, but

Danny Gillman talked him off his proverbial ledge. Everyone's okay, but it's entirely possible that Frank's our man—"

Alyssa interrupted him. "You need to get over here. Now. I'm in the alley behind Maria's office. I haven't been able to get onto the scene, but I think the police have found Winston—and Maggie's body. Bodies. I think Winston's dead, too, Jules."

"Holy crap," Jules said. "When it rains, it pours. I'm on my way. Sam is, too."

Good. She could use a little Sam right about now. A little eye contact, a little connection, the briefest touch of his hand . . . Amazing how something so simple could make the world a significantly better place.

Alyssa hung up her phone to find Douglas watching her. "Jenn's all right," she told him.

"They've found the killer, haven't they?" he asked, but he was talking about Winston, in the basement.

"Go home," she said. "Your parents need you. If we have any additional questions, someone will be in touch."

He nodded and turned, and as he walked away, Alyssa saw the intern, what's his name—Gene—standing in the crowd that was forming. Word was apparently getting out that bodies had been found.

But when Gene saw that Alyssa had spotted him, he quickly faded back, disappearing from sight.

And okay, Sam wasn't even here yet to whisper into her ear about how freaking spooky *that* was. It was true what they said. Criminals—particularly killers—usually had an overpowering urge to return to the scene of the crime.

She headed toward the crowd, determined to talk to Gene, but he was gone.

Which was when her phone rang. It was Carol.

"I'm so sorry I was delayed," the FBI agent said, her voice out of breath. "The head of the New York office called and . . . I'm finally at the dumpster. Where are you?"

"They'll call us," Izzy said, for the four hundredth time, as Maria paced the living room of the hotel suite. "As soon as they get the situation under control."

Robin had taken Ash into the bedroom, because he'd surpassed fussy and moved full-bore into weep-monster of doom.

It was hard to say which was the chicken and which was the egg. Babies were so perceptive, Ash might've originally started fussing because Maria's tension level was off the charts.

But it was also obvious that his crying made Maria more tense. It had turned into an ugly self-perpetuating cycle that Robin was smart enough to try to break.

Izzy could hear him in the bedroom, singing to the kid with a voice that made Izzy's sound like amateur-hour, as—alleluia—Ash brought his diva-worthy outburst down to an occasional mewl or snuffle.

Maria, however, still paced.

As far as wrangling went, Robin had definitely left Izzy with the more difficult of the two jobs. Maria wasn't going to be distracted by funny faces or peek-a-boo, or even the fact that he knew all eighty-seven verses of Don MacLean's "American Pie."

"*A long, long time ago,*" he sang, testing his theory. "*I could still remember* . . . No? I guess a puppet show's probably out then, too."

She looked at him as if he'd spoken to her in Martian, which he had—if he put any faith in the time-honored theories from that book, *Men Are from Mars, Women Are from Venus.*

In his entire life, Izzy had met only one woman who came close to speaking his language and getting most of his jokes, and she still wasn't talking to him, and probably wouldn't ever talk to him again, even when he flew to Germany to see her, which he was going to do in just a matter of days now.

Thinking of Eden made him sad—no. It was beyond sad. It was sorrow that tightened his chest, and he had to look away from Maria and out the window at the low-hanging pewter-colored clouds that made the city skyline look simultaneously starkly ugly and timelessly beautiful.

Maria sat down next to him on the sofa. "You remind me of that Smokey Robinson song," she said, which doubly surprised him. Not only had she stopped pacing, she was talking about something other than was-Jenn-all-right. And then she completely made him sit back, because she started to sing. "*If there's a smile on my face, it's only there, trying to fool the public . . .*"

Her voice was rich and husky and really nice and he found himself smiling at her.

"Have you thought about *American Idol* as a way to the White House?" Izzy asked. "Think of how many votes you could get if you went that route."

"See, you're doing it," she said, unamused. "You're sitting here, and you're terribly sad, but you still have to make a joke."

"I don't *have* to," he said. "I just like to. I mean, what am I going to do, sit around and cry all day?"

She pretended to think about that. "Yeah," she said. "Because that's what people do when they're sad. They cry, and cry, and *cry,* and eventually they're not so sad anymore. You're not the only person in the world who's ever had his heart broken, you know."

"Really?" he said, "because I thought I was. I thought everyone except me always got everything they ever wanted."

"You want to hear something really sad?" Maria asked him, but didn't wait for him to respond. She just kept going. "I'm sitting here, scared to death that my baby brother might hurt my best friend, and at the same time, there's a really dark, ugly part of me that's not-so-secretly hoping that Frankie finally dies." Her eyes filled with tears. "Because it'll be easier for me to achieve my political goals without a drug-addicted, PTSD-suffering brother hanging like an albatross around my neck. How's *that* for sad?"

Izzy nodded. "I don't know if you *win*," he said, "but it's definitely sad. Besides, we don't know that he's the one who made Jenn push the panic button."

"We know," she said. "At least I do. It's got to be Frank. Where else would he go? Stopping first at his dealer's, of course."

Her cell phone rang. It was sitting on the coffee table in front of them and she picked it up. "It's Jenn." She answered it. "Are you all right? Oh, thank God." She closed her eyes, listening to her friend on the other end. "I knew it was," she said. "Is he . . . ? Oh, God, Jenni, I'm so sorry. . . . *Damage* control? Are you *serious*?" She looked at Izzy. "She wants to write a statement for the website—as well as a press release. No," she said into the phone again. "What I want you to do is soul kiss Dan Gillman for me and send him into orbit." She laughed. "Oh, yes, I did go there," she added, but she sobered up fast. "All right," she said. "Yes. It's not like I'm going anywhere. Love you, too. Yeah. Bye."

Maria ended the call, and sat there, as if frozen.

"Is he okay?" Izzy asked quietly.

She met his gaze. "He's alive," she said. "But he's not okay. He's high. And not like buzzed, but out of his mind high—assuming he was in his right mind to start with. And, God, we all know what a good combination it is to mix drugs with firearms, so . . . They think it's possible that he's the one who killed Maggie and a homeless man, too."

And with that, her face crumpled and she started to cry.

But she didn't run away, she just sat there.

So Izzy moved closer. Put his arm around her. It was weird, she was tiny—just a little slip of a thing. It was kind of funny, her personality and presence were so large, he'd thought she was larger.

She reached for him, holding him tightly as she cried on his shoulder, as he rubbed her miniature back with his hand, the way he would've comforted Ash, had that been his assignment.

Not that he was complaining. Maria's hair smelled better, and she was less likely to crap her pants or pee on him, which was a plus.

He could feel the softness of her body against him, the tautness of her thigh against his, and it was remarkable the nothing that he felt. Especially since he was the King of the Comfort Fuck. Women flocked to him for it. It was, in fact, how things had started between Eden and himself. Although he hadn't actually had sex with Eden. He'd just made her come.

And okay, now he wasn't feeling *nothing* anymore. Now he was aching with longing. Although, it had been so many months since he'd last had sex, he wasn't sure he'd remember how to do it.

But the thing was, he didn't want Maria, as beautiful and accomplished as she was.

He wanted Eden, and he wanted Pinkie, but mostly he wanted Eden, because together they could make their own Pinkie, but there wasn't even the remotest chance of that happening if she wouldn't talk to him.

"It's okay," he murmured to Maria. "It's okay to cry. . . ."

"Nicely done, by the way," Jules said as he and Sam jogged back from Jenn's apartment to the alley behind

Maria's office building. "The not-killing-Mick-Callahan thing."

"You noticed that, huh?" Sam sidestepped something that looked remarkably like a cow patty but absolutely couldn't be. Not many cows wandering in this part of New York City. Still, it was uncanny . . .

"Robin calls them car turds," Jules said, as he saw where Sam was looking. "Dirty snow gets kicked up by the tires and stashed somewhere, like in the wheel well or up under the fender, where it freezes. When it starts to thaw, it gets knocked loose, and the car takes a dump."

"And you live in the Northeast by choice?" Sam asked. It was meant to be banter, but he realized even as the words left his mouth that he was unbelievably stupid, and that he wasn't even close to being funny. Jules and Robin lived in Massachusetts because their marriage was legal there, period, the end. It was *the* main reason why Jules, one of the top FBI agents in the country, wasn't working where he should have been—out of the D.C. office under counterterrorist legend Max Bhagat. "Sorry. That was—"

"Are you happy?" Jules interrupted him.

"My side hurts like a bitch," Sam reported. "My feet are fucking cold. Our op's body count is up to two, and someone's going to have to break the news to the client that her brother is at worst a psycho-killer, at best a drug addict, and that lucky person's probably going to be my wife, who'll cry about it after, but only when she's somewhere no one—including me—will see or hear her. So, no, I'm not particularly happy right now."

"Yeah, yeah, but I'm talking big-picture happy," Jules said.

"Big picture," Sam repeated.

"You, Alyssa, Ashton," Jules said. "Haley. Making peace with Mary Lou. Owning your own home. Working for Troubleshooters, with Alyssa as your boss. Not being a SEAL until your knees gave out . . . ?"

"Ah." Sam got what he was saying. And Jules was right. He hadn't taken the path he'd expected to take, but the amazing achievements of the past few years—Alyssa had actually fallen in love with him, married him, and borne his child—far outweighed any of the disappointments. "I'm very happy."

"I am, too," Jules said. "In Boston. With all of its many car turds."

"You tell me that a lot, don't you?" Sam realized. "That you're happy."

"Like a broken record," Jules said. "You can't seem to grasp that I'm beyond good with what I've got, and yet here you are—Alyssa told me—making your own lemonade out of lemons and blithely suggesting that you and Robin and Ash camp out in Italy for a month so that your wife and I can go off without you and save the world."

Sam shrugged. "It'll be easier with Robin. You know, helping out with Ash."

"No," Jules said, "it won't."

"Yes, it will," Sam said, "Mister Don't-Tell-Me-I'm-Not-Happy. *You* don't tell *me* what will or won't be easier for *me, capisce*?"

"Practicing your Italian already?"

"I figured we'd stay at that place where you and I had our romantic getaway," Sam said. He'd taken an allegedly easy assignment, setting up security for a richie-rich celebrity wedding, and had gotten damn near attacked by the bridesmaids, as if in a nightmarish *Girls Gone Wild* parody. He'd repeatedly called Alyssa for help, but she was on assignment on the other side of the globe. She'd ended up calling Jules, who'd flown in for the weekend as the weirdest backup ever.

Sam's continuously flashing his wedding ring and

talking ceaselessly about his wife hadn't slowed down the attacking horde, but Jules, showing up looking fabulous and giving Sam a kiss hello . . . ?

It had done the trick. Instant respect.

"I was gonna see if Ric and Annie wanted to come to provide extra security for Robin," Sam said. Ric ran Troubleshooters' Florida office. He and his wife, Annie, were also good friends with Robin and Jules. "And I thought we should invite Gina and Maxine Junior, too. And their new baby, Piggy-Face. Don't want to leave him out. As long as Max is going over there, with you."

Jules was laughing. "Max and Gina's new baby does *not* have a piggy face. And it's not Maxine Junior, it's—"

"Emma," Sam said. "And Michael, I know. And you're right. The little dude looks more like Alfred Hitchcock."

"All babies look like Alfred Hitchcock," Jules said. "Or Winston Churchill. I got a picture stored in my phone of Ashton, at a few weeks old, looking like he's ready for the sumo wrestling tryouts. Shit."

There was a crowd and a gaggle of police cruisers and unmarked vehicles at the entrance to the alley, back behind Maria's office.

But Alyssa was there, too—standing with Mick Callahan.

How the hell had he gotten here before them?

"I thought he was still in the apartment," Sam muttered to Jules, who knew immediately to whom he was referring, "talking to Jenn?"

Mick had done quite a good job earlier, calming Jennilyn down after she'd reluctantly left Dan in the stairwell with Maria's drugged-out brother.

"Dan's been over there," Mick had reminded Jenn, getting her to sit down with him on her sofa and stay out of the way. "He's enlisted, too—he's not an officer. Way I understand it, that makes a difference. He's got more in common with Frank than most of us here. And what little I know about Navy SEALs is he's a damn good shot, if it comes to that."

Mick's sisterly affection for Jenn seemed solid and real. Warm, even.

But now here he was, standing too close to Alyssa as he watched Sam and Jules approach with those cold, flat eyes.

Alyssa was locked down, her mouth tight, her eyes guarded, and Sam knew that she hadn't waited for them—that she'd talked her way into the crime scene.

She'd seen the bodies, and she nodded at them now.

"It's Winston," she confirmed. "And Mick identified the woman as Margaret Thorndyke, although the official ID will wait for a dental match. But . . . It's her."

No doubt the hole in her chest made the ID official enough for Alyssa.

"The murder weapon's the exact same kind of knife that was stuck in Assemblywoman Bonavita's door a week ago," Mick volunteered. "It's a fucking mess in there. I should've listened to my mother and become a dentist the way she wanted me to."

"What the hell is he doing here?" Sam asked.

Mick, of course, bristled, and Alyssa reached out and took hold of Sam's arm.

"He's helping," she told him, but she also tightened her grip before she released him—clearly sending a message, but what? *Don't* was solidly in there, Sam did know that.

So he didn't. Didn't move, didn't talk, didn't even look at the prick.

Jules asked, "Have they moved the bodies?"

"No," Alyssa said. "I told them to wait for you."

"Good," Jules said.

Sam moved to follow him into the basement, half expecting Alyssa to stop him with another hand on his arm and to tell him that he didn't need to go in there and see the awful things that human beings could do to one another.

But she just looked at him, and he knew she would never say that in front of Mick Callahan.

She also knew that it wasn't a fear of being unmanned, or a need to accept some kind of double-dare that was making Sam follow Jules. He was going in because, as awful as it was going to be, another pair of eyes might see something differently.

And because a case like this wasn't over until it was *over.*

Because they still had Frank Bonavita in custody, where he was going to endure some serious detox, saying things like *They said they saw me kill Maria.* . . .

"They" had written him a letter that he'd hidden in his room with his stash of meth. A stash that had, he claimed, just appeared in his bathroom, as if magical meth-making elves had left it there for him.

A team of FBI agents was already on their way out to Long Island to find out if the letter and stash were just another part of Frank's paranoid delusions.

As Sam stepped through the basement door, he paused, letting his eyes adjust to the dim light and . . .

Holy fuck.

The smell was awful, the sight even worse.

He made himself look, made himself join Jules, who was standing in the middle of the room.

"Our guy," Jules said quietly, "is definitely a showman." He raised his voice. "I want an autopsy on both bodies, and I want it now. Carol!"

"Yes, sir."

"I thought I saw you lurking there," Jules said. "There's going to be interest from the media, and I don't want to be the one that gets questions shouted at him. I don't even want them to know I'm here."

"I'll handle it, sir."

"The statement we're releasing is that two homeless people froze to death," Jules ordered. "I don't want any details leaking out."

"Yes, sir."

Sam followed them both back out into the metal-grayness of the waning afternoon light, where Alyssa was waiting for him.

Mick, thank God, was gone. But not far.

"He's upstairs," Alyssa told him, told Jules, too. "I told him we still wanted to talk to him, because as far as I'm concerned? Winston didn't kill Maggie. In fact, I'm pretty sure he's victim number two."

CHAPTER SEVENTEEN

As Lopez left, locking the door behind him, Danny poured Jenn a glass of cranberry juice and she took it, meeting his eyes only briefly.

She was embarrassed.

Not because she'd foolishly opened the door without checking to see who was on the other side, but because she'd told Frank that she loved Dan.

At the time, he'd been intent on making sure Frank didn't kill anyone, and he'd let it roll, completely, off his back and out of his focus.

But now he couldn't stop thinking about it, and it was making him sweat. It was crazy, but even the idea of talking to her about the way he'd blacked out again was less anxiety-inducing.

Lopez had given him an out before he'd left them alone here in Jenn's apartment. He'd offered to stay so that Dan could go back to the hotel and take some downtime.

Danny had considered it—just picking up and running away. But he wanted Jenn again, desperately. God, he wanted to lose himself in sex that was so good, he couldn't remember the last time he'd had any that was better. And he wanted her badly enough that it trumped the most awkward of conversations. It even trumped the fact that he knew—he *knew*—that if she truly was falling in love with him, the dead last thing he should do was make love to her again, and risk cementing her feelings.

It would be selfish and cruel to do that.

Not that. *This.*

Because he *was* doing it.

Except maybe she didn't *really* love him.

Maybe she loved him as a friend. Maybe . . .

Jenn being Jenn, despite her embarrassment, she led the elephant in the corner into the center of the room, and started the awkward discussion.

"It's worse than getting called *pookie,* isn't it?" she said, adjusting her bathrobe more securely around her and pushing her glasses farther up her nose. She'd been shaking so hard after Frank was taken into custody, that her cop friend, Mick, had suggested she take a hot shower, try to use it both to warm up and to wash away what had been a frightening incident. "The we-both-know-it's-short-term girlfriend dropping the L-bomb on Day Two. It's not only terrifying, it's absurd. It's clearly a very strong signal as to my emotional instability."

As usual, she'd made him laugh.

"Or maybe it's more of an emotional immaturity," she continued. "Either way, alarm bells *are* ringing. I can tell, just from looking at you, that you've pushed your own internal panic button. But you're too gallant to run away."

"There're all kinds of love," he said.

"There are," she agreed.

"I also think," Dan told her as he sat down on the other end of the couch, trying to keep his distance, "that it can be easy to mistake certain . . . biological reactions for strong emotions. You were in serious danger, and I came to your rescue. And your body released all kinds of hormones and endorphins and God knows what-all into your system, giving you a physical reaction that feels a lot like, you know . . ."

She didn't look convinced, so he kept going.

"I know," he continued, "because I feel it, too. It's more than just a woodie, although that's a pretty standard accessory for me, to any life and death confrontation. And again, it's biological. And I feel this shit racing through my bloodstream, the adrenaline and whatever and I look at you, and start getting these messages, like an intercom clicking on at the stem of my brain, saying, *Mine*. I'm possessive to start with. I know that about myself. Add some extra testosterone, and look out. I would've killed him, you know. If he'd as much as turned toward you, I would have dropped him, right there."

"I'm glad you didn't," Jenn said.

"I'm glad I didn't have to."

"So you think," she said, "that while I was in that moment, my body was releasing hormones and adrenaline—"

"I don't just think it, I know it," Dan told her. "Your hands are still shaking. That's as classic a symptom of adrenaline overload as my, you know . . . packing wood."

She smiled at that.

"You also didn't have a lot of time to tell Frank exactly what you were feeling. *Hey, don't shoot Dan, because I like him and we've been having a really good time together and if you killed him I'd be extremely upset, particularly since I'm feeling overwhelmed with appreciation at the way he came to my rescue . . .* Instead, you . . . said what you said. You went concise and used language you knew Frank would understand."

"Ah," she said. "I like that one, too. You're incredibly talented when it comes to rationalizing."

"The key," Dan told her, "is to understand what's going on, and not misinterpret the little voice that says *Mine,* and rush off to Vegas to get married. Because the hormone levels and adrenaline eventually go back to normal, and then you're, like, waking up next to some numbnuts, thinking, *What the hell have I done?*"

"The numbnuts being you," Jenn pointed out, "since I'm completely nutless."

He didn't know what to say to that. She was clearly speaking symbolically, as in she had no balls, i.e., courage to challenge his theories, or to disagree.

"You think I'm wrong?" he finally said.

"I don't know," she admitted. "It just seems so . . . cold. You probably don't believe in love at first sight, either. Unless there's a scientific explanation for that . . ."

"I don't believe in it," he admitted. "I believe in attraction at first sight. I also believe in . . . immediate connection at first conversation. I believe that there's no such thing as an easy relationship and that every time you put two people together, there's going to be sacrifice and compromise. That nobody gets exactly what they want, but if you learn to adapt and be flexible, you'll win more often than you lose. Because your definition of winning will be broad and include more options."

"Then why can't it be a win for you, when I say . . . what I said." She laughed and sat forward. "God, it's not like it's an evil spell that'll destroy the world if it's uttered aloud. Why isn't it a win when I say that I love you?"

Her leaning toward him like that made one side of her robe fall open a bit, giving him a clear shot of the soft curve of one of her breasts.

She didn't have particularly large breasts. They certainly weren't as large as they should have been to make her shaped like an hourglass in proportion to her generous hips. No, she was a pear, smaller on top than on bottom, but big breasts weren't everything, and he sure as hell didn't want her to change anything about her legs and thighs—she had gorgeous thighs, strong yet soft and so smooth when she wrapped them around him. . . .

He'd yet to get her completely naked, but give him time and he would, because he wanted her riding him, her eyes closed as she moaned her pleasure, her breasts slick with sweat as she strained to take him deep, deeper. . . .

Mine.

She was sitting there, watching him with those big eyes, waiting for him to tell her that he didn't want to hurt her. That he wasn't sure if he could make himself walk away from her—which he knew he had to do if she really was falling for him.

Why the hell was she falling for him? For *him* . . . ?

Dan found himself kissing her. He had no idea if she'd leaned even nearer to him, or if he'd been the one to reach for her and pull her close. But Jesus, he *was* kissing her, and she was kissing him back, her arms around him, her fingers in his hair.

She moved even closer, straddling him, reaching between them to unfasten his pants, to find him, as always, ready to go.

She laughed a little. "You weren't kidding, were you?"

She'd let her robe fall open, and there it was, one perfect, dark pink nipple that he licked into his mouth. Her hands tightened around him as she gasped, "Condom . . ."

He bumped into her hand as he reached for one—she'd learned where he kept them. But as intriguing as the thought of her putting it on him was . . . He didn't think he could wait that long. Except . . .

"Jenn, I don't want to hurt you," he whispered. "And unless that was magic cranberry juice . . ."

She laughed. "I'm fine," she insisted, shrugging out of her robe, letting it fall on the floor, leaving her naked.

And Christ, he couldn't say no to that, for so many reasons—the foremost being that she'd take it as a rejection, and he was not going to do that to her. And yes, like the woman had said, he was a master at rationalizing.

He could give himself a list of fifty reasons, but the real one was right here, in his hands, now covered and ready for her to climb upon, which she did as she breathed his name, "Oh, Dan . . ."

And it was all right there, in every touch, every kiss, every moan as she moved, so exquisitely slowly at first, then faster, as she lit him on fire.

His fear when Izzy had called, when he'd run back here and realized she was no longer in her apartment, when he'd waited nearly goddamn out of his mind for the elevator so he could ride up to a higher floor and cut them off before they reached the roof, when he'd realized Frank, who was holding a weapon, was high. . . .

His anger at Frank—that he would put Jenn at risk like that.

His relief when he saw her—that she was all right, that Frank hadn't hurt her.

His joy that she could make him laugh, even then and there in the stairwell, regardless of all his anger and fear.

His confidence that he would, without question, keep her safe.

He wanted to keep her safe.

Her bare skin was so smooth beneath his fingers. Her body was so soft as she cried out his name again, this time as she came.

Head thrown back, body arched, breasts thrust forward, nipples taut, thighs tight around him as she pushed him even deeper inside of her . . . Jesus, she was beyond gorgeous, and he ran his hands up her body from her thighs to her breasts, filling the palms of his hands as she just kept coming and coming around him.

And he came, too, in an intense rush of pleasure that made his blood sing and his ears roar. And despite the additional noise from his pounding heart and his ragged breathing, he heard it, as clear as a crystal bell. His adrenaline and hormones and endorphins all coming together to chime in . . .

Mine.

"Are we sure," Alyssa said, "that Danny Gillman's got it together enough to provide sufficient protection for Jennilyn?"

She and Sam, and Jules and Robin, were sitting in the living room of the hotel suite. Or rather she, Sam, and Jules were sitting.

Robin was lying on the floor. Ashton, who was now happily at his mother's breast, had totally kicked his ass today. The tyke hadn't yet mastered crawling, but he had his own form of propulsion—scooting across the floor on his butt, using his strong little legs to push himself along. In a matter of seconds—the briefest of head turns—the little boy was gone and into God knows what.

Robin had had to monitor him constantly. Gone were the days of putting him in his rocking seat or his swing as Robin quietly sat nearby, reading a good book.

But the real killer was the continuous requests—that upraised precious face and two tiny, reaching hands— for assistance in walking. All Ash wanted to do, for hours on end, was walk around holding onto Robin's hands. Which had actually been fun, the first four thousand times.

Come on, Ash, let's sit for a while and read a book. *Ning-a-nang!*

Hey, Ash, let's play with these nifty blocks. I'll set 'em up and you can knock 'em down. It'll be fun. *Ning-a-nang!*

Ooh, Ashie, I bet you want Uncle Robin to put you in this ugly-ass rented high chair so you can eat some yummy Cheerios.

Ning-a-ning-a-freaking-nang.

"We could put a guard over there, if you want," Sam said, answering Alyssa's question about Gillman, who'd apparently gotten something hot and heavy going with Maria's assistant.

Robin had overheard Maria talking to Izzy about it today. She was secretly thrilled that Jenn would do something so impetuous. It was, allegedly, completely out of character.

Maria, who like Robin was one of those glass-half-full people, was convinced that Jenn had met her soul mate and would be married within the year. Izzy'd argued with her about that for a bit, but he'd finally given up. He was not, he'd agreed, the best person in the world to judge whether or not Dan Gillman would make a good soul mate for anyone.

"But Jenn's place is ridiculously small," Sam added now. "I say let Danny stay with her. For tonight, anyway. As for tomorrow . . . I think we should consider bringing in more members of the team. How's Lindsey feeling? Have you heard from her?"

"She's not out of bed yet," Alyssa told him. "Maybe Deck and Nash are back from Indonesia."

Robin lifted his head. "Wait a minute. I thought this was over. That the bad guy is Maria's brother. The way she was talking about him . . ."

Maria had been convinced that her brother had killed Maggie Thorndyke. That plus the fact that they'd moved her back into her own apartment so she could sleep in her own bed tonight had made Robin assume . . .

Jules spoke up. "It seems unlikely that Frank Bonavita had the ability to do everything that our killer did. Grab Maggie, take her somewhere private to kill her and do his . . . handiwork on her—"

Robin sat up. "But I thought that you found where he took her. To that basement where the homeless man was living. Did I miss something?"

"Sweetie, whoever killed her," Jules told him, "he didn't do it there. There would have been way more blood. Plus she had marks on her wrists and ankles that indicate she'd been bound, prior to her death. But there were no ropes and nothing to tie her to in that basement. The full autopsy report's not in yet, but the entire forensics team agrees. Maggie's body was moved there after she was dead. And whoever put her there knew that Winston—the homeless guy—lived there. Our killer set it up to look like Winston slit his own wrists, but I'm betting we find a major amount of a narcotic in his system."

"Okay, I can see how the theory's implausible," Robin said. "Frank killed Maggie—somewhere presumably *not* in the center of Times Square, then put her heart in his sister's office, sent a postcard, made a phone call, and framed Winston—all while under the influence of a radically mind-altering drug."

"Forget about the implausibility. It doesn't even begin to explain how or why Winston had Alyssa's picture back in September," Sam chimed in. "That's what *I* still want to find out."

The former SEAL usually sat sprawled in his seat, long legs stretched out, his posture and body language enormously masculine and relaxed. But tonight he was sitting up straight, his movements limited and extremely careful. No doubt about it, the man was in some serious pain.

"Do you need some ice?" Robin asked him silently, so Alyssa didn't start in again on Sam taking a shower and getting his butt into bed. Although, truth be told, if Jules had ordered Robin into bed that way, he'd have gone willingly. Of course, they didn't have a baby to feed. "Should I get you some?"

Sam shook his head, just the tiniest little bit. "Won't help," he said silently back.

And, of course, Robin didn't have a broken rib, which could make going to bed a lot less fun.

"Whoever killed Maggie and Winston knew that we were looking at Winston as a suspect." Alyssa's voice rang with certainty.

"I agree," Jules said.

"And you're certain that couldn't have been Frank?" Robin asked. "Hey, here's a thought. Do you know for a fact that he's using—that he's not just a really good actor, pretending to be on meth?"

That question got everyone looking at each other, so he asked, "Is he in detox or in jail? Because if he's in detox, they'll have done complete blood work. But if it's jail . . . Not so much."

"I think they were taking him to a psychiatric hospital," Jules said, reaching for his phone.

"This is why I didn't want to go to bed," Sam told Alyssa. "I wanted to stay up so I could watch the Boy Wonder here solve our case for us."

"But what's his motive? Frank's." Alyssa asked, putting Ash onto her shoulder and rubbing his back, looking for a burp. The kid could belch like a longshoreman and he not only complied but he stayed asleep through it. Alyssa had the magic touch. "If he's looking to ruin his sister's political career, he doesn't have to kill Maggie to do that."

That was true. Frank just needed to run amok.

"Maria mentioned something about a letter," Robin said. "That Frank was sent something through the mail? Snail mail, I mean."

"His parents remembered getting it," Jules reported, his cell phone to his ear. "They said they thought it was something he'd sent away for. You know, that he'd sent someone a self-addressed envelope, because his name and address looked like it was in his own handwriting."

"What?" Sam said, leaning forward but then wincing.

Jules held up one finger as his call went through. "Hey, Carol. Can we make sure that Frank Bonavita was given a complete drug test?" He paused, listening, then said, "Okay, that's good. Make sure I get a copy. I want to know what he was on, and if possible, for how long he was on it. Thank you." He listened some more, then said "Uh-huh" a handful of times mixed with "Really," and then, "Yeah, definitely scan it in and e-mail it to me. Yeah. Thanks." He hung up and sighed—he was tired, too—and said, "We'll have the drug-test info in the morning. And in the land of too-little-too-late, we've verified that Winston was seen—on the webcam footage—outside Nicco's restaurant, shortly after 11 A.M., which was when the killer used Maggie's phone to call Maria."

"But he was bound to be there at some point," Alyssa argued. "He lived in the neighborhood. Did he go inside?"

"No, he did not," Jules answered, "and most of the footage of the people who *did* go in is too blurry to ID. Winston was unique in his appearance, but most people who went through the restaurant door . . . ? The analysts can't even tell if they're men or women." He sighed. "And the bad news just keeps coming. Re: the letter. The team searching Frank's bedroom found both it and his stash, exactly where he said they were. That's good, right? He's being honest with us, at least to a degree. His parents are pissed, though. They don't know how he got the drugs. According to them—and to Frank, too—he never leaves his room, let alone the house. But the parents aren't there all the time, so . . ."

"What does the letter say?" Alyssa asked, smiling down into her sleeping baby's face. "Did he keep the envelope? Was there a postmark?"

"No envelope," Jules said. "Carol's sending a scanned copy. She told me that what they found was handwritten, on a single sheet of notebook paper. It accused Frank of killing both Maggie—and Maria. In fact, it said, *I saw you kill Maria*. But the kicker? The handwriting, again, appears to be Frank's."

"Appears to be." Robin pounced on Jules's words. "You think it's possible that Frank didn't write it."

Jules glanced at Sam. "Occam's razor says he did, but . . . I don't know. I just don't see Frank killing anyone."

"But if it's not Frank, then who?" Robin asked.

"Mick Callahan," Sam said with an extra dash of grim, and all but a growl in his Texas twang. "He saw the case file. He knew we were looking for Winston. He knows the neighborhood. He has the motive—Maria rejected him. His life's in the shitter. His wife left him for his cousin, he lost his job in New Jersey . . . Best he could do was return to his old precinct, which is, as he admits, a giant step backward in his career. He still hasn't found an apartment that he can afford, so he's been living with his parents. He drinks too much and he's got a hair-trigger temper that we've seen up close and personal." He laughed. "He apologized to me—sort of. *I didn't know she was your wife*. Like it would've been okay for him to say those things about Alyssa if I wasn't married to her."

"He's definitely a misogynist," Jules chimed in, "and probably homophobic. He's one of those guys who didn't want to shake my hand, for fear that some of my gay might rub off."

"I hate that," Robin said, laughing.

"But that doesn't make Callahan a killer. I got the same vibe from both Doug and Gene—*and* one of the New York FBI agents," Jules said. "John what's-his-name. It can be a generational thing."

"Douglas," Alyssa chimed in, and when Jules looked at her blankly, she added, "Forsythe. He doesn't like to be called Doug. It's Douglas. He knew Maggie better than anyone, including Maria and Jenn. They ran with the same crowd when they were growing up."

Jules nodded. "For that alone, *he* should stay on our suspect list, too."

"Although he did volunteer that information," Alyssa pointed out. "He seems forthright."

"He's also guilty of wearing a bow tie and meaning it," Sam said.

"And loving the sound of his own voice," Jules added. "But that's not a crime, either."

"He's a personal-space invader," Sam said. "I kept wanting to tell him to move away from my wife."

"Yeah, and maybe if you did it with the right *je ne sais quoi,* he would have broken your other rib," Jules quipped.

"Forsythe?" Sam scoffed. "I doubt it."

"Don't be fooled by the bow tie," Jules said. "There was a solidly put together man under that tweed jacket."

"Excuse me. Should I be jealous?" Robin asked.

"No," both Jules and Sam said in unison, then laughed, Sam adding an "Ow."

"He just creeped me out," Jules said. "Although, I gotta confess, I've reached that place where everyone I talk to creeps me out. Any one of them could be the killer—including Ron Reed with his perfectly prepared alibi report. I mean, I just start thinking why else would he have gone to all that trouble to document his every move. So he's still on my suspect list."

"Gene the intern's at the top of mine," Alyssa said. She told Robin, "Not only did I see him lurking in the crowd outside the basement, but Jules sent some agents out to talk to his parents. No one was home, but they spoke to some neighbors who saw a car idling in the driveway around midnight on the night Maggie was murdered. They said they saw Gene get in and the car drove away. But Gene told us he was there all night."

"So you know that he lied to you," Robin concluded. "At least about that."

"Don't forget Hank Englewood, the UPS man," Jules said. "He was supposed to come in for an interview today, but he was a no-show. Carol called the branch office where he works, and they told her he quit. Just like that. No notice, just good-bye. She got his home address and went out there, got the landlord to open up the place, and he was gone. We've got an APB out on him. He could be our man."

"But what does he want?" Alyssa asked. "Why put Maggie's heart into Maria's office? And why kill Winston at all—unless it's to try to make us think that Winston killed Maggie? But whoever set that up didn't try very hard. It's almost as if they were just playing with us. I mean, yes, let's find and bring in Hank Englewood, but I can't shake the idea that the killer is someone we've already spoken to. And I keep coming back to Gene. Tomorrow, I want to go out to his house. Talk to his parents, see if there's anything else he's lied about."

"We'll check out everyone's alibis," Jules said. He glanced at Sam. "Even Mick Callahan's."

"I still think," Sam said, looking over at his wife, "that until we figure out what Winston was doing with your photo, you need to make damn sure that you're with me or Jules at all times. No more exceptions, no more back-alley excursions with anyone, suspect or not."

"Carol's good, too," Alyssa pointed out.

"Me," Sam repeated, holding her gaze, "or Jules." He paused, then added, "Please."

They sat there, just looking at each other, having some kind of silent communion. God only knew what all they were saying to each other, but it was clearly heartfelt.

Robin glanced at Jules, who was watching him and smiling. And he knew what Jules was thinking. Out of all of their many friends who were committed couples, Sam and Alyssa's relationship was the most solid. In fact, Jules often said that being with them was like taking a master class in communication. They were both leaders, both alpha personalities, and they worked it—hard—to maintain a perfect balance, to make their relationship a true partnership.

"Fair enough," Alyssa said.

"Thank you," Sam told her quietly.

She smiled at him and stood up. "Let's put this baby to bed." She glanced at Jules and Robin. "Good night, guys."

"I'll print out that copy of Frank's letter and leave it on the table out here," Jules told her, "so you can see it first thing in the morning."

"Thanks," she said with another smile, as she closed their bedroom door behind them.

"Is the laptop set up?" Jules asked.

"In our room," Robin said. "It's attached to the printer."

"Bless you," Jules said. He pushed himself up to his feet. "This is turning out to be some vacation for you, huh?"

"Ash is amazing," Robin told him. "He's killing me, but he's . . . really amazing. He's making up his own language and . . . I gotta figure out how to get him crawling. I read that there's a correlation between crawling and developing fine motor skills and reading. It sounds crazy, but when people have strokes, part of their recovery therapy is to learn to crawl again." He laughed. "That's on my to-do list for tomorrow—teach Ash to crawl. As opposed to yours—catch a killer."

"Please baby Jesus, let us catch him tomorrow," Jules said, as he held out his hands to help Robin off the floor.

"Is it okay with you if we bring Maria back here in the morning? That letter with its *I saw you kill Maria* thing has me on edge."

"Of course," Robin said. "She . . . gets a little uptight when Ash cries. I haven't figured out if it's a biological clock thing, or if she's annoyed with herself because she just doesn't like babies—like she thinks there's something wrong with her because of that. Which there's not. Not everyone's meant to have children. I don't know—I like her, though, don't get me wrong. I'm not complaining. I like Izzy, too. He's . . . funny and . . . Thank you, by the way, for not sending me home."

"Come here," Jules said, pulling him in for an embrace.

Robin closed his eyes and held on tight, his cheek against Jules's—who always seemed to know exactly what he needed.

Robin was about to tell him that, when Jules spoke first. "I'm so lucky that you're in my life," he murmured, pulling back to look into Robin's eyes. "On days like today, when I see things that . . ." He looked away, shook his head.

"You can tell me about it, babe," Robin said.

Jules smiled. "I know. I'd just rather . . ." He kissed Robin.

And yeah. Talking was nice, but there were definitely other ways to communicate.

And right now, Robin would *just rather*, too.

He used nearly a full bottle of Purell hand sanitizer after shaking the homosexual FBI agent's hand.

It was a shame, because he wanted to keep his hand unwashed for at least a little while, after touching her.

After waiting so long, he'd finally touched Alyssa.

He'd practiced breathing, slowly, regularly, in the hours leading up to their meeting.

He knew he was a suspect—that was all right. He was prepared. Even if they came out to his house, looking to ask him further questions, looking to talk to his parents, to verify that he'd been where he'd claimed he was on the night of Maggie's murder . . . He was ready for them. He was ready for anything.

He was euphoric, despite the mishap with the unwanted handshake.

It had been more thrilling than he'd imagined to talk to her, to answer her questions, to have her talk to him, look at him.

To have her *see* him.

He'd spoken to her without his voice cracking or wavering—at least not too badly.

And he'd managed, too, not to snarl and tear out the husband's eyes—although he'd desperately wanted to.

And he was glad that he'd looked out of the window in the men's room that cold December day, and watched the homeless man, Winston, shuffling away from the dumpsters, then furtively climbing in through the window, into the basement of that building at the end of the alley.

He knew where Winston lived, and when he'd heard the SEALs talking in the hall outside Maria's office, he knew what he had to do.

It was easier than one would think, to transport a body through the city, although it helped that he had his father's car.

Getting Maggie through the window had had its difficult moments, but he'd managed, and he was there with her, waiting, when sure enough, Winston scrambled home.

The elderly man was wearing only that skimpy hospital gown, and he was shivering and near frozen.

Nearly dead.

But not quite.

It had been exhilarating, knowing that Alyssa was going to see this, find this . . .

And he also knew he'd have to step up his schedule, to move his plan along. She was smart and he couldn't risk her being a step ahead of him.

Because he hadn't been able to resist taking a tooth.

Chapter Eighteen

The morning was another gray one, with a cold rain falling, beating a syncopated cadence on the window and the top of the air conditioner.

Dan had slept better last night than he had in weeks, possibly months. No nightmares, no dreams at all. Just Jenn, breathing steadily, warm and soft next to him.

The one time he'd woken up in the night, he'd known exactly where he was—no disorientation, no sense of panic. He'd gotten up to use the head and, coming back to join Jenn, had fallen asleep again, almost immediately.

This morning, after some slow, lazy lovemaking that had left him smiling, Jenn had gotten up to write a series of statements for the press about Maria's brother's drug use and Maggie's death. She'd even written a speculative one, linking Maria's brother to Maggie and Winston's murders. It was only a matter of time, she'd told Dan, until the truth came out and the story broke. And they had to be ready with honest, concise information.

Her apartment was so small, she sat cross-legged on the end of the bed, her laptop on a tray table as she worked.

She was including facts and statistics about the government's self-admitted failure in treating PTSD—about their lack of readiness in providing sufficient facilities and medical personnel to treat the sheer numbers of servicemen and women returning from war zones with the trauma-induced disorder. Frank had had the additional difficulty of getting care because his condition was labeled "pre-existing," which was ridiculous. But there it was, in his file. He allegedly had something called borderline personality disorder, a condition that was hard to diagnose or even define, and his benefits were cut.

And then, when he'd started self-medicating through drug use . . .

He'd been completely abandoned by a system that was desperately in need of change.

Jenn sat there, calmly giving Danny information about PTSD—what it was and how it manifested itself in a wide variety of symptoms, depending on the person.

Not everyone ended up like Frank, broken and addicted. In fact, most people with PTSD knuckled down, coping with the disability as best they could—raising their families, living their lives.

But the stigma attached to post-traumatic stress disorder often kept servicemen and women from seeking the proper treatment. And there *was* treatment. Doctors had had a huge amount of success with something called eye movement therapy—the idea being that human beings used dreams to process high-stress situations and events fraught with fear or peril. But some people either didn't or couldn't dream properly. Or they compartmentalized the trauma, seemingly in control, when in fact it was back there, unprocessed and manifesting itself in the nightmares or flashbacks or other symptoms of PTSD.

In eye movement therapy, with the assistance of a trained psychologist, a PTSD-sufferer learned to properly process the trauma. It was true that it didn't work for everyone, but the success rate, to date, was noteworthy.

Dan knew what Jenn was doing. She was addressing his unspoken dread that he was destined to follow Frank's path. Although a big difference between them—him and Frank—was that Frank didn't want to go back. Dan's big fear was that he'd be pulled from active duty and that they wouldn't *let* him go back to war.

Somehow, Jenn understood that, too.

Last night she'd gently asked him about his fight with Izzy Zanella in the hotel suite, and he'd told her what he remembered.

"I remember being tired," he'd admitted, "but being afraid to fall asleep because, well, I've been having these really bad nightmares lately." Understatement. Thank God he'd been sitting next to Lopez on the plane during their flight to New York from California. He'd dozed off, and his friend had woken him up before he'd started shouting. "So I was just going to read and, you know, keep the light on."

"What were you reading?" Jenn asked.

He'd looked at her. "What does it matter—"

"It doesn't," she said. "But I'm curious. Don't you want to know what *I* like to read?"

"I know what you like to read," he told her, pointing to her bookshelves. "Romance novels. And they all lived happily ever after . . ."

She laughed her outrage. "Are you mocking me?" she asked. "Like there's something wrong with being happy?"

"It's just such a long shot," Dan told her. "The idea that two people are going to stay married forever, when fifty percent of all couples eventually split up . . . ?" He pointed to her shelves again, with a sweeping gesture. "That means that if half of those books had a sequel, they'd be anti-romance novels, about divorce and despair."

"So what were *you* reading?" she asked again. "Some

treatise on doom and gloom? A horror story where everyone dies at the hand of the brutal killer?"

"Actually," he said, "I was reading a book that, um, Tony recommended. An autobiography by a guy whose parents sent him to one of those, um, you know, ex-gay ministries?"

He'd surprised her. Completely.

"I'm not gay," he said, which was stupid, because if she didn't know that by now . . .

"I know, I just . . ." She started over. "I didn't know if *you* knew that Tony was. Gay. Don't ask, don't tell . . . ?"

"That bullshit doesn't work," Dan said.

Jenn laughed. "Wow, I had no idea you were so advanced in your thinking."

"Should I be insulted?" he asked.

"Yes, actually." She surprised him by agreeing. "That *was* insulting, wasn't it? I'm sorry."

He'd pulled her back onto the bed with him and kissed her. "I'll let you make it up to me."

She smiled into his eyes. "I bet you will. But okay. Let me mentally rearrange what I thought I knew about Dan Gillman. He's a member of Tony Vlachic's gay book club—you know, I didn't even get the impression that you were *friends* with him, let alone—"

"I'm not," Dan admitted. "Not really. Friends with him. And yeah, okay, before I knew about Tony, I was in the don't ask, don't tell, don't want to know school, so then when I *did* know, it was . . . Weird. I had no idea, and suddenly . . . But he's a good teammate. He always has been, and like Lopez says, nothing's changed. He's still a SEAL. There's nothing that kid can't do, and do well—except maybe have sex with my sister, the way that that motherfucker Zanella did."

Jenn laughed at that. But the words she spoke were

serious. "Is that really what's behind the animosity between you and Izzy? You know, I thought you were going to kill him last night."

"I don't know when it started," Dan said. "But it was definitely a problem even before he slept with Eden. We've always clashed. It's a personality thing. I think he's an asshole, and he *doesn't* think he's an asshole so . . ."

She was watching him, as if she expected him to continue, so he did.

"It was bad enough," he said, "that he slept with her. But he let me think that he knocked her up, and then he went and freaking married her, like, what the hell . . . ? Why would he do that? She doesn't even know who the baby's father was. She's always been a mess."

"Maybe he fell in love with her," Jenn suggested. "People fall in love and do crazy things. And I'm not just talking about the people"—she motioned toward her bookshelves—"in romance novels."

"I think he did it to piss me off," Dan said, even though the words sounded ridiculous, even to his own ears.

"That seems drastic," Jenn said mildly. "But I understand why it's upsetting to you. This man you don't like marries your sister, and suddenly, he's part of your family—with a fifty-percent chance of him being in your life forever. Except, she's already left him. And last night, while you're reading, he can't sleep, he comes out of the conference room, sees that you're still up, and says . . ." She looked at him expectantly.

But Dan shook his head. "I got nothing," he said. "It's blank. I remember reading this scene where the author gets thrown into solitary, for, like, a whole week, and then I remember Zanella putting me in a headlock."

And *then* he remembered Jenn staring at him, like he was some kind of loser freak.

"What happened to the book?" she asked.

And wasn't *that* a good question? "I don't know," he said. He got out of bed and dug through his bag, but it wasn't in there. "I must've left it at the hotel."

"So why *are* you reading that book?" Jenn asked.

"My brother," he said. "Half brother, really. Ben. He's, like, thirteen. And he's always been . . . Well. He's just Ben, you know? Only, about a month ago, I get this e-mail from my mother saying can I send more money because there's this special camp that my dick of a step-father wants to send Ben to this summer."

"Oh, no," Jenn said.

"Oh, yeah," Dan told her. "She tells me that Ben's gone goth, you know, black fingernail polish?"

"That doesn't mean he's gay."

"But if he is . . ." Dan shook his head again. "I'm reading this bullshit about what they do to kids in these places and . . . So I send her an e-mail to tell her no, I won't give her the money to do that, but she e-mails me back, going *that's okay, he got a scholarship from the church*. Jesus Christ."

"What are you going to do?" Jenn asked, propping her head up on one hand, supported by her elbow.

"I don't know," he admitted, unable to keep himself from touching her, even just to push her hair back behind her ear with one finger. She had nice ears—just the right size, although she thought they were too big. "I've been trying to call my sister, Sandy, but she's not answering her phone, which isn't a good sign."

She winced. "I'm sorry," she said.

"And yeah, I know, I said she was doing better, and she was," Dan admitted. "Until she dropped off the map again, which is a classic signal that the shit's about to hit the fan. How many times has it happened now? Fifteen? Twenty? And I still gloss it over. I still, you know, pretend there're flowers growing, when all there is is the same old bullshit."

He rolled onto his back to stare at the ceiling. He had to look away from the sympathy in her eyes.

Sympathy—and understanding. She knew, exactly, what he was talking about. And maybe that was why he kept talking.

"I think I kind of snapped," he said, "when I saw Eden starting down the same screwed-up path. She was fourteen, and she was getting drunk. And then she got drunk and slept with this total asshole." He looked at Jenn. "Not Zanella, some earlier asshole. She definitely gravitates toward the same type of loser, though, that's for sure. But I came home for some holiday—I was in the Navy at that point—and all this scumbag could talk about was how he took her cherry." He turned to look at Jenn. "She was *fourteen*."

"That must've been hard for her," she said. "To trust someone that much and then have him betray her that way."

Dan looked at her. "She didn't give a shit. She was walking around in these clothes that made her look like she was selling it on the street, with this hardcore *fuck you* attitude—"

"If *you* found it embarrassing and awful, imagine how she felt, regardless of whatever facade she was hiding behind," Jenn continued. "You were only there for a few days. She had to live there."

"It felt like Sandy, all over again," Dan said. "I couldn't survive that a second time. I don't think I came home for another two years. Jesus, maybe longer. Not until after Katrina, which was a total nightmare. I still don't know what happened to Eden in the Super Dome, and it makes me sick . . . Why am I telling you this? You don't want to hear this."

"When I was six," Jenn told him, "my father punched a hole in the wall. He was angry about something relatively small, like the cable went out during an electrical storm, and he couldn't watch the football game on TV. I was in bed, and I heard all the noise, and I came out to find him and my mother sitting on the floor beneath this big, gaping hole, just crying, and that scared me more than it did when he yelled, you know?"

Dan closed his eyes. "Jesus, did we have the same father, or what?"

She laughed. "Okay, that's an icky thought."

"No," he said. "I didn't mean . . . Ew. I meant, you know, cast from the same mold."

"Phew, that's better," she said, smiling down at him. "I thought you were going to *sister* me. Which would've been one for the record books, let me tell you . . ."

He tugged her close and kissed her, but let her go to ask, "How can you tell me that about your father, and still smile and make jokes like that? Why aren't you crying, LeMay?"

"It happened a long time ago," she told him, leaning in to kiss him again. Her lips were so soft. "I've worked hard to put it behind me. When's the last time *you* went to a meeting, Gillman?"

"Al-Anon?" he said, even though he knew exactly what she meant by *meeting*. Al-Anon was a support group for family members of alcoholics. "It's been awhile." He'd started going post-Katrina, when Sandy had finally gone into rehab. It had helped to hear stories that were so like his own, coming from total strangers.

But he'd never stood up and told his own story. And then he'd gone overseas again and . . . He hadn't gone back.

"Maybe you should think about going again." Jenn must've seen the trepidation in his eyes, because she added, "Or not. We could have our own meetings, right here. Naked meetings. Close with the serenity prayer, and maybe a little extra bonus serenity-inducing activity. . . ."

"Like yoga?" Dan teased. "Or maybe basket weaving. Isn't basket weaving supposed to be soothing?"

"I love it when you smile and mean it," Jenn told him.

Love. Jesus. Okay, keep it light. "Do I really ever smile and *not* mean it?" he asked.

"You do," she said. "At least I think you do." She kissed him again and reached over and closed her laptop with her foot. "What do you say we go get breakfast? There's this diner over near the hotel that makes the best pancakes. If you want, we could stop and pick up your book. Since I've still got some work to do today . . . That way, you won't be sitting around. Or reading one of my not-doom-and-gloomy-enough-for-you romance novels."

"Yeah," he said, as she began packing up her computer, "because I already know how they end. And they lived happily ever after. Although the book I'm reading has a happy ending, too. The author tries to kill himself."

Jenn looked at him. "Oh, big yay . . . ?"

Danny laughed. "No, it *was* good because he ended up in the psych ward of a hospital where the doctors actually followed scientific guidelines. He started to learn that it was okay to be, you know, gay." He sighed. Jesus. "I have no idea what I'm going to do about Ben."

Jenn handed him his pants. "We'll figure something out."

The autopsy reports on Maggie Thorndyke and the homeless man known as Winston came in via e-mail, about an hour after Alyssa and Jules left the hotel.

They'd gone to Maria's office, to check out a framed letter that the assemblywoman said was hanging on the wall. It was from her brother, Frank, and it was—she believed—all anyone would need to fake his handwriting. Provided they had time and patience, of course.

The skills of a master forger wouldn't hurt, either.

Still, Sam remembered seeing it there, in a simple metal frame. Maria had caught him reading it and had told him that that letter was the reason she'd begun her political career.

So Alyssa and Jules had gone out to look at it, while Sam lounged in bed until he couldn't stand it anymore.

He'd just gotten dressed and was about to emerge into the suite's living room to see how on earth Robin was keeping Ash so damn quiet, when he saw the e-mail alert on Alyssa's laptop.

He downloaded the various reports, carrying her computer out to the more comfortable couch. It wasn't exactly breakfast reading, but he plowed through it all, checking first to see what exactly, besides blood, old Winston had had flowing through his veins before he died.

Valium was mixed in with an outrageously high amount of alcohol. And yeah, the docs all agreed with Sam that no way had this man slit his own wrists.

Identification of the homeless man was as of yet incomplete. His teeth were in such poor condition—there were several dense pages on them, focusing on vitamin deficiencies and dental hygiene, comma, lack thereof—so they couldn't consider the results from a dental match to be conclusive. Instead, they were waiting on a DNA test.

With that said, it was highly likely that the dead man would be identified as John Winston Jones, born 1945 in Harlem, served in Vietnam from 1967 to 1970, winner of a whole fuckload of medals, honors, and distinctions—the list went on and on and on. The man was an American hero. No way should he have been living in the street, cold and alone, with his teeth rotting out of his head.

His teeth . . .

The hair stood up on the back of Sam's neck, and he scrolled back a few pages to the info that he'd barely skimmed.

About the man's teeth . . .

And there it was.

The victim had recently lost a tooth, quite possibly earlier in the day or the evening that he was killed, or even shortly before he died.

The medical examiner was aware that both police and hospital reports noted that he'd fallen, suffering a blow to his head. It was entirely possible he'd lost the tooth at that time.

But Sam flipped to the report on Maggie Thorndyke, using the computer search function, typing in *teeth*.

Victim's mouth was badly damaged, as if struck by a blunt object, many of her front teeth broken or missing, one of her molars curiously extracted . . .

"Holy fuck."

"Uh-oh," Robin said. "Daddy said a bad word. Ning-a-nang, Daddy."

Sam looked up to see Ash, holding tightly to Robin's hands as they walked toward him, all smiles and drool and sheer innocent pleasure.

Not so much drool from Robin, though.

"Ready to blow Daddy's mind, punkin?" Robin asked the little boy. "Daddy needs to be ready, too. Laptop to the side please, so we can demonstrate what we've been hard at work on all morning. We were going to master crawling, but Ash had something else in mind."

Sam shook his head, but then nearly tossed the computer onto the couch, because here came Ashton, on his own steam, taking two or three drunken, staggering solo steps before starting to accelerate into a nosedive.

But Sam was there to catch him, lifting him up before he fell. If his side hurt, he didn't feel it.

"That was amazing," he told his son, who was giving himself a round of applause, which was pretty damn funny. "I gotta call your mama."

But he wasn't quite sure what to tell her first—that

their baby boy was walking, or that Sam was more convinced than ever that his instincts had been right.

Alyssa was the real target.

And if he *was* right? The man who'd killed both Maggie and Winston was just getting warmed up.

Izzy went into Maria's kitchen, looking for coffee.

He'd volunteered for the first watch last night, sitting out in the hall as Lopez and Vlachic crashed in Maria's second bedroom.

It was crazy. He knew he was being crazy. Just because the woman had cried on his shoulder didn't mean she was going to try to jump him.

Except he couldn't shake the feeling that she was going to try to jump him.

Maria Bonavita was, hands down, one of the ten most beautiful women he'd ever seen in his life—and that included women he'd seen in movies and on TV. She had a lot going on behind her eyes, which—okay, yes—he found enormously attractive.

But she wasn't Eden.

The coffeepot was nearly empty, and he poured what was left into his mug. The swallow and a half provided just enough energy for him to search for another filter and the ground coffee, and he stood there, leaning against the counter as the new pot slowly brewed.

"Good morning."

Izzy jumped, which made Maria laugh and add, "Sorry. I didn't mean to startle you."

"No," he said, "I was just . . . Um . . ."

She was wearing jeans today, and a long-sleeved T-shirt that hugged her curves, and okay, yes, the woman was stacked. She was also smiling, and even an idiot could tell she was not only used to rendering men speechless, but that she liked doing it—and particularly so to him.

And maybe that was his giant ego talking—the same

Jupiter-sized beast that had pushed him out into the hall last night to avoid any awkward invitations.

As if.

"I thought we were moving back to the hotel this morning," Maria said, as she reached up to get a mug from the cabinet, as he tried not to look at her ass.

"Yeah," he said, suddenly aware that he'd crawled in here straight from bed. His hair was probably sticking up in odd clumps, like Wolverine having a bad hair day. Once it got that way, only a shower would tame it so there was no use attempting to flatten it down. He'd just look like a flipping moron if he tried. "No. We, um, got a call from Lt. Starrett—Sam. He asked us to hold up. He also asked Tony to go over there. Lopez is still here, though. And we've got a team of FBI agents standing guard in the hall. So . . ."

Thank God we're not alone, he refrained from screaming at her.

She'd taken a position directly opposite him, on the other side of that coffeepot. Like him, she was watching it and waiting for it to fill. But she glanced up. "What's going on?"

"I don't know," he admitted. "Sam was in commanding officer mode, so . . . He said to stay put, not let anyone in. When you're in the Navy, when your CO gives an order, you say *Sir, yes, Sir!* Not so much with the *What up, dawg?*"

She smiled. "My father and both brothers were military. Not Navy, though. Two Marines, one Army infantry. But it's pretty much the same. My dad was a sergeant and my mother used to get in his face—*I am not one of your grunts, Victor Bonavita, I am your wife. . . .*"

"The flip side," Izzy said, "is that those of us who're enlisted—the grunts? We follow orders really well. *Honey, will you take out the trash? Ma'am, yes, Ma'am!*"

Her smile broadened. "Why do I get the feeling that following orders isn't exactly instinctive for you?"

"Actually, it is," he said. "I was the youngest in a big family. My survival pretty much depended on my doing what I was told. Not that I always did it."

"You never thought about being an officer?" she asked. "I was talking to Jay Lopez, and he said there was a program in which a qualified enlisted man could make the jump to officer."

"OCS—Officer Candidate School," Izzy said. "Yeah. I thought about it for, like, two minutes. It's not for me."

"Why not?"

"Well, for starters, I'm not exactly qualified. I got into trouble a few years ago, and . . . It's taken me this long to get back on track. I'm a little long in the tooth now, to go O."

"What kind of trouble?" she asked as the coffeepot finished filling with a hiss and sputter.

"I kind of went UA." Izzy filled her mug first.

"Thanks," she said, with a smile and flash of her pretty brown eyes. She carried her mug to the kitchen table. "Tony got doughnuts before he left."

Tony got *wha* . . . ? But indeed, on the table was most of a mighty mixed dozen from the double D. Izzy'd missed seeing it, completely, in his pre-coffee haze. "Bless you, young Tony," Izzy said.

But suddenly, there he and Maria were, like Mr. and Mrs. Brady, sitting across the breakfast table from each other, as he clogged his arteries with a chocolate-covered Bavarian cream, taking the express train to Sugar Shock Land.

"What does it mean?" Maria asked, delicately dabbing her pornstar-worthy lips with a napkin. "You *went UA?*"

"Unauthorized absence," Izzy explained. "It's the Navy's version of AWOL—absent without leave."

"That's a pretty serious offense," she said, frowning slightly, "to have on your record."

Why did this suddenly feel like a job interview?

"Yeah," he said, "it's not. On my record. I pretty much became the senior chief's bitch for a really long time, though." He translated, because he could see she was confused. "A chief's the equivalent of a sergeant in the Army, and the senior chief is like the king of the chiefs. He's big and he's loud and he's mean, and when he said jump, I had to jump. I couldn't blow my nose without asking his permission. But I took my punishment, and earned his trust again, and . . . Here I am. In New York instead of using up my liberty washing his office floor."

She took a sip of her coffee as she gazed at him.

"What?" he asked. "Do I have, like, a bat in the cave?"

Maria laughed. "No, your nose is . . . very nice."

Okay, now he was really scared. "Thank you," he said, standing up. "But my very nice nose and my attractive hairdo and I are in dire need of a shower, so . . ."

She stood up, too.

Dear Penthouse, Why me?

He was halfway to the sink, so he just kept going, keeping his back to her. He rinsed his mug and saw that the dishwasher door was slightly open. Maybe if he simply ignored her, if he didn't look at her, gave her zero eye contact. "Dishes dirty or clean?"

"Dirty," she said, so he opened the door and put his mug on the top rack.

But yeah, okay, she was blocking his route to the door, so he had to look at her, and when he did, she smiled and stepped closer—too close—except she was just getting herself another cup of coffee, but he couldn't back up because the dishwasher door was open now, and in his way.

Instead, he just tried to make himself smaller as he stood in front of the sink, as he tried not to think about how good she smelled—which, was, of course, what women who wore perfume wanted other people to think about. Among other things . . .

He could've escaped by going around her, but it would've been clumsy. And yeah, part of him wasn't really all that scared. Part of him—the Jupiter-sized ego-beast part—wanted to see what she was going to do.

What she did was blow on her hot coffee as she glanced up at him, which made it hard not to think about sex, which was stupid, because it was coffee and she was blowing on it to cool it down—her actions didn't have anything to do with anyone's naked anything.

But okay, now he was standing here thinking about it, and she was a woman, and all women had highly tuned sex-radar, which meant that she absolutely knew that he was, indeed, thinking about sex.

And she didn't move back, and she didn't move back, and she didn't . . .

She put her coffee mug down on the counter.

And she spoke. "Isn't it crazy how, with some people you just have this . . . instant chemistry?"

And there she was, standing there, still too close, her hand now on his arm, her thumb brushing the inside of his wrist.

It felt nice—too nice, and any second now she was going to stand on her toes and kiss him, which, okay, yes, she did. Only Izzy turned his head so that her mouth bounced off his cheek. He pulled his arm free and stepped around her, away from her.

He'd surprised the shit out of her—and she wasn't the only one. Had he really just done that?

"Sorry," she said. She'd probably never been shut down before, in her entire life. "I just thought . . ." She laughed a little as she told him, "I don't know, maybe I could save you another trip to Germany . . . ?"

"Wow," Izzy said. "That's um . . . *very* tempting . . ."

He knew from looking at her that *she* knew he was lying. But she didn't call him on it. She was already embarrassed enough.

So he gave her the truth.

"I'm still in love with her," he said. "With Eden. And I gotta give it one more try."

He went, then, not to take his shower, but to call Lt. Starrett to see if he couldn't trade assignments with Tony, ASAP.

CHAPTER NINETEEN

Sam Starrett was on the phone as Jenn followed Dan past the FBI agents standing guard in the hall, and into the hotel suite.

Whoever Sam was talking to, it was serious, but rather than make them all be quiet, he pointed at Dan, said "Don't go anywhere," then went into one of the bedrooms and shut the door behind him.

"What's going on?" Dan asked Robin, who was sitting on the sofa, giving the baby a bottle.

"Something about teeth in the autopsy reports," the movie star replied. "It's gruesome and horrible, and I'm not sure I really want to know the complete details. You guys want to stay for lunch? We're sending out for Chinese. Maria says there's a really great place nearby that delivers."

Dan glanced at Jenn, as if trying to gauge her reaction to being asked to stay for lunch by an Emmy-award winner, even if it was Chinese all over again. He was willing to stay if she wanted to—she could tell just from his body language.

It was sweet. *He* was sweet.

The way he'd held her hand as they'd walked over here was sweet. The way he smiled, his sense of humor, the way his brown eyes danced when he laughed, and yes, his dazzling good looks and beyond hot, hard-muscled body were all unbelievably . . . sweet.

And she still couldn't quite believe that he was smiling at *her,* that he was kissing *her,* that he was holding *her* hand.

For two weeks. No, not quite. Eleven more days, not counting the rest of today. God, it was going by so quickly—it was happening too fast.

She pulled herself back into the moment. Chinese food for lunch? They hadn't had breakfast yet. She shook her head. "I have work that I need to do," she said, when in truth she didn't want to share her remaining eleven Dan days with anyone—not even a movie star. "We really just stopped in to pick up Dan's book and . . . I thought Maria would be here."

"No, she's still back at her condo," Robin reported as he watched Dan look around—on the tables, on the floor, even under the window drapes that extended from the ceiling to the carpeting. "Sam called a time-out. Again, it's about this teeth thing. I'm surprised he didn't get in touch with you guys."

Dan stopped looking for his book and dug for his cell phone. "Maybe he called while we were in the cone of silence. Jenn's building has this ancient elevator and yep, I got a missed call and a message." He plugged in his code so he could access his voice mail. He listened and . . . "Yes, the message was to stay put. Great. No wonder he didn't look happy to see me."

He pocketed his phone and went back to searching for his book, neatly dropping to the rug as if he were going to start doing push-ups, but in truth to peer beneath the sofa.

Robin obligingly lifted both his feet. "*What* is it that you're looking for?"

"The book I was reading," Dan said. "I'm pretty sure I left it here."

"Maybe someone moved it," Jenn suggested.

"They wouldn't have moved it far," Robin said. "Just out of baby range—onto the table. Or maybe into the conference room. I haven't seen it, but my hands have been pretty full. What's it called?"

Dan cleared his throat. "*Ex-Me*. It's, um, a memoir. I was lying on the couch while I was reading it. Not last night, the night before, and, um . . ."

"*This* couch?" Robin realized. He stood up gracefully, the baby asleep in his arms. "Maybe it slipped behind the pillows."

Jenn helped Dan look beneath the various throw pillows and . . . There it was. It had slid down, along the back of the sofa.

"How the hell did it get back there?" Dan wondered.

"Oh, that's nothing," Robin said. "I've fallen asleep reading, and had my book end up beneath the seat cushion. Or if I'm in bed, down by my feet. Like, I wasn't asleep that long, so how did it manage to migrate so far, so fast?"

Jenn looked at Dan, who was looking back at her. She knew what he was thinking. Was it possible that he'd fallen asleep?

"You should talk to Izzy," she told him.

"Yeah," he agreed. "I should."

"Izzy?" Robin said helpfully, as he settled back on the couch with the baby, who was still miraculously asleep. "He just got here. He's in the third bedroom. I think he just took a shower."

"Thanks," Dan said, looking at Jenn again.

But this time, she wasn't sure what he wanted.

"Should I come with you?" she asked him.

"No," he said quickly. "Nah, I can, um . . . You wanted to find out about Frank." He looked at Robin, since the man seemed to have all the answers. "Has there been any word about Maria's brother?"

But this time Robin shook his head. "Not that I've heard." He shot Jenn a sympathetic face. "Sorry. I *do* know he's detoxing at a psychiatric hospital. Considering what he was on, that's going to take some time. Anyone looking to have an information-gathering conversation with him is going to have to wait, because right now he's probably not capable of putting together a coherent sentence."

"Thanks," Jenn said. "And thanks for helping us find Dan's book."

"Anytime." Robin smiled as they drifted away from him.

Which left Dan eying that third bedroom.

He misinterpreted the concern on her face. "Don't worry," he said. "I'm not going to kill Izzy."

Jenn laughed. "God, I didn't even think of *that.*" She'd been focusing so completely on his fear of what he was going to discover. But if Izzy had purposely and maliciously pretended that Dan had had another blackout . . . "Dan, maybe I should—"

"Call Maria," he said quietly. "I know you need to talk to her. I'll be quick. I'll meet you in the conference room."

"You know, it's possible you had a conversation with Izzy," she pointed out, "in your sleep. And he didn't even know you were—"

"I'm *not* going to kill him," he said again, pulling her close and dropping a kiss on her lips. "Not today, anyway."

Jenn was worried about him.

Dan could see it clearly in her eyes. And she had just the very beginnings of an expression that he knew was going to morph into her apology face—and how weird was it that he already recognized that?

She was sorry, she was going to say, but she knew how hard this was for him. . . .

He shut it all down cold by kissing her again. More thoroughly this time.

And then, as she staggered away—or, shit, maybe he was the one who was staggering. What was it with the weak knees lately?—he knocked on the open bedroom door, even as he went inside.

Izzy Zanella was sitting at the desk in the corner, his hair still wet, eating a salad. He froze as he saw Danny, his fork midway to his mouth.

"Got a sec?" Dan asked, keeping his voice calm even though the mere sight of Zanella was enough to raise his blood pressure.

Izzy was sitting in one of those swivel desk chairs, so he turned to face Dan, but he didn't stand up. He was on high alert though, even putting his fork down, probably to have both hands free in case Danny tried to sucker punch him. But he, too, kept his voice light. "Sure, bro, what's up?"

Bro. They weren't brothers. They weren't even close. But okay. Dan forced his shoulders to loosen up, and made sure his hands were open, his fists not clenched.

"I was wondering if I could, um, ask you a few questions about the, uh, other night?"

Izzy sat there, and he was either the best freaking actor in the world, or he truly had absolutely no clue what Dan was talking about. "The other night?" he repeated.

"When you put me in a headlock?" Dan was unable to keep some snark from his voice. "Ring any bells?"

Izzy relaxed, sitting back a little in his seat. "Yeah, sure," he said. "But you don't have to worry. I was the only one who heard you."

"Heard me?" Now Danny was the parrot.

"I must've been in a light sleep cycle," Izzy said, "because you weren't making that much noise. You were really just talking, man. Hardly more than mumbling. No blood-chilling screams. You're cool."

"I was talking," Dan said, trying to understand.

"It was angry," Izzy said, "but you were keeping it quiet. Kind of low and dangerous. You know, *Get the fuck away from her*. That kind of shit. Whoever you were dreaming of was about to get their ass kicked."

Dreaming.

"Huh," Izzy continued. "I wonder if it was me. You know, the ass-kickee. Because when I went to wake you, you just—bam—took me down."

Danny had to sit, so he lowered himself down on the edge of one of the beds.

And then, as if the miracle of him *not* having blacked out again wasn't enough, Izzy went and apologized.

"I'm sorry for, you know, the lack of finesse in waking you," he told Dan. "I tried a coupla different ways, but you were out cold. Except then you were starting to get loud and I figured *anything* was better than you waking everyone in the suite, right? After Kazabek, I had these nightmares where after I woke up I nearly puked, and I didn't know if you had, you know, something similar going on."

Izzy'd gotten shot in a terrorist attack on the Grand Hotel in Kazabek, in which one of the SEAL team's beloved chiefs had died. Dan had been injured, too, in the same attack—but he'd only been hit by flying glass.

"No," Danny said now. "I, um, can get pretty loud though, so . . ." He made himself meet Izzy's gaze. "Thanks. I'm, uh, sorry I, um, you know . . ."

Izzy shrugged. "No biggie." He smiled. "It had shades of *Not now, Cato, not now*, though," he said, referencing the Pink Panther movies, where the Inspector's servant

Cato would jump out and attack him—for practice—at random times.

Dan laughed a little, too. "I bet. Jesus, and I ended up waking everyone anyway." He shook his head. "I, um, thought I'd blacked out again when you told Starrett we were talking about Eden."

"Oh, shit," Izzy said. "Dan, I am so sorry. It never even occurred to me that you might—"

"No, it's okay," Dan interrupted. "It just had me worried for a little bit."

"Shit," Izzy said.

"No," Dan said again. "Just . . . Thanks for helping clear things up."

And there they sat for a moment, in silence.

Izzy, who'd never been able to stay silent for long, broke it by saying, "At the risk of you going for my throat again . . . *Have* you heard from Eden?"

Jesus Christ. But okay, the asshole *had* seriously helped him out. Or maybe it was the relief from knowing he *wasn't* on the verge of having to give up his career due to frequent and unpredictable blackouts. . . .

"I haven't," Dan answered. "No." He cleared his throat. "I take it you haven't heard from her, either."

Izzy shook his head. "I'm going. Over there. To Germany. After this assignment."

"What the fuck is wrong with you?" Dan asked, but then realized how harsh he sounded. "I mean, why do you do that to yourself? Lopez told me you go all the time, but she won't see you."

Izzy poked at his salad with his fork. "Maybe this time she will."

"Zanella," Dan told him, moving closer, sitting now on the other bed. "Don't you get it? Eden's crazy. You can't possibly win with her. Even if by some miracle you *do* get back together? It'll only be until the next time she loses it again. Or until she decides she wants to trade up. Which she will—as soon as there's something she wants that you can't afford to buy her."

"She's not like that," Izzy said. "You don't even know her, asshole. When was the last time you had a conversation with her, that wasn't you telling her what to do, or blaming her for something?"

It was definitely time to go, but maybe because *crazy* was a default when it came to being a Gillman, Dan ignored his screaming instincts and tried to explain.

"You're right," he admitted. "I don't really know Eden, not anymore, but I know women, and I know this: She's an infant."

Izzy shifted, his disgust apparent, so Dan quickly added, "And no, this isn't me slamming you for screwing around with an eighteen-year-old. This is me saying that the whole running away to Germany and hiding thing is something a twelve-year-old would do, and you know it. Emotionally, Eden's acting like she's in seventh grade."

"Have you ever lost a baby?" Izzy asked, defending her, as usual.

"You know that I haven't," Dan answered. "So why are you asking?"

"Because you have no clue what is or isn't appropriate behavior for—"

"Okay," Dan said. "You win that one. Point to you."

"I'm just saying." Izzy pushed his salad away from him, as if he had no appetite.

"And *I'm* saying, fair enough," Dan countered. "But here's something that I've found when dealing with women—and you can take it or leave it, but for me, it's a God-given truth. And it's that the really drop-dead beautiful ones . . . ? They are all completely insane."

"That's a rather broad generalization," Izzy pointed out.

"Okay, so maybe they aren't *all* insane," Dan gave him

that. "But ninety-nine point nine percent of them are. Because they're taught, from like the time that they're two, that the world revolves around them. And you combine *that* with all the learned diva behavior from watching *Project Runway* and all those other bullshit reality shows where the camera lingers on the prettiest person who cries the hardest or is the biggest asshole . . . And the end result is a woman who is at best high maintenance, and at worst a raving, irrational lunatic."

"So . . . is that why you're forsaking women and going gay?" Izzy was looking pointedly at the book Dan had brought in and set down on the bed next to him.

He flipped it over, so that the title wasn't showing. "Don't be a douche. I'm being serious here. And yes, you're partly right, but I've only sworn off *beautiful* women. When time after time, you keep coming up with a resounding *no* to the age-old question, *Is the fucking you're getting worth the fucking you're getting?* It's definitely time to swear off *something*. But not sex. Thank God."

Izzy shook his head. "I appreciate the fact that we're having this conversation. At least I think I do. But I don't really—"

Dan lowered his voice, glancing back at the door to make sure Jenn wasn't done with her phone call. "Dude, everyone wants to get laid, all right? That's just a fact of life. But there are ways to do it. Strategies. You don't just automatically follow your dick. You use your head with the brain. You find the, I don't know, the chunky girl with the really pretty friends."

He'd done this for years, and he was doing it again, except . . . Somehow, with Jenn, it was different. Better. Probably because the sex was so great. Plus, he'd finally seen her naked and she wasn't chunky, she was statuesque. "She's low maintenance and low drama, plus she's wired to believe that you're too good to be true.

She expects to be dumped, so when you do it, she lets go immediately." As he said those words, he paused—not because they weren't true, but because the knowledge that, yes, Jenn *would* let him go without high drama didn't bring him the reassurance that he usually experienced. In fact, what he was feeling was a twinge of anxiety—what was *that* about? He tried to make a joke. "Unlike Ms. Crazy-Beautiful, who'll spend months blogging about how she had to use a magnifying glass just to give you a blow job."

But Izzy didn't laugh, he just sighed heavily. "I don't want to piss you off, man, but I'm in love with her. I'm not going to Germany because I'm hoping to get laid. I'm going because . . . maybe this time she'll need me. Maybe this time we'll talk. Maybe this time—"

"Excuse me, guys."

They both looked up to see Robin standing in the door.

"Sorry to interrupt," he continued, "but . . . Jenn just left." He looked at Dan. "Aren't you supposed to be with her at all times?"

"Oh, fuck!"

Danny launched himself up off the bed, and Robin stepped back so he could run for the hotel room door. As he threw it open, the FBI agent named John helpfully asked, "Was she supposed to leave . . . ?"

"No," Dan said. The elevators were around the corner to the right, so he shouted, "Jenni! Wait!"

Izzy was on Dan's heels as they both skidded into the little elevator lobby—which was empty.

"Fuck!" Dan slapped the down button, pacing in front of the three elevator doors, even as he dug for his cell phone and punched in Jenn's number. They were up too many floors even to consider taking the stairs. No way could they beat an express elevator to the lobby.

There was nothing to do but wait and pray.

Jenn's voice mail picked up before the elevator door opened.

"Jenn," he said, his voice actually cracking as he left a message. Christ, he was an idiot. "Please call me. I don't know what you thought you heard, but you've got to call me."

The elevator door opened with a ding, and Dan shut his phone and stepped in. Izzy followed.

"What she *thought* she heard is pretty much exactly what she heard," he pointed out.

"Yeah, I know," Dan admitted, his heart in the pit of his stomach, and not just from the elevator free fall, as he mentally reviewed all that she'd no doubt overheard while lurking outside of the door. He purposely hadn't used the word *fat*, but he *had* said *chunky*. "I'm a total dick."

There was a letter, framed and on the wall of Maria's office, from Pvt. Francis Bonavita, to the middle school students of the Chelsea YMCA's after-school program, who'd written to him while he was stationed in Iraq.

In his letter, he urged them to get involved in their government, and to stay involved; to register to vote and never take their civil rights and freedoms for granted. He ended it by asking them to do him a favor and talk his sister—their volunteer program supervisor—into running for the New York State Assembly.

He'd signed it "Peace out, your friend in Iraq, Frankie B."

Alyssa looked at Jules, who was reaching to take the frame from the wall. She watched as he brought it to the conference table, and flipped all of the clips that held the cardboard backing in place. He lifted the cardboard out, took the letter from the glass, and carefully carried it to the machine in the corner, where he made a copy.

"I'm going to have the lab run a comparison and analysis," he told Alyssa. "But I'm pretty sure we're going to find that the second letter is a forgery—Frank didn't write it."

"This is too bizarre," she said.

"More bizarre than cutting out a woman's heart and putting it in a desk drawer?" he asked as he wrote on the bottom of the copy, *I will bring the original back ASAP, Peace Out, your friend in the FBI, Jules Cassidy.*

Good point. She pulled off her jacket because it was just too hot in there. "Are we *really* thinking that Maria's brother is telling us the truth? About everything? That the drugs your team found just appeared in his bathroom?"

Jules put the copy of the letter back into the frame. "We've already determined that our man had access to this office. He could have made a copy of this letter as easily as I just did. Could he have also gone out to Long Island, and broken into Maria's parent's home? If his intention was to frame Frank for the murders, or even just add to the chaos? I say, why not?"

"Why not?" Alyssa repeated. "How about not *why not*. How about plain old *why*? I know, I know, none of this makes any sense—but it's not supposed to. It's supposed to put us on edge, keep us rattled. Well, guess what? It's working."

And yet she'd managed to talk Sam into sleeping in this morning. He knew it as well as she did—sleep helped a body heal. And his caving to her pressure to rest was in direct response to *her* capitulation to his demand that she not so much as go to the store on the corner without Sam or Jules in tow. Which was just as good, since she didn't want *them* out and about on their own, either.

"Are we back to thinking that Maria's the target?" she asked Jules, who'd wisely remained silent during her rant. He'd rehung the picture frame.

But now he looked at her. "You know that scene in

The Princess Bride where Wally Shawn is the guy with the iocane powder—remember that? And he's sitting across from our hero, who knows that the poison is in one of the goblets of wine that he's poured. And Wally goes something like *But I know that* you *know that I know that you know that I know . . .* That's where I feel like we are right now. Trapped in a mind-game vortex, with someone who's completely mad."

"So I'm gonna take that as a *maybe,*" Alyssa said.

"SpongeBob tell you *his* theory?" Jules asked.

"That I'm the target?" Alyssa said. Sam had mentioned that to her last night. "I don't know, Jules. I think that's just his own personal craziness showing. It gets ramped up into overdrive whenever I make plans to go to someplace like Afghanistan."

"He surprised the crap out of me," Jules said. "By offering to let Robin join him and Ash while we're gone. He said he was going to ask Gina and the kids, too. And Ric and Annie for added security—a silver bullet assignment for them, on Troubleshooters' dime . . . ? Pretty sweet."

"Sam would rather be over there, with us," Alyssa said.

"Yeah, but they asked for you," Jules pointed out. "When they ask for him, it's your turn to stay behind."

"*When?*" Alyssa asked.

"If," Jules said with a shrug. "Or maybe when, as in *when* you get the call and delegate the job to your equally competent second-in-command."

"Is that what you think I should do now, for this op?" she asked. Some of the Troubleshooters operatives, people that she'd worked with for years, some of them women themselves, had assumed, now that Alyssa had had Ashton, that she'd be staying far from any danger zones.

"Absolutely not," Jules said. "This one you've got to do. This is where you show everyone that it's business as usual. Get your Helen Reddy on: *I am woman, hear me roar.* Ash needs to know that his mommy has a very important job." He paused. "At the same time, I'm in agreement with Sam. The time for you both to go out on the same high-risk assignment has definitely passed. You know I love Ashton, and God forbid something terrible happens? Robin and I will be there for him, completely. But."

"I hear you," Alyssa said. "Believe me, Sam and I have talked about this a lot. It's just . . . how do you define high risk? And what do we do when we're on a low-risk assignment like this one, when body bags start coming into play?"

"I don't know," Jules answered honestly, as he started going through the mail they'd brought in with them. "I was going to send Robin home, but . . ." He shrugged. "He's safer at the hotel, with Navy SEALs standing guard. I mean, talk about overqualified. *This* is weird. Heads up, I think our man has made contact."

Alyssa moved to look over his shoulder.

Jules was holding a postcard—plain and white—similar to the one that had arrived with the message *Bottom Drawer.*

Maria's address was printed onto a label affixed on the front. And on the back was another message.

Alyssa read it aloud. "The number will be seven."

Jules looked at her. "Oh, goody," he said. "I just *love* riddles from fucking maniacs."

Alyssa's phone rang—it was Sam. She answered. "Hey."

"Where are you?" he asked, extra brusque.

"Maria's office," she reported. "I'm here with Jules. What's up?"

"Check the floor for me," he said. "Underneath the desk—the other one in the outer office, not Jennilyn's. I'm pretty sure when I was down there, on the floor, I saw it."

"Saw what?" she asked, getting onto her hands and knees, phone tucked between her chin and shoulder. Jules was looking at her as if she were crazy. "There's nothing here, not even a dust ball. It's clean."

"I saw a pen," Sam told her, his voice tight, "and a paper clip, and . . . a tooth. I'm pretty sure I saw a tooth."

Dan was calling her again.

Jenn took a deep breath and opened her phone. "Hello?" Now that she'd finally stopped crying, she didn't have to worry that her voice would wobble pathetically.

"Where are you?" he asked.

"I'm running some errands," she told him. She was heading across town to pick up a new batch of business cards from the printers. Maria handed them out by the dozens, so it was actually cheaper to have them professionally made.

Because even though the things Jenn had heard Dan say had hurt her feelings, life still went on.

And it wasn't as if she were surprised by what he'd said. He'd been honest with her from the start. It was just . . . hearing it that way, summarized as a strategy for getting laid . . .

When he'd talked with her, he'd always referred to sex as *making love*. But that was, no doubt, part of his strategy, too. *Find the chunky girl with the pretty friends . . .*

"Where are you, as in give me the address so I can meet you there," he said. He sounded pissed, which was kind of funny. Him, being pissed at her. "Haven't you seen any horror movies? It's when the girl goes off alone that the killer gets her."

"I'm in a cab," she said evenly, "that I'm pretty sure is killer-free."

"Heading where?"

"To the printers," she said, "and then back to the office."

"Where is the printers?" he asked.

"I'm picking something up," Jenn told her. "I won't be there long enough—"

"You will if you wait for me."

"That's not going to happen."

"Someone's supposed to be with you at all times," Dan said tightly. "This isn't a game, Jenn."

Oh, and the irony of *him* saying *that* was just too intense. "You told me yourself that it's just a precaution," she said, instead of laughing hysterically and calling him names. "That if anyone's a target, it's Maria—"

"That was before her brother took you at gunpoint."

"He's in custody," she reminded him as the cab pulled to the curb. "And I'm at the printers. I'll be back at the office in a half hour. If you're really that concerned about my safety, in the middle of the day, in a city filled with millions of witnesses, feel free to send someone over there to meet me. Someone who's not you though, please."

He was silent at that, but then he said, "I don't know what you thought you heard—"

"Is the fucking you're getting worth the fucking you're getting," she recited. "And right now? I'm gonna have to say *no, it's not.*"

"Jenni—"

"And I prefer *big-boned* to *chunky,* thank you very much."

"Jenn, I wasn't talking about you," he said.

"Oh, please," she said. "You like me because I'm smart, remember? Cute but also smart. And you also apparently like me because beautiful women are insane, and I'm not beautiful, ergo I must not be insane. Except I am, because what did I think I was doing, believing I actually had a shot at finding something real—even just for fourteen stupid days—with someone like *you?*"

She hung up because she was crying again. She'd walked out of the suite for the same reason.

She was *not* going to let him know that he'd made her cry.

CHAPTER
TWENTY

Robin wrestled Ash's legs back into his bunny suit, put the baby into his crib for a nap, and went to find Sam.

He was sitting at the suite's dining table, frowning at whatever he was reading on his laptop computer.

He was also wearing a shoulder holster. The sturdy black straps stood out in stark relief against the light blue of his T-shirt.

He looked up as Robin approached, giving him an invitation to speak that was heavily tinged with his impatience. Interrupt him, BW, but do it quickly.

"Did Dan find Jenn?" Robin asked.

"Not yet," Sam said, turning back to his computer, already dismissing him.

"I'm sorry," Robin said, "but the garbage is getting pretty toxic. Normally, I'd just call for maid service to come and get it and put the can outside the door—"

"I don't want you going anywhere near the door," Sam said sharply, his full attention back on Robin.

"Okay, then, I won't," he said. "I just didn't want to come across as a diva. *Empty my trash, bitch!* As if you guys with the guns don't have enough to do than to be my servants."

Sam smiled, but it wasn't quite enough to erase all of his grim. "No one thinks you're a diva. Divas don't change their *own* diapers, let alone someone else's. I'll take care of it. Trash and . . . need some towels, too?"

"Yeah, thanks." Robin nodded and Sam made a note on a pad of paper that was next to the computer.

"Anything else?" he asked.

"You want to tell me what's going on, that you feel the need to be armed?" Robin said. Come to think of it, getting that holster on and fastened must've involved a fair degree of wincing and cursing. So Sam's need to wear it was pretty dang high.

"Jules ever tell you about a serial killer called the Dentist?" Sam asked, leaning back in his seat.

"The guy who took some of his victims' teeth." And suddenly Sam's preoccupation with the mention of teeth in both autopsy reports made horrible sense.

"Not some of their teeth," Sam corrected him. "*All* of 'em."

Ew. Robin didn't say it aloud, but he made a face.

"Yeah," Sam said. "And he wasn't real careful about how he got 'em. He had the tendency to break his victims' jaws. Or remove their lower jaw entirely. And not always after they were dead."

Jules hadn't told him that part.

"Alyssa and I found one of his victims," Sam continued. "We were on this missing persons case. A woman named Amanda Timberman had vanished about six months earlier and . . . The fact that her body wasn't found until then was an aberration from the killer's usual MO. He was into the notoriety, and he always contacted the authorities and the media with the location of the body. *Bodies*—he usually killed in clusters, once every five to nine months or so. It's pretty gruesome stuff—you sure you want to hear this?"

"Are you really sure the same guy killed Maggie and Winston?" Robin countered.

"Nope," Sam said. "I'm not sure of anything. It's all gut."

Robin nodded. Jules, too, relied heavily on instinct and what he teasingly referred to as "his spidey senses a-tingling."

It sometimes helped for Jules to talk about a case—to think aloud and work things through. Despite Sam's earlier impatience, he looked as if he wanted to keep talking. So Robin braced himself for the awfulness of it all as he sat down across from the former SEAL and asked, "So after killing Amanda, he didn't contact anyone?"

"Nope," Sam said again. "But for a while we thought maybe we had him, because Amanda had supposedly run off with this slacker ski instructor named Steve Hathaway. Her father had some pictures of the two of them together. The FBI thought it was a major break in the case—finally a photo of the Dentist, you know? They thought that was why there was no trumpeting announcement about where the body could be found—because the killer knew those photos were out there. But then, months later, Steve-the-ski-instructor's body turns up, also without his teeth, killed around the same time as Amanda. Which was also odd. Steve was the Dentist's only male victim."

"That you know about," Robin pointed out.

"Good point, BW," Sam said. "Although, I do know this—that the FBI profilers spent a lot of time trying to glean as much information as they could from those two murders in particular. They compiled a huge file on both Amanda and Steve. Amanda was pretty much just a bored rich girl, looking for excitement, but Steve . . . He liked to get his kink on. Guy was solidly into three-ways—particularly MMF. The profilers' favorite theory is that Amanda unwittingly picked up the Dentist in some bar, and took him back to Steve's crappy little love shack to get him even more drunk before springing Steve on him and . . . Everyone lost their teeth, instead."

"And the Dentist didn't send out his usual press release about the murders," Robin concluded, "because . . . he didn't want anyone to know he'd had sex with Steve?"

"Or almost had sex with Steve," Sam agreed.

"Does he usually have sex with his victims?" Robin asked.

"About half the time. And it's never violent—at least as far as the autopsies show."

"So . . . it's possible some of his victims go with him willingly," Robin concluded. "He must be handsome or charming."

"That's the consensus."

"Was Maggie . . . ?" Robin asked.

"No," Sam told him. "The autopsy showed no sign of sexual activity or assault."

"But you think it could be the same guy. Even though he didn't take her teeth."

"He took some," Sam said. "He hit her in the mouth with something big and hard. Most of her front teeth were broken or missing."

"I'm not an expert here," Robin said, "but if I'm collecting something the way this guy seems to be collecting teeth? I'm going to want them in mint condition, not all smashed up."

"Unless," Sam said, "he wanted to take a few, but he didn't want anyone to know he was taking them. It's a good cover, the old baseball bat to the face."

"Crafty," Robin agreed. "Of course the alternate explanation is that it's not the same guy."

"Alyssa's been tracking the Dentist since we found Amanda," Sam told him. "Which was back in the fall of 2003—the year we got married. Jules hooked her up with the special unit that's been hunting him, and she's gone out to nearly all the crime scenes since then. His usual MO isn't two bodies, by the way. It's more like three or four. He trolls a town, usually one with a mall, and he takes his first victim from the parking lot. He keeps her alive while he uses her cell phone to pick his other victims. Theory is he sometimes makes *her* pick them for him. He makes her call them—one at a time. She tells them her car broke down on a deserted road, she's scared, she needs them to come and get her right away.

"And if they come alone—and they usually do," Sam continued, "he overpowers them and takes them to a house that he either rents or breaks into, somewhere out in the middle of nowhere, and he kills them and he takes their teeth—usually in front of the first victim, who's still alive. And then he makes her call someone else, and if she won't, he sends a text message to someone in her phone book, telling them that her car broke down on a different deserted road, yada yada, and he keeps going until one of them's smart enough to bring their father or their boyfriend. At which point, he calls it a night, and goes back to that first girl he snatched, and he kills *her* and takes *her* teeth. And then he sends an e-mail to the FBI—sometimes directly to the AIC for the case—a guy named Pete Quincy. He gives them the location and the number of bodies they'll find when they get there."

"God," Robin said.

"Yeah," Sam agreed. "And here's the latest newsflash. Remember that postcard that said *bottom drawer*? There was another one in the assemblywoman's mail today, saying *The number will be seven*."

"Holy crap," Robin said. "*Seven*? Was there a—"

"Nope," Sam said. "That's all it said. Lys thinks it might be a copycat—someone who knew about the number *and* about her involvement in the case, and wants to make it look like the Dentist is back, but . . . See, he never sent anything through the mail before this. Contact was always through e-mail. There're other things, too, that were purposely kept from the public, in case of a copycat, and those aren't lining up either, but . . ."

"You still think it could be him," Robin said.

Sam nodded. "Alyssa just keeps saying, why would he change his MO?"

"Why *would* he change his MO?" Robin asked.

"Because he nearly got caught," Sam said. "See, a lot of experts thought the best way to fight this prick was to educate the public. Alyssa and Jules agreed. So the FBI, in concert with state and local police, launched this huge awareness campaign. They also worked with malls across the country, to increase security, making it harder for him to make that initial snatch.

"Fast forward to August, 2007," he continued. "He made a mistake and grabbed a woman named Betsy MacGregor, in a suburb of Chicago. She was a teacher at the local high school, and she'd helped launch their safety program. And just as she'd told her kids to do, she'd programmed 9-1-1 into her phone under some name like Heather or Ashley. So she called the police and gave them the whole *My car broke down* story. The emergency operator knew enough to realize it wasn't a prank, and the locals tried to set a trap to catch this guy."

"I'm guessing they didn't," Robin said.

"Nope. They don't know what happened for sure, but he probably checked Betsy's phone and saw what *Heather's* number really was. He not only got away, but Betsy's body was never recovered," Sam reported. "There was a massive search effort, but . . ." He shook his head. "To say that Alyssa was disappointed is a huge understatement. She wanted to see this guy burn. It was then—a year ago last August—that he went dormant. He went completely dark. No contact with anyone, no news about Betsy's body. Not even an e-mail saying *Nyah, nyah, you can't have her back*. One group of profilers believes he suicided, but . . ."

"You don't think so," Robin said it for him.

"Nope." Sam was somber. "I think he's still out there. And I don't think he's been dormant. I don't think he's gone all this time without killing. I think he's changed his MO to not taking all of his victims' teeth. Jules is spooked, too. He put in a request to get information about any unsolved murders of young women—the Dentist's main target group—between August '07 and now, in which the autopsies reveal damage to any of the victims' teeth. I think he loves taking all the teeth, but I think he *needs* to take at least one."

"Where are they?" Robin asked. Now he was spooked, too. "Jules and Alyssa?"

"They're visiting the office staff at home today," Sam said. "All of the male interns and Doug What'sHisName and even good old Mick Callahan."

"Wouldn't it be smarter," Robin said, "to just round them all up and bring them in—and *then* see if their basement is ankle deep in blood?"

"There's this little thing," Sam told him, "called probable cause, and these other things called warrants that the FBI is trying to get back in the habit of using more often. In order to get a warrant you need probable cause. But on the other hand, if you knock, say, on Mick Callahan's door and he invites you in . . . ?"

"As long as he doesn't invite you in while holding his dental extraction tool behind his back," Robin pointed out. "You're really okay with Alyssa doing this?"

Sam wasn't, but he was pretending—hard. "Jules is with her," he said. "And she's going to be calling me, to check in. Every twenty minutes. Here's a question for you. If you were a serial killer and you took your victims' teeth . . . What would you do with them?"

"Like . . . make placemats out of them, or glue them onto the bases of all the lamps in my house?" Robin asked, but then answered his own question. "That would make them hard to travel with. You gotta figure this guy has to be ready to pick up and leave at a moment's notice. How many victims has he . . . ?"

"Thirty-seven," Sam said. "That we know of."

"Holy shit," Robin said. That was a lot of teeth. "Would that many even fit in a shoebox? Maybe a big one—a really heavy one, too. Plus, you'd want to keep them dry, or maybe even shellac them, or coat them in some kind of plastic, because otherwise they'll decay."

"But would you carry them around?" Sam asked. "In your pocket. You know, just a few . . ."

"Oh, definitely," Robin said. "So you could touch them when you're out in the world, pretending to be sane. You could fondle them and no one would know . . ."

Sam was looking at him oddly.

"Sorry," Robin said. "Actor. I'm just . . . I've never played a serial killer, but if I were going to play *this* one, I'd want some prop teeth in my pockets so I could, you know, reach in and . . ."

"Fondle them," Sam said.

"Yeah," Robin grinned, but then pushed away the character. "Sorry. That's pretty awful. Thinking that someone who killed thirty-seven people is out there walking around like he's normal . . . ? It's even worse if you think he's been working in Maria Bonavita's office."

"Even more awful," Sam said grimly, "if he's walking around with teeth *and* a picture of Alyssa in his pocket."

"You think it's all somehow connected," Robin said. "That picture of Alyssa that Winston had . . . ?"

"I do," Sam said. He picked up his cell phone and dialed Alyssa. She was twenty seconds late.

She picked up on the first ring. "I was just going to call

you," she said. "Jules is on his phone with the local police. There's a body in the dumpster, back behind the assemblywoman's office. We've got an appointment in five minutes that I don't want to cancel, so will you go check it out? And Sam . . . ?"

"Yes, ma'am," he said, because although she made certain they were equal partners, particularly in bed at night, right now she was in team leader mode.

"If Mick Callahan's there," Alyssa warned him, "try your best not to get arrested."

His father had kept his car in quite good condition, thank goodness.

He drove it now, out of the garage that made their home worth at least another quarter million—pity he wouldn't see any of that—stopping to close and lock the door tightly behind him.

His plan was to use one of the female interns. Wendy or Belinda. They really were completely interchangeable, as far as he was concerned.

But he knew where they lived. He'd given them a lift home from a fundraiser, back in October.

He had his Taser. Getting one or even both of them into his car would be no problem, especially since he'd gone to that website that showed him how to boost the electrical charge, and how to remove any restrictions as to the length of time of the Taser blast.

Thirty seconds just wasn't long enough to do what he needed it to do.

But he'd already fixed that.

He would have liked for it to have been Maria. She had such pretty teeth. He would have liked to have watched her cry while he talked to Alyssa on her phone.

His plans had changed since he'd met Alyssa, since he'd talked to her and breathed in her sweet perfume.

He wanted her to talk to him knowing who he was—the Dentist—and knowing what he was capable of doing, what he *would* do, if she didn't meet his demands. *Come alone* . . . Of course, she wouldn't. He didn't expect that. So he'd have to kill the girl. He couldn't wait.

He'd been busy late into the night, moving Betsy—it was finally time for him to give her back. But he wouldn't text message the FBI with her whereabouts. Not until after he'd grabbed an intern or two and gotten on the road.

He'd spent most of the morning at the bank, closing out his parents' accounts and moving funds—getting much of it in cash. Because even if he did this right, they would now know who he was, and his access to his trust fund would cease.

He was going to take Wendy or Belinda—or both of them if he could manage it—and he was going to lock them in his trunk and drive west. He would know when he'd reached his destination. His inner bell-like toll of certainty would tell him it was the right time and place.

And then he would call Alyssa, and she would talk to him. He would make his demands, and she would fail to deliver, and he would hang up and kill the girls. And he'd call her back and tell her about it, and it would be better than he'd ever dreamed it could be.

He didn't need to risk it all, he didn't need to die. And when he finally tired of it again—*if* he tired of it—he would find Alyssa. Her husband wouldn't be able to keep her under guard forever. And he would find her and take her if he could. If not, he'd just die with her. He just needed to—

Wait, was that Jenn?

He hit the brakes, squealing to a stop—his good fortune holding, as there wasn't another car behind him to rear-end him. He put the car in reverse and backed up, pulling to the curb because . . .

It was.

It was Jennilyn LeMay, all by herself, lugging a heavy-looking bag down the street, obviously heading toward the office, which was over on the next block.

He'd made some noise with his tires, and she'd spotted him, too. And he looked and he looked, but he didn't see any of the Navy SEALs that were supposed to be following her around.

As she came closer, he saw that her eyes were red behind her glasses, as if she'd been crying, and he knew.

He *knew*. What to do, how to do it.

She'd seen him, and he waved her closer, lowering the passenger side window and leaning over so he could talk to her.

"Get in," he said, before she could speak, before she could ask him what he was doing there. "Jenn, quick, we've been looking all over for you. There's been an accident. One of the SEALs—Gillman—he was hit by a car."

"*What?*" she said, aghast. "When? Where?"

"It happened in front of the hotel," he said. "The Hilton." And he saw that she believed him because he knew the name of the supposedly secret hotel, and he had to work not to smile, to continue to look concerned. "He was upset and didn't see the taxi. It just happened. Maria called me. He's in bad shape. A head and neck injury." Oh, this was fun! "The ambulance took him to the hospital. Get in, I'll drive you over there."

She got in, nearly pulling the door off its hinges in her forceful haste, fumbling through her purse for her cell phone—no doubt to call Maria, which would never do.

So he tased her.

And as she slumped in her seat, he knew she could still hear him, so he told her, "He's fine. I was lying. You're the one who's going to die."

He gave her the injection. He'd dosed it for the interns who were petite as opposed to queen-size, but it would do for now.

But then his phone rang, and he looked and it was . . .
Alyssa.

As if she somehow knew.

He answered, trying to control the excitement in his
voice.

And she asked him if this afternoon would be a good
time for her to drop by and speak with his parents. She
would confirm his alibi and check to make sure that
both he and they were safe, all at the same time.

She made it sound as if he were not on her suspect list,
but he knew that he still was.

And again, he *knew.* What to do, how to do it.

Of course, he said. His parents would be delighted.
His mother would make tea. Oh, no, he knew it wasn't
necessary, but she'd insist.

In about an hour?

Perfect. He'd make sure his father was up from his
nap in time.

"Change of plans," he told Jennilyn as he hung up the
phone, and he put the car in gear and headed back home.

It was ball-curdling, dick-shriveling freezing out.

Izzy finally gave up and called Dan, who answered his
phone not with *hello,* but with, "Do you have her?"

Now was not the time to make jokes, so Izzy gave it to
him, straight.

"She hasn't showed," Izzy told him. "So, no. Sorry,
man. I've been standing here—I'm out front again—for
like forty minutes and—"

"You're sure she's not inside already?" Dan asked, his
tension evident in his voice.

"I'm sure," Izzy said. "I checked—three times. I called
her cell, no answer. I called again. I walked over to her
apartment. She's not there, either. I found out the name
of the printers, called them, confirmed that she picked

up a delivery and left. I haven't checked, um, the assem-blywoman's apartment, though. . . ."

"I'm there now," Dan told him tersely. "Jenn's not here, hasn't been here."

"Then . . . I'm guessing that she doesn't want to be found."

"No," Dan said. "That's not—"

"Dude, I know you're—"

"No," Dan said again, more stridently. "She told me that she'd be at the office. She *said* she would."

"And no woman anywhere has ever changed her mind," Izzy said, which okay, *was* kind of a wiseass thing to say. So he tried to soften it by asking, "What should I do? Should I stay or should I . . ."

But Danny had already hung up.

"Go," Izzy finished. He put his phone and his hands back into his pockets and headed for the hotel.

Dan ran into Lt. Starrett on the sidewalk in front of the hotel.

"I was just gonna call you," Sam said, holding up his open phone. "Tell me you found Jenn."

"I can't do that, sir," Dan said. "I'm sorry—believe me, I am, but I don't know where she is."

"God damn it." Wherever Sam was going, he was in a hurry. "You're with me," he ordered, and Dan had to double-time it to keep up.

"I'd really like to keep looking for her, sir," Dan started, but Sam cut him off.

"I suck at this," he said, "so I'm just going to tell it to you straight. The local police called Jules. There's a body in the dumpster outside of the assemblywoman's office."

Dan heard the words. He knew what they meant. And he knew what the trepidation in Sam's tone meant, too.

"It's not her," he said, but his voice sounded strange to his own ears. "Oh, Jesus . . ."

"It's probably not," Sam agreed. "But we've got a missing woman, and NYPD's got a body, so . . . We've got to go check it out, whoever it turns out to be. It's too much of a coincidence, body turning up in *that* dumpster, day after Maggie and Winston's bodies are recovered a few buildings down . . ."

Sam may have kept talking. He may even have—like Izzy often did—burst into song. If he did, Danny didn't hear him.

All he could hear was his own heartbeat, the sound of his breathing, the rhythm of his boots on the sidewalk as the city blocks went by.

He didn't know whether to hurry or lag, because as long as he wasn't there yet, it wasn't Jenn in that dumpster. He wouldn't let it be.

Ah, but God, what if it was?

Despair and loss clutched at him in a near-overpowering wave, but then he felt Sam's hand on his arm, and he looked up, surprised to see that they'd already made it over to the office. He'd nearly walked right past the alley entrance.

"You okay?" Sam asked.

"Yes, sir," Dan lied.

Once again, there were police cruisers and unmarked vehicles, lights spinning, in the alley. Once again, a crowd had gathered.

Dan followed Sam, and they pushed their way over to where a uniformed officer was keeping the onlookers back from the crime scene.

"I'm Starrett, with Troubleshooters," Sam said, but the cop was unyielding—until one of the FBI agents who'd come to Maria's office—Carol—stepped forward. With a nod, they were through.

But then Sam stopped Dan, his voice not unkind. "Maybe you should wait here."

Dan shook his head. "I'd rather not, sir."

Sam sighed, but he nodded. And Dan trailed after Sam as Carol led the way to the police detective who was apparently in charge.

"The victim's female," the man told them, and Dan wanted to stop listening. He wanted to walk away. He didn't want to know. But then the man added, "She's been dead for quite some time . . ."

And the rush of relief, so swift and fierce, made him lightheaded, that the rest of the detective's words seemed to come from far, far away. ". . . it's hard to tell how long exactly, because the body appears to be frozen."

"There's a bag over her head," Carol added. "We're waiting for the photographer to get pictures before we open it or attempt to ID the—"

Sam somehow knew Danny was on the verge of falling over, and interrupted Carol to tell him, "Why don't you take a few minutes?"

"Thank you, sir." Dan stepped away to dig for his phone, to try calling Jenn again as he leaned against the side of a nearby building, grateful for its support. But he went right to her voice mail, so he left a message.

"Please, Jenn," he said. "Call me. I know you're mad— you should be. What you overheard is . . . It's what I do. And I pretend to be honest, but I'm not, because it's just a game. It's not real, it never is, except . . . it's different this time. With you." Jesus, he sounded like every lying sack-of-shit idiot on the entire face of the planet. Except this time he *was* telling the truth. "Look, I just had the crap scared out of me. There was a body in the dumpster and I thought it might be you and . . . Please, baby . . ." He couldn't help it—his voice actually cracked. "Jenni, come on. Just call so I know you're all right."

*   *   *

When Jenn woke up, she didn't know where she was or how she'd gotten there.

She was on the floor of a dimly lit room, with dark wood paneling on the walls and an ornate hardwood floor, with what looked like an Art Deco–era chain of darker wood inlaid around the edges.

God, her head ached and her arms and shoulders hurt, and something hard was biting into her wrists, but she couldn't move her hands. With a flood of panic, she realized that they were tied behind her back. Her feet were tied as well, and a gag was actually in her mouth, wicking the moisture, making her tongue feel swollen and her throat sore and dry.

She had to be dreaming. She felt strange, as if she were partially floating, and she tried to make herself wake up. This had to be a nightmare, it had to be. But try as she could, she couldn't seem to open her eyes.

Because her eyes were already open.

Sobbing, she pulled herself up so that she was sitting, taking her weight off her arms and wrists. And that helped, but not a lot, because as she looked around, even with her glasses gone, she realized that there were no windows or doors—just that relentless paneling, as if she'd been put here and the room built around her.

Around her and a huge table that sat pushed off to one side.

And she realized, with dread, that the awful, faintly metallic smell was from the dark stains on the floor and on that table, and that the splatters on the walls . . .

It was blood.

And Jenn began inching her way around the edge of the room, searching for a crack in the paneling that would reveal a door—and a way out.

This wasn't a dream. Someone had brought her here—

someone who was going to come back and add her blood to the floor and walls.

"Can we get a warrant?" Alyssa asked as she and Jules picked their way carefully down the still slippery sidewalk of a neighborhood that was right out of one of *The Thin Man* movies. Nick and Nora definitely had lived in this quaint part of town. And while some of the owners had converted their ornate townhouses into condos, dividing the multistory mansions into four or even five separate apartments, some looked unchanged.

Oh, to have a few million dollars in disposable income. . . .

"I'm not sure I can find a judge who will agree that *Alyssa has a bad feeling about this man* is a sufficient reason for a search warrant," Jules told her. "What we *can* do is assign a team to watch Gene's house and as soon as anyone appears—either Gene or his parents— we bring 'em in for questioning."

Alyssa had been sorely tempted, while walking around the outside of Gene's parents' ramshackle Victorian house in Brooklyn, to tell Jules to look the other way while she did a little non-government-regulated investigation of her own.

"That's assuming they're going to appear," she pointed out now.

"True," he said. "But if they don't, that gives us the probable cause we need, so we win."

"No," Alyssa argued, "we lose because we have to wait. And if Gene *is* our guy? While we're waiting, his trail is getting colder."

And if Sam was right—and she wasn't yet convinced that he was—Gene Ivanov was also the vicious serial killer known as the Dentist.

And here they were. In front of the house where Douglas

Forsythe lived with his ailing, elderly parents. And suddenly, she didn't feel quite so bad for him. It wasn't as if he were stuck with them in some seven-hundred-square-foot one-bedroom apartment. This was one of the unaltered townhouses. Douglas had a good seven *thousand* square feet with which to stay well out of his parents' way.

"Let's make this as quick as possible," she told Jules as she went up the steps to the massive front door. They still had a scheduled visit with Mick Callahan and *his* parents, and they were running behind. The trip back from Gene's house in Brooklyn had been fraught with traffic. Everything in New York City took three times longer than it ought to, and she needed to get back to the hotel to feed Ashton or to use the pump or she was going to ruin yet another shirt.

But before they reached the landing, the door was thrown open, as if Douglas had been waiting for them.

But instead of a welcoming smile, the man looked distraught. His hair was a mess, his glasses crooked, tears on his face. He was holding a cell phone in hands that were shaking. "I'm trying to call 9-1-1," he told them. "But I can't get through. My mother—I think she's having a heart attack!"

Alyssa looked at Jules, who was already taking out his own phone. He also took the opportunity to do what she'd already done—to unfasten the velcro that locked his sidearm in place, making it easier to access, should he need it.

"I'll call," Jules said. "I'll get through."

"Where is she?" Alyssa asked as she stepped through the door and into a marble-tiled two-story foyer, with a chandelier the size of a Volkswagon Beetle hanging overhead, above the curve of an elegant staircase.

"The kitchen," Douglas told her.

There were doors leading in all directions, not to mention that set of stairs, so she said, "Show me."

He led the way—Jules was right behind them—past a formal living room and through a dining room with a massive wooden table and seating for what looked like sixteen. All the shades were drawn and that, plus the gloomy day, filled the place with shadows. But when Douglas held open the swinging door into the kitchen, stepping back to let her go in first, the room was brightly lit and warm, a kettle whistling on the stove, a tinny-sounding radio playing some big band hit from 1940, and something with chocolate and cinnamon baking in the oven.

And yes, there in an open, old-fashioned pantry, was a small figure, wearing a brightly flowered housedress, crumpled on the floor.

Alyssa reached into her jacket and locked her weapon back in place—a safety precaution—as she crossed to the woman, who'd fallen onto her side, her face down, her legs curled almost oddly beneath her.

Her hair was gray and strangely matted with what looked like blood. "Looks like she hit her head when she fell," Alyssa informed Jules, but as she reached to check for the woman's pulse, she was cold to the touch—not just cool but *cold*.

This woman was dead. She had been for quite some time, and Alyssa moved to see what, as Sam would have said, the fuck . . . ? And she caught sight of the dead woman's face and recoiled in horror. Someone had taken a knife to her, cutting open her cheeks and breaking her jaw so that it hung down, her mouth permanently open in a horrible silent scream.

Her teeth were gone.

Alyssa had seen that awful mutilation before—when she'd discovered Amanda Timberman's body, jammed into an ancient refrigerator in a cabin in the mountains of New Hampshire.

Dear God, Sam was right.

She reached for her sidearm, shouting, "Jules!" but it was too late.

Douglas tased her—but it was unlike the numbing trial blast she'd voluntarily experienced when Troubleshooters had had mandatory Taser training. It seized all of her muscles—all of them, not just her upper body, but her legs as well. And she crumpled to the pantry floor, taking out a shelf of spices and cans of soup, willing herself to move, to fight, to scream, but unable to do anything.

Jules was on the floor, too—Douglas must have tased him first—the shrillness of the teakettle and the music masking both the electrical charge and the sound of him falling.

And she felt Douglas groping her, taking her weapon and her cell phone.

He looked down at her; paralyzed, she could do little more than gaze up at him.

And he smiled and said, "Isn't this fun?" and hit her in the head with her own sidearm.

And the world crashed and popped and faded to black.

He didn't know what to do about the FBI agent.

He'd taken both of their guns, so he *could* shoot him, but he'd never owned a gun, and didn't quite know how to use it. Besides, shooting him would mean there'd be blood spraying everywhere, and he didn't want that.

It was bad enough that the tasering had made the man drool. He'd read on many websites—after the fiasco with the freak in New Hampshire—that it wasn't just blood that carried the AIDS virus. It could be transmitted from other bodily fluids, too.

He'd gotten himself tested and retested after taking the homosexual ski instructor's teeth, after being elbow deep in his blood and gore, but luckily he was clean.

Still he'd learned his lesson.

He now carefully tied up the FBI agent, just as he'd

done with Alyssa—hands behind his back, ankles bound. He used an extra length of cord to tie together the ropes around both his wrists and ankles, pulling it tight so that his body was bent backwards, his hands and feet touching, so that there was no chance of his working his hands around in front of him.

The man was starting to rouse as the effect of the Taser finally began to wear off. So he quickly rummaged through his *mère*'s cabinet and found a plastic bag that was big enough. He put it over the abomination's head, to protect himself from any flying spittle as he tasered him again. And again.

But the son of a bitch now pissed himself, which was disgusting and problematic, because now he couldn't touch him to move him, but . . .

Then there it was—so obvious—the solution to his problem.

He merely had to tie—tightly around the man's throat—that plastic bag that was already covering his head and face.

That would, most definitely, do the trick.

Alyssa was still unconscious, too, but he spoke to her anyway. "Shall we go, my dear?"

As he picked her up, he couldn't resist pulling back her lips to touch her pretty white teeth.

The cop that Jennilyn had a crush on—Mick Callahan—showed up just as the body was being moved out of the dumpster and onto the ground.

The dead woman had been frozen, but apparently only after she'd started to decompose. It was awful—even just the bit that Danny could see. She was in a strange, near-fetal position, her knees bent up to her chest—probably the better to fit her into a standing freezer.

The detectives were getting ready to cut open the bag that was over her head. It was one of those tan, plastic grocery-store bags, and it concealed her face. Dan didn't particularly want to be close enough to see her when they took it off.

He wanted to find Jenn, but despite his many messages, she still hadn't called back.

Neither had Alyssa or Jules called Sam. Danny knew that the former SEAL lieutenant was getting more and more concerned about his inability to reach them, too. And Callahan's appearance in the alley just put the frosting on the cake.

For Dan, too. Jenn *liked* this asshole. Jesus, was this actually jealousy he was feeling?

"I can't help but notice how the bodies didn't start piling up until *you* hit town," Mick said to Sam. He stood with his legs slightly apart, and that plus his smirk punctuated his words. The man was clearly trolling for a fight.

But Sam kept it together. He made himself smile, even though it didn't come close to touching his eyes. "That's pretty funny."

"I'm not kidding," Mick said, his eyes as cold as Sam's. "You think *I'm* a suspect? Well, now I think *you* are. How do you like *that*?"

I think you're a fucking douche bag. Dan could see the words written all over Sam's face, but he didn't have a chance to say them, because one of the other detectives announced, "Victim's got what looks like a wallet in the back pocket of her jeans."

"Her name's Betsy MacGregor," Sam told them, ignoring Mick. "She's from a burb outside of Chicago and she's been missing since August, 2007. She was abducted by a serial killer known as the Dentist, who's still at large."

"Illinois driver's license," the other detective said, as he opened the wallet, "belonging to one . . . Elizabeth MacGregor."

"How the hell did you know that?" Mick said, even as Sam said, "Shit."

"I didn't want to be right," the former SEAL officer added. "Betsy was this bastard's last victim—that we know of, anyway. Before Maggie Thorndyke, that is."

"The *Dentist*," Mick repeated, folding his arms across his chest. "I suppose you're going to try to pin that on me, because I just happened to mention the other day that my mother wanted me to—"

"No one's trying to pin anything on anyone who doesn't deserve it," Sam said. Dan knew he was trying to be diplomatic, but he couldn't keep his disgust from his voice. "I'm trying to help catch a killer who's been carving up his victims since 2001. What are *you* doing here, Callahan?"

"Jesus Christ," gasped the detective who'd cut open the bag, and *Jesus Christ* was right. Dan turned away, having gotten only a glimpse of what was left of the poor woman's face.

"Alyssa and I found another of his victims," Sam said tightly, and for once Mick Callahan had nothing to say. "A girl named Amanda. He left her looking a lot like Betsy, here."

One of the FBI agents vomited behind the dumpster as Dan focused on his phone, taking the opportunity to dial Jenn's number again.

But again, she didn't pick up.

"Jenni, just call me back," Dan said. "Please."

"He takes their teeth," Sam said quietly. "Believe me, seeing this is something that you'll never forget. I never did. So if you're done screwing with me, Callahan, I'd like to go find my wife, so we can catch this motherfucker."

Mick's face was pale as he nodded. "On July 30, '07, my father had a heart attack. It was a bad one. He was in the hospital—Mt. Sinai—for the entire month of August.

I was there, with him, every day." He cleared his throat. "But if you still think I might be the monster who did this, then I'll make your job easier and I'll go in right now, and I'll sit in the police station . . ."

Dan didn't hear what Sam said to Mick, because—finally—his phone vibrated. It was Jenn, sending a text message. But the relief didn't last as he read the words . . .

Alyssa has nice teeth.

"Lieutenant," he interrupted Starrett, as the realization of what that message meant chilled him to the soul.

Holy Jesus, the son of a bitch had them both.

CHAPTER TWENTY-ONE

Jenn played dead as the door she'd found in the wall opened.

She hadn't figured out how to unlatch it—it was possible it was locked from the other side—but she *had* found it.

Without her glasses, she couldn't see very far. Still, she squinted, peering out between her eyelashes at the shape of a man carrying something—some*one*—into the room.

He put whoever it was down, almost gently, onto the floor, then went back out again. It sounded as if he were sending a text message from her phone, the keys making familiar bell-like tones. But he shut the door tightly behind him and the sound was gone.

Jenn waited. Five seconds, ten, fifteen . . . By twenty, when the door didn't open again, she shifted around, moving awkwardly—but moving—toward the person on the floor.

It was Alyssa Locke.

Whoever the man was, he'd tied her up, too. Alyssa's hands were secured behind her back with the same kind of rope that held Jenn, her ankles also bound. And it looked as if he'd hit her. There was blood on her head, in her hair.

With the gag in her mouth, Jenn couldn't speak, but

she could make sounds, and she did so now, nudging Alyssa with her head, trying to get her to wake up.

Please, God, wake up. . . .

And then, thank you, *thank you,* Alyssa's lids began to flutter and she opened her eyes, pulling away from Jenn with a gasp, and then looking sharply around.

She wasn't gagged and she said, "Jenni. Are you all right?"

Jenn nodded yes, which was pretty stupid, because she was the furthest thing from all right that she'd ever been in her life, although granted, now that Alyssa was here, she was doing much, much better.

Except, they were both tied up.

"Turn around, turn around," Alyssa commanded, her voice low in case the man could hear them, and Jenn scrambled to obey, because—yes! Alyssa shifted, too, so that her back was to Jenn, her fingers working to explore the rope that chaffed against Jenn's wrists. But then she shifted again, and Jenn knew she'd turned so she could look at the knot.

She moved again, and Jenn felt Alyssa's fingers again— icy cold against her skin.

"We are going to get out of here," Alyssa told her, over and over again, in that same rich, low, soothing voice. "We are *going* to get out of here. . . ."

Sam didn't allow himself to think.

That monster had Alyssa, and he couldn't think about what that meant, because if he thought about it too hard he'd know a terrible truth—if this son of a bitch *had* somehow taken Alyssa, then Jules was dead.

He was out of Mick Callahan's car and running up the steps to the house where Douglas Forsythe lived, Dan and Mick on his heels.

He was filled with a sense of dread. Forsythe surely knew that Sam and the entire FBI knew that Alyssa and

Jules had come to his house. So why send that text message, unless he was long gone?

In the car, Sam had called Izzy, who was back at the hotel, telling him to fire up the computer that held the GPS tracking system. He and Alyssa both had GPS systems in their phones that allowed them to be traced, provided they stayed close to their phones.

The front door was locked, and Dan put his shoulder into trying to break it down, but he bounced off, while Sam went for the window.

He was up and through it with a crash, feet first, as the FBI team members were yammering about warrants.

Mick was right behind him, an unlikely ally, his weapon drawn, like Sam. The cop stopped to unlock the door in a palatial foyer, letting the FBI in, and checking the ancient security control panel that was by the door.

"Security system is not activated," he reported, before Sam shut him up with a finger to his lips.

But Dan had gone through the other window with an equally loud crash, with Carol right behind him, and they both came out of what looked like an old-fashioned front parlor, with their weapons held at ready.

Sam again signaled that he now wanted silence, then gestured with his sidearm for Mick and Carol to go upstairs. He and Dan—used to working together—would sweep through the rooms on the first floor.

He could hear music coming from a room in the back of the house. Dan nodded, he heard it, too, as they went through a living room and a formal dining room.

The place was right out of a horror movie, with uncomfortable-looking antique furniture that had to be worth a fortune. Except there were no cobwebs or dust. At first glance, at least, it seemed clean.

Sam found a door that was locked with the kind of ancient but still effective latch that couldn't be opened from the other side, not even with a key, so he went past it.

There was light—and that music, from some kind of badly EQ'ed radio—coming from behind a door that didn't have a knob or a latch. Sam didn't break stride as he glanced at Dan, who nodded. He, too, was ready.

Sam swiftly pulled the door open rather than pushing it, hoping for the element of surprise, but the kitchen—it was a kitchen and it was much smaller than he'd expected—was empty. The only people in there were lying on the floor.

And, shit, one of them was Jules. He was tied so tightly he was bent almost backwards, and he had a plastic bag over his head.

"Agent down!" Sam shouted, as Dan quickly moved toward the other prone figure.

"Jesus!" Dan exclaimed.

"Tell me it's not Alyssa or Jenn," Sam ordered the younger man, as he saw that Jules was still alive, he was breathing—he'd managed to tear a hole in the thin plastic with his teeth.

"It's not," Dan confirmed, his voice tight. "It's another victim like Betsy, but . . . elderly and . . ."

Sam ripped the bag the rest of the way open, pulling it off Jules. And even though the FBI agent looked like death warmed over, he immediately said, "Douglas Forsythe. He has at least two handguns, and a handheld Taser set on holy fucking turbo."

"And Alyssa," Sam added, as he used one of the kitchen knives to cut the rope that tied him, and Jules nodded.

"And he also has Alyssa," he agreed grimly.

"Did you see Jenn?" Dan asked.

"No," Jules answered, rubbing his wrists. "I'm sorry. When we approached the house, Forsythe opened the door, appearing to be in distress. He told us his mother had had a heart attack, so we came in to assist. He tased me first, while Alyssa was tending to his mother. Is she dead?"

"She's been dead for a while," Dan reported.

Jules nodded. "I went down and hit my head, which was when he must've tased Alyssa. I'm telling you, I've been tased before, but that thing was juiced—the world went black and white. I couldn't scream. I couldn't make a sound—I couldn't fucking *breathe*."

"Second and third floors are clear," Carol reported as she came into the kitchen. "No forensic evidence of homicide. And an ambulance is on its way." She nodded to Jules. "Glad to see you, sir."

"What I really need," Jules said, looking down at himself, "is a new pair of pants. He tased me again—I was pretty sure he was going to keep doing it, and I didn't think I'd survive, so I kind of . . . went for full loss of bodily control, in hopes that he'd back off. Which he did. But now I'm soggy . . ."

"Does this place have a basement?" Dan asked.

"Back this way," Sam said, leading the way to that bolted door that he'd bypassed.

But Mick had already found it and opened it, and sure enough there were stairs leading down. A light switch had been flipped on, and okay. This was where the dust and cobwebs lived. Still, the stairs were clear enough to make Sam believe that someone had made use of them somewhat regularly.

The wood creaked as he went down into the basement, Dan right behind him.

It was cold and damp and it smelled like one of those museums that Alyssa loved to visit—old houses where Lincoln or Mozart or Mark Twain had lived. It smelled ancient and mildewy, but it didn't smell of death.

"Nothing," Mick announced. He put it differently than Carol had. "No puddles of blood or piles of teeth. Although we did find this."

This was a row of three new-looking freezers, their Energy Star stickers still on their doors.

"Two are empty," Mick told him. "The third holds Dougie's daddy—at least that's the assumption we're working with. Elderly man, no teeth . . ."

Sam nodded. "Suspect is armed with Alyssa's SIG P226 and Cassidy's Browning BDM, as well as a super-juiced Taser," he told the police detective and the other agents who came down there.

Aside from those gleaming white freezers, this part of the basement could've been a museum, with an old time workbench, and an array of tools—from a garden hoe to a pickax to an ancient crank-roller washing machine.

The far part of the basement was a garage, with two sets of arch-shaped carriage house doors that were hinged on the sides and opened in the center. They led out into a back alley. There was room for two cars in the garage, but only one was parked there. It was a museum-worthy Pontiac, dating from the early 1970s, and neatly covered with an oilcloth.

Mick pushed at the doors on the empty side of the garage, and as they swung open, Sam's heart sank.

"This was unlocked when we got down here," Mick reported.

"We need to find out what other car was registered in either Forsythe or his parents' names," Sam said, "and we need that info now!"

"Already on it." Carol was behind him, phone to her ear, Jules behind her. She turned to him. "Sir, with all due respect, you need to—"

"I know what I need," Jules told her.

"I'm not sure you do, sir," she insisted.

Sam didn't hear the end of that argument, because his phone rang. It was Izzy calling from the hotel.

"Starrett here," Sam said. "Tell Robin we found Jules, he's okay, but Alyssa and Jenn are still UA. Tell Tony to bring over the weapons case and a pair of Jules's pants,

ASAP. When he leaves, you lock that door behind you and do not open it for anyone, not even the FBI agents in the hall, not under any circumstances. If someone tries to get in, shoot to fucking kill. Do you hear me?"

"Yes, sir."

"Now, give me some good news, Zanella," Sam ordered.

"GPS puts Alyssa heading north on the Henry Hudson Parkway," Izzy reported, "moving at forty miles per hour."

His dread increasing, Sam repeated Zanella's words.

"Can we set up a road block?" Mick asked. "Or a checkpoint at the toll?"

Izzy must've heard him, because he told Sam, and Sam repeated, "They're already past the toll booth."

"DMV doesn't have another vehicle on record for either Douglas, John, or Danielle Forsythe," Carol interrupted, "which doesn't mean Douglas didn't have a second car registered under an assumed name. And here's a useful fact—John and Danielle Forsythe also own property on Lake Mahopac. It's about an hour north of here, just over the Putnam County line. You'd get there by taking the Henry Hudson to the Saw Mill to the Taconic."

Sam shook his head. "That's too easy. He wouldn't go there. He'd know it's the first place we'd look."

"We don't have a lot of options," Mick pointed out.

"Let's start by following Alyssa's GPS," Jules said. "Carol, alert the State Police, as well as the locals in Lake Mahopac."

"Already doing it, sir," she said.

"I need a car and driver."

"I've got a car," Mick volunteered.

Jules turned to Sam and Dan. "You gonna come with or stay?"

"I'm in," Dan said.

"We'll find them," Jules said, picking up on Sam's uncertainty. "This is Alyssa. She's going to kick his ass."

But Sam wasn't convinced.

"Oh, good, they're leaving," Douglas said with a smile that made the hair go up on the back of Alyssa's neck.

He'd come back in, wheeling three large suitcases with him, which he'd stacked neatly against the far wall, then covered with a heavy-duty plastic painter's tarp.

Alyssa had heard him coming, and she'd pushed herself back to where he'd left her. Jenn had moved, too—they were both playing unconscious.

Through her eyelashes, she'd watched as he dragged in a case of bottled water, and several grocery bags that looked as if they actually held food. Healthy snacks like rice cakes and pita chips. He brought in a cooler, too.

As if he were planning to stay here, in this windowless room, for a while.

"I know you're awake," he'd told her, "but if you want to pretend otherwise, that's fine with me."

It was strange—he was Douglas. She'd sat and interviewed him. God, she'd walked out to the dumpster with him, just the two of them, and she hadn't been even slightly afraid.

And yes, he'd been on her suspect list, but he'd been way at the bottom, beneath Mick Callahan even. He'd fooled her—completely. He was smart, he was cunning, and he was completely psychotic.

He was the Dentist.

Her brain stuttered through her choices, her options. Stay silent and wait, because Sam was coming. She knew he was coming. And Jules was somewhere, too, because he wasn't in here with her, and oh, please God, don't let this monster have slashed his throat, like he did with all the others. . . .

She pushed aside her fear and grief, because she was

alive and Jenn was alive, and right now her job was to make damn sure that they both stayed that way.

She could beg for Jenn's life, but this man had no soul, no conscience, so appealing to him for mercy would be worthless.

She could try to figure out where the hell they were—they were still in his house, she was sure of it, and yet she'd clearly been wrong about much of this so far.

So she opened her eyes and spoke, making her voice even and calm. "What is this place? The floor is lovely."

She'd surprised him—that was good. "Isn't it?" he asked. "It's a prohibition room. Back when alcohol was declared illegal, the owners renovated, and built this hidden room. They stored their wine here, and even brewed their own beer. They had dinner parties in here—the room was built around this table. Mother and Dad once tried to get it out, but it didn't fit through the narrow doorway."

So they *were* still in his townhouse. Which meant that Sam was going to be here, soon.

"He won't find us," Douglas told her, perceptive as always. "Your husband. The room isn't big enough. It was designed to fit in behind the closets and the kitchen pantry. I found it, myself, when I was a child—just by chance."

Alyssa was silent, just waiting, because this man, the Dentist, did love to talk.

He didn't disappoint. "Besides, he's not going to stay here long enough. I gave a taxi driver a very generous tip to take a package—with your cell phone in it—to a pizza parlor in a little town about an hour north of here. I imagine he'll be chasing that." He laughed. "I almost feel bad for him."

She heard it then—the crash of a window being broken. And she drew in her breath to scream—*Sam!*

But she didn't make a sound because Douglas was on

top of her, shocking her with that souped-up Taser that made the world shudder and shake with searing pain. And when she stopped buzzing and regained at least some of her senses, she discovered that he'd gagged her.

And damn it, he'd realized that she'd begun to loosen the binds around Jenn's wrists.

"Look what you've gone and done," he said, tsking, as he pulled the ropes so tightly that Jenn made a sound of pain behind her gag.

Alyssa tried to make noise—please God, let Sam know they were here—but Douglas zapped her again, and again the world went dim.

She fought it, though, and saw him smile, heard him say, "Oh, good, they're leaving."

He adjusted the plastic tarp over his suitcases and got out a deadly looking knife. God, they were in trouble. . . .

But Alyssa turned to look at Jenn, who gave her solid eye contact.

It wasn't over until it was over, and they weren't done fighting yet.

Sam was dragging his feet.

Dan wanted to scream at him. *Let's go! Let's move!* But Sam lingered in the foyer, looking back toward the kitchen, as if maybe he wanted to grab a sandwich for the ride north.

Mick was already in his car, engine running. And Tony was there with the Troubleshooters' weapons case, helping Jules replace his stolen sidearm, and making sure they had all the ammunition they needed.

Dan grabbed a few more clips himself as Jules ran inside to change into the jeans that Tony had brought for him.

"Get in the car, sir," Dan called to Sam as Jules came back out.

And then, alleluia, Sam jogged down the steps, behind Jules. But he didn't get in. Instead he motioned for Mick to pull down his window, which the detective did.

"There was a bolt on the basement door," Sam said. "When I went past, I thought it was locked. Were you the first one through that door?"

Mick nodded. "I was," he said. "And it *was* locked."

"It doesn't make sense," Sam said. "Douglas takes Jenn and Alyssa into the basement—to the garage—puts them in his car and . . . Goes back upstairs to lock that door from the inside? He left the garage doors unlocked. Why would he bother? Did he really go back inside, lock the door, leave through the front door, walk all the way around to the back alley, go in through the garage, and only then make his escape?"

Dan wanted to get moving. "If he had the key he could've locked it from—"

"No," Sam cut him off. "It's not that kind of bolt. There's no way to unlock it unless you're *inside* the *house.*"

"It was locked," Mick said again. He turned off his car.

"What the hell . . . ?" Dan said. "We need to—"

"The kitchen's too small," Sam announced, as if that fucking meant something important.

"Shit, you're right." And now Mick was out of his car, and he and Jules were following Sam up the steps.

But Sam turned to stop them and put a finger to his lips. He wanted silence.

"*Jesus,*" Dan said, but he followed them because the alternative was to stand there on the sidewalk with his thumb up his ass.

"I just want to find Jenn," he whispered to Tony, who was right behind him.

"I think that's what we're doing," Tony whispered back, pointing to the bolt on the door that Sam had been talking about.

The kitchen's too small—so what if the kitchen was too small?

But Sam and Mick and Jules were walking silently back and forth between it and the dining room and the living room, turning on all the lights.

Which was when Dan saw it, too. The *kitchen* was *too small*. It should have extended another ten feet from the back of the pantry.

There was another room—a hidden room—here on the first floor of this big house.

But how the hell were they going to get in? They didn't have time to explore and find the equally hidden door. That psycho could be carving up Jenn and Alyssa right now, right behind those very walls. . . .

Sam motioned for Tony to bring the weapons case over, and Tony snapped to it, opening it up. Whereupon Sam reached—yes—for the small chunk of C4 explosives.

For what he was going to do, they wouldn't need a lot.

Except these walls were old. God only knew what was behind the plaster. Possibly horsehair. They had to assume they were plenty thick.

One blast might not be enough.

But Danny remembered seeing a pickax in the basement.

He ran to get it while Sam set the charge.

He liked it when they bit him, hard enough to draw blood, so he always gave them a chance to do so. He had his Taser in the event that they latched on too tightly, so he was never in real danger.

But here they were, hidden away in his kill room, where he'd brought Monsieur Henri, Tinkerbell, Jolie, and Maggie Thorndyke all to their magnificent, snarling ends.

He wished there was a drain in the floor, and a shower so he could wash. After killing Maggie, he'd had to wipe himself down very carefully, so as not to get blood on Mère's carpeting in the hall outside his bathroom.

And he also wished he could remove Jenn's gag, so he could see and feel her sharp little teeth, as she felt the bite of his knife.

But he couldn't, because there were still people in the house, moving quietly around, no doubt putting the gay FBI agent, Mère *et* Papa in body bags. He wondered, briefly, what the FBI would do with the freezers that he'd bought upon his return home. They were still almost new. Barely used.

He liked the idea of some unknowing person buying one of them and using it to store their ground beef and frozen vegetables—never realizing that this freezer they'd gotten at such a great bargain had been used, for months, as a tomb.

He also liked the fact that Alyssa was pretending that she wasn't afraid. Or maybe she really wasn't—he liked to think that was possible, too. That she was, in fact, as strong as he was.

But it was far more likely that she would crack when he took his knife to Jennilyn.

If Alyssa's gag was off, she'd beg. And plead. And bargain. And cry.

He was going to make her cry before this was over, before this ended.

And it *would* end, one way or another.

If the house emptied, he'd kill Jenn here and leave her body for them to find, while he and Alyssa drove west. He would keep her alive a little bit longer. It was not his original plan, but he liked having her watch him work.

And he wanted to hear her scream.

Of course, there was always a chance that someone would find them—that someone would realize they hadn't left the city after all. In which case he would kill Alyssa immediately, even as his own life ended.

Either way though, Jenn was going to die right now.

It was time to do it—to see if he could make Alyssa Locke cry.

Sam was coming back.

He was going to come back.

Alyssa knew it. She believed it, believed in him.

He would realize that she and Jenn and this monster were all still here, and he would . . .

Come . . .

Back . . .

But she was also terrified because she knew that they were out of time.

He was going to start cutting Jenn, and she would not let that happen.

Alyssa rolled, pushing herself toward Jenn, getting in front of her, next to her, but he just laughed and kept coming.

They backed up, together, Alyssa's shoulder against Jenn's, until they finally hit the wall and there was nowhere left to go.

He reached down, still laughing, and easily—with his left hand, because his right held that knife—took hold of the ropes that bound Alyssa's ankles, and he dragged her back, away from Jenn, to the other side of the room.

She flailed, trying to kick him, and he laughed again.

"Oh, I *knew* you'd make this fun," he said, and he turned back toward Jenn—and the world exploded.

The explosion threw Jenn back, and she hit her head against the pedestal base of the big table hard enough to see stars.

Her ears were ringing, and chokingly thick smoke and dust was everywhere, but light—bright light—was shining through.

She could see the shadowy, backlit shape of a very big man, wielding what looked like some kind of ax, swinging it and crashing through what was left of the wall.

She turned, looking for Alyssa. Where *was* she?

And there she was—she'd been flung back into the far corner of the room, where she lay motionless.

But there was Douglas, in the middle of the room, pushing himself up onto his hands and knees, shaking his head as if to clear it from the confusion and chaos, pushing himself even further up onto his feet. And the light glinted off of the knife he still held in his hand.

As Jenn watched from beneath the table, he turned toward Alyssa and threw himself at her.

Jenn tried to move, tried to get between them, tried to do for Alyssa what Alyssa had done for her, but she wasn't fast enough.

But she didn't have to be.

Because Sam was there, with that pickax. He'd broken through the wall, yet he still swung just as hard, one more time. He connected with Douglas, stopping him literally dead in his tracks before that blade touched Alyssa.

She had to turn away, because, God . . .

"Jenn!"

And there was Dan. He, too, had come through the wall, part of the cavalry, to save the day.

He pulled off her gag, and he grabbed one of Douglas's bottles of water—they were rolling all over the floor—and gave her some to drink.

"Thank you," she said as she started to cry.

"It's okay now," he told her. "Everything's okay." And he picked her up. He actually *picked* her *up* in his arms and carried her out of there, out of that room, out of the house and into the cold, welcoming fresh air of the late afternoon.

She could hear sirens—ambulances and fire trucks both were on their way.

But Dan just sat down on the steps leading up to Douglas's house and, after making sure that she truly was unharmed, that she hadn't been injured either by Douglas or that blast, he kissed her. And kissed her.

And *kissed* her.

CHAPTER
TWENTY-TWO

Alyssa was going to be all right.

They were all in the hospital—Alyssa and Jenn and Jules.

Jules—who'd been both electrocuted and nearly asphyxiated by a notorious serial killer, and was acting as if it were all in a day's work.

Robin sat at the side of his husband's bed in the ER, grateful that this had happened in New York City. If this were a hospital in Cleveland or New Orleans, he'd be forced to sit out in the waiting room, because his marriage wouldn't be recognized and he wouldn't be considered a family member.

But this *was* New York, and Jules had neither been electrocuted nor asphyxiated to death, all of which was extremely good news.

The doctors had hooked Jules up to an EKG, to make sure the blasts from Douglas Forsythe's illegally altered Taser hadn't done any damage to his heart.

It hadn't, thank God.

Alyssa and Jenn had both gotten their hearts checked, too. And Alyssa was having a CAT scan, because she'd hit her head in the explosion that had saved her life and Jenn's.

But she was conscious and cognizant, and with Sam's

help had taken a shower. Robin had brought clothes from the hotel for Sam and Alyssa both. Apparently Sam taking a pickax to the serial killer's head had had extremely messy results.

"What I don't get," Robin said, "and believe me, I'm not complaining, but—"

"Why didn't he kill me," Jules finished for him. "Why a bag over my head instead of cutting my throat? And it wasn't a very thick bag—it was one of those produce bags from the grocery store. I tore it easily with my teeth."

"But if you had been unconscious," Robin started. It would have killed him.

Jules squeezed his hand. "I wasn't."

"Thank God."

They sat there for a moment, then Jules said, "It was because I'm gay. I mean, I don't know that for sure—we'll never really know. But I think he was, I don't know, afraid of me . . . ? It sounds crazy, but . . . You know, maybe he was one of those people who think that everyone who's gay has AIDS and . . . He was something of a germophobe, that we *do* know. Lots of bottles of hand sanitizer around the house."

"Well hooray for ignorance," Robin said.

"He kept the place really clean, too," Jules told him. "I mean, usually when you think *serial killer,* you think of someone insane, living in a cave or a basement, in their own filth."

Robin laughed. "That's the difference between the two of us," he pointed out. "I don't generally think about serial killers."

"That's a good thing," Jules assured him.

"So he was clean," Robin said, "but he was still insane. I mean, keeping mom and dad in freezers in the basement? How come no one noticed they were gone?"

"Carol told me that when he came home back in May, he terminated the contracts with his parents' hired help, and told them his folks were going to winter in Florida. No one checked to find out if that was true. I guess they didn't have many friends."

"That's kind of sad," Robin said.

Jules nodded. "Our theory is that he brought Betsy's body home with him—that he carried it with him since he killed her, buying a freezer to store it wherever he went. Apparently he had access to a significant trust fund. We could probably figure out where he stayed over the past year and a half, by finding the properties across the country in which the tenant paid in cash and bought and left behind a full-size freezer."

"So he spent all that time," Robin said, "targeting Alyssa?"

"That's Sam's theory," Jules said. He had three suitcases with him in his secret room. Two were filled with money, but the other held photos and information—a lot of stuff about Alyssa. He had details about Sam and Ashton, too. Scary.

"He was definitely behind that forged letter that was sent to Frank Bonavita," Jules continued. "He had samples of Frank's handwriting and some earlier drafts of the letter in his suitcase. Along with a pretty big bag of meth, probably to keep Frank supplied . . . We're doing an autopsy, but I don't think we're going to find he was a user himself. I'm guessing he had it to control Frank—in case he needed someone to take the blame or create a distraction."

"What about the teeth?" Robin asked.

"They were in that suitcase, too," Jules told him. "Although he did have a few in the pockets of his pants. Lab is going to do DNA tests on all of them—see if there are any victims that we didn't know about."

"He's definitely the one who killed Maggie, right?" Robin asked.

"Yeah, and Winston," Jules said.

"I figured," Robin said. "I mean, otherwise you wouldn't have let me leave the hotel."

Jules shook his head, apology and regret in his eyes. "Some vacation this turned out to be, huh?"

"The you-not-being-dead part ranks it right up among the very best."

Jules sat up and reached for him, and Robin went into his arms.

Izzy stayed behind at the hotel with Ashton.

That was the plan. He'd hang with the baby, while Lopez escorted Maria to the hospital, to see Jenn.

It was crazy, everything that had gone down—Sam Starrett blowing the shit out of a wall and then splitting open some deviant serial killer's skull with a single well-placed blow, in order to save the life of his wife and another innocent woman.

It was the kind of thing that, if this were some B-grade horror movie, Sam would have gotten there a heartbeat too late, and Alyssa would have died. And then, in killing the killer so gruesomely, Sam would have become possessed by the man's evil spirit, and thus would begin his own horrific killing spree, offing all of *his* victims in the very same way, with a brutal blow to the head with a pickax.

But this wasn't a horror movie. Alyssa was very much alive, although the story of her rescue wasn't one either of Ash's parents would be telling their little boy anytime soon.

Izzy had just put the munchkin down for a nap and was looking forward to a little shut-eye himself, when there was a knock at the door.

Grateful that he no longer had to enforce Sam's shoot-to-kill order, Izzy went to the peephole and . . .

Hmm.

It was Lopez—and Maria Bonavita.

He opened the door, thinking that Lopez had forgotten something, but it was Maria who said, "Hi, may I come in?"

"Uh," Izzy said. "Sure? Come on in. *Please* come in." He looked at Lopez pointedly.

But the bastard shook his head. "I'll wait in the hall," he said.

"Thank you," Maria said—it was clearly something they'd worked out in advance.

Which left Izzy awkwardly closing the door behind her. "S'up?" he said, playing the stupid card—as if he didn't know why she was here.

"May we sit?" she asked, not waiting for him to respond as she went into the living room of the suite. She was still dressed down in jeans and a sweater. She'd taken her coat off before she'd knocked on his door and she held it over her arm.

He let her sit first, then took a seat as far from her as possible.

"I want to apologize," Maria said, "for my inappropriate behavior this morning. I know you're still married and . . . I should have kept my distance."

"Apology accepted," he said, standing up.

But she didn't get to her feet, which was a rather huge clue that there was more to come.

So he beat her to the punch. "I won't tell anyone," he promised her. "I know that as a politician you've got to be careful about this kind of thing, and I will absolutely keep my mouth zipped and—"

"No," she said. "That's not . . . I don't care about that. Well, I *do* care, but it never even occurred to me that you'd . . ." She exhaled hard. "Wow, okay. Thank you. For not telling anyone. I appreciate that. But I wanted to . . ." She stopped again. Crossed her legs. Tapped her fingers on the armrest of the sofa as she looked at him. "Will you please sit?"

"I'm good standing," Izzy said.

So she stood up, too. "Look," she said. "Here it is: I want to have a family. But my political career is taking off, and I work 24/7 and . . . I'm heading to Albany and probably Washington—I mean, *if* I survive this thing with the Dentist being one of my major donors and volunteering in my office—which, granted, is better than my brother being a murderer—"

"Spin that you helped catch him," Izzy said. "Don't be the victim, be part of the team of heroes who caught the bad guy."

Maria looked startled, but then nodded. "Yeah," she said. She smiled. "Yeah. Thanks."

"You want a family," Izzy asked her, "or you *need* one?"

She didn't answer right away, but when she did, it was with honesty. "Both," she admitted. "But you're right. Need more than want."

Izzy nodded. He'd been thinking about it since she'd hit on him, and he now knew exactly what this was about.

Maria was still young but, like she'd said, her career was kicking into high gear. Right now it was clear that she had no time for a baby, or even for a husband or boyfriend—which was a perfectly fine choice for her to make. Still, as a politician, having a family was perceived to be important.

That had to be a weird consideration, even though male politicians married trophy wives—usually those with money—all the time.

But a woman with political aspirations . . . ?

It would definitely serve her better to have a kid soon, and get through those early childhood years before running for governor or senator or whatever she had in mind.

"I assume you're looking for more than a sperm donor," Izzy said.

Maria laughed. "I've got plenty of volunteers for that. So, no. I'm looking to get married."

"The polygamy thing could be a problem," he pointed out. "During the vetting process, someone will probably find out."

"Obviously," she said, "if it ever got to that point, you'd have to get a divorce."

The word hit him, like a punch to the gut.

"Look," she said again, "I'm not talking about running off to Vegas tomorrow. Obviously we'd need to get to know each other better. And maybe it wouldn't work. But . . . maybe it would. What I *do* know is this—I like what I've seen, enough to think it's worth a try."

He started to speak again, but again, Maria cut him off.

"I know you still hope to reconnect with Eden," she said, "and I really hope, for your sake, that you do, but if you *don't*—"

"This is crazy," he said.

"No, it's not," she countered. "I like you, you like me—and you're great with kids."

She was serious.

She was also gathering up her jacket and purse. "That's all," she said. "That's what I came here to say. I'm not looking for an immediate answer. I just wanted to put the idea out there, and make you realize you have other options if your plans fall through. So, think about it. And, you know, call me, if you find yourself unmarried."

She was halfway to the door before he spoke.

"You're *that* certain you're never going to fall in love again," Izzy asked her. "That you'd be willing to give up the possibility, by settling for someone you merely like?"

"Yes," she told him. "I'm that certain."

And with that, she walked out the door.

*   *   *

It was weird being home, in her little apartment.

After being checked and poked and prodded, the doctors had finally released Jenn from the hospital. Dan had come with her, unlocking her door and disarming the alarm system, as if he lived there, too.

He was on the verge of taking off his jacket and hanging it on the knob—which was rapidly becoming his place for it—when she stopped him.

"You should go," she said.

He honestly didn't understand, as if she'd spoken to him in some foreign tongue.

So she put it a different way.

"I'm really not up for having anyone stay tonight," she said.

"But . . ." He stopped. "Really?"

Heart in her throat, Jenn nodded.

"I thought you, you know, accepted my apology," he said.

In the hospital, he'd told her, over and over again, how sorry he was—not just for saying what she'd overheard him say to Izzy, but for doing exactly what he'd described. He'd found and seduced the chunky girl with the much prettier friends.

They'd sat there, in the hospital, while she'd waited to find out if her heart had been damaged from the electrical blasts she'd received, and Dan had admitted that when this had started—just a few short days ago—that his goal had purely been to get some. Since he found her attractive enough—and yes, his bluntly honest words had made them both wince—and since she seemed to be on the same page, it had seemed like a win/win.

"But then," Dan had told her, "it changed. I don't know what happened. But it did. And Jenni, it's not just about sex anymore. God, when I thought you were dead . . ."

He'd kissed her then, and she'd kissed him, too, because it was impossible to *not* kiss Dan Gillman back.

And maybe she would've been okay with him coming home with her and spending the rest of his two weeks in her bed, but then he'd gone and said it.

"Jenni, I think I'm falling in love with you," he'd whispered, and she knew in that moment that she didn't have to wait for the doctor to tell her.

Her heart *was* damaged.

She didn't say it right then, because there were too many doctors and nurses coming in and out of the room. Maria dropped in to see her, too, and Robin, and even Sam and Alyssa.

But now Jenn told Dan, "You helped save my life today. Remember your theory? The one about the hormones and adrenaline?"

He shook his head as if to dismiss it, but she pressed.

"You rescue me, and then you say . . . what you said, that you're in love with me, and you expect me to believe you?"

"Yes," he said, as if that would end the discussion.

"How was it you described it?" she asked. "Your brain is receiving some deceptive little signal saying *Mine*. But it's not real."

"It is," he said.

"But what if it's not?" Jenn countered. "God, Dan, I really, *really* don't want you waking up in a few months going *who's this numbnuts lying here next to me. . . .* "

She was fighting him with his own logic, his own theories, and he was not happy about that. "It's been a bitch of a day," he said, desperation in his voice. "Can't we please just call a time-out and talk about this in the morning?"

Jenn made herself shake her head. "I don't want two weeks or eleven days or whatever you've got left, Dan. I just don't. I want more than that."

"That's what I want now, too," he said. "I do, Jenni—"

"Okay," she said. "Then call me when you get back to the States."

He was flummoxed. "What?"

"Yeah," she said. "Yes. This is how we'll do it, okay? You go, and come back. And if you do . . . Then I'll believe you."

He was starting to realize that she was serious. "I'm going to Afghanistan," he said, which made her stomach twist. "I won't be back for months."

"Give me your address," Jenn said. "I'll write." She forced a smile. "I'll send you packages."

"Jenni," he said.

She waited, but he didn't seem to have more to say than that.

So she told him, "When you get back, give me a call. If you want."

"And you're just going to be, what?" Dan asked. "Waiting for me?"

"Yes," she said. "But I won't wait forever. Just for this one time. I'll find out from Savannah when you're back, and if you don't call me, well, that'll be that. So you don't have to feel guilty if you change your mind."

He put his jacket on, but did it really slowly. "I don't want to go," he said. "God, Jenn, come on. What if this guy Mick calls you?"

"Well," she said, "if *Mick* calls, all bets are off. George Clooney's on my exception list, too, and—look at you. I'm kidding. If Mick or George calls, I'll say, *Thank you, but I'm sorry, I'm in love with Dan Gillman and I'm waiting for him to come back.*"

And great. With her own words, she'd made herself start to cry.

"Jenni," he said again and reached for her, but she stepped back, away from him, wiping her eyes dry.

She could do this. She *had* to do this.

"This is where we find out if you trust me," Jenn told him, using the very words he'd said to her in the stairwell, with Frank. They were the words that made her leave him there—because she *did* trust him. Very much.

He just stood there, looking at her, for a long time.

"I'm serious," she finally said.

And he nodded. "I'll be back."

"Okay," she said, but she knew that he knew she'd believe it only when she saw it.

He opened her door. But then he shut it again, and he grabbed her and kissed her, long and sweet, before he let her go.

"I'll e-mail you with my APO," he said.

And he walked out the door.

Alyssa stood at Ashton's crib and looked down at her son.

He was smiling in his sleep, and it was hard not to smile back as she watched him.

"He's dreaming about his momma," Sam said softly, as he put his arms around her waist, hugging her from behind, his chest warm against her back.

She turned to face him, and he held her tightly, his broken rib be damned.

"God, I was scared to death today," he breathed. "When Danny got that text message . . ."

"I was scared, too," she admitted. She pulled back to look at him, to push his hair from his eyes, to look at him searchingly. "Are you really okay?"

He nodded. "I'm not going to lose any sleep over killing Forsythe," he told her. "Not a minute. It's the fact that I nearly killed you in that blast that's gonna give me nightmares."

"He was going to kill Jenn," Alyssa told him. "I was trying to stop him, but my hands and feet were tied. And he was just laughing. . . ." She shook her head. "Your timing was perfect."

"I was sure I'd lost both you and Jules today," Sam told her.

"And I was so sure it was Gene Ivanov," Alyssa said. "If I'd thought it really could've been Douglas, I never would've turned my back on him. It was a foolish mistake."

"A human mistake," he corrected her. "You know Gene turned up—did Jules tell you?"

"No," she said. "Where?"

"He was in the hospital. He got himself shot. Apparently Hank the UPS man was running drugs, and he'd blackmailed Gene into making some of his deliveries. So you were right about Gene hiding something. He told the police that he was intending to come back to the office and confess his involvement, when you got tied up in the discovery of Maggie and Winston's bodies."

"I saw him in the alley. And I thought . . ." She'd thought he was the killer—the Dentist—when all along it had been Douglas Forsythe. "I wish I'd seen you," Alyssa said, "the way Jenn described you, coming straight through the wall."

He smiled. "I have to confess, I went a little caveman."

"Every now and then," she said, "I could use a little caveman."

"Aha," he said. "The truth comes out. It's all *Sam, don't beat up the cop,* and *Sam, don't get arrested,* until the caveman saves the day."

She laughed, but it faded as she lost herself in his eyes. She stood on her toes to kiss him again. "I knew you'd come," she told him softly. "I knew you'd find me."

"Always," he told her, and he kissed her back, then shut their bedroom door.

AUTHOR'S NOTE

Quite a few years ago when I wrote *Gone Too Far*, the Troubleshooters book that ended Sam and Alyssa's story arc, my editor suggested that we include a short story featuring these two extremely popular characters in the back of the next book (*Flashpoint*). We could let readers see how their lives were going after they'd won their happily-ever-after.

I liked the idea, but I was wary. Writing short—stories or articles or even birthday cards—is hard for me. (Just see how long this author's note is . . .) Plus, I was also adamant that I *not* write something inappropriately light and fluffy, like "Sam and Alyssa Get a Puppy."

So I stomped around my office for a few weeks, thinking about these two characters, and pondering all of the changes that Alyssa surely had to deal with, with Sam-the-optimist now permanently part of her life.

And I wrote what I thought was a short story in which Sam and Alyssa handle a missing persons assignment for Troubleshooters Incorporated. They go to New Hampshire and search for a wealthy young woman who appears to have eloped with her ski instructor.

Alyssa ends up finding the woman's mutilated body stuffed into the refrigerator of an abandoned cabin. It's a chilling, disturbing, upsetting experience for her. And in the aftermath, as Sam does his best to give her support, she realizes that living with her husband has started to change her. She really thought that they'd find this young woman living happily with her lover, probably in a little house with a picket fence and a flower garden. (And plenty of puppies.)

The short story ends—or at least I thought it ended—with Alyssa in Sam's arms, watching the sunrise, welcoming a new day. The killer was, however, still at large, because, come on, people, it was a *short* story.

So okay, after *Flashpoint* came out, I waded my way through the ocean of reader e-mails that asked me about that "excerpt" from the new book with Sam and Alyssa and the serial killer that I'd named "the Dentist." (Note to my own dentist: Nothing personal, Mark.) When would that book be out, many readers asked, and what was it called?

I tried, for years, to convince readers that this really was just a short story.

FYI, I've written about a dozen Troubleshooters short stories since that first one. And none are about anyone getting puppies, although some are significantly lighter than people finding dead women in refrigerators. I've learned (the hard way!) to give them titles, which help readers believe that they are, indeed, short stories and not excerpts from upcoming books. But I do mention the Dentist—still at large—in at least one other story.

I think I probably always knew that someday I'd bring the Dentist back, and let Alyssa and Sam go head to head with him. Because I also knew that Alyssa—as happy as she was with Sam—was not going to rest until she brought this killer to justice.

So that, dear readers, is the story behind *Hot Pursuit*. Which brings me to the story *after Hot Pursuit*.

I'm going to anticipate a frequently asked question

that I'm expecting to get after this book comes out, and say, *yes*.

Yes, you'll be seeing more of both Dan and Jenn in the next book. Their story is not yet over.

You'll see more of Izzy, too. And Eden. I don't have a title yet, but watch for what's looking to be the sixteenth book in my Troubleshooters series.

It's also going to be the *final* TS book—at least for a little while. I'm going to be taking a break from the series for a bit—although I'm hoping to release an anthology of all those Troubleshooters short stories that I've written, with a few brand-new ones thrown in. Just to tide you over.

Because, yes, I know. How could there be a final Troubleshooters book while I've left all those characters unattached? Lopez. Jazz. Commander Lewis Koehl. Martell, Joe Hirabayashi, Hobomofo . . . (I know he's new, but aren't you dying to meet the Navy SEAL with *that* nickname? I am, too.)

Visit my website, www.SuzanneBrockmann.com, for news about new releases and reissues of older books.

Oh, and one last *Hot Pursuit* FAQ that I'm anticipating . . . Yes, Tony V. *is* involved with exactly who you think he's involved with. And it's going really, *really* well.

Be on the lookout
for the next pulse-pounding novel
in Suzanne Brockmann's beloved
Troubleshooters Inc. series . . .

BREAKING
THE RULES

Navy SEAL Izzy Zanella's story

Coming in Spring 2011
from Ballantine Books